LOVE AT WAR

A NOVEL BY JAY VOLEK

I have always wanted to write a book and this, my first, is dedicated to my late mom Jean who inspired me with both her encouragement and criticism, my sister Sharman who nurtured within me both a love for literature and thirst for knowledge before even starting primary school and my little sister Karen. Thank you Karen for your loving, caring nature and for all the things we both know you have done for me over the years.

To my immediate family, I hope you are proud of me for this one. Everything I do, I do because of you.

Johannesburg, South Africa, January 2024

+++ PLEASE NOTE THERE IS A GLOSSARY OF YIDDISH AND SOUTH AFRICAN TERMS AT THE END OF THE BOOK +++

Foreword

As both an educator and researcher, two questions have been central in my professional work:

- How does learning happen (and how can we best facilitate this)?
- What counts as knowledge (and whose knowledge counts)?

In reading my brother's first novel, I have also asked myself:

- Why is it important to tell stories?

Using *Love At War* as a platform, I provide some personal answers to these questions below:

I believe that storytelling is one way of learning about ourselves and our worlds. In other words, we tell stories not just to entertain and educate, but also to make sense of our own lives and those of others around us. Before science became the hallmark of knowledge, people told myths and fairy tales to explain how they thought the world worked – like why the sun arose in the east – why certain things happened as they did – like pandemics – and about who we are and become during our lives. In this way, stories become explanatory narratives – and may even be used to predict the likely consequences of our choices and actions.

Both the author and the readers learn from storytelling. The author sometimes learns as the story unfolds on paper or laptop – often in unexpected, rather than planned, ways. The readers learn through following the narrative – and identifying with the characters and their lives.

In *Love At War*, we follow the story of a period in the main protagonist's life and, alongside him, we consider the choices he faces. Ser in Durban, South Africa during apartheid, David's personal choices are inextricably bound up with the wider political context. Elements such as his birth identity, family and culture, his aspirations as a professional tennis player, and his emotional response to meeting a woman he had initially viewed as part of a quid pro quo transaction to further his tennis aspirations, are entangled with nationalist imperatives in South Africa and Israel.

Through our reading of the novel, we learn that life holds unexpected complexities that give rise to inner conflicts, and also that friendship sustains us and that love sees us through. The choices David makes during the narrative further shape both his identity and his life trajectory.

It is through reading his story that we recall and reflect on our own life experiences and choices. For me, I loved remembering elements of my life in Durban while reading: the lazy days in the sun on the beaches, walks on the promenade, outings with my mom to the *Three Monkeys Café* and, later, with friends to *Legends r*estaurant. In this way, I have learned that the power of story is enhanced by the detail of place, of dialogue and of descriptions of the mundane – even the smell of the washing powder used by Emma.

Jay has used the writing process as an opportunity to "pull together" many strands of his own life experience and to weave these into David's story – to make sense of these so that his readers can also remember and reflect on what makes us, ourselves. So, stories are a form of knowledge as important as science, in helping us to learn about our world.

Dr. Professor Sharman Wickham, Stellenbosch, South Africa, April 2024

Chapter 1

The gentle Durban autumn sun woke David just before 8 a.m., tickling his face softly like a delicate feather. In his daze he managed to figure that, in his exhausted stupor the previous *Shabbat* evening which his parents had hosted, he had unsuccessfully tried closing his curtains as he had slumped into his welcoming bed. His last memory before falling into a deep sleep was the familiar fresh, lavender smell of the washing powder the family's long time domestic maid, Emma, would add to their laundry. It now permeated sweetly from his duvet and sheets. He could also vaguely hear the shutting of the front entrance door and the distant excited strains of his parents, Solomon and Lara Oppenheim. It being Saturday morning, they were setting out for their weekly *Shabbat* morning walk for prayers at The Great Synagogue in Musgrave Road.

His mother, Lara, a product of a secular, Czech Jewish family of academics and traders who had fortunately escaped Hitler and his gang of Nazi thugs by being hidden by their gentile neighbours in their little village of Lostice in Moravia, before being smuggled out through Switzerland, and eventually to relatives in South Africa. His maternal grandfather, one Abraham Langer who they called Big Abie, whom his mother loosely described as being religiously observant but mostly not, had totally rejected the possibility of a deity existing. Both his brothers and two younger sisters had been murdered at Auschwitz and Big Abie had from that point rejected *HaShem* or any notion of a divine power. Solomon Langer or Uncle Sol as the family called him, was a tough, streetwise and shrewd operator and unlike his sister Lara, who never mentioned a word about the atrocities of the camps, was very vocal of the horrors of Auschwitz, Dachau and Theresienstadt. Uncle Sol was a staunch Zionist like his own parents had been and thanks to his great success in his various business interests had already purchased frontline property in Tel Aviv, where he hoped the family would one day make *Aliyah*.

When he was younger David remembered Sol repeatedly telling him, "David, now listen carefully my *boychik*, this is *not* our home. Only Israel can be our home, the *only* place where Jews can be safe, nowhere else. We can't rely on

HaShem. We must make our own plans to get there and defend our nation if necessary."

David liked teasing his mother that in spite of Uncle Sol's atheism and her largely secular upbringing, his father had transformed her into a *frum* Jewess in her old age. This wasn't always well received by her unfortunately.

As the sun now started to warm his duvet, David reflected how shortly after his *bar mitzvah* he had joined ranks with his Uncle Sol in rejecting the notion of any supernatural being, who depending on our earthly behaviour, was going to send his puppets to either Heaven or Hell. His parents were shattered when he broke the news to them and that, going forward, his only commitment thereafter was a promise to regularly attend Shabbat dinners, which to date he had honoured. At the time he remembered telling them with a subtle grin "I promise you that I'll attend *Shabbos* ... religiously." It was the most difficult conversation he had ever had with his parents and his beautiful, younger sister Leah's more recent stricter observance of her Judaism, didn't help ease his guilt either. Still he was at peace in his heart with his decision and so that was the end of synagogue attendance beyond the odd family *bar mitzvah*, *bris* or wedding.

The previous evening and in honour of David's return from 2 weeks overseas, his mother had invited a crowd and had really outdone herself with a beautiful spread, including the *gefilte fish* and freshly baked *challah* which were his favourites together with the fresh Norwegian salmon. His lovely mother had also not missed the opportunity to invite the Rabinowitz's, including their attractive and intelligent daughter, Loren, a second year psychology student at David's alma mater, the University of Natal, Durban campus.

The dinner conversation was, as is usual over *Shabbos,* lively and entertaining and Loren Rabinowitz had obviously gone to lengths in making herself up. Even David in his distracted state thought she looked quite stunning. After his long flight home from Israel via Europe, and having eaten his mother's delicious cooking, the only thing on David's mind was sleep and lots of it. In any case, the only person who was on his mind that night was Shakira Mahomedy and their conversation of that afternoon in Mitchell Park. In all honesty she was the only thing David was thinking about since he had left her a few hours earlier.

Chapter 2

With considerable effort David managed to rouse himself to make the trip downstairs to seek out some leftovers from dinner. Surprisingly there was still some of the Norwegian salmon so he lightly toasted two bagels and made salmon bagels. Jew food as his Gentile friends, of whom he had many, would call it. Thank God for Jew food David thought munching on his delicious snacks whilst admiring the beautiful view of Durban's city and harbour from the lounge. He loved his birth and hometown where he had grown up. When away from home plying his trade as a battling semi-pro on the Challenger tennis circuit, he would often feel homesick and look forward to his return trips. It wasn't exactly the right outlook for an aspiring professional tennis player trying to break into the top ranks of his sport, but Durban was his emotional home, his sanctuary.

The fancy Italian coffee machine which he had won in Rome a few months before as part of his prize money for reaching the semi-finals, alerted him that his cappuccino was ready. He collected it from the kitchen and retired to his bedroom. He was pleased with his improvements and general level of play but the last fortnight in Morocco and Dubai had been both emotionally and physically gruelling, especially 2 drawn out 3 setters on the red clay in Morocco. He had scraped through both of those, requiring tense third set tiebreakers in both and now he needed rest. Still, making the finals in Morocco where he had narrowly lost to the top-ranked Spanish clay court specialist and then to a young upcoming Yank in the semis in Dubai, had been rewarding, not so much financially but the points he had accumulated would catapult him on Monday into the top two-hundred men players. For the first time he felt maybe he did belong on the main tour where he would at least be able to make a decent living.

His bed was still warm when he got back into it after closing the curtains tightly this time. With his hunger satisfied his mind wandered inevitably back to Shakira and their conversation. They had met in David's final year of his Bachelor of Commerce degree where he was majoring in Business Finance, having been pushed into it by his uncle Sol, whilst she was studying towards a chartered accountancy qualification. David's alma mater, the University of Natal, was within walking distance of the family home and had offered David a full tennis scholarship which entailed free education in return for representing the university in the tennis leagues. It was a huge relief for David as he wanted to spare his mother the embarrassment of asking her brother, his Uncle Sol, for funds for his university education. David had only learnt recently that Uncle Sol had been his sponsor for his primary schooling at Carmel College, Durban's only private Jewish school. It also made sense to him now why his parents had been so openly accepting of his request to rather transfer to and attend Durban High School, the top-rated *goyische* public high school. After his shock announcement of no longer attending *shul* David was certain they would deny him this request, but instead he was amazed to find them both rather encouraging of it. Now he knew why. The last thing his proud mother wanted was for her brother to see her husband as a *rachmones,* unable to pay for their son's university fees.

David, as with most of the male students in his commerce lectures, noticed Shakira instantly. She was a Durban Indian but could quite easily have passed for Persian with her radiant, olive skin, long, thick flowing black hair and captivating green eyes. She was outwardly shy and almost aloof, only keeping company with a small group of conservatively-dressed Muslim girls. Although quite liberal, owing to Apartheid, white students were still a clear majority which made her exotic looks all the more appealing to the opposite sex, and she seemed to know it. Unlike her contemporaries she wore traditional western garb including jeans and dresses, and damn fine ones too. She was quite clearly a fashionista and on the rare occasion she wore a headscarf it made her look more like a Persian Grace Kelly rather than a conservative, little Muslim girl. Rumour had it that her father was one Ismail Mahomedy, a clothing and textiles *macher*, who apparently was a pro-Palestine supporter who donated large amounts of cash to their cause. Certainly no friend of the Jews or Israel.

Truth be told, David's first meeting with this beautiful creature would never have happened without Dov's request and assistance. David was shy around girls in spite of his good looks, almost awkward, and he found her beauty intimidating as did most of his friends. Fortunately he had been given the best background information available on her and he was amazed and intrigued to learn that they had a common passion – music! He could hardly believe that considering one of his Muslim Finance tutorial mates had explained to him that western music was considered *haram* in most conservative Muslim homes. So armed with this vital bit of precious information David plotted his approach. It still took him some time to pluck up the courage to put his plan into action.

Chapter 3

For once in his life his timing was perfect and he moved confidently and swiftly in claiming the seat directly opposite her in the crowded Student Union's cafeteria.

"Hi! This seat isn't taken by any chance, is it?" David asked coolly, beef roll and Coke in one hand and a bundle of vinyl under his other arm.

"Nope. Help yourself" she whispered gently, only making brief eye contact with him. Even that brief second of looking into her beautiful green eyes startled him. He could feel his cool, confident façade starting to crumble instantly and his palms began to sweat. He almost stumbled taking his seat but then composed himself. He slowly placed down his plate with his Coke and then strategically placed the pile of vinyl half way on the table between them. Pretending only to be interested in eating his food, he managed to notice an initial quick glance at the vinyl, followed by a more protracted stare.

"Is that, is that really the *Japanese* pressing?" she suddenly blurted out, definitely not whispering this time.

"Wow! You like early Bowie too?" David responded almost nonchalantly, pointing to Bowie's 1972 pressing of "Ziggy Stardust and the Spiders from Mars", sitting strategically on the top of the pile.

"What? Girls don't listen to Bowie, the ultimate musical chameleon?" came her unexpected and almost cheeky retort with the sneakiest of grins. Now she was staring directly at David.

"No, no, that's not what I was implying at all, it's just not a lot of ... well, quite a few, uh ..." David stammered, without wanting to put his foot any deeper into his mouth. Oh God, now she's thinking I'm both a sexist and Islamophobe, were his only thoughts.

"You mean nice Muslim girls, don't you ?" she shot back but with a wider, unmistakable grin this time that gave David the distinct feeling she was playing him, whilst she picked up the record from the pile.

"You do know this is out-of-print and a collector's item? I've got a German pressing but it's got nothing on this one. I've also got "Diamond Dogs" and

"Hunky Dory" on import." David had grown up listening to them both and grinned back.

"Well, I'm shocked *and* impressed. You are welcome to look through the pile if you like? I enjoy a wide range of genres so there may be something else that appeals to you" David stuttered again as he looked more intently at her beautiful face. He was impressed that she only had a little lipstick on but otherwise no make-up, yet still looked so naturally alluring. He watched her flick through the pile, still with the wide grin and looking up occasionally at him, taking in his expression.

"I have all of these and you're right, a wide range of genres."

After a pause, she looked at him again and asked earnestly this time, "So how big is it?"

"How big is *what*?!" David, almost choking on his beef roll, managed to get out.

"Your record collection, white guy? What did you think?" she said, half giggling.

"My vinyl collection? Of course, yes. Last count was over two-thousand odd. I'm a bit of an audiophile and been collecting since I was 5. And you?"

After thinking for a bit all she replied with was, "A lot more" and then burst out laughing.

David just stared at the mesmerising creature sitting opposite him, caught speechless at her utter beauty amplified to its maximum by her laughter. She was astonishing.

"Well, now that you have my attention white guy, you may as well tell me a bit about yourself. You see any white guy who happens to have "Incognito" in his collection can't be half-bad" she said, breaking a moment's silence.

"You have more than two-thousand records in your collection?!" was David's only response and Shakira Mahomedy burst out laughing again at this. This time a big, loud, hearty laugh and in that moment David felt a warm, soothing feeling coming over him. He had never experienced this before with a girl or with anyone.

And then in a flash she was up and ready to go. "White guy, here's my name and number" as she slipped him what at first glance looked like a business

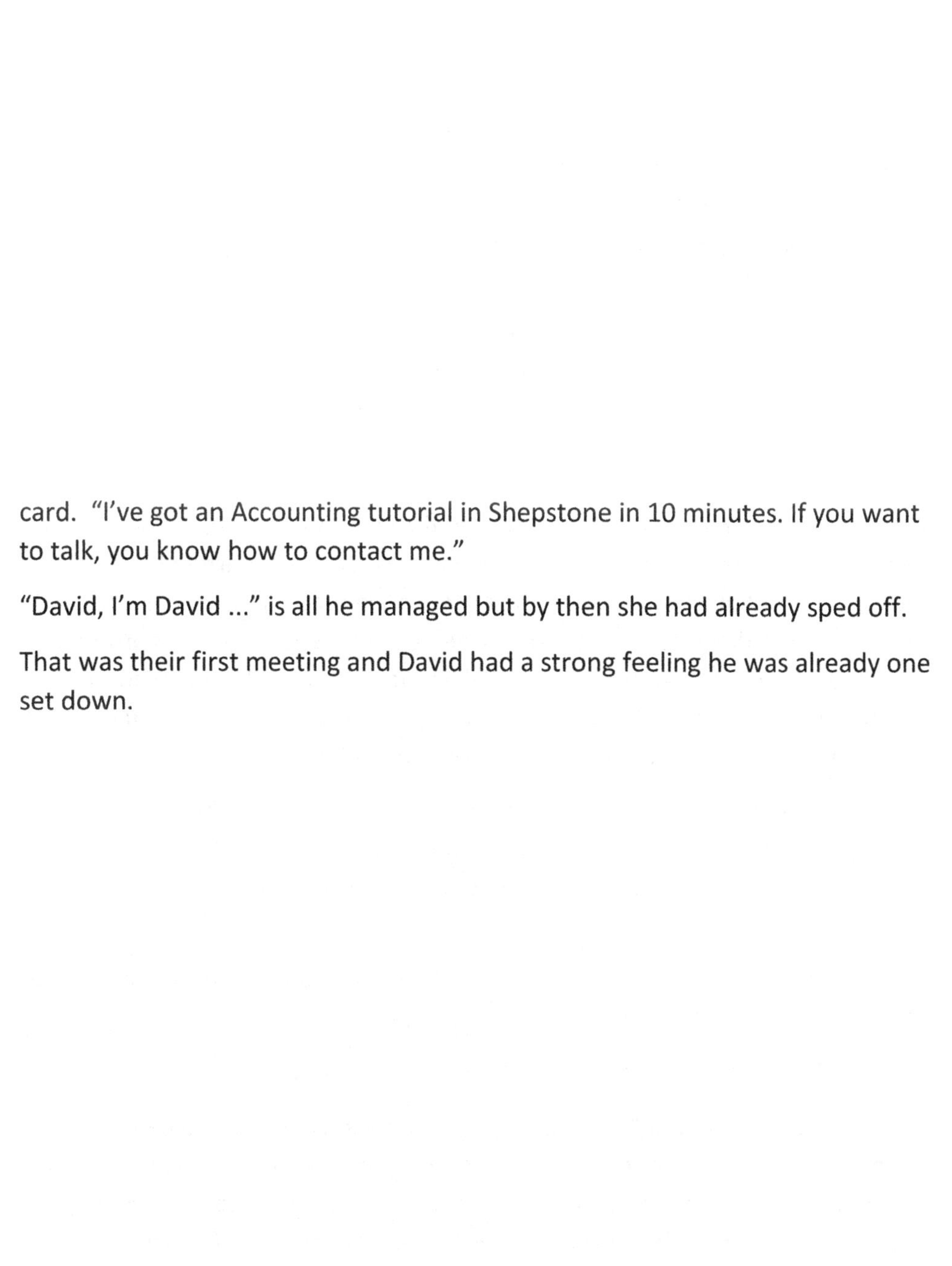

card. “I’ve got an Accounting tutorial in Shepstone in 10 minutes. If you want to talk, you know how to contact me.”

“David, I’m David ...” is all he managed but by then she had already sped off.

That was their first meeting and David had a strong feeling he was already one set down.

Chapter 4

David was awoken later with the distinct feeling of someone leaning over him. He was right.

"C'mon sleepy head, just because you've been playing a bit of tennis doesn't give you an excuse to sleep all day! Mom's put lunch out on the table and they've been hoodwinked into inviting some poor, starving wretches back with them from *shul*. I need some help with one annoying wretch in particular please. You know who I mean!"

Leah Oppenheim was 4 years her brother's junior and although she was beautiful in a most un-Jewish way with soft, gentle cheekbones, beautiful blue eyes and gorgeous, curly hazelnut-coloured hair, personality-wise she was anything but gentle. She was a gifted student with a genius IQ who had jumped two years ahead in primary school. Their family joke being that she might very well graduate high school before David, and not because he was failing either. In spite of his sister's bossiness he loved her deeply and admired her intelligence and quick wit, even if the latter had landed him in precarious positions defending her on more than one occasion. Leah loved her brother equally and even though his rejection of *HaShem* infuriated her she adored him for all he was as her big brother: courageous, kind, intelligent and loyal to their family. Still, she liked to tease and boss him about.

"Well, hello to you too, my little *frummie*. How was *shul*? Did Rabbi Goldstein manage to put everyone to sleep again? Did he go on about the horrors of mixed marriages leading to the downfall of the Jewish tribe?"

" Well, Mr Big Shot Tennis Player, if you didn't act like such a *putz* and dropped your heathen ways, you could attend with us on *Shabbat* and find out yourself" she shot back, whilst spreading his curtains open.

"Jesus, what time is it?" he asked, through half slit eyes.

"Well firstly, you shouldn't take their Lords name in vain as it could be disrespectful towards your *goyische* girlfriends, and secondly, to answer your question, it's time for you to get up. I seriously need your help with Myron, you know what a *schmuck* he can be and the sooner we get rid of him the sooner we can get some alone-time to chat. Believe it or not, I really missed you these

2 weeks and there's something specific I need to talk with you about, but it can wait." She pulled back his duvet and then turned to leave.

"Just to inform you, my darling sister, that I didn't miss you one bit, but in spite of your barbs it'll be my pleasure to rid you of that *schmuck* Myron Hirschowitz. He was an arrogant nerd at Carmel and he's only regressed from there. Tell mom I'll be down for lunch in 5 minutes. Please close the door behind you."

True to form Leah exited without closing the door whilst David pulled on a pair of Levis and threw on a Sergio Tacchini T-shirt. It had delighted Dov when David had told him Tacchini were prepared to offer him a clothing sponsorship for 2 years. Head followed shortly thereafter with a racket deal, which for Dov meant the agency no longer had to pick up David's bills for tennis apparel and rackets and he was quite sure that Nike was about to make a similar offer for shoes, which meant a further saving for them. There were other benefits they provided though, like the tricky knee operation in Tel Aviv by one of the world's best knee surgeons. He had waited until December last year when the tour had shut down to get the operation done and it was so successful he was able to travel for the Australian Open qualifiers, early the following month. He frustratingly lost in the final round of qualifiers to an Afrikaans guy he had beaten before in the juniors, but the kid had grown into a 6'5" giant with a booming serve. That day the giant had boomed down 26 aces from the clouds and that was that. The knee had held up well though and enabled David to achieve his most consistent run of good results since joining the tour. His clay court season had established him as a player to be feared amongst his fellow contemporaries and with the French Open just a few weeks away Paris was looking his best chance yet to make a main ATP tour draw, and a major at that too. This could really be it.

"Ah, thanks for joining us sleepy head" his mother said, while putting a roasted chicken and what looked like a delicious green salad on the table.

"Good *Shabbos* to you too, mom. That looks delicious and I'm starving."

"*Shabbos,* Davie. Come greet our guests and then sit down" his soft-spoken father added. His father, Solomon, his Uncle Sol's namesake, was a serious, studious Professor of English who had suffered years of dismay at his son's rejection of *HaShem,* never mind Judaism, and then there was the decision not to continue his studying beyond his undergraduate degree - for now anyway.

His decision instead of joining the tennis tour was just too much for his father as he despised sport which he considered egotistical and selfish. The only positive was that it didn't require a cash outlay because as far as his parents were informed, David, being part of the SA squad, was being sponsored by Tennis South Africa. David was certainly not going to confess that it was in fact Dov and the agency shelling out the shekels for him, or that Dov wasn't really his part-time Israeli "coach" or anyone's coach for that matter. If he in fact ever did explain that one, it would be in much later years to come when his careers both on the tour and with Dov and the agency were up.

David wished their guests *Shabbat Shalom* including a smug-looking Myron Hirschowitz, endowed in his *tzitzit* and *yarmulke*. The way he looked at his sister annoyed him and in a different place and not on *Shabbos*, he would have enjoyed wiping the smug grin off his pale, freckled face. David had really been looking forward to a quiet lunch with just family after the busy activities of the previous evening, and now he had to be sociable with the Hirschowitz's of all people. He could already see Leah having to restrain her tongue from delivering some well-timed insults at Myron, who was all but letting his tongue drool while admiring her. It was so obvious that Mrs Hirschowitz had ambitions of matching her nerd of a son to his beautiful, smart sister since she had become *frum.* He could just imagine them latching onto his kind parents at shul to force a lunch invitation out of them. The father, a very successful surgeon, was a total bore and almost put them all to sleep describing in detail the intricacies of his recent operations in his monotone voice. It was at times like these that he wished his Uncle Sol, with his usual tactlessness, was here to cut Dr Hirschowitz's stories short with some outrageous Holocaust joke that would leave these *frummies* shocked in disbelief, in turn leading to a short lunch. Instead the lunch dragged on for endless hours until the Hirschowitz's finally decided *they* were ready to leave. David would have excused himself after he had finished eating but he couldn't do that to Leah and endured another two hours of medical stories, and Mrs Hirschowitz interrogating poor Leah.

Once the ordeal was over David jumped in the shower to get ready for a secret dinner date with Shakira Mahomedy at a Turkish restaurant just off the busy strip in Florida Road. He still couldn't believe that 6 months into seeing her as regularly as he could when back home from the tour, that she still made him so nervous and giddy before a date. It was no longer just her natural beauty and sensual body that excited him, but the whole package. She was just as sharp and witty as she had been that first conversation they had had in the SU.

She was indeed shy and the first time he had called her, after holding back for a week, she wasn't nearly as bold as she had been in person. She was almost coy and allowed David to carry most of the conversation. She hadn't seemed too surprised upon answering his call, almost like she was expecting it, like she was hoping he would call, David hoped. He broke the ice by asking her if she had bought anything interesting to add to her collection. She hadn't, she had replied and had been especially busy with a large volume of varsity work, it being her final year of her Bachelor of Commerce degree. They exchanged some more small talk until she cut to the chase.

"Look, Mr white guy, I'm not really in a place to talk freely right now but are you going to ask me out on a date or what ?" she seemed to whisper into the phone.

"Of course I want to, I just didn't know if that's something I could ask you?"

"Please don't tell me you gay? That would be rather a waste of a nice, white guy."

"No, no, I'm definitely straight and by the way my name is actually David. I tried telling you last time but you had left already" he said, embarrassed to his core at her unexpected directness.

"Well, actually David, next time wait until I'm actually around before telling me your name, and secondly, let's meet at Legends in Musgrave for dinner Friday at 8:30 p.m."

David's heart dropped at her mention of Friday night. He had promised he wouldn't go AWOL on *Shabbat,* and so far over the years he had kept his word on that. He also didn't want to say no to Shakira and miss out on the opportunity of a date with this beauty. It was a bit too early to explain he was Jewish and inviting her to *Shabbat* dinner that night with his family was definitely out of the question. His mind thought overtime and he then suggested 9 p.m. rather, at the same venue. He would stay for *Shabbat* dinner and then tell his parents he had an important TSA meeting to attend. They would be more receptive to that.

"OK then, actually David, 9 p.m. this Friday at Legends and you better not be late" he heard her giggle.

"Oh no, I won't be. I'm always prompt" he replied seriously.

"I was only kidding, actually David. Bye now" and she cut the call.

It was hardly the first time he had nervously called a girl to take her on a date and he knew that generally the opposite sex didn't find him unattractive, but this was certainly the first time he had been handled by a girl. It excited and intrigued him and *Shabbat* couldn't come fast enough for him, but not for the usual reasons.

He was now two sets to love down with his only consolation being it was a best of five.

Chapter 5

David arrived early at Legends Restaurant in Musgrave Centre in the upmarket Berea neighbourhood. His old high school, DHS, was within walking distance and the restaurant was a popular haunt for Durban's young and trendy jetsetters. The proprietors were old family friends and he was glad that the father Billy Budd was at the welcome desk when he entered.

"Hello young man, been a while. You jetting all over the world playing your tennis, right?"

"Hi Mr Budd, nice to see you again. Yes sir I've just come back from Morocco and Dubai" David replied, respectfully.

"Aw c'mon with that Mr Budd stuff. I've known you since you were in nappies. Please call me Billy, man. So, who is this chickita who's joining you tonight? She must be something for you to have especially booked the VIP room and be 20 minutes early, *nogal*? And on *Shabbat* too?" Billy Budd asked with a big grin on his face?

"Not Jewish either I bet! Don't worry I won't mention a word to your folks about your *shiksa*!" Billy said teasingly, still with the big grin.

"Actually, it's a first date and I would really appreciate if you kept *shtum* about it to my parents. Please, Mr Budd" David managed to stutter out, his cheeks starting to warm from embarrassment.

"Sure thing *boykie*, but remember this is the *only* restaurant for any dates OK? What does she look like by the way so we'll know where to escort her when she arrives?" Billy asked, whilst gesturing to a waitress.

"Oh, don't worry Mr B ... Billy you'll *know* when she enters" David said confidently, regaining his composure.

"Sheryl, please escort this young man to the VIP room and *best service* for them, not only is David a close family friend, but he's got the *chutzpah* to invite Miss Universe on a first date" winking at David.

"Thanks so much Billy" David replied, as he followed Sheryl to the VIP room.

The restaurant was always full of Durban's most beautiful people, young, athletic and naturally bronzed from the outdoors. David couldn't help but notice two Jewish girls whose names he didn't know but recognised, look up from their table and give him a bit of a looking over.

The VIP room was all his friends had made it out to be and more. It was at the very rear of the restaurant but raised so its lucky diners could still get a full view of the restaurant and its patrons. The decor was stunning and the walls were covered with pictures of Hollywood legends like Marilyn, Grace Kelly, Humphrey Bogart and his favourite, Marlon Brando, in a scene from "The Godfather." After Sheryl had seated him, taken his double whiskey and soda order and closed the room's door, David could barely hear the hum of the main restaurant area. He was pleased about that because he wanted to hear every word his date had to say to him. He very seldom drank but he needed a double whiskey to calm his nerves a bit. He wished he didn't get so nervous around the opposite sex. He must remember to ask his father one day if it was genetic.

David had specially booked the VIP room not only because it was quiet and private but because he could also see her arrive from its perfect outlook. He wanted to be prepared in every way. In order to help that along it didn't take him long to knock back his drink. He didn't want her arriving at their first date with him swigging alcohol. He popped a few mints into his mouth to try rid himself of any evidence.

The whiskey was just putting a nice buzz on him when a black Mercedes Maybach pulled up and a beautiful woman in a black designer dress got out of the passenger seat. It was 9:09 p.m. and she was fashionably late. David didn't care. Even passers-by outside the restaurant stared. She was perfect for Legends, looking like she was an old school Hollywood actress. She gathered her dress and walked swiftly towards the entrance, nonchalant about the attention she was receiving. Clearly turning heads wasn't new to her thought David. As she entered and Sheryl was leading her to the VIP room, he was hardly surprised how most of the room turned to look at this beauty. She was wearing a sequined, long black dress that was glimmering and hugged her slim, curved body. She wore a classic white pearl neckless around her neck which accentuated her gorgeous, olive skin. She wore black, high heel designer shoes and had a very expensive looking shawl slung over her one shoulder and what looked like a Louis-Vuitton handbag in her hand. David had no doubt that it was the real thing and not one of those fakes the marauding gang of Africans in Rome were always trying to sell to him. But it was her beautiful face that captivated him. She had put on a bit more make up this time but not much more, maybe some eyeliner because her eyes were so piercingly green that he noticed them as she entered the restaurant. Her black hair was pitch black and flowing and accentuated those green eyes. She had plump red lips and high cheek bones which didn't hurt either. David had never seen a more beautiful face, not even those on the posters hanging in the VIP room could compete. He wished he had time for a second drink because the buzz was starting to go and he could feel his hands starting to sweat.

As Sheryl opened the door to the VIP room for her, David rose to greet her but suddenly felt underdressed even though he was wearing his one and only Hugo Boss jacket which he had bought in Dubai after his recent wins. He thought it went well with his jeans and sneakers. Anyway, it was too late.

"David, I'm so, so sorry I'm late. This after telling you to be prompt!"

"Well, Miss Mahomedy, fortunately you look stunning so you are forgiven" replied David, whilst pulling her chair out for her to sit in.

"Thank you, David" she said gently as she followed his lead and sat down.

"This is just beautiful" she said taking in the room. "You must be quite somebody to get a reservation here at such short notice and on a Friday night too. You know how to impress a girl. I know people who've only been able to get a reservation months in advance. What's your secret?"

"No real secret, I know the owner Billy Budd" David tried to say as matter of fact as possible.

"Well, all the same I'm very impressed" was her reply, whilst removing the black and bronze-tinged silk shawl.

"I hope you don't mind but I took the liberty of bringing you a little gift?" he said, handing over a wrapped box of Sally Williams chocolate-coated nougats.

"Not at all and that's so sweet of you, pardon the pun"

"And I made sure they are *halaal*"

"You only eat *halaal*?" she replied, as they both laughed.

"I see you like to tease, like in the SU ..."

"Truth be told, I only eat *halaal* at home but anything and everything when I'm not."

"Me too" he replied, and they both laughed at that.

"No seriously, my dad is strict at home even though if she had her way, my mom wouldn't care. She was brought up in a secular home in Iran and anything went, to be honest. When the Revolution started she and her family escaped to relatives in Durban. She met my dad here."

"Oh wow! That's quite something, leaving your home like that" said David, sounding very interested.

"Yip, especially because they were secular, *Shia* Muslims coming to a predominantly *Sunni* Durban community" she explained.

"So, pardon me for asking but is your dad *Sunni,* then?" he asked politely.

"Oh yes, and very *Sunni*! He prays 5 times a day without fail and won't eat anything unless its *halaal*. In fact if he knew I was out to dinner here with a white guy, he would probably hunt you down and shoot you! I'm supposedly at my friend Miriam tonight and going out for coffee with her and her brother EB in town. I especially suggested Legends because it isn't *halaal* so not too many Muslims, if any."

"Ah, makes sense now" said David, "but let's get back to that part about the shooting bit ..."

"Just teasing again, but he wouldn't allow this which just makes it all the more exciting actually."

"So you saying it's actually working to my advantage?" as they both laughed again. She looked especially beautiful when she laughed and smiled.

"I hope I can make you laugh all the time" said David.

"Oh yes, and why's that?"

"You just look so incredibly beautiful when you smile Shakira ... I've never seen more beautiful eyes than yours" David blurted out before he could change his mind.

After a moments silence she responded with, "Is that what you tell all the girls you invite to the VIP room at Legends?" looking up in earnest at him now.

"Well, I've never been in this room in my life before tonight and I've never told anyone, anywhere, that they are beautiful ... besides you" David said, gently placing his one hand on top of hers. From the look he gave her she knew he was telling the truth. Even David was shocked how instinctively he had done this but he was so attracted to her he couldn't help himself.

Sheryl broke the silence as she entered to drop off menus and to take their drinks order.

"I think I'll have a glass of French champagne, please" Shakira said.

"Really, you sure?" David asked, surprised.

"It's the only thing I drink and I haven't had one for months so please indulge me."

"Of course" David said. "Sheryl, please can you bring us a bottle then? I'm sure we'll have decided on food by the time you back."

"Perfect, I'll bring a bottle and 2 flutes now" Sheryl said, moving back to the door.

"Well, now that I've told you about my family, let's hear a bit about yours, David Oppenheim ..." Shakira asked.

David was quite taken aback that she knew his *surname*. He wondered who she had been talking to. She was smart and obviously knew he was Jewish. Well, seeing as his cover was blown so early there was no point in holding back he decided.

"Well now, for starters I happen to be Jewish." He stared directly at her to gauge her reaction but there was nothing other than that cheeky grin she had flashed at him in the SU.

"That makes you all the more interesting, David ... now tell me something I don't already know."

This girl was absolutely blowing his mind and he was really regretting not having had that second whiskey and soda. It took him a bit longer than usual to gather himself.

"My family are mostly Holocaust survivors from Czech. Many of them didn't survive but fortunately my parents escaped the camps and made it here. I have only one sibling, my younger sister, Leah, who is the only really religious one in our family although I guess you could describe my parents as being observant. I'm the black sheep of the family as I decided shortly after my 13th birthday I was atheist, like my mom's older brother."

"Well I for one am delighted your parents survived and feel so sad for those ones who didn't" she interrupted in a delicate voice, "but please continue."

"I went to Carmel College for primary school and DHS for high school before starting a Bachelor of Commerce at UND. My dad's an English professor there and my sister, Leah, is a first year philosophy student there too."

"Your dad taught me English 1 in first year, actually. He's a brilliant man. Quiet and a deep thinker. I also see where you get your shyness from."

"Yes, my dad and sister are the clever ones with genius IQ's. I'm the dummy in the family, for sure" he said, laughing.

"I somehow doubt that but let's get back to your story."

"OK, well I really enjoyed all the typical school sports and I did pretty well at tennis, so I dropped the others and focused on my tennis from 12."

"So what exactly does "pretty good at tennis" mean?" she cut in.

"It means pretty highly ranked nationally ..." he answered.

"So, what *was* your national ranking then, David?" she persisted.

"Ja, it was pretty high ... actually it was number 1" David admitted shyly, knowing only too well she would not stop with this line of questioning until he had given her the truth.

"Wow! I'm sure your parents must have been so proud of you?"

"My mom yes, but my dad not so much. He finds sport in general is silly and thinks there are far more important, serious things in life like studying, teaching or joining a profession. He thinks being called a professional sportsman is an *oxymoron* so he has no interest in my tennis."

"And your sister?"

"Oh she adores me and would support me in anything, even something she didn't like, so I'm lucky I have her."

"And what about your mom? What does she do? Do you look like her because you don't look like your father?" she asked.

"Yip, I'm from her side, the Langer's, not the Oppenheim's and I take after her brother, my Uncle Sol. I think you would like him, he's a helluva character who's always making people laugh. He saved what he could of his family from the Holocaust and my mom thinks it affected him so profoundly that he never married and had children, so he treats Leah and I like the kids he never had. To answer your question about my mom, she's always been a home executive taking care of us all, especially my father who is married to his research and work. She does a bit of voluntary work at the Jewish Club when they need help but looking after us lot at home is a full-time job."

"So my little birds also tell me you quite the tennis pro and you not far off breaking into the big time" she teased.

"Ha Ha, tell your little birds, thanks for their kind words and support but next year I join the Challenger tour with a ranking in the eight-hundreds only. Very few make it and move up to the ATP tour level where you can make a half-decent living. My father is furious with me as he thinks I'm wasting my time and money and should continue my studies and enrol for Honours in Business Finance, followed by a Masters. I'm really sick and tired of studying. It's his and Leah's thing, not mine. My Uncle Sol very kindly spoke to my father and assured him that whatever TSA doesn't cover of my expenses, he would carry. It was the only way to console him. That, and assuring him I would only play for 2 years, and if my results are not good enough to make the ATP tour, then I will continue to further my studies."

At that point Sheryl entered and took their food orders. Shakira ordered a green salad and calamari mains and David stuck with his dependable fillet with pepper sauce on the side and chips. They had been so engrossed in their conversation that neither of them had touched their champagne so David proposed a toast.

"So, here's to our families and their good health, wealth and most importantly, happiness."

"That's lovely, David" she said, as they clinked glasses.

"Well now that you know everything about me let's talk about *you* and *your* family a bit."

"Sure" she replied, "but before we do that there's something important I need to ask you. It's quite personal but been on my mind this week so I need to ask."

"You don't think a first date is a bit too early to propose?" David joked.

"No David, I'm being serious. You see you aren't the first Jewish guy I've gone out to dinner with and certainly not the first white guy either" she said earnestly.

"Oh Ok, I didn't see that one coming" he said, feeling a tad deflated.

"David, after high school I spent 2 years living in Paris studying art and literature. My mother had done the same as a young girl before the Revolution and she knew I would love the experience. My father being the typical overprotective Muslim father was totally against it but my mother persuaded him that if I stayed with her cousin's family in Paris, I would be carefully taken care of. He accepted this compromise so off I flew, away from my family for the first time in my life. Paris was everything my mother had told me it would be and I immersed myself in the French culture. At the end of my first year I met and fell in love with one of the senior art students, Jared Rothschild. Jewish, and yes, those Rothschild's, if that's what you wondering. He was exciting, intellectual and worldly, and as the French say full of joie de vivre. We had to do things under the radar, meeting at the Louvre or coffee shops which made it even more romantic and exciting. He showed me a whole new world so different from my suffocating, conservative Muslim life in Durban. He took me to his family's wine estate in Champagne, which is where I got my penchant for French champagne. He opened my eyes to another world and the longer we dated the more deeply we fell in love with each other, and the more risks we took, until ..." Her voice lowered as her eyes started to water.

"Until?" David asked gently, not sure where this was going.

After composing herself she continued. "Until one of his father's business associates saw us in a small café in a romantic moment. We didn't even notice that *we* had been noticed until Jared was summonsed to a dinner with his parents, where they confronted him about me. They said they were disgusted with him for associating with a Muslim girl, whose father was an ardent anti-Zionist and rumoured anti-Semite. Jared had fought them trying to tell them that he was in love with me and I was a beautiful person whom he was intending to introduce them to. They would have none of it and threatened to disinherit him if he didn't end our relationship immediately. This was so hard for him because he was very close with his family but still had the courage to tell them he was not prepared to break it off, and he didn't care for the money." Shakira took a second to sip of her champagne and then continued.

“When he told me this I was both broken-hearted and also angry. I was angry and humiliated because even growing up in Durban never once had I been insulted for my religion, my culture. I couldn’t believe in multicultural France that I would ever be subjected to such insults. Look, I’m going to cut to the chase here so I can get to the main point. I loved Jared too much to cause this issue with his family for him, and even though he wanted to make a go of it, I broke it off. It broke my heart.”

“Oh my God, that took such bravery and must have really been hard. A very unselfish act which tells me how deeply you must have loved this lucky guy. I’m not sure I would have been able to do that but then again I’ve never been in love with anyone before” David managed to get in.

“Yes it was awful, especially because we would still bump into each other in the corridors of art school but please let me finish and get everything out before I lose the courage to get to the main point.” She paused for a couple of seconds, seemed to blow out her breath and then looked deeply into David’s eyes. “I wasn’t going to tell you all this, certainly not on a first date. We’re really only strangers and who knows where it may or may not go but then on my way here, I changed my mind. You see David, my heart couldn’t handle another heartache like that. I promised myself I wouldn’t fall for another Jew after my turmoil but now look at me on a first date with you and enjoying myself. There was something so gentle and caring about your eyes in the SU that day that it brought back a warm feeling, like when I was with Jared. And of course it didn’t help you had those incredible albums” she said, and for the first time they both cracked smiles.

“I didn’t think you would phone but was pleased when you did. I was also conflicted so I shared our brief meeting with my best friend Miriam. She was happy but concerned for me just in case you phoned to invite me out because somehow or other she knows of you and that you are Prof O’s son who is obviously Jewish. Miriam is literally the only person in Durban I’ve ever discussed Jared with. She reminded me of the heartache and my vow never to date another Jewish man again and yet here I am sitting next to you, loving every minute. Just FYI even until you phoned I was going to turn you down gently, and then forget we had ever met. I heard your voice and then I couldn’t help myself. I think it ended up with me even asking you out ultimately” she said, which had both of them laughing again.

"Yes you did and I'm certainly not used to that, especially from a nice little Muslim girl!" he said leading to further laughter.

"Well, as my father would tell you I'm anything but a typical little Muslim girl. When I phoned Miriam straight after our call and told her I had no intention of going on a date with you, and yet the opposite just came rolling out my mouth, her only response was "Girl, trouble with a capital T."

"She sounds like a character and I like her already" said David.

"David, I need you to be completely truthful with me now. I don't want there to be any confusion or mixed signals. I don't want the heartache later. Should this thing go any further I will need to know upfront that this won't cause issues between you and your family later? We are from opposing sides after all. I mean a Jew and a Muslim, right?"

Half laughing, David countered, "That's the exact same question I was going to ask you tonight."

"Phew! Well at least we are on the same page on this thing" she said, as she seemed to relax and fall back into her chair.

David leaned forward and moved his hand towards hers, and this time she did the same and his much bigger hand wrapped around her delicate, slender fingers. It surprised and delighted David at the same time.

"I was so worried how you would take this and I'm so relieved you're not insulted" she said.

"Alright, so this is *my spiel*. I'm religiously atheist and culturally Jewish. I love Israel and so I'm pro Zionism. I'm not insulted at all with your question as the Jewish-Muslim thing was inevitably going to come up. Like you I think it is better early on, although I didn't anticipate it this early on. My family is largely secular except for Leah who has become a lot more religious over the last year. They are for the most part very liberal and open-minded, and although my mother would love me to marry a nice Jewish girl, she would accept if I didn't. She trusts my judgement. So full disclosure. Firstly, you can probably tell I really like you and sincerely hope we can do this again. Secondly, next year I will be spending quite a bit of my time travelling overseas on the tour and that may not be fair on or suit anyone looking for a serious relationship".

"Yes, and thirdly?" she asked.

"Thirdly, I'm starved and Sheryl is about to enter with our food" David said, laughing as Sheryl swung the door open, both hands carrying plates.

"I'm so sorry it has taken this long but we are full and the kitchen is working overtime" said Sheryl, sounding a bit ruffled.

"Absolutely no issue, I didn't even notice the time actually" said David, whilst Sheryl set their meals down and refilled their glasses.

"Me neither" said Shakira with a smile on her face.

"Actually, before Sheryl interrupted me, I was going to say I really hope none of what I've said is objectionable to you because I would like to see you again. Shakira, I can't tell you more than this, or offer you more than this for now. It's a bit too early for me now, but should things go further I will have no issue having you for *Shabbat* dinner and introducing you to my parents. I've always been my own man and my family knows and respects this."

"*Shabbat* dinner? *Oy vey*, you trying to convert me already David?" at which they both had a hearty laugh.

"You forget I had a Jewish boyfriend so know some basic *Yiddish*" she added.

"You keep on surprising and impressing me. Here's hoping I can teach you a few more *Yiddish* phrases" he chuckled.

"So, in light of your full disclosure I need to do the same. Firstly, thanks for your honesty. I can see you are a sincere man. Secondly, I think I do kind of like you ... a little bit" she said with an impish grin.

"Thirdly, I would like to see you again and it doesn't need to be the VIP room at Legends. I'm actually not that high maintenance although I do like French champagne. Finally, certainly until I'm sure of things, I cannot tell my family. It's too complicated. My brother Mo, who dropped me here tonight and genuinely thinks I'm here for coffee with Miriam and her brother, would kill me and probably you too for lying about this. He and I are close and I'll tell him when the time is right, should that become necessary."

She leaned forward in her chair and this time stretched out with both hands across the table. David took both her hands in his, electricity running down his back. She gazed deeply into his eyes with her seductive green eyes and said "OK, so Mr Jewish tennis pro, we are going to move forward slowly with this thing whatever it turns out to be. It is one minute before 12 a.m. and these 3 hours have whizzed by. I've so enjoyed the dinner and your company but Mo is collecting me at 12 a.m. sharp, outside. We can't be seen together but phone me soon please. I want to hear from you."

As they both stood up and David moved to pull her chair out for her, she moved closer to him and kissed him briefly on his lips. It sent shock waves through him and he could do no more than watch her paralysed, as she swished up her dress and disappeared through the VIP room's door.

True to form the black Maybach arrived at 12 a.m. precisely and he watched her jump in before it sped off. He slumped back in his seat still in shock trying to digest everything that had happened in the last 3 hours. He could still taste the sweetness of her lipstick on his mouth. It took him a few seconds to register that Sheryl was in front of him asking him if he wanted anything else or just the bill.

"Uh, yes please bring me another double whiskey and soda and the bill with it. Your service was great too by the way."

"No problem. Billy was right about Miss Universe. Your lady is absolutely stunning and I hope everything went well?" asked Sheryl, whilst removing the empty plates and bottle of champagne.

"Uh, yes thanks. I think it did" said David, still half in a stupor.

David wolfed down his drink, put on his Hugo Boss jacket and settled the bill with Billy Budd. He gave David a high-five about his stunning date and asked him when he should make a reservation for the next one.

"If I had my way it would be tomorrow night sir" which caused Billy Budd to chuckle and slap him on the back.

"You've got a beauty there *boykie,* hold on to her" Billy Budd said, whilst holding the entrance door open for him.

David wished his folks good night when he got home and went straight to bed. His mind was reeling and as his best friend Derek would say, "That chick is a total mind fuck." He knew exactly what he meant now. He knew as tired as he was the only thing he was going to dream about was the beautiful Shakira.

Before he finally nodded off his last thought was; 3 sets to love, game, set and match.

Chapter 6

David arose early the Sunday morning after his wonderful evening's dinner at the popular little Turkish restaurant off the busy Florida Road strip. Once again he had arrived early and watched as the black Maybach dropped her off exactly at the arranged time. He had chuckled watching all the attention she attracted as she exited the vehicle, whether it was only just the handful of car guards milling around or the little old lady taking her dogs for an evening walk. It made him proud that she was his, even if he wasn't sure how he had got so lucky.

She had worn a pair of body-hugging, dark brown leather pants with ankle boots and a black T-shirt with a white denim jacket. Even when she dressed casually, she looked like a model. Her fashion sense and style were cutting-edge and she had even helped David pick out a couple of Tacchini outfits for the tour. If nothing else he would look amazing for the main draw at the French Open. He had received the news that both he and 2 others had been given wildcards for the main draw after the withdrawal of a few of the regular tour players due to injury. After watching his heroes like Bjorn Borg and Mats Wilander winning titles on the red clay of Roland Garros, in 2 weeks he would be playing on the same courts they had graced. His Uncle Sol had immediately bought business class flights for the whole family and booked 4 rooms at a swanky hotel, about 30 min walk from both the Eiffel Tower and Roland Garros. This time his mother didn't argue with her brother and accepted his kindness graciously as she felt this was deserved. She had made many sacrifices for David over the years and finally he was proving his worth. Even his father had seemed delighted but then David had reasoned it was most probably all the wonderful museums he would be able to visit rather than the tennis. When he had let Dov know, he was genuinely delighted for David and really excited as he had never actually been to the French Open before. Jokingly, he put all of David's recent successes and his first major tournament invite, down to his "coaching". When he had broken the exciting news to Shakira she had jumped into his arms, the tears of happiness pouring down her gleaming cheeks. "I can't believe I have a boyfriend who is a tennis legend!" she had shouted for everyone at The Three Monkeys coffee bar to hear. "My boyfriend is going to be playing at the French Open tennis soon. His name is

David Oppenheim everyone, and you've got to look out for him please!" she burst out again, this time even louder.

David, cheeks bright red from embarrassment, didn't know where to hide and especially when the coffee bar had broken out into loud applause. Quite a few of the old, little Jewish ladies came up to him wishing him *mazel tov,* promising they would be watching out for him on the television and how proud they were of him. Shakira was beaming from ear to ear, delighted at all the fuss that was being made of her understated, shy boyfriend.

David threw on his tennis gear, grabbed his racket and clothes bags and quietly headed out the door. The family was still asleep and he didn't want to wake them. Soon he was flying over the hills of South and North Ridge roads in his green Alpha GTV which his friends coined "The Green Mamba." Except for a couple of early bird joggers the roads were empty and it wasn't long before he was parking in the road next to MPTC. It was a perfect June morning in Durban and the early morning sun shimmered off the perfectly painted tennis courts.

As was usual, David was early and no doubt his hitting partner, Lionel Perreira, would be late. It suited David as it gave him a bit of extra time to stretch out all his muscles before what was bound to be another gruelling workout with Lionel. They had grown up together on the tennis courts of Mitchell and Westridge Park, battling things out on the court since they were eleven years old. Lionel was both his closest tennis friend and greatest rival. Within the Natal junior tennis community their matches had been legendary, attracting crowds to watch them duke it out. Practice partners, doubles partners and good friends off the court, had no bearing when competing against each other in tournaments or even practice matches. Neither of them gave an inch and most matches went the full distance with both usually playing their best tennis and putting on a spectacle for the crowd. Their first final against each other had been in the under 14 final of the annual Coca-Cola juniors at Westridge Park, played during a boiling hot and sticky January. It was Lionel's first final and he was a bag of nerves and had not even managed to win a game off David, which David would sometimes remind him of when Lionel got a bit cocky. Their next final was 3 months later and both Lionel's game and control of his nerves had improved markedly and he had beaten David in a thrilling match in which David had been seeded to win. This set a pattern throughout their junior rivalry with David winning one encounter and then Lionel the following. They knew each other's games inside out and every match became closer and more exciting. When their junior careers ended they were drawn in their head-to-head matches although David had the pleasure of winning their last club champs match in another tense encounter. That hadn't stopped them from going clubbing to Zodiac to celebrate their rivalry later that evening. After high school they had gone their separate ways though, David to study business in Durban and Lionel to Auburn University, on a full tennis scholarship to study graphic design, another one of his passions. David had been so impressed with Lionel's painting of Ivan Lendl's beautiful backhand for his final year Art project that he had arranged through his father to have it displayed in the foyer of his university's Art Department, for everybody to admire. Now they had both graduated and Lionel had come home to visit his folks before joining the Challenger tour like David. They had not seen each other for almost 2 years although they had still caught up with each other with occasional long distance telephone calls. David was delighted Lionel was back in Durban for a few weeks as he needed 2 solid weeks of tough practice and work outs before the French, and it would be also great to catch up with his buddy.

"Always early hey shit-for-brains, nothing changed with you!" Lionel shouted as he bounded down the steep stairs towards David and the main show courts.

"You right about that *schlemiel,* you still always late" David replied with a big grin on his face, genuinely happy to see his old pal.

Lionel gave his old friend a big bear hug and kiss on the forehead.

"You looking good Davie! You been working out or what?"

"Genetics brother, genetics ..."

"*Kak* bro, those muscles aren't in any of your family" Lionel laughed back at him.

"Well I see your hair has grown a lot longer but otherwise you're still the same sack of shit you were when you left us a few years back" David said teasingly.

"Bro, I feel like I've put on about fifteen extra pounds the last 2 weeks thanks to my old girl's cooking. I need to really work hard now so I hope you've brought your A game fucker? I've been seeing some pretty impressive results in Morocco and Dubai and I guess I should congratulate you for the French bud. Seriously though, I'm really happy and proud for you that you're getting there. Roland Garros is a helluva tournament and your baseline game is perfect for clay."

"You better not make any excuses and be there for my first match as it could also turn out to be my last" David laughed back.

"Of course I'll be there. It won't be the last Davie, you *Yids* are the Chosen don't forget, so you'll do just fine. You lot have the luck of the Irish too, but on steroids."

"Well maybe not during the Holocaust so much ..."

After an awkward silence staring at each other, they both burst out laughing.

"I've got a bunch of tickets for you and any of your college mates by the way, or any significant others if that happens to be the case."

"Actually, there is someone. American chick I started seeing in my final year. We still trying to decide where we are now that my student visa is up. I don't want to just marry her for a green card. Complicated like most of my other ones" Lionel chuckled.

"Well, I'll buy us lunch afterwards and I'll tell *you* about complicated on steroids" David laughed.

"OK Davie, let's get hitting. I want to see what it feels like to smash a French main draw pro" he said, baiting David.

"You mean like when I *klapped* you double bagel?"

"Fuck off, shit for brains! That was like a thousand years ago" Lionel barked back as he popped open 2 cans of new Dunlop balls and moved towards the baseline.

The sun had now risen high above them and people were starting to arrive for breakfast in the restaurant in the park. An elderly couple had also sat down on a bench above the courts to watch them hitting. The balls whizzed over the net, snarling with topspin and then almost floating with sliced backhands, as David and Lionel warmed up their strokes. A few more interested onlookers had entered the club and were watching the two young men. Lionel had classic, free swinging strokes imparting less spin on both sides than David's. David was especially envious of Lionel's single handed backhand, in the mould of Lendl's, which Lionel was able to hit winners with from anywhere on the court. Lionel had always been physically stronger and he seemed to have really filled out even more in college and was hitting the ball harder and deeper. David was both mentally and strategically superior and had always relied on his guile in his wins against his great rival. The gritty Challenger tour had forced David to up his game, especially his serves, both first and second. His return of serve had improved tenfold on both sides and he would need all of it to return Lionel's booming first serve. As they practiced serves he also noted that Lionel had picked up a nice little first serve slider in the deuce court where he would take some pace off and hit wide to the forehand with a bit of slice. College tennis had been good for Lionel, it was obvious.

"OK Davie, call it bro. Heads or tails?" as Lionel sipped on a pink concoction he had brought back with him from the States.

"Heads as always!" shouted David.

Lionel flicked the 50 cent coin, caught it and inspected it. "You lose again, tails. I'll serve bud. You happy starting that side or you want to swap ends?" Lionel asked.

"Nah, I'll stay. Good luck *china*. You going to need it!"

The quality and competitiveness of their play must have been high because within 20 minutes a small crowd had gathered around the show court, watching the combatants duelling. In spite of spending most of the previous week resting, David did not take long to shrug off the little bit of rust he had. The Challenger tour had toughened him up. Playing for your livelihood was a step up from just playing for the glory of it at an American college. David's game was sharp, especially his much improved return of serve. He was able to read Lionel's serve easily and sent forehand and backhand winners sizzling past Lionel as he charged the net. He could see the look of surprise on his opponent's face and by discouraging him from serving and volleying he had him exactly where he wanted him, on the baseline. David sent some deep looping topspin forehands to the middle of the court making sure he gave his opponent no angles to generate and then if anything short came back he would pounce on it and whip his next shot to the corners for a winner. It was just a question of time before David broke his opponent's service and it came from a beautifully disguised and directed backhand lob that Lionel could only admire as it fizzed over his head and dipped inside the baseline, with a few feet to spare.

"You shit, where did that fucking shot come from?" Lionel muttered under his breath so the spectators couldn't hear but just loud enough so that David could. They swapped ends with David serving for a 5-3 lead which he did quite easily. Lionel then battled it out to hold his serve and David followed through by holding his to finish off the set 6-4.

"Yeah, nice Davie. Let's have a brief break and then see if you can do that again. I see the tour has made a tennis player of you. You used to have a pretty *kak* serve but now you've developed a bit of a weapon there" Lionel said, wolfing down as many electrolytes as quickly as he could.

"Had no choice Li, I was getting murdered on serve when I first joined the tour, on both first and second serves. I came back home and got Clive to spend endless hours helping me get more wrist action and suddenly the extra power and zip came too. When I returned to the tour I suddenly started beating the same dudes who had smashed me a few weeks earlier. All I can say is, thank god Clive is still around".

Clive Jaikins had been David's second coach after Joan Johnson and before retiring had been David's most influential coach. He had taken an extra interest in David as he recognised his talent and hunger.

"Did he help you with your returns too? You reading my serve better than ever and I think I'm serving the best I've ever served in my life!" asked Lionel quizzically.

"Nope. I took a few days off and watched Agassi at the Italian. I don't think I've seen a better returner since Jimbo" David replied, referring to Jimmy Connors. "It's all about anticipating and quick eye-brain reactions. I'll give you some drills which will help you big time".

"Please, I'm going need every bit of help I can ..."

For the first time David noticed the one-hundred plus spectators they had attracted who seemed to be egging them on for another set of tough tennis.

"OK Li, you up for another set of being smashed? C'mon' let's give them a show. This feels like we teenagers again playing against each other at Westridge, don't you think?"

"Not at all. You didn't have a demon serve when we were kids" Lionel said laughing and moving to the baseline to start the second set off serving.

The second set was a lot tighter as Lionel had figured out how to counter the looping top spins to the centre of the court. David nevertheless had other tricks up his sleeve and started varying his strokes, one second sending some low, acute-angled slices, followed by more top spin drives and then flat rather than topspin shots to the centre of the court. Besides the regular clapping and occasional gasps as either player hammered winners, David could sense the crowd was really getting into it because they were even starting to call out the score. They both managed to hold serve until 6 games each which required a tiebreaker to decide the set. This was where David appreciated the benefits of the constant week-in-week-out rigours of professional tennis. He broke Lionel twice and held his serves to close out the set 7-6. The crowd seemed to rise in unison and gave them both a standing ovation for the spectacle they had provided for free. It also dispersed as quickly as it had arrived. They probably starving for a breakfast and got side tracked into watching them compete, David thought.

"Nice, you got me this time bro. So now I believe it's 9-8 in your favour" Lionel teased and they both laughed.

"No, no, we start with a clean slate in big time tennis my boy. So 1-0" said David enjoying the friendly banter with his old mate.

For the next hour they did court drills retrieving balls from all corners of the court and returning them to the centre of the baseline. They followed that with David's favourite, kangaroo jumps, and then finally running stairs. David could feel some of the fatigue of his overseas battles in his muscles but he still loved the lactic acid after-burn and the warmth of the sun on his skin as they both collapsed on their towels on the court. Lionel glugged the last of his pink drink, sweating like crazy and trying his best to wipe the salty sweat from his eyes.

"Sure beats the crap out of an office job, hey Davie?" he managed to get out, breathing heavily.

"Please tell my old man that bud. The *ballie* thinks this is just an ego trip I'm on and all rather silly. Thinks I'm wasting my time and I should be studying further! He doesn't understand the feeling after 3 hours of pushing ourselves to the limit" replied David in between deep breaths.

"Your *ballie* will come round at the French dude. That place is infectious and he'll have a better understanding about our love for this crazy game, you'll see."

"I hope you right, bro. Let's go shower and change and then you can tell me about this chickie you're seeing and I'll tell you about my rather complicated situation too, over lunch."

"Davie, I always thought you may be gay. Don't be shy, it's not so complicated these days for gay men to come out of the closet!" Lionel said, laughing his way to the locker rooms for a much needed cold shower.

"*Schlemiel*!" was David's only response.

Chapter 7

David felt like opening up the Green Mamba a bit so decided to drive them up the coast to the clubhouse at Prince's Grant. The view from the restaurant was as magnificent as ever with the beautiful, green and luscious golf course rambling before them, and the dark blue of the Indian Ocean behind it. The sky was a deep blue with puffy clouds up high. Durban sure was putting on a show today.

"Bro, the Green Mamba still hauls ass man. I just hope there were no hidden cameras otherwise you ain't making the French or any other tournament for a while. If the traffic cops catch you doing that speed in the States that's the end of your car and your licence."

"Thank god we aren't in the States, then" David replied laughing.

They were seated outside by a waitress and placed a drinks order. "He only drinks pink drinks" David said teasingly to the waitress.

"Actually he's right, bring me an extra-large rock shandy, please" asked Lionel.

"Make it two, please" David requested, "and some menus too".

Whilst waiting for their food and drinks Lionel told David about Tammy whom he had met in his final year. She had transferred from Alabama because Auburn had a better graphic design department. Unlike his other couple American girls it had started off as a friendship with Tammy. She was impressed with his work and was looking for guidance and a mentor. She knew absolutely zero about tennis which was a plus because it's the last thing a tennis player wants to talk about with a significant other. Quite by chance Tammy was as big an obsessive as Lionel about Depeche Mode and dance music so they immediately bonded over that. In spite of not wanting to start a serious relationship in his final year of college the more time he spent with her the more he realised how special she was and his feelings progressed from just friendship to romance.

Tammy, he said, was a typical southern girl from a lovely southern family from Wilmington, North Carolina. She took him to their family home for a

Thanksgiving weekend and he bonded immediately with her father who was a massive soccer and tennis fan. It was obvious from her mom where she had got both her looks and kind, loving nature from.

"Davie, she's perfect for me bro, absolutely perfect but there's complications. Firstly, my study visa is up so I can only return as a visitor for a maximum of 3 months a year. Alternatively, I get lucky with the green card lottery which is a long shot or finally we get married. We're both a bit too young for that and with the topsy-turvy life of the tour ahead of me I wouldn't want to put her through that. It wouldn't be fair on her although if I proposed I think she would accept. Thing is Davie, for the first time in my life I'm in love with a girl" he said dropping his shoulders a bit.

"Li, I'm hardly an expert on the topic with my short-lived romances but I think with love you have to forget the head and just go with the heart. It's risky and could lead to a lot of heartache for the both of you but that's what we tennis players do all the time. We take risks because the prize is worth it" David offered.

"Funny bro, my old girl said I should talk to you about this one. She thought you would be able to shine a light on my predicament. I have to admit I've missed our chats these last few years".

"Now what would you *goyim* do without us *Yids* shining our light on your predicaments!" replied David causing them both to burst out laughing.

"So now you know all about my Tammy let's hear about your better half. Who is he?" Lionel asked mischievously.

"Well I'm just going to get this out of the way early. You know how I've always told you my mother would love me to settle down with a nice little Jewish girl, right? So guess who this *schmucko* finds for himself?"

"Davie, it's not like you haven't dated a gentile girl before though!"

"Here's the thing though Li, she isn't gentile ..." he said, sheepishly.

"*Mazel tov*! Finally a nice Jewish girl for your mom!"

"Lionel, she's neither of those ... she is Muslim!" David blurted out before Lionel could go any further.

"*Schlemiel*! What the fuck are you thinking? Davie, these people hate you lot bud. Not only is she from a different *religion* she's also from a different *race*! You do know in theory you could be arrested for this?!" Lionel shouted out, shaking his head. "When you told me *"complicated on steroids"* I had no idea you would be talking about *this* fucked up. I hope you haven't told your old lady yet? Lara will disinherit you and send you into exile."

David had anticipated this outburst as his mate had certainly not been the most open-minded or progressive citizen when he had lived in South Africa, which is why the south of the USA probably suited him far better than California.

"Li, firstly she looks Persian or Mediterranean so I'm not worried about us being arrested. Although her father is quite religious the rest of her family are not, and if anything are almost secular, especially Shakira and her brother. Secondly, she's the most beautiful girl I've ever seen and when you meet her, you'll see. Thirdly, she's incredibly intelligent and will qualify as a CA within the next few years. Fourth, she's independent so has no issue with me gallivanting around the planet on the tour and if anything is really encouraging of me to break in to the top 100. Fifth, she's so funny and just gets me. Sixth, neither of us have told our parents yet because we wanted to get through at least 6 months to see if we still like each other. We do. In fact I'm also in love with someone for the first time in my life. Oh yes, and FYI, Lara and Sol are a lot more open-minded than you may believe!"

"Jesus Christ, Davie! Do you know what you getting yourself into? Granted Shakira is a really beautiful name but have you forgotten you're Jewish and she's a Muslim?! I think it's my duty as your long-time friend to give you a good *klap* on your head with my racquet. I expected a bit of a story from you but this is just a total mind fuck" said Lionel, still dumbstruck.

"I hope you trust my judgement Lionel. She's truly amazing this girl. She's wise and worldly beyond her years and she has no issue that I'm Jewish. In fact she's dated a Jewish man before when she was studying in Paris. If anything she's fascinated with the whole Jewish culture. I want you to meet her bud. You see we made, or at least *she* made a very important call the other day after our 6 month anniversary. She told me in spite of the obstacles in front of us and her heartache from her previous relationship with a Jew, she wants to make a go of it. She wants to introduce me to her family and get their blessing. She also wants to meet my family and attend a *Shabbat* dinner."

"Oh my God, Davie. Just wait for me to quickly get my racket out the car. Now I know you've completely lost your mind. *Meshuggeneh* you used to call me in Jewish, right?!" Lionel asked, flabbergasted.

At that David burst out laughing. He didn't think his friend had remembered any of the Yiddish he had tried to teach him in their youth.

"Bro, you have to meet her. I can't really explain otherwise. She doesn't wear a burqa and ride a camel. You'll really like her. She's no different from us."

"If your old girl finds out that I'm a co-conspirator to this she will kill me Davie" at which they both chuckled breaking the tension a bit. "OK I'll make you a deal. I'll meet this Shakira chick but if I give her the thumbs down you move on and find a nice Jewish girl instead, OK?"

"It's a deal!" David replied, completely confident once he met her Lionel would approve.

"So then, I suppose you better tell me about her" Lionel sighed, realising he was not going to change his friend's mind easily, if at all.

Through lunch and then for a further hour David talked obsessively about Shakira. How once he had learnt about her passion for music he had laid his little plan for their first meeting in the SU. He spoke in great detail about their first date at the VIP room which really impressed his friend. He was just as shocked as David had been that she drank champagne and about her relationship with Jared Rothschild in Paris. He told his friend about her delight at him receiving a wildcard for the French and how she had embarrassed him but in the nicest possible way at the Three Monkeys coffee bar.

"Wow! And all of this whilst graduating university *and* playing the circuit? You've been really busy, bro."

That wasn't all but David couldn't talk about Dov and the agency. Not only could that endanger both of their security but Dov's too.

"So now I'm pretty intrigued to meet her. When can we arrange something?" Lionel asked.

"Frankie sent me a bunch of VIP tickets for Ronnyz for next Saturday. They having a reunion party and I know you'll love it. Keen to do it?" suggested David.

"You kidding? Of course I'm in! Auburn doesn't exactly have many dance clubs so let's do it" Lionel replied, excitedly.

"Shit Li, you know we've been talking for almost 4 hours now. Time to rock 'n roll in the Green Mamba."

David paid and left a generous tip for their waitress. Soon they were flying south on the N2 highway in the Green Mamba,a Depeche Mode CD blasting out from the Alpine front loader. It was awesome to have his mate back for a bit and life was good thought David, laughing as Lionel Perreira threw his long hair about rocking it out to his favourite band. Life was indeed exciting.

Chapter 8

David arrived home after dropping Lionel at his parent's house and went straight to Leah's room. They had hardly chatted one-on-one since his arrival home and he felt bad. In many ways he was her closest confidant as it was difficult for her to see her usual group of friends as often since becoming *frum*. He knocked twice on her bedroom door and he heard her gentle voice replying to enter.

"Wow brother, going by the colour of your cheeks I would have to say you got a serious overdose of vitamin D today!" she said, always full of cheek.

"Yip, Lionel Perreira being the main culprit. Bugger had me running to all corners of the court!" David responded.

"Yes, I already heard. Maddie's mother was part of the crowd watching you two this morning. I hear you two boys put on quite an exhibition for the early risers. Maddie is still interested in you by the way."

"*Oy*! I really thought I had dissuaded her from any such notions. No Jewish girls for me though, my darling sister, they expect a proposal by the second date. Next time I'll wake you up early and you can umpire our next practice match. I would love you to come watch."

"I don't know if my nerves can withstand a crowd watching one of your matches. What if I make a mistake?"

"As long as it's in my favour it's no problem" David said with a grin. "Anyway it was really awesome practicing against Lionel after all these years. It was even better winning both our sets but I predict with his beautiful game he'll be top 100 within 18 months. The Challenger tour will see to that. So, I know I haven't had much time for a quiet chat with you Leah and I know there was something you wanted to discuss, so here I am".

"I appreciate that David, you've had a lot on your plate and mom's kept you busy too. Yes, there a few things actually but let me start with the first one. You know that, except for a silly little thing with Julian Goldstein, I haven't really had anything serious with anyone. Problem is something has changed but I'm in a bit of emotional turmoil right now. Actually, I feel like a wreck. I've done a good job of hiding it from everybody, even you, but I need someone to talk to about this and you're the only one who has always understood me. It's bad enough now that since I am practicing my faith a lot more seriously my friends think I have lost it, but if I tell them what I'm about to tell you ..." she trailed off.

"Go for it Leah, I'm listening. You know I won't judge you. Just whatever it is don't tell me you are thinking of marrying Myron Hirschowitz. I couldn't handle that!"

"David, please! I need to have a serious discussion. This is really important" she replied, with tears forming in her eyes.

"Sorry Leah, I didn't mean to make light of it" he apologised.

Before continuing she took a deep breath and blew it out.

"OK so I've met someone. In light of the religious changes in my life he's the last person I expected it to be. David, he's not Jewish. Not only that but he happens to be a very religious Christian!"

"*Oy vey*!" was David's only reply, certainly not expecting this from his sister.

"It feels like *HaShem* is on the one hand blessing me, and on the other hand cursing me" she replied.

"How the hell did this all happen? And when?" asked David, still shocked.

All David could keep thinking was how on earth this could happen to both of them and at the same time too. Their parents would disown them both.

"He's at varsity with me also studying philosophy ... theology too" she mumbled.

"Jesus Christ, Leah. Don't tell me he's studying to be a priest?!" David blurted out at her.

She didn't need to answer. He could tell by her crestfallen head and the tears streaming down her cheeks that he was. In that moment she looked so helpless and lost that he picked her up and just hugged her in his arms. At that point she just burst into huge sobs.

"I didn't mean to David, I really didn't mean to fall in love with him ... not a Gentile!" she cried out between sobs. Underneath her tough exterior he always knew his little sister was nothing more than a gentle, kind and loving soul. He had never seen her this vulnerable before.

"Leah it's OK, really. It could have been worse, it could have been Myron Hirschowitz" he said to make her laugh a bit, which she did.

"So tell me about this *goyische* priest and then let me decide whether I go beat the living daylights out of him or not" David joked again, trying to lighten her mood.

"Well for one thing before he attended church this morning he tells me he was almost late, watching my pro tennis brother swatting balls all over the place with his mate. You've got a huge fan if nothing else. His whole family are tennis nuts and think you are the bees' knees" she said, with the first sign of a smile on her face.

"I'm glad I have at least one fan then" laughed David.

"Two actually. Michael and me" she laughed back.

"As I was saying, we met at varsity. He's also studying Philosophy and Psychology, it is part of their instruction. I wouldn't even have noticed him except for the philosophical discussion he started with Prof Greenberg in one of our lectures. David, they had us so enraptured in their discussion that for almost the full lecture the entire class sat mesmerised. As you know I've read everything ever published by Freud, Nietzsche, Baudelaire and too many others to mention, but the exchange between these 2 intellectual giants was on another level. I felt like I was still at kindergarten level following their back and forward arguments. David it was beyond thrilling, like 2 academic gladiators flexing their muscles. I suppose how that crowd felt watching you and Lionel scrapping it out this morning but instead of rackets this was with their minds. Just when we thought Prof Greenberg had him in a corner, he would pivot and come back at an angle nobody expected and suddenly Prof would be on the back foot. When I stared at this boy I couldn't believe it was the same person whom I had hardly noticed before. David, the passion of this young man for the truth and understanding was painted all over his face. He left me and many others in that lecture hall desperate for more after the alarm sounded for the end of the lecture. I have never seen Prof Greenberg look flustered and this young guy is a *first year student*. Total mind fuck like you often say my brother."

"So, he's a smart priest-in-training. What else?" David asked.

"Well he's a horsefly like you. He matriculated a few years after you from DHS. He's very bright and was Dux of his year. His father is a scientist and a very famous one with many inventions and patents to his name. Apparently made a fortune out of them in the area of medical science. He and Michael don't get along. The father is an atheist like you and expected Michael to follow his career path in the Sciences. He cannot believe Michael is studying Theology let alone believing in *HaShem*. Michael says if he hadn't won a scholarship his father would have refused to pay for his Theology studies. He's read more than anyone I know and is interested in everything whether it be astrology, politics, travel, sport, food, religion obviously or whatever. He's a typical Aquarian like you, always needing to understand and always looking for the truth in everything. I think this was the attraction of *HaShem* and religion for him, understanding the truth. Oh and he's fascinated by Judaism."

"So how did you guys first meet?" David asked, thinking back to his first meeting with Shakira.

"It happened quite by chance. I was sitting directly behind him in one of our lectures and my Siddur prayer book slipped out of my bag and fell at his feet. He picked it up, stared at it, stared at me and said deadpanned, "You don't look very Jewish."

"I was so astounded that all I could say back to him was "Well you don't look very clever!" she burst out laughing with her brother.

"What a great pick-up line. I must try that sometime" said David, laughing.

"Whatever I said worked because he was almost kicked out of the lecture he laughed so loudly. I was so embarrassed and tried desperately to apologise but he wouldn't let me. He said later it was the first time he had ever been called stupid and he loved it. I've learnt subsequently that Aquarians have this offbeat sense of humour and Michael personifies this. He tells me stories that have me in hysterics, like literally rolling on the floor, but sometimes I'm not quite sure if they are stories or not. David, you would love his wicked jokes and the pranks he plays on people. He loves to stare expressionless at people after he's told them a story, just to observe their reactions. It's like he takes as much pleasure in that as he does from the actual telling of the stories. He's just so fascinating" she went on.

"That day after retrieving my Siddur he insisted we go for lunch so he could ask me some questions about Judaism. It turned out he had taught himself Hebrew in order to read the original text of the Torah to understand the Bible correctly. It didn't take him long to figure out he knew a lot more about our religion than I did so the teacher quickly became the student. He was even able to explain a few passages in a simple way that Rabbi Goldberg had battled with. But David it wasn't only his brilliant mind that captivated me. It was his deep love that he had for *HaShem.* It's something that I haven't even truly felt with our rabbis. His clarity of thought and unequivocal belief in *HaShem* gave me such a feeling of calmness and certainty. It was like his brilliant mind had cut through any doubts I may have ever felt."

"He sounds pretty interesting but what's the deal with you guys now?" David asked.

"We've been seeing each other regularly since then, like every day at varsity and whenever possible on Sundays after he's returned from church. David, we're very close and getting closer. At first I tried to fight it and stopped meeting or talking to him for 2 weeks, but every day he would drop a letter in my lap during lectures. I couldn't resist reading them and they were so beautifully written and heartfelt that I had to go back to him. I couldn't deny my feelings and that I was in love with him. If anything he's the one who has brought me closer to Judaism, not Rabbi Goldberg. He has a way of explaining the big things, the difficult things about *HaShem,* so simply and clearly. You are literally the only person I have discussed Michael with and I've gone through moments of guilt, anger and utter loneliness. I'm still trying to understand why the first man I had to fall in love with isn't Jewish. Thank goodness you are home David. I felt I was losing my mind and it feels so good to tell you. I'm sorry if it feels that I'm dumping a lot on you but I don't know anyone I can trust like you."

"Look, I'm no Dr Phil relationship expert but I think you just need to relax and let things take their natural course. So if you feel love for someone, then love them, so what if they aren't your religion. The mere fact that on a planet of 8 billion people you've got lucky enough to find someone who makes you feel this special, I say that can't possibly be wrong Leah. I mean it's hardly like he's trying to convert you, right? He sounds like a good kid and I'd be happy to meet him if you like?"

"David, I would love you to meet Michael and I know he would like to meet you. He's already asked me a ton of questions about you and tennis. He wants to hear the nitty-gritties of life on the tennis tour, how you finance things, what diet you on, how you prepare mentally for a match and so many other questions. I told you Aquarians need to know and understand everything" she said laughing.

"I think he sounds like the only guy I know who can match you intellectually, my darling sister."

"Oh no, no, no ... this dude is many levels higher" she replied.

"OK, before you go sleep there's something else" she smiled.

"Jesus, I don't know if I can take any more surprises Leah!"

"This won't take long. It's just that for a couple months now I've noticed a change in you. You seem a lot more relaxed in spite of the pressure you must be under. You seem content and happier than I've ever seen you. I think it's the reason you are achieving such amazing results too. But I've also noticed amongst all that, a bit of unease too, like you have conflicting emotions. Is there anything you want to tell me, my brother?" she asked seriously.

Leah knew him only too well. She had always been able to read his moods, far better than his parents anyway.

"Even though you were so tired *Shabbos* two weeks ago whatever happened that afternoon before dinner left a sparkle in your eyes which I've never seen before. I know it wasn't Loren Rabinowitz although she was looking very hot that night, and just for you by the way. You hardly even gave her a look and so whoever was occupying your mind must be very, very special. Then, the way you rushed out last night for dinner with that same sparkle in your eyes ... David, I'm not blind. I know you have met someone special even though you've done your best to hide her."

After a long silence David finally answered.

"Leah, I'm not ready to talk about what I'm going through yet until I understand it fully myself. Of course, once I do you will be the first one I will talk to about it. I promise you."

"You OK though, David? That's all I want to know" she asked, sounding concerned.

"I'm really fine Leah and you were right. For the first time in a long time I am happy" he replied giving his little sister a hug and kiss on the forehead.

“Maybe I take you and your priest out for dinner this week. I’ve been wanting to go back to the Roma revolving restaurant for a while now so maybe Wednesday evening?” he asked, moving towards the door.

“I’ll check with Michael tomorrow but I’m sure he’ll be delighted” she answered.

“Good night Leah. I’m so glad we had some time together tonight.”

“Good night my big brother. I’m so happy you back home with us for a bit. I feel so much better now I cannot tell you.”

Chapter 9

David rose early again the Monday morning. He had set his alarm for 5:30 a.m. so he could do some early training sprints on North Beach. He knew he was going to be doing a lot of sprinting around the red clay at Roland Garros and he would have to be in tip-top shape for that. As a junior David had found the sea sand the best place to do this type of aerobic training as it not only improved his speed but also strengthened his ankles at the same time. The sun was just starting to break through as he hit Berea Road heading east to Durban's famous central beaches.

Early mornings in Durban were David's favourite. He loved the chirping of the birds in all the trees along Manning Road, the multitude of early morning runners training for the city's annual Comrades marathon along with the many cyclists. The sea would often be full of surfers even at this time of morning, many of them scholars or students catching a wave before school or college. but also quite a few office workers and businessmen. Durban was a city that rose early wanting to make the most of its daylight and beautiful nature that it had been blessed with.

David's route took him past the Indian part of the CBD and taxis full of workers for the many retail stores, offices and factories, were rushing to drop off their customers and then to collect more. Durban's Indian community was the biggest of any major city outside of India and they were an important part of the fabric of the city. David reflected how they had arrived largely as indentured labourers to cut the sugar cane for the colonial sugar farm estates dotted all over the province's north and south coasts. Through sheer tenacity and back-breaking work the first generation immigrants had educated their children to become doctors, lawyers, accountants, dentists as well as smart businessmen. They had left an indelible mark on the city with their food and culture and David admired them for their achievements. The Muslim community, unlike the majority of Hindus and Tamils, had come to South Africa and Durban specifically, as merchants and not labourers. Over time they had come to dominate the clothing and textile industries together with the Eastern European Jews, David's tribe. David's Uncle Sol, who was an early shareholder of SA Clothing, the dominant Jewish-owned clothing manufacturer, often spoke of his business with the Lockhats, Mahomedys and Paruks who were the doyens of the Muslim clothing community. In fact, he even remembered Uncle Sol telling him that he had invested money in some of their operations. At the time David couldn't understand that but then Uncle Sol had said to him in an accent right out of the *shtetl, "Boychik*, beeshniss is beeshniss. One day you'll understand."

David opened his driver's window and he could hear the hustle and bustle of the streets, as well as the smell of incense and curry spices. He knew he was home, his true home where everything was so familiar and welcoming. Soon he was passing Kingsmead cricket stadium which was the home of Natal cricket and had hosted many important cricket tests until South Africa had been banned from international sport because of its stance on Apartheid. Before long he could smell the crisp salt air and he knew he was close to the beaches.

The sea was quite flat but there was an amazing wave forming just off the pier at the Bay of Plenty, famous for hosting the annual Gunston 500, Durban's contribution to the ASP Tour. It was at this very beach that David had watched his boyhood surfing idol, Shaun Tomson, win the title and become surfing world champion. Whilst it wasn't that much of a surprise for a Durban boy to win it, it was certainly a surprise for a Jewish one to do it. In fact Uncle Sol had told him that ever since G-d had parted the Red Sea for the Jews to escape the Egyptians, Jews had left anything to do with water for the Gentiles, and that's why they had chosen the desert of Israel.

The beach and the lovely promenade was full of joggers, cyclists and surfers heading to jump off the pier to the backline. There was even a group of old Chinese people doing tai-chi on the lawns outside The Cattleman restaurant. David was soon doing his sprints, jogging 20 metres and then sprinting 10 metres. He alternated like this for the distance between the 2 piers, a distance of approximately one-thousand metres, and then stretch out his body for 10 minutes. He timed himself for 60 minutes and then feeling quite exhausted, he jumped into the crisp Indian Ocean to cool off his burning muscles. It felt so exhilarating to body surf in the shore break for half an hour and then rinse himself off in the open showers on the edge of the promenade.

Drying off on the promenade wall with a towel draped around him, his mind wandered to Dov. They had met at a SAUJS meeting he had attended on campus in his final year at UND. It had been at a time of heightened tensions in the Middle East. After the routing they had received in the 1967 and 1973 wars and the revolution in Iran, the Arabs had rearmed themselves and anti-Israel hatred was building again. After being caught with their pants down on Yom Kippur the IDF had vowed it would never happen again and had invested huge sums of the tiny nation's budget on military intelligence. Israel did not have the luxury of a second chance. The IDF and Mossad had to have access to vital enemy intelligence before any attacks occurred and they also had to have the latest armoury to ward off any encounters. Whilst David had noticed Dov at other SAUJS's meetings, he had just assumed he was just another Jewish student concerned for Israel's safety. He had been approached by Dov the first time in the university gym, a real sweaty, stinky room with no air conditioning. It worked for David because anybody who worked out there was serious and certainly not there for the décor or to socialise. David would do circuits focusing on building core strength as well as shoulder strength, essential for stability on a tennis court. Occasionally he would do a few bench-press reps for his chest and arms but he mostly preferred reps with lighter weights. On this particular gym day he decided to end off an excellent session with a few bench- presses. Lying horizontally on the bench, just before he made his second press, Dov appeared from behind him, lightly supporting the pole in his hands.

"Howzit! You should never bench-press without a partner, bud. I've had friends seriously injure themselves. Broken sternums, pulled pectoral muscles, all sorts. Let me help you now" he said in his nasally Johannesburg Jewish accent.

"Oh OK, thanks. Very kind of you" David responded, pushing up hard.

He finished a set of ten and then called it quits.

"I saw you last week battling with these and thought to myself, no man I can't let this *Yid* kill himself. Next time I'll help him" he said to David, grinning.

"Many thanks, bro. So what's a Jo'burg Yid like you doing in a nice place like this?" laughed David.

"It's that obvious hey?" chuckled Dov.

"Oh yes! Where in Jo'burg you from?" asked David curiously.

"Sandton. The new Tel Aviv, you know" and they both laughed.

"I did army for 2 long fucking years and then finished a BCom at Wits last year with law majors. Got *gatvol* of Joburg and the family so decided I'd do my LLB here. Except for the humidity, this place is a *jol* and I'm loving it. I saw you at the SAUJS meeting about Palestine 2 weeks ago by the way."

"Yip, I go every so often when my conscience gets the better of me. Your face is familiar. I'm David by the way, David Oppenheim" David said holding out his hand for Dov to shake it.

"Cool, I'm Dov Mendelson. Lekker to meet you brother" said Dov whose hand felt more like a huge baseball mitt than a hand. He was a big unit but not with any obvious fat on him, just big.

"If you finished your workout can I buy you a Coke or something at the SU?" asked Dov. "I don't really know anyone here and certainly very few Jews. The Durban ones are a real closed-off cliquey bunch."

David knew exactly what he meant by that and was one of the reasons he left Carmel all those years ago. The Durban Jewish community was so introverted and rather incestuous. Durban as a whole was a difficult place for a newcomer to break into. The school system was a strong one in Durban and life bonds were formed in high school. David detested that Durbanites felt they could sum up a person simply by asking them which school they had attended. From that one piece of information they would instantly assume a stranger's income group, political ideology, quality of education and general standing in the community. Talk about judging a book by its cover, David thought.

"Sure, I've got an hour now if you do?" asked David, towelling the sweat from his brow.

"*Schweet,* let's do it man" Dov answered again in typical Jo'burg-speak.

Once comfortably seated in the SU cafeteria Dov proceeded to tell David about his life. He was a few years older than David and had seemed to have lead the typical Sandton Jewish upbringing, having attended King David High School in Linksfield. After matriculating he had spent a year on a kibbutz in Israel trying to figure out exactly what he wanted to do with his life. He had met a girl on the kibbutz and one year became a second year on his kibbutz, but once the relationship had fizzled out he had decided to return home and get his military service out the way. He had loved the physicality of the army and after his basic training in Upington he had been selected for an officer's course in Oudtshoorn. The course had gone so well that he had then been selected for a parabats course in Bloemfontein which had been followed by a stint in Angola.

David noticed how excited Dov seemed when he spoke about his time in the military which was the complete opposite for his Jewish friends who all tried to postpone their national service for as long as possible. He couldn't quite imagine the big unit floating on a parachute, but maybe they had an extra, extra large one for Dov. He went on to talk about the combat they had experienced in the bush war in Angola where they had jumped in the dark so the enemy couldn't get a visual on them. He told David with great amusement how one of his colleagues had landed in a tree and they had teased him about leaving him there for the duration of the trip, where he would be perfectly safe from the lions.

"Jesus, you sound like you really miss those days. I would have wanted to get out of there as fast as possible" laughed David.

"Bro, you don't understand the camaraderie and friendships you build when you fight together as a unit. Your life is in your team's hands and so you become a band of brothers. You learn so many important lessons like for instance how to live off the land. You can throw me anywhere in the bush with nothing but my clothes and I'll never have to miss a single meal. I know how to make fire, how to track and catch wildlife, and how to find water. How many clever professors here know how to do that?" boasted Dov.

"I also know how precious life is and how easily it can be taken. I buried more friends than I care to tell you about, some kids as young as 18 years old. I'm proud of having fought on the border for my country David. Whilst you and the rest of the country were going about your normal lives we army guys were making night jumps and shooting up the terrorists so you could enjoy your lifestyles. War is a terrible thing but sometimes it's necessary to keep your country and its people safe. I don't think there's a more honourable thing for a man to do than protecting his people" Dov concluded.

"Were there any moments when you didn't think you were going to make it out?" David asked his new friend.

"Yes, but *HaShem* was always protecting me. It wasn't my time."

"I wish I had your faith in a divine power, bud. I like a lot of our traditions but I have never been able to get my head around the idea of a personal God. Organised religion just seems so archaic in our modern world and too synthetic, man-made. I don't think you survived because of a deity Dov, I think you made it out because you are a damn fine soldier. If I had to go to war I would hope you were in my team. Then maybe this *putz* would survive."

"David, I have a very strong notion that you under-estimate yourself. I've watched how disciplined you are in your workouts in the gym and how you are able to push yourself even when you're in pain. Those are also the hallmarks of a good soldier. Anyway enough about war, I overheard some of the *okes* in the gym saying you're going to play the pro tennis circuit next year?" asked Dov.

"Well, it's not in fact the main tour but the qualifying tour for the main tour. It's called the Challenger Tour and the money isn't great but it's the points you really play for. You do well and accumulate enough points then you get to qualify for the ATP tour without needing to qualify for any of the majors. Then you making some decent bucks and you can call yourself a true professional."

"So how do you finance all this? Do you have a sponsor for all your gear and airfares and hotels? I would imagine all this must be lank expensive or do you have a rich family helping you out?" asked Dov.

"My family are anything but wealthy, I assure you. My old man is an English professor and academics are not flush. My mom is a stay-at-home housewife so my dad's salary is the only household income. Fortunately I am talking to a few racket and clothing sponsors to help me with my gear as you call it, and my Uncle Sol is helping me a bit with travelling expenses. It's damn tough without a sponsor or a rich daddy to make it on the Challenger tour never mind the main ATP tour. There are no guarantees but I'm going to push it for 2 years and hopefully I can get into the top one-hundred players" explained David.

"Interesting, I may have a solution for you David but it doesn't come for free. It would cover all your costs from equipment and apparel to your travel expenses and take all that pressure off you to concentrate on your tennis, but it would require a *quid pro quo."* Dov's tone had changed from casual to serious.

"I don't know if I follow you? What do you mean? Are you suggesting you will finance my tennis? What exactly do you mean by this *quid pro quo*? Sounds like my current tennis scholarship where I represent UND in the tennis league?" David asked, with the distinct feeling that Dov knew more about him than he had let on.

"No, no, no David this is far more serious than UND allowing you a free education in return for you playing tennis for them. It's far more important

David. It could save many, many Jewish lives. In fact not trying to be dramatic but it could even save a country. David, I am a law postgraduate student here but I'm also quite a lot more. David, I work for our people. I'm *Mossad* bro" he said in a whisper.

Dov stared intently at David's shocked face looking for any signs he gave off. After a few moments silence he continued.

"David, I know more about you than even your family do. I can tell you that you were second in Hebrew at Carmel in standard 5. I can tell you that your mother and not your father or sister has the highest IQ in your family. I can tell you things about your family and friends that you don't even know. I work for *the* best and smartest spy agency in the world, David. I also know in spite of you being an atheist, you love Israel and the Jewish people enough to agree to what I'm about to propose to you. David the Jewish tribe needs you, Israel needs you" said Dov, still whispering, but now with an almost pleading tone.

"*Me*? *Me*? I think you have the wrong David Oppenheim, bro!" responded David, half laughing.

"I'm just some ordinary Jewish kid from Durban who can play a bit of tennis. I'm definitely no spy and certainly no soldier! What are you talking about?" said David, in a confused tone.

"David, you have all the right qualities to be an intelligence officer. You don't know it but we've been observing you in great detail the last year. I was even watching you play in that match against Stellenbosch last week. I loved the way you used your cunning to outdo that big Dutchman by the way. David, you are smart, loyal to our people and probably because of your tennis you handle pressure situations very well. These are all the traits we are looking for, and the fact that you will be a full-time pro tennis player next year is perfect cover. The agency will pay all your expenses and we will never interfere with any of your tennis. It's a win-win for both of us" explained Dov.

"It's true I'm a proud Jew but I have zero experience of any kind in spying" laughed David.

"That's where we help David. We'll start by helping you with Arabic, you already speak Hebrew well enough to pick it up quickly. Where we need you, you may very well need to understand it to understand messages being sent.

Messages that, if intercepted in time could save thousands of Jewish lives in both Israel and the Diaspora. Then we'll ..."

"Whoa, wait just a second Dov! I haven't agreed to anything yet. I'm certainly not going to live in the Middle East spying on Arabs for you. I've got a tennis career ahead of me, hopefully for the next ten years and besides 5 years of fucking Hebrew was bad enough for me" interrupted David.

"No, no bro I'm not talking about targeting in the Middle East, I'm talking about here, Durban, which is why I'm here too. Let me explain before we decide anything" said Dov.

David was not too happy when Dov said *we* decide. He didn't like the word *targeting* either, having never fired a single shot in his life.

"Bro, it's hardly news that we've had an uneasy relationship with the Arabs. You will recall from your visit in your standard 9 year and the one and only *Habonim* trip your parents forced you on, that we are permanently at war with our enemies. They are intent on destroying us, bro. The 1973 war was a much closer thing than our government has told people. David if we had lost that war they would have obliterated us and Jews would no longer have a safe homeland of their own to escape to from another Holocaust. There is a rise in anti-Semitism worldwide and soon Jews in the Diaspora will no longer be safe. We cannot allow our enemies to destroy our last refuge, bro. We need you David to help us, *your* people, David" pleaded Dov.

"Go on then" asked David still sounding sceptical.

"David, the Durban Muslim community have been sending large amounts of cash out of this country in the form of foreign exchange to finance their Palestinian brothers. The money, most of which is supposed to go to aid NGO's, is being intercepted by terrorist groups like Hezbollah and Hamas amongst others, who are using it to buy arms rather than food and medicines. With the imminent fall of Russia there are already all sorts of nuclear warheads and dangerous weapons available for these fuckers to buy on the black market. Mossad have managed to neutralise some of these deals but not all. If this continues much longer they will score enough firepower to blow our little country and its people off the face of this planet. David, we can't, we won't allow this to happen".

David and Dov just stared at each other for quite some time both trying to assess the other. He could just imagine his Uncle Sol's delight at his being chosen by Mossad to intercept messages for them. His mother on the other hand would go ballistic and tell him to have nothing to do with spying. His father wouldn't really care and would probably insist on them rather paying for another 3 years for him to study.

"Dov, you come to me pretending to be one Jew helping another do bench presses in a gym, and then next minute you are asking me to spy for fucking Mossad? Have you heard the term "mind fuck" before? Well, this right here is a mid fuck on steroids, OK. What the fuck do you think I should say?" David eventually responded, and feeling quite angry his life had been disturbed like this.

"David, your reaction is *exactly* what I anticipated. When Mossad interviewed me whilst I was living on my *kibbutz* I felt all the feelings you are now going through. We will never force you to do anything you don't feel comfortable with. We will totally understand if this is the last meeting you want but I think I know you well enough that you won't do that. David, I see you in me, and after letting things settle a bit you will come to the same conclusion that I did. David, we have a responsibility to do this for our people" Dov ended.

"Look, my head is spinning right now. I do need time to digest all this craziness you are proposing. I just have one question. How the fuck do you expect a Jew to infiltrate the Muslim community?"

"So, to answer your first question. Let me touch bases with you in a week. The answer to your second question. Your target is a very, very beautiful girl who is the daughter of a suspected donor of these terrorist groups. We need you, through your relationship with her, to find out how and who. Believe me, when you see this chick you will thank me!" laughed Dov.

"She's *Muslim*?" David asked in disbelief.

"Yip, she is" responded Dov.

"Oy vey, bro! I don't even particularly like dating Jewish chicks and you want me to start a relationship with a Muslim one?" David asked, shocked.

"Mark my words, should you accept my proposal, you'll thank me!" laughed Dov, as he collected his things and stood up.

“I’ll see you in a week, my brother” is all Dov said, before leaving the SU cafeteria.

David sat very still, totally shocked. The only words he could think of clearly. Total mind fuck!

Chapter 10

Late afternoon that Monday, David met up with Lionel at Mitchell Park Tennis Club again. This time Lionel was on time which was surprising. Rather than play a couple of sets Lionel suggested he show David some interesting new drills his college coach had introduced him to before he graduated. In return he asked for the exercise David had used to improve his return of service.

"Bro, these drills are going to sharpen your game like a samurai sword. You going be so ready for that Spanish *oke* you'll gut him like a fish. Best part for you is I only charge 10% of your winnings!" Lionel boasted, stretching his hamstrings.

"So 10% for that match against Figueras only then. Sounds fair, send me your banking details" laughed David.

"No, no *china* 10% on *all* the matches you win at the French. Based on what I saw yesterday and the workout I'm going to give you the next 2 weeks, I think it's only fair. You are good for the last 16 at least, Davie boy" said Lionel.

"Deal bro! If I get that far you will have earned every cent of that 10% the way I'm going to grind you in Durban" joked David.

"OK, shut up then and move to the other side of the court so I can secure my investment and show you these drills. They're specially designed for you pushers glued to the baseline. It's all about strategy, a physical game of chess as it were" explained Lionel.

"But Li, you've never played a game of chess in your life" David teased his friend.

"Just shut up and move please, you *meshuggeneh*!" shouted Lionel.

For the next 2 hours Lionel put David through his paces with 3 different drills coach had shown Lionel. The drills were novel and David understood their full benefits for a baseliner like himself. Lionel had brought with him a basket full of balls and standing at the net he had David scrambling from side to side, screaming out instructions to him.

“Move, move, c’mon you lazy bugger. Imagine you’re already a set down to Figueras and you need to make him respect you, fear you. C’mon, c’mon, Davie boy” Lionel barked.

The first drill was designed to not only move David around the baseline but disallowed him from hitting two of the same shot in a row. The name of the game was variety of stroke to keep the opponent off balance and make him feel as uncomfortable as possible. He was the only person in discomfort, David thought, as the late afternoon humidity set in and the balls kept on coming. He was surprised after his early morning run that his legs still felt strong and he seemed to glide about the baseline. It was in all likelihood the endless hours he had endured on the clay courts the last few weeks that had built his stamina.

“OK shit-for-brains, you’ve earned a 10 minute break and then I *klap* you with a new drill. What did you think of that one by the way?” Lionel asked.

“Jesus, it certainly gets one thinking. I like it and you were right, it’s perfect for baseliners” replied David, sweat pouring off his brow.

“Here, drink this. It’s a concoction coach invented. It’s got virgin coconut oil mixed with a bunch of some electrolysis stuff. Nectar of the gods he said” said Lionel, throwing him a full bottle of the pink stuff.

“Electrolytes, Li” David corrected him.

“Yeah, exactly what I said” Lionel grinned back.

Surprisingly, the pink concoction was not bad tasting and David glugged down half the bottle.

“Now watch how you move around the court, bro. I’m not sure I should be giving away all my trade secrets like this” said Lionel half-joking.

“You mean *coach’s* trade secrets, right?” teased David.

“That’s going to cost you, cheeky bugger! Your ten minutes is done, now kindly piss off back to the baseline for some more death” Lionel teased.

The second drill was all about improving reactions on the baseline. David would face the back of the court and when Lionel shouted he would spin around and need to react to where Lionel had hit the ball. At first it was really tough, but once David had learnt how to spin about faster, he was soon able to master it and even Lionel was impressed.

"Impressive Davie, I see you even anticipating where I'm going to go now."

The drill continued for 30 minutes and David could feel the first strains of tightness in his calves.

"I thought you said this pink stuff has electrolytes in it, bud?" he teased Lionel as he finished off the rest of his pink drink.

"Listen, coach made the quarters at Wimbledon and the semis at the US in his day so I would like to think the *oke* knows his stuff. Have you not thought you're just unfit?" Lionel replied, defensively.

"So what's the last drill then coach?" David asked.

"Coach? You could never afford me!" Lionel joked.

The final drill was the most unexpected of them. Coach had explained to Lionel that one of the most underutilised but effective shots was the often-maligned moonball, where the player on the baseline lobs up high with plenty topspin a moonball. Lionel explained that not only did it change the pace, but if struck correctly, was an offensive stroke because it was tiring for the opponent to return.

After 40 minutes of hitting moonballs to each other they were both exhausted. David's shoulders were really feeling it and even Lionel looked like he had had a great workout.

"Well done, Davie! I'm really impressed you got through all three of those drills alive. Very few of my college mates could do that and certainly not for as long as we did. Let's take a thirty minute break and take a stroll to the tearoom and grab some Cokes. I don't know about you but I need a serious dose of sugar after the moonballs".

"Great idea, Cokes are on me" replied David.

As the two rivals walked across the park to the tearoom Lionel spoke about the conversation he had the previous evening with his family about his Tammy. He had reflected on David's advice about taking risks where the reward was worth it.

"You know my old girl worships you Jews, bro. She reminds me often you *okes* have the highest IQ in the world, but then I reminded her that I have you as a mate who brings the average down!" he laughed.

“Hey, hey I never said I was the sharpest tool in the shed but I would at least like to think I’m sharper than you!” David shot back.

“Relax Davie, I was just kidding. Anyone who graduates with a Bachelor of Commerce in Finance can’t be that dumb. Anyway my point was going to be that I think you right and I should just run with it with Tammy. I would love you to meet her and if you make the US Open this year I’ll fly her to Flushing Meadows to watch.”

“Li, after a couple months on the Challenger I foresee you qualifying too. Your game has come a long way since juniors and if I can do it, you certainly can too. You just need the week- in week- out competition to sharpen up one or two areas but otherwise everything I’ve seen looks solid. We can’t afford full-time shrinks but I’ve read a couple books on mind-over-matter that you should read. When I was getting a bit down on myself when I first joined the tour they helped me build my confidence again. You will quickly realise that unlike juniors and maybe even college, where we were the hot shots, that in the pro ranks everybody was a hot shot in their day. Every match is life or death, dog eat dog. Nobody cares about your junior or college ranking. They just want to roll you over and move on to the next guy. I’m just warning you so it doesn’t catch you by surprise, like it did me. The intensity of the pro ranks is something else, Li” David explained.

“So when did you feel like you were breaking through then?” asked Lionel, taking in everything his friend was saying like a sponge.

“Bro, that’s a smart question. It happened in Rome in the second round. I was playing the top seed, a French dude who had won the French as a junior. I went in without much hope and then when I was a set and 4-3 down with him serving, something just clicked. I suddenly thought to myself at the changeover that if I could push this guy close with a losing mind set, then why couldn’t I beat him with a positive one. From that moment, everything changed in my head and it translated onto the court. I was moving better, anticipating better, serving better. Actually I was just doing everything better. I broke his serve for 4-4 and never looked back. The dude was so shocked that his game went to pieces whilst mine soared. After that he only won one more game and stormed off swearing in French at anybody he came into contact with. Li, it’s a cliché but so true, at this level it’s 90% in the mind. Never forget that” said David.

“Wow! I wish I had been there to witness that one” was Lionel’s only response.

"Yip, me too. But I was lucky to have good support from the crowd as he wasn't very well liked" laughed David.

After quenching their thirst on a couple of Cokes they headed back to the courts where David explained the intricacies of his eye-brain exercises. David explained how he had contacted Dr Cheryl Gordon from the High Performance Sports Institute as she had done wonders for some of the South African pro golfers, and was also working with the batsmen and slip fielders from the national cricket team. She had explained that it was not difficult to improve one's reactions and ability to anticipate using a couple of very simple exercises. The primary objective was to have the eyes pass signals as quickly as possible to the brain so it could compute the best reaction, and send that signal to the limbs to execute the necessary actions. After completing her exercises repetitively, just like muscle memory, the brain would then learn to anticipate events and repeat actions, instinctively. David had found this all to be accurate and the results were showing in his return of serve.

David spent 30 minutes running through the drills Cheryl had taught him. Lionel seemed really excited and felt that these drills would add to his game. He was really motivated and hungry to prove his worth on the Challenger tour. He felt a lot better that he would have his more experienced friend to guide him into a softer landing on the tour. They had always been the greatest rivals but unusually for the competitive tennis circuit, they not only respected each other, but had a genuine friendship too.

"Davie, the next 2 weeks I'm going have you playing the best tennis of your life. The beauty is that the pros don't know you, they don't know your game whereas you've watched them play plenty. That Spanish *oke* isn't going to believe what has hit him your opening match at the French. I've watched a bit of him and your baseline game is far superior, and I'm not just saying that. Just think, he may be the highest seed to fall in the first round and to an unknown called Davie Oppenheim. You couldn't have dreamed up a better script!" laughed Lionel.

"You bloody well better be right, Li. Let's go shower and then you can buy me a meal for a change, *schnorrer*! And no more tennis talk for the day, we've done enough of that for the day" said David, ambling towards the change rooms.

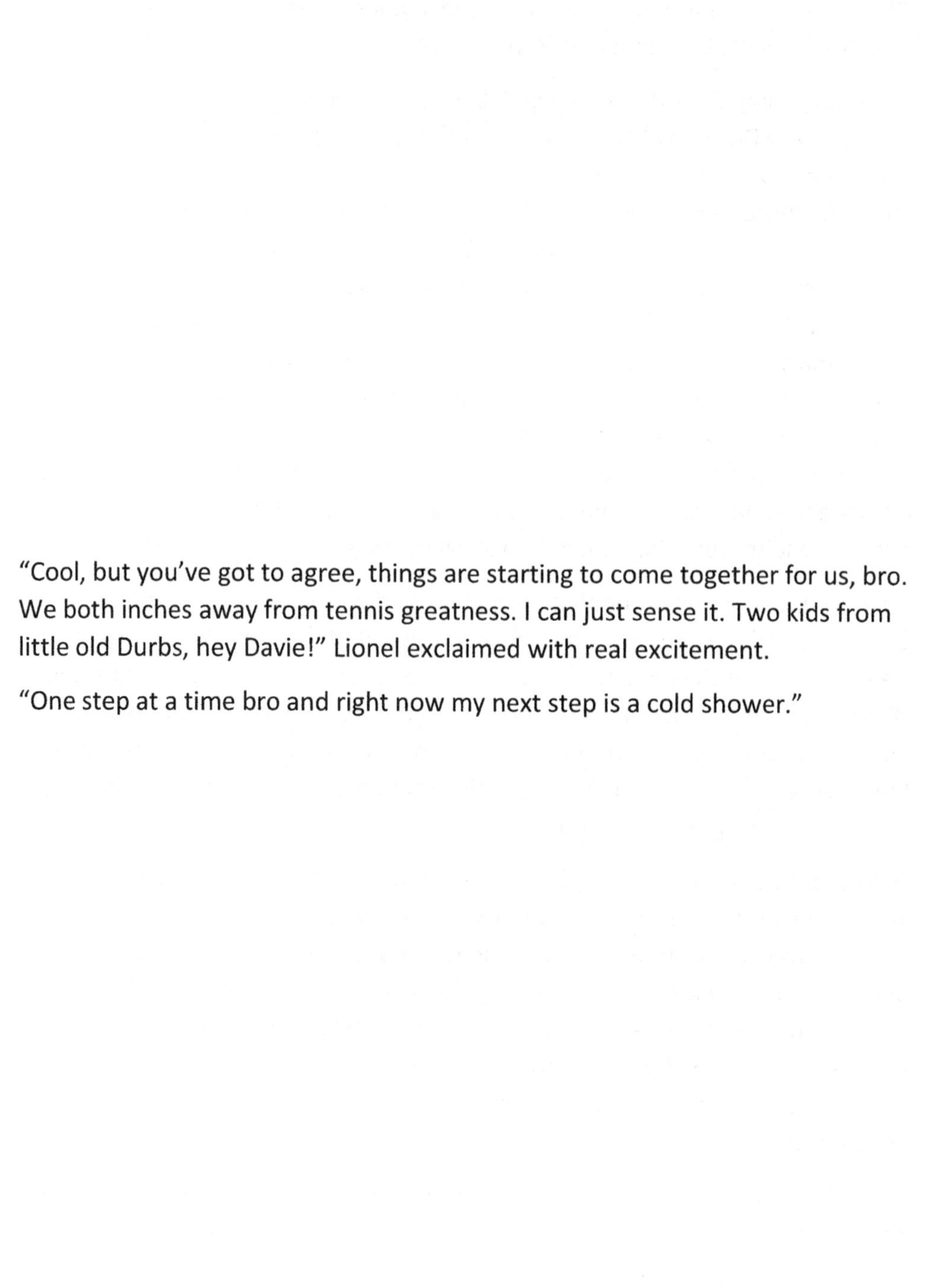

"Cool, but you've got to agree, things are starting to come together for us, bro. We both inches away from tennis greatness. I can just sense it. Two kids from little old Durbs, hey Davie!" Lionel exclaimed with real excitement.

"One step at a time bro and right now my next step is a cold shower."

Chapter 11

True to his word Dov contacted David. He was eating lunch in the SU after a long morning's session about the inflationary and deflationary effects on the SA economy, when out of nowhere Dov plonked himself down next to him with 2 Cokes in hand. He startled David at first, as for the 3 previous nights he had managed to relax and not think about Dov at all. As tempting as Dov's financial assistance had first appeared David had other options available like his Uncle Sol's offer, so his first instincts were to forego Dov's offer. Still he couldn't get their earlier conversation out of his mind. A certain level of guilt had started to infiltrate his mind about how he had forsaken his religion, but that didn't entitle him to forsake his people. As Dov had explained, this was about saving many lives and so much more than tennis. Surely there was somebody who did believe in *HaShem* and far better suited to Mossad's expectations than him. I mean after all he had told Dov he had never shot a weapon in his life before but was now expected to go out into the field and spy on so-called 'targets' in the Muslim community. He hardly knew a thing about these people except their equivalent of *kosher* was called *halaal* and their god they called *Allah*. Oh yes, and that virtually all of them hated his people and wanted them wiped off the face of the planet. They weren't exactly going to be welcoming, these so-called 'targets' of Dov's.

As the week wore on David's conscience was starting to play on him and he started considering Dov's offer more seriously. He could always lay down some conditions and that he would not be able to consider assisting Dov if it meant doing anything against his humanity or conscience, even if he was an atheist. He would tell Dov he would not hurt anyone and especially if it came down to killing a 'target'. That type of violence was against his principles. The only time physical violence was justified was in self-defence and David had only resorted to that once, when a stupid kid on the first day at DHS had called him a "dirty little Jew boy". David had never faced anti-Semitism before and had instinctively punched the *schmuck* with an incredible left hook, which sent the kid to the floor crying. At first David had felt awful about his response but then later he realised by setting a marker word had gotten around the school not to fuck with Oppenheim, the boxer. That proved to be the first and only bit of anti-Semitism David had faced throughout his DHS years. Regardless of this bit of bravery David abhorred violence of any kind and would need to make this crystal clear if he was going to assist Dov.

"Howzit bro! Come with me to the back there where it's more private and quieter" instructed Dov.

They made their way to the back of the cafeteria where the view onto the Durban harbour was incredible and where the campus radio station music was also much softer.

"So, you had a good week then?" asked Dov, sitting down.

"No Dov, you made sure of that I'm afraid" replied David, straightforwardly.

"Ha! I know exactly what you mean. When they first approached me on my *kibbutz* I went through all the same emotions you must have gone through. I remember it vividly. First, was I was angry. Like why drop all this on little old me. Then there was the guilt, that except for just taking I hadn't really done anything for our people, especially considering half my family were murdered in the *Shoah.* At that stage, like you, I too hadn't received any military training and wasn't ready for any Mossad stuff. My plans after breaking it off with my girlfriend were to return home, get my law degree and then start my career at my uncle's big commercial practice in Jo'burg, and hopefully get out of army conscription somehow. I didn't want my plans disrupted" Dov explained.

"So instead you're disrupting mine!" David half-laughed.

"David, I've spent endless hours researching and studying you. I already know what your answer is going to be even though I gave you the option of an out. You are more like me than you may know. Before my instruction, I too was an atheist like you. I too had a deep love for my people. It may be hard to believe but I too have a gentleness and caring for people in my heart" said Dov.

"Oh yes, so then seeing as you know everything, what is my answer?" asked David, feeling annoyed.

"David, don't be angry with me. I want us to have a great relationship and I also want the best for you. You are an amazing person and you are going to become a very famous professional Jewish tennis player. I for one am going to do everything in my power to make it happen"

"OK, before we go any further I have certain conditions. First and foremost, I'm not going to be involved in hurting anyone and definitely not killing anyone.

That goes against all my principles. Second, if at any stage this 'targeting' thing starts interfering with my tennis, I'm out, and thirdly, I don't want *any* of my friends or family brought into this. If any of those 3 conditions aren't acceptable to you, I suggest you just fuck off now and we never met!" David said determinedly, staring directly into Dov's eyes.

Dov listened intently and then broke out into loud laughter.

"David! Except for the tennis, those are almost exactly the same conditions I gave my handler, bro!" he said, still laughing.

"Given how serious your fucking request is I don't think that's very funny, dude! Don't just assume you've now just become my 'handler' too!" said David, unimpressed.

"Bro, I'm sorry man! Forgive my sick sense of humour, really."

After he had managed to compose himself he looked straight at David and said, "I'm not going to be your *handler* David. I'm going to be your part-time, Israeli tennis coach."

This time it was David's turn to burst out laughing.

"My *tennis* coach? Tennis coach? Dov, please! I mean what the fuck *you* know about tennis. I'm not playing at amateur level any longer. I mean you say you know how serious I am about achieving greatness in the game and now you want to pretend to be my coach? My contemporaries will kill themselves laughing at us!" David said, with tears of laughter streaming down his face.

"Hey, hey now, young man! I will have you know I did play a bit in my day. I played in the B team in matric for King David" Dov replied, defensively.

"Oh my god! This is getting worse and worse bro. Dov, the blind school used to beat King David tennis back in the day and now you want to start coaching a soon-to-be pro? I would rather pay you *not* to coach me!" David said, starting to guffaw again.

"Bro look, I am not a tennis coach but I'm reading every coaching book and watching every coaching video available on the market. I've also got Amos Mansdorf on call any minute I require him. I shouldn't even have mentioned his name so that's only between the two of us" said Dov.

"Well, why don't they provide Amos as my coach then?" asked David.

"David, I could answer that but then I would have to kill you right after! Let's just say he goes a lot higher up the ladder, OK" Dov responded.

"Amos is *Mossad*?" asked David, shocked.

"No more about him now" Dov said in a stern voice.

"So, Mr David Oppenheim, are we doing this thing or do I have to find another nice Jewish boy?" Dov asked knowingly.

"There's one last non-negotiable condition I need you to say yes to, otherwise you can still go fuck off" David said, with a small grin on his face.

"What else?" asked Dov, surprised.

"That if you're going to be my "tennis coach" you don't dare to ever try give me any tennis advice!" at which they both broke out in laughter.

"So, we got a deal then?" asked Dov, reaching out a hand.

"OK coach, we go for it then!" replied David, shaking his hand.

"*Baruch Hashem*! You had me sweating a bit there, bugger!" laughed Dov, with obvious relief on his face.

"Now I need you to sit closer to me so I can show you some photos. I didn't want to show them to you before you agreed to my proposal because it would almost certainly have caused you to change your mind if you were thinking of declining. She's very special this one, and you'll see why now" he said, pulling a file from his backpack.

"You mean my target is a *she*?" David said scornfully.

"Ha! Not any old *she,* this chickie, she's very special in many ways. Listen, she's the hottest chick I've ever seen in my life, way above your pecking order I might add. Fortunately we have intel that will open that door for you though."

Dov opened the file and showed David the first of a few enlarged photos. The face looking back at him was shockingly beautiful especially her beautiful green eyes. David immediately recognised her from campus. He didn't feel so bad that Dov had said this girl was out of his league, because she was out of every male students' league on campus. Dov was also smart in *not* having shown him these photos before he had given a final answer, because this beautiful creature would have swayed any man to agree to the assignment. Dov slowly flicked through the pictures. There were quite a few of her taken on different days on campus, one of her walking 2 golden retrievers with some guy, another of her playing badminton with friends and even some of her in a one-piece bathing costume, swimming lengths in an indoor pool. A beautiful face and a nice, slim, athletic body David thought.

"Well, she's not *ugly* at least" David said, trying not to be that impressed.

"Bollocks, bro! She's got every Indian and white guy out there trying to get into her pants but she's not interested. Her old man is very, very strict and religious and her brother has to chaperone her wherever she goes, except on campus. You should kiss me I've given this chickie as a first target. You don't want to know the *drek* I was given my first time" scoffed Dov, "but maybe I should be happy to hear that from you because then there's no chance of falling in love with her."

"So what, you want me to follow her around campus and report on her?" asked David.

"Nope, I can train a monkey to do that. Our real person of interest is her old man, one Ismail Mahomedy and his friends, not his daughter, Shakira. Getting friendly with her will lead to the father and hopefully shed light on how money is being moved to our enemies and by whom exactly. The father is legitimately an honest businessman who has made an absolute shitload of money from the *shmatta* business. He imports and exports clothing and textiles from all parts of the world. He is regarded within his community as the country's sheikh of clothing and textiles. Surprisingly, our contacts within the local tax department tell us that he's honest and declares all his income. Our friends at the bank say that his foreign exchange inflows and outflows tie up exactly and that he's 100% *kosher*" he explained to David.

"So, if her old man is so honest, why even bother looking at him? There must be others who are better to pursue, surely?" asked David.

"Our people are saying that in recent chatter this guy's name keeps on popping up. They are convinced he is the kingpin, the main source of the foreign exchange the terrorists are receiving. Our intelligence guys are the best in the world and if they have info this guy is involved, then we roll with it" said Dov, looking about just to ensure nobody was in earshot of them.

"So my role will be to befriend this Shakira chick and see what comes back from my contact with her?"

“Wrong again my friend. We need you to start a *romantic* relationship with her not just a platonic friendship. We need you to get so close with her that she even invites you to meet her father, who from our reports is a big tennis nut. Apparently he was a pretty good junior in his day but between the apartheid system and his poor family there was really no chance of him going very far, so he quit both school and tennis and started trading. He’s a real character this dude and I think if he wasn’t our enemy we would like him”

“So, I’m going to go back to the beginning part of all that. You said a fucking *romantic* relationship, right?” David asked, totally bewildered.

“Dov, you do know I’m Jewish and she’s Muslim, right? I shouldn’t need to remind you that they’ve been trying to kill our people since 1948? Now you just blurt out that you expect me to form a romantic relationship with someone whose father is assisting terrorists, and whose daughter probably hates us too? Is this a script for The Bold and The Beautiful because it’s sounding more and more ridiculous the longer you go on” said David.

“I know, I know. The first time Moshe discussed this with me I also thought they were *meshugge,* but then after letting it sink in and digest a bit I realised that it’s brilliant. David, we have information that will at least open the door for you with this chick and then we need you to work your magic to take it further.”

“What information do you have because I’m quite shy around girls?” David asked, sounding unconvinced.

“She and you have one common passion that will open the door. You see like you she’s a music nutter, in fact much more than you. Music is one of the few vices her father has allowed her at home. He probably thinks it’s better to keep his beautiful daughter at home listening to music than cavorting with infidels outside. Our tax friends also advised us that amongst the many businesses her father is invested in as a silent partner, is Manhattan Music, which is one of the biggest importers, wholesalers and retailers in South Africa and where you yourself have purchased many of your records since you were a *pisher.* Everybody seems to think the business is owned by the Vaheds, who are close friends of the family, but the Mahomedy’s own 60% of it. Interestingly, your chickie does the accounts for this particular operation for which she receives records and CD’s as compensation. She would rather receive records than cash which tells you what music means to her. We hear she also compiles lists of titles for their buyers to source. From what we've seen Manhattan has the largest collection of collectibles and out-of-print titles by a long shot, and apparently those can bring in a big profit for the seller. Like you, she also listens to a wide range of genres."

"Wait a minute, how do you know that I have a wide range in musical taste? Please don't tell me you've been in our *home*?" asked David.

"Bro, before we approach someone we need to be 100% sure for both your sakes and ours. We will never just throw you out there if you don't have the right stuff. We have to be sure David" replied Dov earnestly.

"Well, as per my one condition, that's the last time you ever do that unless I give you my permission. From here on, my family and my friends are off limits, or I'm out Dov!" David insisted.

"Of course bro. Now we are satisfied you have all the right characteristics we won't intrude on your private life again, promise" Dov responded, half apologetically.

"Good. Then carry on."

"David, we feel if you approach Shakira using your common passion of music as your bait she will be interested, especially if we source some irresistible out-of-prints and collectibles. She's not as shy or aloof as she gives off. Her mother's family are actually quite progressive and are of Persian background. Shakira and her siblings were born here. She has a few casual friends and only one close one called Miriam. She's also close with her older brother who has a bit of a love and hate relationship with the father. He didn't want to join any of the fathers businesses to prove his worth, but apparently he's turned out to be a bit of a wannabe gangster, nothing too bad but not 100% *kosher* like the father. We trying to find out more detailed information about the relationship but that's all we know for now."

"Do you know whether she's had any relationships *at all*?" David asked.

"She doesn't seem to have had anything here but she lived in Paris for a few years at one point and she may have had something there, but we are still looking into that. Take it at this stage that the old man has prevented that from happening."

"Oh great, so now I'm supposed to try be her first!" laughed David

"Look, she could have been a total dog but instead you got the most beautiful chickie on campus, and besides you're not going to fall in love with her. Once you've got what we need from her you'll break it off and that will be that" said Dov.

"Before we can even consider your first encounter we need to put you through your paces at HQ and get you learning Arabic too. The father and many of his friends speak it quite fluently so it's important you can understand it. Mossad want you in Israel for induction training in a week today. They have even arranged for 2 top juniors to practice with you and a dietitian wants to spend time with you and completely change your poor eating habits. She says you are eating crap which is why you are battling with your stamina on the court. You will never make it in the majors where they play best of 5 sets. We also have a shrink who will help you with the mental side of things which will also improve your tennis. There will also be a lot of physical training involved so it's going to be no holiday camp but will get you fitter than you've ever been. I really think you will enjoy this a lot more than you realise, David. They have even arranged some sightseeing trips so you can understand our peoples' history better. It falls over your university vac so you won't miss any lectures either. Our contact at TSA will provide a letter you can show your folks that you have been selected for a 2 week training program in Israel. They won't suspect anything that way. My handler Moshe will take good care of you there I can assure you. You'll love him, bro, he's one helluva character!"

"Our second meeting and you people have everything already planned out for me. You not messing around I see" David responded.

"David, there isn't a soul at Mossad who doesn't regard your contribution as anything other than lifesaving. There's nothing the agency won't do to protect you and support you in this quest. As we get further into this you will come to fully understand your role. David, you are doing this for *our people* and their survival. That makes you a very important person. I want to meet with you in future in a room upstairs on the 3rd floor marked Economics Society. Here is a key to the room. Not only will we meet there at prearranged times but if you ever feel you are in trouble, there is a phone hidden in there which you will use to phone HQ who will in turn send agents to collect you. Depending where I am at the time it may or may not be me but whoever it is will make sure you are safe. Hopefully we never have to receive that call from you. Anyway, I will meet you there next Tuesday at 5 p.m. after your last Finance lecture. Just tell your folks you eating out with varsity mates that night" instructed Dov, handing David a single key marked Economics Society.

"I will give you the full run down on Shakira Mahomedy and I'll also bring the bait" said Dov.

"Bait?" asked David.

"Yes, some very hard to find and extremely rare, not to mention expensive, records!" laughed Dov, "and you can keep them afterwards too" he finished.

"Cool. Before we go there is something I'm curious about though. I want to know how you broke into our home?" asked David.

"Nobody broke into your home David, your mother let us in" answered Dov.

"What?"

"We interfered and disabled your house alarm and then when your mother phoned the alarm company we intercepted the call and pretended to be the alarm company. Two of our guys were let into your house by your mother wearing branded overalls. Once inside, they went through the rooms 'looking' for the fault and took pictures, unnoticed, of whatever they needed. Then when they were done we reactivated the alarm. No damage done" laughed Dov.

"Cheeky buggers!" David responded.

"Tuesday next week 5 p.m. sharp, bro. We have lots to get through. It starts now" Dov replied, whilst standing up.

David left their meeting with the distinct feeling that he was in for a long haul. In tennis terms, definitely a 5 setter.

Chapter 12

David woke at 5 a.m. on Tuesday morning. He could feel the after-effects of his tough workouts of the previous 2 days. The beach sprints of the previous morning had really stretched his ankles to their limit and the last thing he felt like doing was repeating the exercise this morning. He knew that his first round Spanish opponent, Juan Figueras, a tough clay court veteran, would not be skipping his daily grind in pursuit of tennis glory, so he reluctantly pulled his body out of bed.

He was relieved he had packed his workout bag the night before and after a quick wash he quickly found himself in the good old Green Mamba, hauling himself off to North Beach. For a change David flicked over the Alpine to one of the local news channels. He immediately recognised the news reader as one of his former Carmel classmates whom he had one of many brief flings with. She was talking about some riot in one of the Johannesburg townships before moving onto a story about Israel. David immediately turned the volume a bit higher. Apparently there had been trouble in the West Bank again as well as a failed suicide attempt on a school bus in Jerusalem. What kind of a sicko would honestly want to blow up a group of innocent school kids David thought. The threatened *intifada* that the agency had warned both David and Dov about was indeed imminent. They had been instructed to be extra cautious with their movements as some of David's intel was starting to pay off and the enemy were starting to be suspicious. Fortunately they were only looking within their own camp for a mole but it wouldn't take long before they widened their investigation. This had caused both of them a bit of anxiety and they had decided to hang a bit low on their work for a little while. Let the dust settle a bit as it were so that the Arabs might put things down to coincidence. His smart sister had picked up this concern from David as well as the first traces of conflict David was now feeling about his growing relationship with his beautiful girlfriend.

As the Green Mamba ate up the miles passing countless early morning joggers and cyclists, David's mind wandered back to his meeting with Shakira of the previous Friday morning at Mitchell Park. She had been so happy to see him after his 2 weeks overseas. She came running up to him in the park and jumped into his arms. He loved the warmth of her body and familiar smell of her perfume as she dived into him.

"Oh god, I've missed you more than you can imagine!" she shouted, planting kisses on every part of his face.

"I think I know because I missed you even more!" David shouted back taking in every bit of her in his arms. He could feel the warm, soft tears on her cheeks.

"I'm going to have to travel with you soon on this damn tour, Mr Oppenheim, because I can't handle being apart from you for this long" she cried out.

Ever since their first date at Legends they had either seen each other or spoken on the phone nearly every day. The only times he hadn't spoken with her was when he hadn't been able to find a phone in time overseas or because it was too late and he didn't want to wake her household. They had arranged specific times that he would call so that none of her family would answer first. On the one occasion that her mother got to the phone seconds before her, Shakira had told her mother that he was her Finance tutorial leader who had important information for the exam. David had been startled how similar the mother's accent was to her daughter's. They had both attended elocution lessons and sounded like proper English ladies, not even white South Africans, never mind Durban Indians. Shakira had told him how they were both fluent in French and when they didn't want her father to understand their conversations they would talk French to each other and explain to him they didn't want to lose their French and needed to practice. Her father was not entirely convinced, she said.

"Now tell me in detail about your trip, my sweetness. Those odd calls here and there I'm sure don't do it justice. I've always wanted to go to Morocco and the souks of Marrakesh, not to mention Dubai for some shopping. My dad is tired of the shopping lists I give him and having to declare it all at Jan Smuts Customs. Come on, I want it all, even the part about all those beautiful girls flirting with my tennis champion" she said, more excited than he had seen her in some time.

"OK, OK, OK my darling, give me a chance!" David chuckled, his heart getting that warm feeling every time he was around her. He felt so good at how much she had missed him. It was so true that absence had made their hearts grow fonder. Over the past couple months they had fallen deeper for each other and they had also formed a deep bond. His girlfriend was highly intelligent and far more worldly than him. She was very well read and he couldn't help but think that she could be best friends with his Leah. They would be able to discuss philosophy for endless hours as well as religion. David was astounded at her depth of knowledge of all 3 monotheistic religions. He was almost embarrassed how in so many ways she knew as much if not more about Judaism than he did. She was really fascinated too about the Christian Jew the Gentiles referred to as Jesus Christ, their saviour and son of God. Even though he had done his high schooling at a Christian school, David knew very little about this man or his history except that he was regarded as the messiah by them and they were awaiting his return to save the world. He was even more shocked to learn that the dude was seen as a prophet by Muslims. She also spent some time telling him about Islam's revered prophet, Mohammed, and his history. The manner she explained about all the major religions was fascinating and more of a history lesson than lecturing about a deity. Leah would have been fascinated.

"Firstly, I never come empty handed as you know" he said.

"Just such a Jewish thing Mr Oppenheim!" she laughed excitedly.

"I also have a nice surprise for you! Actually two, but let's see yours first" she continued excitedly.

David hauled a couple of packets out his Head bag.

"Please don't tell me tennis balls from Morocco!" she laughed.

"Not tennis balls, no! Here we go, you open the first one" he said, passing her the first beautifully wrapped gift.

His prize money on his last trip had been half decent and that combined with the agency's contribution, he had managed to rustle up enough to buy her a gorgeous dark maroon, slinky silk dress in Morocco. It wasn't one of the designer names but it had Shakira written all over it. With all the time they had spent together he knew it would be a perfect fit for her nimble body.

"David, oh my God! This is just my size and what a beautiful colour! David, this must have cost a fortune, you really shouldn't have. You are just starting out on the tour and need your money!" she cried out.

"For my beautiful and smart lady! You deserve it and I can afford it. It is the right size?" he asked.

Shakira stood up and put it against her body.

“It’s absolutely perfect. You know my body now” she said shyly.

“Right, next packet please” he instructed.

She delved into the packet and unpacked a gorgeous box of mixed Turkish delights and chocolate-coated dates. He knew those, along with the Sally Williams chocolate nougats, were her absolute favourites.

“Oh my god! My mother has been pestering my father for months to buy him these on his Dubai trips. Thanks my angel, these are my favourites and you didn’t forget.”

“It’s my greatest pleasure and I hope your folks enjoy them too but please don’t tell your old man I *smokkeled* through Customs! Now onto the last. It’s the smallest but my favourite” he said, beckoning to the final, exquisitely wrapped box.

She held the box in her hand, all the while staring intently into her boyfriend’s eyes with that big grin of hers.

“Come on, come on now, let’s see it” he laughed.

The look on her face was so precious when she lifted the gorgeous white gold necklace with heart on it out of its box. She held it in her hand whilst playing with the heart. He was happy he had allowed Dov to talk him in to engraving their initials on the back of it.

“David, my love, you make me so, so happy!” she exclaimed throwing herself into her arms.

This time he took full advantage of the moment and felt her warm lips opening with his and her gentle tongue hungry for his. They kissed passionately, her hand massaging the back of his head as he pulled her closer to him. For the first time in his life David knew the feeling of a deep love. This was the girl he had always been waiting for but never knew it.

“This is the best present I could ever have received from anybody. And there I was thinking on some days that I was missing you so much more than you were missing me. Thank you for this my darling, it makes me feel so loved and missed” she said before searching for her lover’s warm tongue again.

They kissed each other for some time before just hugging and holding each other.

"Right, time for your pressie then!" she said, and handed over the backpack she had been carrying rather awkwardly.

David unzipped it and there inside were a dozen records.

"Wow! How did you know I like records?" he asked, laughing.

"Come on now, hurry up and check them out" she laughed.

David could genuinely not pull them out fast enough. One after the other was a collector's item, starting with a German 180g pressing of The Beatle's "Sergeant Peppers" album which David knew for sure cost a good couple hundred dollars. There was also a limited release live album of The Doors which David had drooled over at Manhattan Music and was displayed in a locked, see-through cabinet. It had a sign, NOT FOR SALE AT ANY PRICE, next to it. David opened the sleeve and sure enough in black ink there were the signatures of all 4 members of the band. Shakira knew David was crazy about the band's music and especially fascinated with the tragic lead singer, James Douglas Morrison, more commonly known as Jim Morrison or The Lizard King as David called him. Shakira liked and was very familiar with their music but did not know The Lizard King's history but was impressed with David's intimate knowledge of him. He spent many hours keeping her in hysterics, regaling her about some of Jim's crazy antics especially in Los Angeles and Miami. She was impressed how many books and articles David had read about him and how he would sometimes out of nowhere drop a few lines of the man's poetry here and there, but when least expected. She liked them and especially a few of the lines from an early piece which David told her had been written whilst he was still at school, called "Horse Latitudes". The opening line of "When the still sea conspires an armour" and, "In mute nostril agony" had both a darkness but also a beauty about them at the same time. She understood her boyfriend's fascination with Jim. In their own ways they were both artists, Jim, a musical poet and David, a tennis one. She had watched a few of his varsity tennis matches and how he covered the court like a panther, instinctively knowing what his opponent's next move would be. There was also a thing of beauty about how he would magically strike the ball to all sides of the court and then suddenly and unexpectedly, like a magician, glide a soft-as-a-feather drop shot to outmanoeuvre his poor opponent. He played like a poet and it was a thing of beauty to watch. Like a physical game of chess played to a piece of classical music she had told him, much to his embarrassment.

"Jesus Christ, Shakira! This is too much man! How did you even get hold of this?" he asked her.

"It's not too much, my angel. Let's put it this way, my clever father has all kinds of connections and he was owed a favour, so there you go!" she laughed, enjoying the look of delight on David's face.

"Now you have a real piece of The Lizard King with you with his signature" she laughed again.

"I didn't even receive anything vaguely as expensive as this for my *bar mitzvah,* not even from my Uncle Sol. I will treasure this forever, I promise you!" he said, almost turned to tears.

"You better, there's only thirty of those in the world!" she teased, loving how much she had been able to surprise him.

David went through the rest of the pile which had some of his favourite artists like Led Zeppelin, Dave Grusin, Lee Ritenour, Sadao Wattanabe,a very hard to source Japanese pressing of Fleetwood Mac's "Rumours" album as well as a German pressing of Steely Dan's fantastic "Gaucho album." An audiophile's wet dream thought David, but on steroids.

They both laughed and expressed their joy at such lovely gifts and being home together again. Shakira spoke about the increased volume of work for her final years of study for her Diploma in Accounting, which was to prepare her for the Chartered Accountancy Board Exams the following year. She was reaching the stage David had his final year at university and just wanted to get it over and done with. She had been offered articles with a couple of Durban's auditing firms but hadn't made a final decision. Since her brother had not joined the family business after dropping out of university, her father was putting pressure on her to either join the business as their financial director or else get married. He had already picked out a potential husband for her, some kid named Mohammed Vahed, the son of a business associate and friend of her fathers. Her brother hated him and thought he was a little pompous shit who didn't deserve her. That didn't exactly help his cause of patching things up with their father she said but she was grateful to her brother for defending her. Her father was very upset and told her that the kid had studied law at Harvard and now was in the process of setting up what would be the most successful law practice in the country, handling the legal affairs of all the major Muslim businesses. He also came from a very respectable and devout family. Still she didn't like him because her brother was right about him, and she also didn't care for his money. She would make her own way in life and not rely on any man to look after her, she told David.

"I'm a very lucky man to have such a beautiful girlfriend with a generous heart and such great taste to go with it. You've really spoilt me" he said, with obvious gratitude.

"My darling, there's something else I have for you and it's quite serious" she said in a more earnest tone.

"Serious? Should I be concerned?"

"David, sit down and give me your hand and just stay quiet for a minute" she said.

"David, I haven't told you this yet but I'm very in love with you" she said, looking into his eyes and pausing.

"That first date of ours I told you that I wasn't ready to promise much and wanted us to just go slowly and see if things developed from there. Well so much for that because I counted only 3 days in the last 6 months that we either haven't seen or spoken with each other. I had promised myself too that I would never date another Jewish man after Jared, yet here I am and happier than I have ever been. I cannot hide my happiness and my mother has been asking me all the usual awkward questions and trying to figure out which Muslim boy has finally caught my eye. We also said we would reassess our relationship if it was still going after 6 months. It has been 6 months now. David, I love you and I want to explore us so much more. I can't think of anyone I would rather spend my time with" she said, pausing once more.

"David, I don't want to hide our relationship any longer. I want to bring you home and introduce you to my parents and to meet yours!" she managed to get out before she began to gently sob.

He held her tightly in his arms and picked her up and put her in his lap. The tears were streaming off her face onto his like the Victoria Falls. At that very moment he felt closer to her than he had ever felt to anyone before. This was the last thing he expected to hear from her but it made him very happy.

“Hey, hey, my angel, this is a happy moment, don’t cry please. You see I feel the same way about us and if you feel the timing is right, I’m happy to introduce myself to your family” he said gently, stroking her face lovingly all the time.

Her tears came to a stop as did her shaking.

“Oh thank God” she said, now sitting upright with a beaming smile. “I wasn’t quite sure you felt the same way. I’ve been so nervous to tell you this that I almost phoned to cancel today. You’ve made me the happiest girl in the world today, my David” whilst planting a juicy kiss on his ready lips.

“Which *schmucko* would reject a beauty like you!” he laughed, tickling her.

“I only hope your father doesn’t kill me so we can explore each other better. You warned me about him on our first date, if you recall?” he teased.

“Ha! Ha! We will tell my mother first and then she will know how to handle him. My dad can never say no to her, she’s too precious to him. He will definitely hit the roof at first but he always calms down later. My mother will make sure of that. You know the saying, happy wife, happy life!” she said laughing.

“How do you think *your* family will handle it?” she asked.

“Well let’s see. My mom will at first be disappointed that it’s not a nice little Jewish girl to give her Jewish grandbabies, and my father feels I’ve let him down doing my own things so many times, I don’t think he’ll care. It will take a bit of time for them to come around about you being Muslim but my folks are open-minded and my mother trusts me to make good decisions. I haven’t disappointed her yet. My sister, Leah, I think will love you. She’s very smart like you and will love anybody who is good for me. I think you may have a much tougher time with *your* family than mine” said David.

“I promise you, once my mother has prepped my dad he will be putty in your hands, David. As my mom says, his bark is far worse than his bite. Don’t forget I’m also a daddy’s girl so I too know how to talk to him. He will realise that anyone I love as much as you must be a special person. By the way, I even heard him say to my mother whilst reading the sports section of The Daily News, that there’s a new upcoming South African tennis kid who is making his way in the pro ranks. I almost burst with pride because I knew he was talking about you. Believe it or not but he was a pretty decent player in his youth and when he travels overseas he does his best to co-ordinate it with one of the big tournaments. Funnily enough, there is a South African Jewish family now living in the UK, who were involved in one of my dad's businesses who offer him debenture seats for Wimbledon every year. I remember the one year he took my brother to watch a men's final?"

"No ways, which year?" David interrupted her.

"I think it was 1980. Borg and somebody else" she answered.

"Oh my god! That somebody else would have been the legendary Johnny Mac, real name John McEnroe. That was one of the greatest men's finals of all time Shakira. Do you know how famous the 4th set tiebreaker is?" he asked, flabbergasted.

"Well, they did say it was amazing!" she exclaimed.

"Amazing doesn't do that final justice! It's an all-time classic that match. I would have donated body parts to have been there that day!" he laughed.

"Oh no, no, no you wouldn't have my darling. You see I need all of you!" and they both laughed loudly as they hugged each other.

"So, I'll need to sit my mother down next week and have the big chat about us. I'll wait until everybody is out the house before I drop the bomb. It'll take her a few days to come around and a few days more to conceive a plan to tell my father. I know he will blow up at first and he probably won't even look at me for a week. Then he'll start to calm down and think rationally. Our big advantage is your tennis and my mom and I will push that big time, especially the part about you making the main draw at the French Open. I will then slowly start opening up to him about you, and how I feel about you. David, my dad is a strict father but he's also got a heart of gold, just like you. He too was once in love and with a Shia girl, which was borderline *haram* in his family. To make things even worse, a bride had been chosen a few years earlier and so he was engaged to marry her. You can only imagine the drama when he told his poor family that he was in love with a Persian. Fortunately for him he left school early and went out into the business world, so was the family's sole breadwinner as his father had passed on at a young age. They could hardly kick him out of the house and they had to accept his decision. His 2 uncles tried to interfere but my dad is very strong-willed and he had made his decision. Who knows, maybe it is fate that I am following in his footsteps, although on a more radical level. My mother has often told me that I am a lot more like him than I care to admit, especially my stubbornness. I have a good feeling that he will have a déjà vu moment and remember when he first fell in love with my mom and how well that decision worked out for him. If he doesn't remember, I promise you that I will remind him!" she laughed.

"I think you are like him and not only your stubborn side which I've seen ... and happen to love about you. I think you are both very determined and focused people who will always be successful in life. It kind of helps you are smart too. I totally understand why he ultimately wants *you* to replace him as captain of the ship one day. I can see you in the role of CEO of a global business and your CA qualification will help you in that endeavour" he said.

"And so you wouldn't have an issue after the tour as being a stay-at-home daddy? I promise you I'll give you a life of luxury" she giggled, teasing her lover.

"Can I sign on the dotted line now please?" David replied.

They spent the next few hours with David describing in detail the souks he had visited in both Marrakesh and Dubai. He told her at times how he felt he was back in Durban with all the bright colours of the clothing and silks the merchants had displayed and some of the familiar smells of spices he would smell when shopping for bargains in Grey Street. There was also the sweet smell of incense everywhere except when passing one of the many perfume shops which wafted out a smorgasbord of delicious scents. It was purely by chance he had wandered down a little alley and out of the corner of his eye had spotted her dress. He was so excited to see that it was her size and her signature look that he had even forgotten to haggle with the shop assistant, which was very unusual for his people. He would have liked to have spent more time wandering the markets of both cities but he progressed much further in the tournaments of both cities than he had expected so his time was quite limited.

He went on to tell her about the challenges of beating players he had no knowledge of. He had called those matches play-as-you-go in that as you got further into the match you would slowly start to learn your opponent's game. There were so many hungry young kids who had quit school to take a chance at making it into the big time. He wasn't sure what these kids were being fed but they were tall and strong and were out to make a name for themselves. David had knocked off two of them in his recent sojourn but only after they had pushed him all the way. He told her how his game on clay felt like it was coming together and he was mentally starting to see things differently on court, especially when trailing his opponent. The work he had put into action from the training Dr Berkowitz had given him in Tel Aviv, as opposed to Dov's, had made all the difference. Now, even when match point down, David still had the self-belief to come from behind and win. For David this was a huge victory as anybody who has played the game professionally knows, the mind is ninety-percent of winning.

They were both so engrossed in their conversation that, when by chance David checked the time, he was shocked to see it was an hour before *Shabbat.* They packed up their presents, this time with David carrying the heavy backpack, and made their way to their cars, hand-in-hand. David gave her one last long hug and kiss on the lips and opened her door.

"OK, so I'll see you tomorrow night at 8 pm sharp then. Don't be late my angel!" he teased, giving her some of her own medicine.

"I won't, Mr Oppenheim. One other thing" she hesitated.

"And what's that?" he asked.

"*Shabbat shalom* to you and your family, my David" she said.

"*Shabbat shalom* to you too, my Shakira!" he said, smiling and closing the car door.

So this is it thought David. This is it.

Chapter 13

David took the elevator up to the 3rd floor of the offices of the SU. At the beginning of his final year he and a bunch of his Commerce mates had decided to form the Commerce Students Council which had as its main stated purpose to represent the position of Commerce students on campus. Amazingly, the rector had gone for it and allocated them a room directly opposite Dov's, but with the best view of Glenwood and the Harbour. He made one other fatal mistake by allocating them a very decent budget and opening kitty of R20,000.00. The CSC was responsible for inducting the freshers, as first year students were called, and David and his pals thought there was no better way to do that than a massive bash on the cricket fields the Friday evening before lectures started in earnest. For Commerce students their budgeting skills were shocking and needless to say the entire budget barring R5,000.00 was blown on said induction party. Its true success, the Council had explained, was in creating lifelong bonds and possible parenthood amongst the freshers participating. What they failed to mention was the inebriated state of all the students of both sexes, including the CSC's committee members, and the possible partaking of copious amounts of narcotics. The CSC members were informed that attendance at the first year commerce students' first day lectures, was shockingly low, to the point the CSC committee had been questioned if it was a first day prank. The committee of course vehemently denied any such thing and put it down to students still trying to orientate themselves. If nothing else the opening bash had made them extremely popular amongst the freshers, who eagerly awaited the next party.

Fortunately for the CSC, David was able to get his Uncle Sol to purchase nearly a thousand t-shirts of overruns from his buddies at SA Clothing, on which they had printed a picture of a man passed out with empty beer bottles surrounding him, with the caption BE WILD BE FREE B COM printed in large letters underneath him. After the party the T's sold like wildfire even at a crazy three-hundred percent mark-up so the kitty was replaced almost as quickly as it had been depleted. The CSC reasoned the cost of the bash had been nothing more than marketing expenses to generate t-shirt sales. This had at least bought them some more time with the authorities. The sad truth was that except for getting one of the shitty finance lecturers booted off campus their facility was only used as a coffee joint or to hustle the odd starry-eyed fresher for a tour of the facilities.

By mid-year the Rector had wisened up to this and withdrawn all their privileges, deciding on a disbandment of the CSC until the following year.

As David laughed at the memories and inserted the key Dov had given him for the Economics Society, he could smell the familiar marijuana smoke wafting from both the Hobbit Society as well as the Campus radio station, both at the end of the corridor. Nothing had changed thought David.

The Economics Society was certainly a lot neater than their room had been and most certainly better furnished, because it had furniture. Dov was seated towards the rear of the room, glued to a monitor screen. He looked up briefly from the monitor.

"Ah there he is, my tennis protégé and exactly on time. I hope the marijuana smoke hasn't put you on a different planet. Those *okes* at the end of the corridor are mental. You know about a month ago they managed to *smokkel* a couple of those little Shetland ponies in here to race them up and down the corridor. They called it The Dunhill July races except it's not Dunhill they smoke. *Meshuggenahs*!" laughed Dov, shaking his head.

"Hi Dov. Well then not much has changed on the 3rd floor" responded David, also chuckling.

"Ja, I heard about you naughty buggers getting booted from next door. Campus is still going on about that mega bash you *okes* organised" he said, still laughing.

"Listen, we ultimately stayed on budget so I don't know what the big deal was about it" laughed David.

"OK David, pull up that chair I need you to see this" he said, gesturing to the monitor.

"David, most of what I share with you will need to be memorised. We don't like things in writing so there's no comeback or stealing of information. Everything stored on our mainframes is encrypted and I will give you your own login details now so that if you need to access any files or receive messages you will be able to do so anytime, by yourself. There are only 3 of us in Durban who have access to this room, you, me and Carol Levine, who is one of us but to everybody else a doctoral student. She was recruited from the *kibbutz* like me. Your parents know Carol's family from the Jewish Club. Her father is Jack Levine, the attorney" explained Dov.

Carol's name was not too familiar to David but the minute Dov mentioned Jack Levine, the attorney, David knew immediately who he was referring to. Everybody did. Jack Levine had been a political activist during his younger years and had represented many political prisoners who had been held in detention illegally, often tortured by the vicious Security Branch. He was revered by those in the community for whom the memory of the *Shoah* was still fresh. They looked at Jack's work as standing up for the weak who were being treated like animals by the Apartheid regime, much like the European Jews had been treated by the Nazis. He had overheard his parents often discussing the great work this pious man was performing for his fellow man.

"So, how often does she come in here?" he asked.

"Here's the other thing. In order to make our undercover roles seem more legit we work independently of each other mostly like we are 3 Jews from different groups and not a team. I don't socialise at all with Carol. She has no set hours and she just gets on with her life as a doctoral student. She's very smart and has done some amazing work for us already but being a woman she wasn't well suited for your assignment" Dov went on.

"Ah, so now I know who to blame for my predicament" laughed David.

"Carol is totally in the loop about you and your assignment and no doubt you two will meet here at some stage but right now all you need to know is she's a doctoral student doing her research in Economics. Before we get to your immediate target I want to start with her father, Ismail Mahomedy" said Dov.

"Any relation to the clothing Mahomedy's who had a big shop in Berea Road? As a kid I used to buy my Crown shirts, Tiger jackets and jeans there" asked David.

"No. He was from the poor Mahomedy's, not those rich ones, although he could probably buy those ones out with the loose change in his back pocket now. David, he's worked his way up from literally nothing and has shareholdings in at least 50 companies that we know of and many also in the name of white nominees, quite a few who are Jewish. He owns almost half the buildings in town although they are off balance sheet and through all his various investments essentially controls the clothing and textiles industry in

Durban. You won't believe it but we uncovered that he owns fifteen percent of SA Clothing. They backed him when he first set out in business by extending him a line of credit when none of the *goyim,* or even his own people, would offer him a cent of credit. He never forgot that and when they were going through a cash flow crisis in the early 1980's he bailed them out by buying 15% of the shares. Without that investment SA Clothing would have been liquidated but instead today it's a going concern. It's not all charity though because he makes money by supplying them with textiles from his Chinese factory and those numbers are substantial. But the most impressive thing is he has achieved all this doing *kosher* business" explained Dov, eyes still glued to the monitor.

"That is impressive. Does this dude have any vices then?" asked David.

"Patience please, we are getting there" Dov replied.

"Now I want you to look very carefully at this worksheet of all the companies he's invested in, his percentage shareholding, his title in each one of those and the dates of his shareholdings. This may come in very useful later" instructed Dov.

David ran down the list on the computer screen. The companies were split by industry and size. David was shocked at the names that came up in all sorts of industries, from the obvious clothing and textiles, to furniture, to lighting, to sporting goods, to airlines, to home entertainment and even a pest control company that his family had once used. David was shocked at the number of Jewish companies that were listed. That really didn't make sense and David questioned Dov about this.

"Bro, I estimate at least half of these businesses either were, or still are, Jewish firms. How can a guy who is supposed to despise Jews so much have invested so much in Jewish businesses? I mean he could have just invested his clean money in blue chip shares on the JSE and got a better long term return with much less risk attached. That doesn't make sense on any level" David asked.

"You see this is why we have you on board David! You are asking the right questions which we hope you will find the answers to. Is he just a really nice guy showing loyalty to Jews for the early start in life they gave him? Does his shareholding in these firms come with a more sinister motive seeing he can look through their records at any time to understand the operations? Is he planning on controlling Durban's Jewish businesses at some point or to take them over completely? Is he just anti-Zionist and not anti-Semitic? These are the big questions we need answered and we know you are just the right man for the task" said Dov, now looking at David directly.

"As you can see from the book value, which as you will know only too well is a very conservative valuation, this man is worth approximately $2B. This man with his money and his global businesses is in a perfect position to finance the impending *intifada* and siphon dollars to these terrorists. We have to stop him if he's responsible and HQ are convinced he's the culprit, the *macher"* said Dov no longer joking.

"Jesus, $2B is a huge amount of money! He's not far off the Oppenheimer's and it took that family generations to accumulate that" said David, feeling shocked.

"Yip, the *oke* is a machine, between praying 5 times a day and working his *tuches* off I have no idea where he finds the energy for anything else. I've got a bunch of photos of him here for you to check out. Get a bit closer. I want you to have a good look at him" said Dov, gesturing to him.

David started with ones of him as a very young man carrying what looked like a pile of stacked shoe boxes in the middle of the Indian CBD of Durban. In spite of what looked like a menial job he was smartly attired. His youthful face had the determined look of someone who was going to match the position of his suit in a short time. He was very fair skinned and had the looks of one of those Bollywood stars. He definitely had the demeanour of someone who was going to achieve greatness in some form or another.

The next set of photos were of him playing tennis in all-whites. The old wooden Dunlop Maxply tennis racquets and white fluffy tennis balls also gave the time period away. David estimated it was shot in the late 1960's or early 1970's. Judging by a shot where he was addressing the ball on his forehand David could see he could play. There were also photos of him playing golf, slightly older than the tennis ones. From the vegetation alone David could see it was a Durban course. If nothing else this dude knew how to dress David thought as he examined the photo. He noticed that as part of the group were two very Jewish-looking players. This would have been Papwa Seegolam Golf Club thought David because no local white club would even consider allowing non-whites to use their facilities. David always found it ridiculous on the odd occasion when his old DHS classmate, James Edwards, had invited him to join their four ball at the famous Durban Country Club, where the Indians were good enough as caddies but not considered good enough to play. Ironic that at Papwa it was no issue for whites to play but no chance they would be allowed to caddy.

The photos then moved on to a young dapper Ismail standing in between the then Chairman of SA Clothing, Mr Harold Sackstein, and the MD of the group, Mr Myron Jacobs. He was so youthful they looked like his grandfathers, David thought. He immediately recognised the two faces as being the two Jewish gentlemen in the photo at Papwa. This kid who looked no older than twenty years of age in the photo was going places fast.

"These 2 gents from SA Clothing were the guys who extended a line of credit to Ismail. This allowed him to go from 2 to a total of 20 clothing factory outlets within a space of 2 years, David. Eventually he was buying nearly all their overruns and rejects and the joke was that he should have called his outlets the SA Clothing factory shops and not Grab-A-Garb, his chosen trading name. Myron Jacobs became particularly close with him and provided the seed capital for Ismail's second venture, his chain of hardware outlets" explained Dov.

David's family knew the Jacobs family well. The great grandparents were Lithuanian Holocaust survivors, arriving penniless in 1946 after being turned away from Israel by the British. The following generation had started up a small clothing shop on the border of Indian town and the white CBD and one of the sons had studied to become a pharmacist. David's family had supported Jacobs Pharmacy in Pine Street for years and even had an account with them. Over the year's 1 chemist shop had become 8 and the family had become very wealthy. The clothing side of the family business had also prospered and they had moved into manufacturing for some of the big chain or department stores, as they were known at the time. This was ultimately how SA Clothing Industries had started, David's father had told him. The wealthy Sackstein family from Johannesburg had later joined the business and sent Harold to help manage daily operations. David didn't bother explaining this history to Dov who in all likelihood knew everything anyway.

Dov flicked through photos of Ismail outside a number of different hardware stores with Universal Hardware & Builders Supplies emblazoned above them. David knew the name well. It was no longer just a couple-of-stores operation, but had scaled up to being a national chain.

"How the hell did this kid without a matric qualification start up a clothing empire followed by a hardware one?" asked David amazed.

"David, the same can be asked of a number of Jews. Take your school buddy, Brett Nankin's father, Solly. You know he was a Jewish orphan who ran away from Joburg at fourteen years of age. An old Gentile man took pity on him when he arrived in Durban and gave him a job as an assistant at one of his gas stations near the Durban beachfront. It wasn't more than 2 years later he became an equal partner in that station and a further 2 years later he had increased the number of stations to 12. The old man passed away without any relatives soon thereafter and left everything to Solly. At the age of 18, Solly owned nearly 30 gas stations around Natal. You know the rest; clothing, communications, motor vehicles, hotels, race-horses etcetera, etcetera" Dov explained.

"Yes, Solly was something else!" said David.

"So think of this guy as their Solly equivalent" said Dov.

"Maybe we should call him Solly Ismail then?" joked David.

"I'm not too sure either of them would have liked that!" laughed Dov.

Dov moved on to some photos of Ismail on his wedding day. His bride was young and beautiful and together they looked like movie stars. If Ismail was fair-skinned, the mother was even more so. She and her family looked very different from Ismail's. They just looked a lot more polished and sophisticated, and a lot happier too at the union than Ismail's. There was a picture of just the two of them that was very revealing, David thought. He had never been in love before himself but he was sure if there ever was such a thing, it was the way these two love birds were staring at each other. In a picture of the bride only, David thought she looked different from most Durban Indians, possibly Lebanese or Syrian even. Whatever she was, she was certainly as beautiful as Ismail was handsome. A well suited, handsome couple, David thought.

Dov then moved along to newspaper clippings from both the white and Indian press covering Ismail's business exploits. He was often seen pictured alongside the doyens of white business of South Africa whose names he immediately recognised. He was the only non-white director serving as director on listed companies' boards. David concluded that they needed his money as a risk-taker and that this was the only way Ismail was going to break into mainstream, big time business. He stuck out like a sore thumb in these group photos not so much as being Indian but rather because he was so much younger than the stiffs. David could only imagine the amount of racism and prejudice he must have endured sitting in board meetings with these stiff old codgers. Yet without him the show couldn't go on and so they would have no option but to pretend and kiss his *tuches.* His favourite photo of these was Ismail sitting front row next to the Chairman of SA Breweries for the director's group photo from the early 1970's. He was the only director with a broad grin, which made him seem even more charming. It made them all look like boring stiffs.

"So young Ismail is now breaking into the big time of white corporate business here as you can see, David. He has enormous financial clout behind him in the form of his own personal wealth as well as the financial support of his close Jewish backers. He's able to infiltrate the WASPY, mainstream, corporate world because they need his money and as an Indian the *goyim* don't see him as a threat like they do Jews, so they reluctantly take him in. With the backing of Apartheid they think they can control him. So in the process of all this Ismail continues to multiply his wealth tenfold along with the wealth of his silent partners. For Ismail and his Jewish friends it's a win-win situation. Huge global multinational SA firms like SAB, SAPPI and a couple of the big mining ones would have been nothing today without our people and Ismail, David" explained Dov.

Dov then moved on to a photo of the happy couple holding what was probably their firstborn, followed by another of a second born. In that picture they were supporting their little boy who looked no older than 3, maybe 4 years old, who was holding what must have been his sister in a pink blanket. The family were beaming from ear-to-ear, delighted at the birth of the new little one. Dov confirmed to David that this indeed was Shakira Mahomedy's day of birth and to commemorate it Ismail had bought his wife a brand spanking new Mercedes S Class, one of the first in the country and certainly the first in Durban. The next series of photos showed the kids older on holidays in Cape Town, on a cruise ship somewhere in the Nordics, at Madame Tussauds, up the Empire State building and quite a few other overseas locations. The little girl was beautiful even from a young age. She was very much a daddy's girl with Ismail holding her in virtually every photo. David could just tell he was obsessed with his little girl and would give her anything she wanted.

The next batch of photos were all of Shakira growing up. She was sporty and there were pictures of her playing netball, swimming in what looked like a school gala, sitting atop a beautiful black horse in full riding regalia as well as playing badminton in her early teenage years. It was obvious that as she grew older she became even more attractive and was almost a splitting image of her mother with her exotic looks. She had the same olive skin and dark green eyes as her.

"Shakira may appear to have been spoilt from all these photos, what with all these overseas trips and her own horse, but her father made sure she went to a government school just like all the other kids. He could easily have sent her to any overseas private school in England but he wanted his daughter to understand that just because her family was rich, it did not make her special. She attended the Overport Islamic School as did her older brother, Mohammed. She is not only very beautiful but is also very bright and matriculated with straight A's and was Dux of her school. From what we've learnt she's the top Accounting student in 3rd year too, so you better sharpen up your general knowledge if you plan on keeping up with this chick!" Dov joked.

"Does she have any interest in tennis?" asked David.

"Nope, but luckily for you her old man does so you need to play that card to the fullest when you hopefully get to that stage?" said Dov.

"I don't plan on asking her father for her hand in marriage, Dov!"

"No schmucko not that. I meant when you hopefully are invited home to meet her father!" laughed Dov.

"Ah OK, I think I shot the gun there!"

"With the daughter you will use your love and knowledge of music as your bait. Through her family's controlling interest in Manhattan Music she has been able to put together a nice collection. Fortunately for us the father is so kosher that every record she takes is accounted for in their computer system and is taxed. I say fortunately for us because our computer geeks have hacked into their mainframe and I have a listing of her collection from the last 2 years. There are about 800 titles listed here and if we cross-reference them with yours, there are many commonalities. If you look at this page here you will see about three-hundred plus records you both own, so you have quite similar tastes in music which is a very handy thing" Dov said.

David ran his eyes quickly down the list, admiring their common tastes. She owned as many Bowie albums as he did which was impressive. An Indian chick who liked ska was very unusual thought David running through names like The Beat, The Specials and Selecter. He was glad to spot some Doors albums, The Doors being his favourite rock band. What was obvious to David was that she enjoyed as wide a genre of music as he did. This girl was full of surprises.

"We have begrudgingly spent a large sum of money sourcing some extremely rare and difficult to find collectibles from a collector in Brazil. If these things aren't bait to an audio nut like her then I don't know what will be. Apparently it's a rare copy of Bowie's Ziggy something-or-other" said Dov, moving towards a cabinet.

"You mean Stardust" said David.

"What?" asked Dov.

"The Bowie album is "Ziggy Stardust", possibly his most famous of the 70's!" replied David.

"Whatever bro. As long as it gets this Shakira chick's attention you can call it Ziggy Mahomedy for all I care" chuckled Dov.

He had extracted a square box from one of the cabinets and placed it before David.

"Well, c'mon open the fucking thing then" he gestured.

David opened the box and pulled out one collectors' item after the other. First out was a very rare Japanese pressing of "Ziggy Stardust" that Dov had been alluding to. It was mint and still smelt new. David handled it like a professional, treating it like a baby rather than a record. Whilst holding it gently at its edges he examined it for any signs of warping. He could see Dov shaking his head out of the corner of his eye and hear his chuckles.

"Bro, I hope you handle this Shakira half as delicately and lovingly as you handling that record" teased Dov.

"Dov, you have no culture but coming from Jo'burg what can one expect" David shot back at him.

"OK, c'mon move on for Chrissakes! I can't take you fawning over that thing any longer" said Dov with disdain.

The collection of a dozen or so records was incredible including another out-of-print copy of an early Incognito album which David had been on the lookout for.

"So HQ expects you to take special care of them because after she's seen them we need them back to recover the money" said Dov.

"Tell them to get fucked, OK! I'm not giving them back or paying a cent for these! Tell HQ or I will to debit them to the danger pay account or as a present from *our people,* OK!" shouted David.

"Relax, relax man! I was just teasing for fuck sakes. HQ says you can keep them. We'll put it down to goodwill" laughed Dov.

"I don't care what the fuck you put it down to, they not coming back from my collection. Nobody comes between me and my music, you should know that already" said David, slowly starting to calm down.

"Oh believe me we do, bro. Any person who has so many records strewn about his room to the point one can't tell whether the walls are painted or have wallpaper on them, has to be a total music *meshuggeneh!* We also know that to have accumulated such a collection by the age of fifteen years old, didn't exactly come through *kosher* means? We happen to know the fifty cents per record you charged your school pals, recording everything on that Nakamichi Dragon tape deck that you also purchased with your recording fees and *bar mitzvah* money. Moshe thinks that's classic Jewish *seichel* and was another reason he thought you were perfect for this assignment, truth be told" teased Dov.

"Is nothing sacred or off-limits with you lot?! I'll have you know that virtually all that cash and more was re-invested in to more records and hardware to support artists. I didn't use it to go on fucking skiing holidays in the Alps or fancy clothes" responded David, feeling embarrassed and exposed.

"David, I'm joking. We couldn't give a camel's ass about your recording gig. If anything we are in awe at your talents for spotting a gap in the market. You are one of us now and never forget that. Besides, you just increased your collection by a further very valuable records!" laughed Dov.

That instantly made David feel better and he delicately placed them in the bag Dov had especially sourced for him. They fit snugly in the bag and David was able to transport them easily.

"Alright, we running out of time now but before we go I need to show you a few more recent photos of our friend, Ismael. You will notice that gone are the beautiful YSL and Lanvin suits of his youth. They have been replaced by more traditional Muslim garb. He's no longer clean-shaven and is sporting a beard and *kippa*. You'll always see him with prayer beads and not a calculator in his hands. At some point in the 80's he made *hajj* to Mecca and came back a changed man. And at that point we think the trouble may have started for us" explained Dov.

The difference between the younger and older Ismail was quite stark. He barely resembled the younger man. The beard made him look much older especially the bits of grey starting to dominate it. The eyes had lost the gentleness and his general demeanour was of a very pious and serious person. Even with the beard he still looked handsome but now it seemed that was unimportant to him, certainly compared with his photos in his youth. The change surprised David. Whatever the man had experienced on his pilgrimage must have been very powerful to have changed him to this degree. He looked more like a *mullah* than a businessman, David thought.

"Amazing hey, David! The *oke* has done a complete one-eighty. We think he was approached by the Iranians and PLO whilst on *hajj* and they were able to get inside his head. Since then he's not only transformed his look and dress but he's been quite vocal within their community about the plight of the Palestinians and the usual anti-Zionist rhetoric. Two weeks ago the *mufti* of his local mosque allowed him to address the congregation and he spent the better part of an hour slating Israel as being an illegitimate, colonialist state and the 51st state of the United States. He was critical of the local Muslim community for not doing enough to assist their Palestinian brothers and came very close to calling for *jihad* against both countries for what he considered crimes against humanity. He was very cautious not to attack Jews in general and kept his focus strictly on Zionists and Israel. In fact he was quite open about the fact that Jews, not even his own people, had assisted him to start his first business and how these people who had fled the Holocaust had kindness in their heart and backed the underdog. They understood persecution after being massacred by the Nazis but with the accumulation of huge wealth their children had lost their way and at the same time, hardened their hearts. It was amazing, he told them, that the very ones who had suffered persecution had now become the persecutors. They had short memories and were no longer god-fearing" explained Dov.

His speech had a profound effect on the gathering and he received a standing ovation from the congregants. Many of them had approached him afterwards wanting to shake his hand and offer their support. The agency had learned that some of the congregants had pledged substantial financial donations for their cause. Ismail Mahomedy was a powerful speaker and commanded respect within his community and his message had a profound effect. He was a man to be reckoned with and the *mufti* knew this only too well when offering him the podium.

Dov moved on to other photos of Ismail taken in Gaza and the West Bank, some with leaders of the PLO and others with him with Hamas and Hezbollah militants. The manner in which they embraced him made it obvious that he was an important person to them. Dov even showed him holding an AK47 automatic weapon surrounded by a group of jubilant Hamas militants most of whom still looked in their teens to David. The metamorphosis of Ismail was frightening. He had gone from being an almost secular Durban Indian businessman to so-called freedom fighter within a very short space of time. What was more frightening to them both was that he wielded financial might which could be directed at their people, and not in a good way. Now it dawned upon David who his real target was. It was the father and not the daughter, who would only serve as a conduit. The gravity of his task at hand was only beginning to become apparent to him. This was no game.

"Right, I think we've covered enough for today, bro. When we next meet I'm going to test your memory. You welcome to come back and go through the files I've left in a folder named BORG on the C drive. You'll need to login with these details" Dov suggested as he showed David his personal login details.

"You got them, David? Now remember do *not* write them down, anywhere!" instructed Dov in a serious tone.

"Should you in any way compromise yourself we will deny all knowledge of you and the office lock will be changed immediately and your login details deleted from our systems. You will be on your own, David. Stick to the script, our rules, and we will do anything and everything in our vast powers to protect you. Do you understand me clearly?" Dov asked, not joking.

"Understood Dov" replied David.

"Cool bro. Let's meet Friday 4 p.m. before *Shabbos*. Enjoy the records in the meantime" he chuckled, gesturing to the door for them to exit.

After they parted company in the crisp early evening David walked briskly through Shepstone and took the escalators down to the student parking where he had left the Green Mamba a few hours earlier.

His mind was racing with both trepidation and excitement. This was much bigger than he had realised. All he kept on thinking was, this is it, this is really it! No turning back now!

Chapter 14

Their second date had been a far less formal affair with a most unexpected ending. Shakira had suggested meeting at a curry joint in Queens Street in the old Indian part of town. They made the best bunny chows in town Shakira told him. Bunny chow, a proprietary Durban invention by poor Indian indentured labourers working the cane fields, was comprised of a dug-out quarter or half loaf of bread replaced with a curry of choice and often served with sambals. It was David and his clubbing mates' choice of early morning food after returning from a stonking evening of sweating on the dance floors of Zodiac, Ronnyz or Faces night clubs.

Their port of call for this delicious concoction was the infamous Johnnie's Chip and Ranch in Overport, open 24 hours a day, 365 days a year. David's filling of choice was mutton and he liked it hot being the standard most Indians ordered as. His friends could barely handle the mild version but David loved the taste and the sweat pouring from all parts of his head and face as he ate his half mutton bunny with his fingers. His close mate, Mark Hodes, who had followed him from Carmel to DHS and then on to study Commerce at UND, had once tried a hot bunny and had almost wound up in hospital. David laughed picturing the flood of sweat pouring off his poor friend's forehead. David had tried to stop him half way through his bunny but the taste was too good that Mark had insisted he was fine to finish it. It had not ended up well for Mark when the bunny reared its ugly head a few hours later. He suffered such bad dehydration that it was a very close thing he hadn't ended up at St Augustine's Hospital on a drip. Mark had learned his lesson and from thereon out he stuck to mild versions only.

When David arrived at 7 pm he was surprised that not only had Shakira beaten him to the venue but she was seated next to another couple. When she caught sight of him she got up and walked towards him and gave him a big welcoming hug.

"Hello there, Mr Oppenheim! Come on, I want to introduce you to my closest friends Miriam and her brother EB" she said, taking his hand and leading him to their table. Her hand felt tiny in his but sent shivers through his arm and David could feel that familiar warm feeling coming on.

Miriam and Ebrahim stood up and politely introduced themselves and shook his hand before sitting down again.

"So you are the famous David Oppenheim my friend hasn't stopped talking about for the last week" Miriam teased.

"Miriam! Please!" Shakira cut in with embarrassment.

"Oh ja? Well pray please tell more. I'm all ears" chuckled David.

"Actually, I've seen you around campus and a friend of ours said you are clever Prof O's son. You really don't look like him though I must say" Miriam said looking him up and down.

"Phew! For a second I thought you were going to say I don't look clever like him! It's true, I look like my mom's brother" David explained.

"Well your uncle must be quite a hottie then!" Miriam teased further.

"Jeez, the *wit ou* has only just met us Miriam and you already giving the *oke kak* man. Give him a chance to at least get to know us man!" her brother cut in.

Both girls and David laughed at that. David was very familiar with the Durban slang the local Indians had developed over the years. It sometimes was a combination of a number of local languages spiced up with a bit of Urdu or Gujarati and even some Arabic too.

"So *bhai*, don't let these *cherries* take advantage of you. You got to stand up for yourself *bhai,* otherwise they will walk all over you, especially this one" he said gesturing to his sister.

"I'll be certain to keep that in mind, EB!" David laughed, enjoying the banter.

"So David, spill the beans then. We want to know what you think of Shaks. Isn't she the most beautiful woman you have ever seen?" asked Miriam.

"She's even more beautiful than that" David answered instantly whilst reaching out his hand for Shakira's.

"Ooh, smoooooth!" laughed Miriam.

"So not only handsome but romantic too, I see. Nice one, girl!" she said making to high-five with her now very embarrassed friend.

"OK, OK, forgive me. I'll stop the teasing but I'm really impressed you sitting there just taking it. Any Muslim guy would have run out the door already! You may just prove to be a keeper" she teased a little more.

A waiter approached to take their orders much to David's relief. He allowed them to order first before he ordered his favourite half-bunny, hot. They all looked at him like he was crazy including the waiter.

"Sir, we have mild and medium too, not just hot" explained the waiter.

"Yes, I'm aware thanks but I always order my bunny hot" replied David.

"Yes sir, no problem to do it hot then sir" answered the waiter still in obvious shock.

"Well check out the legs on this *charou,* ladies! *Bhai*, you must have been an Indian surely in a previous life. You must be the first *wit ou* on the planet to order a hot curry. Now I'm impressed. Next thing you'll tell me is you drive a GTi with low suspension and Brospeed exhaust!" at which everybody burst out laughing.

"No, no GTi for me. I can only afford a 10 year old Alpha GTV called The Green Mamba" replied David.

"Nothing wrong with a GTV, man! That's a real driver's car if ever there was one. When they released it in the late 70's it was miles ahead of its time" said EB enthusiastically.

"You just made a friend for life, David. My brother here is a total petrol-head and bugged our dad endlessly until he gave in and bought Shakira's brother's second hand GTi. There isn't a thing he doesn't know about cars. Ayrton Senna is his idol" said Miriam.

"EB, you welcome to take the Green Mamba for a spin anytime you like" offered David.

"*Bhai*, I will definitely take you up on that offer. I love those old cars" answered EB.

David noticed Shakira lounging back in comfort with the familiar little grin on her face. He realised meeting her friends like this, without any warning, was her testing him. She wanted to see how easily he could fit into her little world. She had invited him to a part of town he wouldn't have frequented and with a group of total strangers. He had more than impressed and surprised her with how comfortable and easy-going he was, especially for someone she regarded as a bit shy. She was no less shocked at him ordering a hot curry when she only ordered it mild. He was totally cool with their banter, even Miriam's, which sometimes wasn't very diplomatic. He had had a haircut since their first date which made him look more like Shakrul Kahn than a nice little Jewish boy. David's hazel eyes and thick wavy black hair, together with his high cheek bones, were reminiscent of her favourite Bollywood actor. Although clearly a man there was a boyishness, almost an innocence to him, which she found attractive. He also had long eyelashes which any girl would have killed for. To finish off he had a very athletic body with strong forearms, in all likelihood from his tennis, and a chest that she just wanted to reach out for and touch whenever they were close. He was gentle and kind too with his words and actions. The more time she spent with him the more the ice wall she had formed at the end of her relationship with Jared, began to melt. She had no intention of breaking this one off early. It would need to run its course she had decided.

"Shaks says you are off to play the pro tennis tour next year?" enquired Miriam.

"Well, it's actually the tour to get into the main tour. If you do well enough on the Challenger tour you then accumulate enough points to make the main ATP tour. At that point only can you really call yourself a full-time pro. The money on the Challenger tour won't get one too far in life" laughed David.

"So how do you rate your chances then? I can only manage how many great players must be out there trying to break into the big time" asked Miriam.

"I think I've got a decent chance, as good as anybody. I'm fortunate that I am being sponsored by Tennis South Africa for my travels and I hope to have an Italian brand sponsor my clothing and Head for my rackets. Nike for my shoes may be a bit tricky but I've written them too. If I honestly didn't feel I have a shot of breaking into the top 100 I wouldn't put myself through what's coming. I've given myself two years and if it doesn't work out I'll finish my Honours in Finance" said David.

"*Bhai*, top 100! That's amazing man. Can I get your signature now please before you become a big shot and don't even remember me?" joked EB.

The waiter arrived with their meals, which looked delicious and smelt even better. The waiter waited until David had scooped his first finger full of his hot mutton bunny. He was at the same time both delighted and surprised when David gave him the thumbs up. He wandered off chuckling and shaking his head at the crazy white man. David loved the freedom of eating with his fingers. He watched as Shakira delicately ate her bunny with such grace so as not to spill any sauce on her clothing or the table. When she looked up and noticed David watching her, she smiled and winked back at him. Before he could register, she was dabbing at the corners of his mouth and his lower lip where he had spilt some of the spicy hot sauce. She took another serviette and this time wiped some of the sweat on his brow. She had been right about this place. It was the best bunny chow he had ever tasted. She poured him a tall glass of water and passed it to him. He was happy to receive it because the curry was piping hot and had a real bite to it. He drank the glass of water in a few swallows and his friends laughed loudly at him.

"*Bhai,* I hope this isn't your friend Mark's revenge and all!" laughed EB and the girls followed suit.

"This is the best bunny I've ever had, man! I know I'm sweating like crazy but it was so tasty" laughed David.

"Have another glass of ice water, my darling" said Shakira passing him another glass she had already poured.

"David have you ever been into this side of town before?" asked Miriam.

"I've been a few times, not often. I've bought clothing for myself in a few stores in Grey Street. My mother was quite well known for buying linens and silks here when I was a young kid. She used to take me along and I was amazed how the shopkeepers knew her by name, and some even knew my name. I go jazz dancing at The Octagon with some of my crazy friends every now and then. This whole Apartheid thing is a lot of bullshit and many of my people just ignore it anyway. Theoretically, the Security Branch could arrest me for eating here tonight which is ridiculous" replied David.

"Have you ever crossed the colour line before?" Miriam asked more seriously.

"No, but not for any other reason other than Apartheid making it illegal" he responded.

"I know it may feel exotic and exciting to be with Shakira but if you are really serious about her you will need to understand the consequences for her if there's a problem. You see the only punishment you will face as a white guy will be a telling off, but for a non-white it's a different story. You are both lucky that she is olive-skinned with green eyes so could easily pass as Mediterranean or even Persian but you will still need to be very cautious. When she told me you had booked the VIP room at Legends for your first date I thought it was quite risky, especially for a first date. It did help when she told me the owners are family friends of yours but my advice is to proceed a bit more cautiously, at least for now. Shaks is very important to us. She's more like a sister to EB and me" she said.

"OK guys, c'mon let's talk about something happier than this" pleaded Shakira.

"Well I just want to finish off by saying that Shakira was right about you, David. You are very nice and kind of sexy too so if things don't work out with her, you know where to find me" at which they all burst out laughing.

"David let me order you some ice cream with fried banana, it'll cool you down some more, my darling" said Shakira, as she wiped more sweat from his face.

"I'm in for that! I think I've sweated more from that bunny than any tennis match I've ever played" laughed David.

"So David, I'm delighted to hear you like The Octagon. It's a really cool place that plays amazing jazz to dance to. The three of us sometimes go on a Thursday night for ladies night so we should maybe think about doing that some time. You must see your lady jazz it out by the way. You may need to go for some lessons and sharpen your skills before joining us for a night there" teased Miriam again.

"I don't know what to say. Shakira is just so full of surprises that just when I've got over one, she hits me with another. I would love to join you guys there. I must also just forewarn you that Jews invented modern dancing. There's two things we come out the womb doing. The first is asking the paediatrician for a discount and the second is tango dancing. You want to see me on the dance floor, believe me!" said David, having his group in hysterics.

"So Fred Astaire has got nothing on you then?" laughed Miriam. "You must be the only hot bunny chow-eating, jazz dancing white guy on the planet. I can't wait to see you at the Octagon, truly!" she continued with tears of laughter rolling down her cheeks. "One thing is for sure, if the tennis doesn't work out, you definitely have a career in comedy. I haven't had as good a laugh as this in forever" she said dabbing her eyes and cheeks with a serviette.

"Right then, I have a proposal. You guys take me to Octagon for a ladies nite and I'll introduce you to Zodiac or Ronnyz for a bit of high-energy dancing. What do you think?" asked David.

"No ways, so not only are you Fred Astaire but you also John Travolta too now!" Miriam burst out laughing.

"*Habibi*, have you got a brother for me, please?" she burst out. holding her sides with laughter.

"Hey, hey, hang around a bit longer and magic will happen" replied David, good-naturedly.

He liked Miriam. She was a tiny little thing but feisty and full of good humour and fun. Any thoughts that meeting any of her friends might be awkward were a thing of the past thanks to Miriam. She had given him the tick of approval which was a big deal for his new girlfriend, and besides he really was enjoying their banter.

"You lot are too much! You going to give me stomach cramps you carry on like this" EB piped up.

"David, honestly *bhai,* you are the first Jewish *oke* I've really spoken to and you have changed my opinion of you guys I think. I've always seen your people as very serious, business-minded people definitely not full of jokes and fun like you" he said, looking at David.

"EB, what you mean is that we not all money-loving, greedy businessmen, right?" David asked with a straight face before bursting out in laughter.

"Man, you should have seen the look on your faces!" David teased, slapping his thighs.

"I really got you there!" he continued laughing as they all joined in, probably more from relief.

"I think my tribe are probably one of the most complicated civilisations in history. Try explain to a non-Jew how a Jew can be both a Jew and an atheist for example. So many people don't understand that Jews are an ethnoreligious grouping and not solely a religion. So in my case I was born Jewish as my mother is an Orthodox Jew, but religiously I'm an atheist which means I don't believe in a personal god. Regardless of my atheism, no rabbi could stop me from getting married in a synagogue or being buried in the Jewish section of a cemetery. It's really complicated which might explain better the high percentage of Jewish shrinks" said David.

"If it's not too personal, David, how can you not believe in a higher power or this "personal god" you speak of? Within my home we have always just grown up believing in an Almighty who gave us the Koran through our prophet. I have lived by those rules which made sense to me and something I've just accepted and never questioned" asked Miriam, intrigued by David.

"It's probably a topic requiring a whole evening which I hope we have the opportunity of having one day. I'm so happy for you that it makes sense to you and is a good fit for you. In many ways I envy you Miriam. I envy your faith. You see the 6M Jews who died in the Holocaust also had faith in what we refer to as *HaShem*, your *Allah*. You see both our books refer to the Jewish people as being the Chosen, chosen by god to shine a light upon the nations to show them the righteous way. I'm afraid their faith in a deity was blind and only those of them, including some of my lot, who used their common sense rather than looking to *HaShem* to save them, managed to escape. Some of my mom's Langer family who chose to stay behind in their *shtetl's*, little *dorpies* as we know them here, were completely obliterated. Entire families were wiped out in Auschwitz and other concentration camps, all the while expecting to be saved because of their faith. I'm sorry but the only thing my people were Chosen to be was victims of the Nazis. If *HaShem* existed then 6M Jews would not have been slaughtered by those Nazi murderers!" David insisted.

"Wow! Now I can understand exactly why you feel you do about god. I guess for Muslims our equivalent would be the Crusades. Here's the thing though David, and it doesn't take away the pain of 6M poor souls, but just like our people survived the Crusades and prospered, the Jewish people also survived and have been even more successful. I mean look at all the great Jewish scientists who have won Nobel prizes. You don't think god didn't play a hand in that?" asked Miriam gently.

"That's a great argument Miriam and yes, my people are the ultimate survivors. We have survived and outwitted our enemies for four-thousand years and we are still here. But Miriam, 6 million poor, innocent souls? Did it have to be *half* our people? Is god really *that* cruel? Do you know how many incredible minds among those 6 million Ashkenazi Jews? Do you know how many cures for dreaded diseases may have been discovered by the doctors and physicians amongst those victims? 6 million is too many for me Miriam" said David quietly.

"Even one is too many, my darling. All I can say is, I will say a prayer tonight for your family and all the families who had people murdered in that atrocity. I'm so grateful your parents escaped because now I have you in my life" said Shakira, kissing David's hand whilst holding it tightly.

"Yoh, guys! This is *heavy* stuff man. Let's get back to the sunshine, please!" said EB who had been sitting back listening to the conversation intently.

"Just excuse me for a second I just need the loo!"

"Cool. Is everyone done eating and drinking? I'll call for the bill?" asked David.

Everyone nodded in unison.

Mo beat David to the punch and paid for their dinner en-route to the bathroom and when he came back he suggested it was time to depart.

"EB, that's very kind of you to get the dinner. I'll buy next time though, OK?" said David.

"*Bhai*, no problem man. You can do a favour for me and drop Shaks off home? She lives closer your side of town than us" said Mo, giving David a little wink. It wasn't quite the truth but David appreciated the gesture and wasn't going to say no.

Once outside they said goodbye to each other and Miriam even reached up and gave David a peck on his cheek goodbye.

"Now you look after my friend, Mr Travolta!" she said, before climbing in to EB's souped-up Golf GTi.

"They really like you, David. I knew that would be the case. I have good taste after all" she smiled, looking at him.

They were zipping along the hills of the ridge towards her family home on the border of Overport and the Berea. She was loving his heavy foot and giggling nervously. She guided him into a cul-de-sac and at the end of the road David saw a monstrosity of a home.

"Don't go to the end of the road yet, just park here for a bit" she asked.

He did as she asked and turned off the ignition. The only lights in the road were shining from the mansion a little further ahead of them.

“That was such an awesome evening. The food was delicious and the company even better. I’m really glad to have met them, thank you” said David looking at her.

“OK Oppenheim, that’s enough talking now. I want you to kiss me. Kiss me like I’m your first” she said.

Totally unexpectedly, she nimbly moved on top and straddled him, throwing her hair back. David could see those green eyes he had fallen in love with and those sweet red lips he had only briefly tasted on their first date.

He pulled her even closer to him and could feel her breathing deeper. His lips touched hers gently and his tongue playfully tickled her top lip before moving to the bottom one. Her lips parted fully and her warm tongue hungrily devoured his, pulling him deep into her mouth whilst she pulled on the back of his head. David could feel himself harden as she straddled herself ever closer to him and he knew she could feel how much he desired her. David’s entire body felt electrified. He had never felt this way before with anyone including his first kiss with Debbie Leibowitz just before his *bar mitzvah*. She had taken her jacket off and he could feel her erect nipples pressing against his chest as she kissed him even deeper. David realised she had not been wearing a bra and her breasts were warm and gentle to the touch as he lifted her silk shirt and felt them. She was breathing heavily into his neck, kissing it gently as he felt her nipples harden further to his touch. She knew he wanted more but she whispered softly in his ears “I want you too, my darling, but not tonight, not yet, please just go slowly with me. This is too important for me to just rush”.

After they had finished kissing they just hugged for a while. They were a perfect fit thought David as she straddled him stroking his hair.

“I’m scared David. The way I feel about you I think I’m in deep, deep trouble. After the hurt with Jared I didn’t think I would ever feel this way again. You know how hard it has been for me to study this past week because you were the only thing on my mind. I so badly want to talk to my mom about you but I manage to restrain myself. She even made some remark this week that I seem to be happier than usual. I don’t think she suspects anything yet but it won’t take her long. She knows me too well” said Shakira.

"When can I see you again? I can't wait long and it's almost impossible sneaking about at varsity" asked David.

"Soon, my darling, soon. I have to get home now. Wait for me to get in and then wait another minute before you pass my house. I don't need anyone seeing your car yet. Not until we are ready, David" she said.

David watched her as she put on her jacket walking towards the monstrosity. He watched her enter the grounds through the huge electric gates before turning to give a quick wave to him. He gave it a few minutes before he turned on the Green Mamba and took off.

She wasn't the only one who was in deep, deep trouble he thought as he took to the hills of the ridge again.

Chapter 15

It was Wednesday and David skipped his early morning stretch and sprint session on North Beach. His ankles were starting to feel stiff and he didn't need to injure himself before his big introduction to the ATP tour. He would suggest to Lionel that they repeat the skill drills after a best of five practice match in the morning. He needed to train his mind to five set possibilities. Gruelling, emotionally-draining 5 set possibilities on the slow, red clay of Roland Garros.

It was common knowledge that the players had called the French Open the toughest of all majors to win. So many great champions had won on every surface but clay. One of his heroes, Johnny Mac, had come so close against Lendl in the final in 1984. After surprisingly serving and volleying his way through the tournament he had led Lendl by 2 sets to love but somehow conspired to lose the last 3 sets, and that was it. He would never have a chance to win the French again although as consolation he annihilated Connors in perhaps the most decisive and beautiful display of serve and volleying tennis Wimbledon's famous centre court had ever been graced with. It was an incredible year for Mac, who managed to lose only 4 matches the entire season, including revenge for his French Open loss against Lendl at the US Open.

He received an early morning delivery of his Sergio Tacchini tennis kit which Shakira had helped him choose. He couldn't open the FedEx boxes quickly enough. The styles were all brand new and smelt so fresh when he took them out of their plastic packets. He quickly tried on some of the shirts and shorts. Perfect fit. He had asked his sponsor for a size up of one or two styles just in case, but he had earmarked these for Lionel. It was the least he could do for his old rival who was putting in a lot to prepare him for the French. He put 2 sets of shorts and shirts in a Tacchini-branded packet for his pal as well as 2 sets of matching socks. He was sure Lionel would be delighted. He had always loved Tacchini as a junior but didn't have the money for it. He would wear a different set from the two he put aside for Lionel today and get Emma to wash all the others immediately. He would smell like lavender on the court for the rest of the week!

David had suggested at the end of their previous session that they play sets and then if they were still up for it, do some of the drills they had taught each other. He wanted to be match fit but he also needed to start preparing his mind for 5 sets of warfare. They had also decided to move for the morning's session to their old tournament haunt of Westridge Park which held so many memories for the both of them.

Surprisingly, Lionel had arrived slightly early, as David guided the Green Mamba into the parking next to the 3 show courts on the upper level. As David looked out over the tennis complex, composed of a number of different clubs, a sense of nostalgia hit him. Almost every court held a memory of a different match, mostly victories but also one or two heart-breaking losses too. Except for the stadium court where David had ballboyed for the likes of Jimmy Connors, Roscoe Tanner and his favourite, Vitas Gerulaitis, the rest of the courts were hard concrete with a real grittiness to them. David loved them, they suited his baseline game perfectly and he had won his first tournament there at the age of 11. He remembered that first final against Sean Tilbrook, a kid from Pietermaritzburg whose family had fled Rhodesia the previous year, played on one of the lower courts. They had really battled it out and he had scraped through in 2 very tight sets. That seemed both like yesterday as well as years ago now David thought, taking his gear out from the trunk of his car.

"So now who's late, bro?!" Lionel greeted him, stretching his hamstrings out on the court.

"I'm one minute early, you dick!" laughed David.

"I haven't come empty handed like you either, you *schnorrer"* said David, throwing him a big white packet with the Tachinni logo on.

Lionel looked curiously in the packet and pulled one garment out at a time in utter amazement.

"Fuck sakes, Davie! Is this really for me? Tacchini, my favourite!" he said, tears welling up in his eyes.

"I managed to convince the rep I needed to try a size up too so these are yours. You should try them on, bro" David suggested.

Lionel needed no further encouragement and within seconds it seemed he had exchanged his outfit for the first Tacchini one, socks-and-all. The first style was a new one designed specifically for Wilander for the French and David was sure not even Wilander had practiced in his yet.

"Perfect! Absolutely perfect fit, Davie! You are not only a scholar but a rock star too, my friend! Thank you so, so much" Lionel said, giving his old pal a big bear hug and peck on the forehead.

"This style must be brand new man. I've never see it before!" he shouted with joy.

"You're right for once in your life. It is part of the new Wilander range, designed especially for the French" explained David. "I had Shakira help me pick them out from their catalogue".

"Well she may not have taste in guys but she certainly has fine taste in tennis clothing" teased Lionel. "I'm going to wear these for our match this morning. There's no way I can lose looking this good" he joked.

"Davie, I brought you something too" he said, scrounging in his kit bag and producing 4 frozen bottles of his favourite pink concoction. "I think the way I'm feeling in my garb you going to need these more than me".

After 10 minutes of stretching exercises they moved to their respective baselines and went through their warm up routine. By this stage the grounds staff had started to arrive and were curiously eyeing out these 2 kids whizzing shots backwards and forwards. They were clearly not club players and it didn't take long before they had attracted a small gang of them.

David loved being back on his home ground as it were, at Westridge. The May weather was stunning, warm but not humid. His game was well-honed and he felt relaxed and loose so decided to play with freedom. Lionel had never seen David play this loose or free and before he knew it David had taken the first set 6-3. By now the retired little old ladies who played regular club morning tennis were arriving and the majority of them had decided that watching the two young men fight it out was far more their cup of tea than playing themselves. One of the old girls shouted out to them asking for the score.

"This *schlemiel* somehow stole the first set 6-3 from me, but we are playing best of 5 so I'll still take him in 4 sets, mam. You look like a gambler so put all your bucks on me, OK my dear!" Lionel shouted back at her.

"Thank you my son. We loving it! You two young men play beautifully. What are your names?" the old goat croaked out.

“Mam, I’m Lionel Perreira and this *schlemiel* is David Oppenheim. He’s playing in the French Open in 2 weeks so you should remember his name!” shouted Lionel.

“Oh, I will my son. I’m also Jewish tell him” she croaked back.

“Davie, I just made you a lifelong fan, my boy. You better perform” laughed Lionel.

After downing half a bottle each of the pink stuff they continued.

Lionel came back strongly in the second set sending down a high percentage of booming first serves and deft, first touch volleys. He won the crucial seventh game of the set by breaking service and held on to win the set 6-4. So set all. Whilst taking in more electrolytes at the break David couldn’t help but feel a sense of déjà vu. It was like they were back to their teenage years trying to kill each other on the hot Westridge courts. The little crowd had started to swell and he even noticed 2 photographers approaching them.

“Guys, howzit! We are from Natal Newspapers. One of the club ladies phoned us to let us know you guys were out here training. Don’t worry to introduce yourselves, we remember you from the juniors. Do you mind if we sit inside the court and take a few shots for this afternoon’s edition? We’ll be quiet and respectful and you won’t even notice us I can assure you” said the taller guy.

“Fine by me” said David who had got used to this type of attention already.

“Only if you make me look better than him!” joked Lionel and both photographers laughed.

“Before you kick off the next set can we have one of the two of you together, please?” asked the shorter man.

The two rivals got closer, arms around each other’s shoulders, and gave their best smiles.

“Lovely, just perfect chaps” they said firing off a couple shots before taking seats next to the umpire’s chair.

By now David noticed a mixed crowd of about three-hundred gathered around their court, some seated on the hard concrete steps, others on the grass verge at the top of the bank, and a bunch of others standing wherever there was room. David chuckled thinking he should ask Lionel to go around with a hat asking for donations towards their expenses. He wouldn't put it past his friend to do so.

David thought the 3rd set was possibly the best set they had ever played against each other. There was nothing in it. The rallies became intense and longer, every shot like it was a decider. They were totally zoned into it and so was the crowd. The old Jewish lady was applauding every point David managed to scrape. Lionel raced to a 5-2 lead in the tiebreaker decider only for David to claw back into it with 2 stinging forehand crosscourt forehand returns followed by a delicious drop shot and gorgeous forehand flicked lob, which he held back on until the absolute last second. It didn't stop there and went backwards and forwards with each of them holding multiple set points until David finally clinched one of his after a protracted baseline rally of twenty-three strokes.

They both fell down on court and lay on their backs, exhausted. David didn't even notice the standing ovation the crowd was giving them or the two photographers who were now right on the court trying to get photos of them lying prostrate on the hard, hot concrete. They barely managed to drag themselves to their chairs to towel themselves off and drink their pink drinks.

"You fucker, you just don't know when to give in, do you?" said Lionel in between large successive gulps. "I don't think I've ever seen 2 better forehand crosscourt returns from anyone that you smashed in that breaker. It's that bloody drill I gave you!" he barked out and they both packed up laughing.

"Jesus, can you never just put it down to my talent, just *one time*, Li" David pleaded whilst pouring ice water over his neck and head.

"Get fucked! On this court you get nothing from me, even if you did give me Tacchini this morning. The one good thing about this first shirt being so drenched is that I get to change into the other one" he said, taking the new one out of its packet and putting it on.

"Listen, I know we are both gassed but I can see this lot are impatient for the next set" said David gesturing to the crowd who were staring intently at them, clearly indicating they were going nowhere.

"Gassed? I'm not gassed! I still have 2 sets to win, Davie!" he shouted, picking up his Wilson racquet and heading to the baseline.

David just smiled looking at his old friend heading off with his super confident and cocky walk. Nothing had changed.

Lionel learned much to his dismay that no amount of pink drink was enough to replace the toughness David had built on the tour. The first break came in the second game courtesy of a low dipping forehand return which almost hit Lionel on the shoe as he tried desperately to reach down for it. It stayed down and not even a dwarf could have scraped it back over the net. David smelt blood and with every game he felt his rival's resolve weakening. It was all in the head Lionel, David reminded himself as he pushed his weary opponent around the baseline before ending the set and match with a flattened-out, down-the-line forehand winner.

The crowd clapped again but this time more out of disappointment because they were hoping for a fifth set. The honest truth David thought was that neither of them could have made a final set. As relieved as he was that he had managed to finish it in four sets he was also concerned how he would cope on clay in a fifth set. It was something he would need to solve and quickly.

The 2 photographers seemed very happy with their shots and thanked them both. They told them they were going to try get a picture or two of them in for the afternoon edition of The Daily News, or the following morning's Natal Mercury, or possibly both. They handed out their business cards and promised enlarged copies of prints for them.

"I hope you guys realise you are making history today by photographing the early days of a future French Open men's singles champion here" Lionel said nodding towards David.

"We can see that, Mr Perreira" the shorter man responded. "Before we go do you guys mind signing autographs for my kid, please? They are both tennis crazy and also play at Mitchell Park. They won't believe I got to watch and photograph you lads today" he said, handing out a diary and pen to them.

The signs were there for all to see that the two friends were on the brink of becoming something in the tennis world. They could sense it too and it reflected in the air of confidence they carried about them on the tennis court. It was a sense of certainty, a sense of clarity in seeing, and believing in your destiny. After all, it was all in the mind.

"Alright, how about we take a drive up the coast again to Ballito this time and grab a lunch, bro?" suggested David after they had towelled off. The crowd had slowly dispersed and only a couple of the old ducks had decided to take to the courts for a bit of a hit. Westridge seemed like it also needed an afternoon breather after the excitement of the morning.

"Cool, let's go get some nutrients back into our systems. It's a huge difference playing beyond 3 sets man! I thought I was going to throw up the 4th set the way you were moving me around the baseline. That nasty little disguised drop shot didn't help my legs either!" said Lionel, packing the last of his kit away.

"Ja, I think we skip any drills this afternoon. We've both had enough sun for today. I think any more time on the court we both going to end up with dehydration and kidney stones and that isn't going to help our cause" laughed David.

It wasn't long before they were doing some low-flying up the north coast freeway, the Green Mamba chewing up the miles of lush, tropical greenery of the coastal forest and cane fields surrounding the highway. Lionel pushed an old Zodiac mixed tape in the cassette player and pumped up the volume. The old classic high-energy Italian beats thumped from the car's audio system and brought back fun memories for them both. Lionel had missed Durban and the memories it held for him even if his future and destiny was no longer tied to it. It had been a very important stepping stone for both of them but with the impending political changes and the international tennis circuit opening doors, they knew big changes were coming for both of them. Durban would always be their emotional home but now the world was their oyster and they were 2 ambitious young men determined to grab all the opportunities thrown their way.

They found an inviting bistro on the main promenade overlooking the dark blue Indian Ocean with its occasional white, fluffy surf. It really was a perfect day with only the occasional cloud floating in an otherwise blue sky. They ordered Cajun chicken salads and drinks from their waitress and then settled in for a chat.

"I spoke to Tammy last night, by the way" said Lionel.

"Oh yes. And?" asked David.

"So, I told her if she was still interested, what with the amount of travel involved with the tour, I would still like to keep our relationship going. I was relieved to hear she felt the same way. She still has 2 more years of college left and if we are still together by the time she graduates then we will look at the next obvious step, but only at that point" he explained.

"Smart move, bro. The time apart will prove a good test for the relationship. If it can handle the stresses of being apart then it'll handle anything. Without having met her the way you have described her and your relationship with her family, I think you're a good fit. At least you don't have the religious differences or racial thing to contend with" said David.

"Very true and I have no idea why you would even consider doing that to yourself, Davie. Surely, just being Jewish is tough enough? I think you're a masochist wanting to put yourself through all this with this Shakira chick. She really has to be something to want to have to deal with all the complications you've had to start with."

"Believe me, bro, in the early days before it got so serious, all those thoughts went through both our minds but in spite of all that, the attraction was just too strong. It's ridiculous that something we have which is so natural and pure is looked down upon by our society both racially and religiously. It's fucking absurd that our government considers us a crime and our religions consider our union as undesirable. It's like we are still living in the Middle Ages in this country" David rattled off with obvious irritation in his voice.

"Well, all of this just makes me so much more curious and excited to finally get to meet her. I know you, Davie and I trust your judgement in people. I mean you're best friends with me after all! I'm so looking forward to meeting her at the reunion on Saturday night. I hope you don't mind but I did discuss your lady with Tammy last night. I just wanted her take on it as an objective outsider" said Lionel.

"So what are her thoughts, given the fact she is from the American south of course?" asked David.

"Bro, she's not from the *deep* south where they still wear white hoods!" laughed Lionel. "At Auburn there are plenty of mixed race couples. It's not quite free-swinging California or New York where any old thing goes but there's definitely no Apartheid. Tammy said love has no colour, no boundaries. It's not a science experiment governed by binary laws. She says the heart doesn't lie and should never be contained. The heart will do what it needs to do" he said to David earnestly.

"I agree with her that it can't be controlled sometimes and this is one of them, Li. Both Shakira and I have decided to go with it even if it ends up with broken hearts for both of us. The only person who gets me even close to Shakira is my sister. She has picked up the change in me the last couple months and is asking all the right, awkward questions which I haven't been ready to open up about yet ... until now. I'm just not sure whether to do it before or after the French is all, but it's time" said David.

"After! Definitely after, bro! You don't need the complications and distraction during the tournament" Lionel piped up.

"Yip, I'm thinking the same thing" replied David.

"She broke the news earlier this week to her mom. Her mom already knew she had met someone. They're close and very alike so that wasn't that much of a surprise, but the part about me being Jewish definitely was. She was disappointed because she was convinced it was a friend of the family's blue-eyed boy who had been asking a lot of questions recently about her. Apparently her father approved of him and his family too as he ticked all the right boxes. She immediately gave Shakira all the usual, rational reasons as to why she would be setting herself up for heartbreak, but when she saw the depth of her feelings for me she became more open. She told her that she had no issue with me being Jewish and that her family had Jewish neighbours they had been close with in Iran. The problem is the father who has already felt let down that she had turned down the Vahed boy he admired so much. To then have his daughter choose a Jew over him is going to be a tough pill for the old man to swallow" said David.

"Oh my god, I can only imagine being told that" Lionel laughed.

"Anyway, the mother wants to meet me in private she told Shakira. She said that before she even contemplates telling her husband a private meeting with me is non-negotiable. And if I'm serious about Shakira that I meet her brother Mo too, although that can be with Shakira and not just one-on-one" David said.

"Fuck sakes, Davie! When is all of this going to happen?" asked Lionel in amazement.

"We've set down a time for next Tuesday when the mother usually attends a morning book club, so we can only practice that afternoon, by the way. I guess after that meeting I'll know whether I have a girlfriend still or not. I'm actually more nervous for that then facing Figueras, Li" he said, half-laughing.

"We're going to meet at the back of the Musgrave Centre library. The one good thing about that is she won't be able to shout at me!" he joked.

"Rather you than me, bro! This is all just a bit too bizarre for me but if there's anything I can do to make things easier just shout. You are right though, that meeting will decide whether the relationship goes forward or not, so you better be on your finest behaviour. Do the Jewish thing for starters and don't arrive empty-handed. A nice bunch of chocolates to break the ice will at least win you some points!" he joked with David.

"Funny you should mention it! Her favourite sweets are Turkish Delights from Dubai and by chance I happen to have a box or two of them still in my drawer so hopefully that will break the ice" David laughed.

"Now you thinking smart, bro! Put on all your David Oppenheim charm too. I mean it's worked on her daughter, right?"

"I'm just going to be myself is all and if that's not good enough for her then so be it. Too tiring spending your whole life trying to please others and be someone you not. That's what I love about Shakira. I'm just me around her and that's all she wants" said David.

They spoke for another hour about their families and about playing a 5 setter, but this time at Mitchell the following morning. Just before the sun was about to set they settled up their bill and headed back to Durban.

After dropping Lionel off at his parent's home he set off for the university campus. Shakira had a late afternoon tutorial session and he had arranged to meet up with her in the law library so she could give him more details and an update about her conversations she was having with her mother about them.

One thing was for sure he thought as the view of Howard College got closer and closer. Nothing about his life was simple.

Chapter 16

He spotted her in her usual place on the second floor of the law library, hidden away in the corner deep in study. He sneaked up behind her and then quickly placed his hands over her eyes.

"Guess who?" he asked, giving her a bit of a fright.

"David, you scared me!" she shouted and turned around to give him a juicy kiss on the cheeks.

He loved the familiar cherry taste of her lipstick and the sweet smell of her Calvin Klein perfume. He pulled her up from her chair and hugged her tenderly.

"Wow! You look like you've been on the beach the whole day, my darling. People pay a lot of money for a tan like yours" she joked.

"Shakira, we played our hearts out at Westridge this morning. I managed to scrape through in 4 sets and just as well because neither Lionel nor I could have made a 5th. We were both gassed!" he said.

"I know all about this morning, Mr O! Look here" she ordered as she opened up her bag and brought out that afternoon's Daily News. There on the front cover was a picture of David and Lionel hugging each other under the heading, "Banana Boys headed for tennis greatness." Even though David could feel his cheeks warming he had to admit it was a really good picture of the two of them smiling. The photographer had managed to also capture a part of the crowd in the background.

Shakira gently removed the paper from him and read the brief article.

"David Oppenheim and Lionel Perrerira put on a fine display of professional level tennis whilst training at Westridge Park tennis stadium this morning. They are both graduates now, Oppenheim from the University of Natal where he studied commerce, and Perreira from Auburn University in Alabama, where he was on a tennis scholarship and studied Graphic Design. Both are now pursuing professional tennis careers on the Challenger tennis circuit. Oppenheim has been on the tour for a number of months already and has improved his ranking to one-hundred and eighty-two on the ATP rankings. As a result of his recent excellent results from the clay court season he has been granted a wildcard for the French Open beginning next month. The two players are well known as rivals throughout their junior careers and are considered to have top 100 potential. Tennis is very much alive and kicking at Westridge Park again!" she read.

"And there you thought I just wanted you for your handsome face, my darling" she laughed, kissing him on his lips again.

"Well, I didn't expect front page when these dudes were taking pictures this morning!" laughed David.

"Well, I think I cleared out the newsstands this afternoon. Miriam arrived for afternoon lectures with a copy and then during recess we zipped down to the Francois Road tearoom and cleared their stock. The owner thinks we are nuts but I don't care. I can't wait to drop a copy on my mom's lap when I get home tonight and watch the look on her face!" she said, as they both giggled.

"I've got a couple copies for you and your family too, my darling" she said as she proceeded to extract more copies from her bag.

"I hope your family and especially your father is very proud of you and your achievements, David. Take a few more too for your pal Lionel and tell him from me he looks very smart in his Tacchini outfit" she said.

"Thanks, my angel, I'm sure he and his family will be delighted to receive these. I'm hoping that this picture may even motivate Tacchini to give Lionel an early sponsorship. Actually, he *really* looks good in that style" laughed David.

"So, before varsity I had another chat with my mom about you. She's impressed your dad is the famous Prof O from UND. Your dad is highly respected amongst her peers so if nothing else your dad has scored you some early points. My mom always enjoys the whole Wimbledon, strawberries-and-cream thing every year with her book club, who they should rather rename the Gossip Club the way those women go on. She mentioned to them that I have a university friend who has qualified for the French and it turns out a few of them know you from your junior years and told her what a nice-looking boy you are. So things are looking a lot more positive for you Mr O for next Tuesday" she giggled.

"I don't know. This feels more like the pressure to perform with the expectations starting to build" David replied.

"Just be yourself my darling, just be you. You are enough just as you are" she said lovingly.

"I envy you that you've at least broken the news to your mother. The longer it goes for me the more nervous I'm getting to face the big day. The only advantage I have over you is that I'll get it over at one sitting. I spoke to Lionel and he agrees with me that I should rather wait until the French is over" said David.

"Well, on the positive side at least, you will have my family out the way before the French. My mother I think will tell my father next week after meeting with you. She's such a smart one that I know she has already probably devised a plan how to handle him."

"Jesus, I really hope so" said David, nervously.

"David, my dad had to fight for my mom's heart. Not only did he have to fight his *own* family but he also had to fight off many wealthy suitors too, she told me. His kindness and pure heart not to mention his refusal to take no for an answer is what won her over. He will do anything for her and she knows just how to handle him, don't worry" she reassured him.

"I'm thinking of telling Leah this weekend. She deserves to hear it before my parents. I'm still toying with the idea though. You two will get on like wildfire I'm positive of that, probably gang up on me too!" he laughed.

"I can't wait to meet her either. It will be good to have another girlfriend besides just Miriam in my life. I love her and EB to bits and would do anything for them but sometimes she drives me insane with her craziness. You know what I mean!"

"I love her too, she's a hoot!" laughed David.

"Whilst on the subject of Leah there's something I feel I can tell you about her even though it was not for repetition. This has to stay between us only though, Shakira" he said.

"Of course, my darling, what is it?"

"Leah has become quite religious the last year or so, like I've told you. My mother has even had to create a kosher kitchen in our home for her even though as a kid Leah ate bacon and prawns. She prays 3 times a day and is what we call *shomer Shabbat* in that she won't drive or work over the Sabbath, or even switch on lights for that matter. She's gone and met someone who also has a strong faith and made her even more observant which would have been all good and well, except for one small little catch" explained David.

"Small catch?" asked Shakira, curiously.

"Actually, big catch! You see this guy is a Gentile and what's more he is studying theology and considering the priesthood!"

"*Oy vey,* OMG!" Shakira exclaimed, shocked at this revelation.

"You can say that again! Can you only imagine if she and I both had to drop our bombshells on our parents on the same night? Even my father who is totally laidback and open-minded would hit the roof. They would disown us both on the spot" he laughed.

"Well you damn well better not do that to them! I can't believe it has happened to the both of you and at the same time. David, you had better tell your sister ASAP about us. You two will need to co-ordinate your coming-out of the closet as it were, very, very carefully. Just how serious is she about this guy and do you know him?" she asked.

"Nope, I'm going to take them out for dinner tomorrow night so I'll meet him there for the first time. I've never seen my sister like this before, she's totally in love with him. She tells me he's a bit of a genius and it sounds like she fell in love with his mind. The dude taught himself to speak Hebrew within the space of a year! It took me 5 years of it at Carmel to become semi-literate so he must be pretty smart. It sounds like he read the whole Torah in Hebrew which makes him more Jewish than me!" he laughed.

"Did you not pick up something before?" asked Shakira.

"Well in retrospect I should have asked her more questions when she was becoming more *frum* because now I see it must have been his influence. She was on that path already but I think his deep conviction in God encouraged her further. I mean, not that it's a bad thing, right?"

"Only if he's not trying to convert her?" replied Shakira.

"Ha! If anything I think he'll be the one being converted!" at which they both laughed.

"Maybe you should suggest that to Leah" said Shakira.

"When it comes to religious discussions I've learnt not to get involved, believe me. Anything to do with religion is worse than a hot, political potatoe! They must do whatever they feel is right" he said.

“Well, I still think it’s best to talk to her at the earliest. You two are close and she felt comfortable enough to discuss the situation with her priest with you” she said.

“You right. You’ve convinced me. I think I’ll tell her after Shabbat lunch on Saturday afternoon before we go out partying at Ronnyz with Lionel” said David.

“Good David, just do it and get part of your coming-out done. She may even be able to give you advice about how best to break it to your folks after the French Open. It’s getting late now so best if you drop me off before my tribe starts wondering where I am” she said.

“Shit, later than I thought it was! When I’m around my beautiful girl time always seems to fly by” he said, kissing her on her luscious lips.

“Flattery will get you everywhere, Mr O!”

Chapter 17

David wafted his way through the cloud of marijuana smoke on the 3rd floor of the SU for his next meeting with Dov. He removed the key from his pocket and opened the door. He was surprised to see Carol Levine in the room along with Dov, who was sipping on a can of Coke.

"Hi David. Meet Carol. She says she knows of your family" said Dov.

"Hi Carol. Really nice to meet you in person. Dov has told you me a little about you" said David politely extending his hand out of courtesy.

"Hi David, great to meet you. My father knows your mom from the Jewish Club and your dad took me for a semester when I was doing my undergraduate" she replied.

"I think I know a lot more about you than you know about me!" she laughed. "I'm a fan by the way" she said.

"I haven't done anything yet, though" said David puzzled.

"I mean a tennis fan of yours. I follow the game closely although I could never play the game. Too difficult for me. Hopefully one day your *faux* coach takes me to a major with him to watch you play" she giggled.

"Hey now, enough about this so-called, "faux coach" thing. I told both of you I played for the King David B team in Matric" replied Dov, defensively.

Both David and Carol burst out laughing.

"OK, enough already you two, we've got some serious stuff to talk about. David, I invited Carol to this one because since we last chatted our people have heard a lot more chatter coming from Durban over the air waves and they want us to speed up the op. Today Carol may be able to give us a woman's perspective about breaking the ice with Shakira. We need you to make your introduction to her ASAP" explained Dov.

"Before you arrived Carol and I were on the same page that it should happen at varsity and in the cafeteria where she usually unwinds in between her lecture breaks. Often she will sit alone if she has some reading to do which is better than if she is with her friends. We also discovered that she's been desperately searching for those records I gave you especially that Ziggy one. If you show her that one even a *schlemiel* like you has a chance with this chick!" he joked.

"But David, you've got to do it so naturally and matter-of-factly that she suspects nothing" said Carol.

"If you can get her talking about music you will be A for away bro. I think you are one of the few people I know who can match her knowledge of music. Once she starts talking about music then she loses her shyness and apparent aloofness. She's smart too and can hold her own in a conversation so don't necessarily keep everything to music" said Dov.

"Unless she asks specifically don't bring up the Jewish thing. Rather leave that for a bit later. So on that point just introduce yourself as David. You can tell her your surname down the line" added Carol.

"I think with a girl like her you've just got to be yourself. She's too smart for the usual guy bullshit. Don't give her too much all at once. Put out little bits of alluring bait at a time and let her digest on them rather than throwing everything in the dam at once. So you start with the records, especially that Bowie one. Let her do the talking then you follow her lead. You want to be a bit mysterious. Let her be the one to do the thinking" said Carol.

"She speaks French fluently bro so anything you can think of about that would be good. Maybe you can talk with her about Roland Garros and Paris" suggested Dov.

"No Dov, remember little bits of bait at a time. I think David should just make his intro about the records. Any other stuff can come later" interrupted Carol.

"You know what? You are quite right, Carol. Stick to the records only David. Besides, music alone could keep you two *hakking* all afternoon. She does quite a bit at Manhattan Music besides compiling the accounting records. The 2 buyers take her lead as far as suggestions are concerned, especially things like back catalogue and collectibles, out-of-print stuff. She takes care of the import side too with their overseas vendors which probably explains why they have the largest collection of imports in their inventories. Her brother Mohammed supplies them with all their dance and club stuff as he is invested quite heavily in clubs around the country so is familiar with that scene. Manhattan are by far the leaders in the club music scene and he's doing a tidy trade with them judging by the figures. That and the business he generates from the clubs probably explains how he is able to pay for the Maybach he moves around in. The kid refuses to take a cent from the old man. Trying to prove he can do it on his own we think and we are still looking a bit deeper into it. It seems like he's close with his mom and Shakira but there may just be an issue with him and the father. For an owner in the nightclub scene he appears to be remarkably clean but not as clean as the father though. We don't think he discloses all his business to the tax authorities but other than that he's clean with no links to the usual drugs and prostitution by-products. He definitely has zero interest in his religion although he's very protective of his family and especially his little sister. Next time we meet we should have a lot more on Mo which you could very well meet if you succeed with his sister. Oh yes, one other thing about the brother. He's not a particularly big guy but as a teenager he was an MMA champion. Fought something like thirty amateur contests, no losses and twenty-four knockouts, so be nice to the guy!" laughed Dov.

"Great, thanks for that last bit! So now I have not only a fundamentalist, anti-Jewish father to worry about but a wannabe-gangster, MMA champion brother in the way too? There I was thinking it was just going to be my shyness to overcome" said David.

"David, you're going to do just fine. You have all the right credentials for this one. Dov and I checked you out thoroughly and you are perfect. This girl is going to love you and so will her family later. Just be yourself" reassured Carol.

"Next time we will cover the brother and mother in detail. They will form an important component especially the mother because we predict it will be her to break the news that their daughter is serious about a Jewish man. His family were disappointed at him choosing a Shia bride when he had so many Sunni girls to choose from but he loved her so dearly that he went against their wishes and married her anyway. He'll do anything for her" said Dov.

"Before you leave I have your plane tickets too. You'll also find an Israeli passport in their as well as a few telephone numbers in case you have any issues. Fly out of South Africa on your SA passport, your Israeli one to enter Israel and then your SA one on your return. You won't be flying El Al but connecting via Istanbul to Tel Aviv. Moshe's guys will collect you before immigration and take you to Moshe. For this trip he wants you to stay at his family home. It's a great honour David. If it wasn't for this man and his bravery, Israel would probably have lost the war in 1973. For you to be staying at his home should tell you how important you are seen by him and the agency. Your letter from TSA is inside your passport. Give it to your parents" said Dov.

"How will I know Moshe's guys?" asked David.

"Not important. They will know you and when you see them you will immediately know it" chuckled Dov.

"OK that's it for today, guys" said Dov, handing an envelope to David as he stood up.

"And David there's quite a bit of cash in there too for your expenses. Please don't spend it all at once and try bring back some change. We're going through a recession after all!"

The meeting concluded and soon David was heading back to the Green Mama.

Things were moving fast and he could see they were about to get complicated too.

Chapter 18

"I see the Green Mamba still loves the smell of the hills on the ridge!" laughed Leah as David floored it en-route to the little kosher restaurant his sister had booked at.

"More like she loves the smell of petrol! I've only been back a few days and I'm already through 2 tanks" laughed David back at her.

"I think the driver probably has a lot to do with that" replied Leah gripping her seat belt as they shot through the Tollgate bridge intersection heading through the Berea suburb.

"How was your practice with Lionel today? Was he surprised to see his photo in the Mercury this morning?" she asked.

David had surprised his parents the previous evening with the copies of the Daily News Shakira had given him but then his mother had given him a bigger surprise by leaving a copy of the Natal Mercury on his floor that morning. One of the kind photographers had dropped off a very early edition with his mother that morning as well as some enlarged prints for him and Lionel. He was delighted to see that they had chosen a classic picture of the two of them lying prostrate on the court after their match with the heading, "Game, Set and Match!" The article was very similar to the one in the sister paper but also mentioning his first round French Open opponent by name. They also mentioned his coach was Dov Mendelson which David found extremely amusing. He could only imagine the local coaches scratching their heads trying to work out who the fuck Dov Mendelson was.

"Yeah, when I told him we were in the Mercury too, his mom went rushing out to get a few copies before they got sold out" chuckled David.

"You two are just *practicing* here and already creating a royal ruckus. You can't believe how many calls we had this morning. Mom must have taken at least 20 plus calls from all her friends going on about you. She was smiling like a Cheshire cat when I went running off with dad to varsity this morning. She has already sent a few of those prints off to Natal Arts & Crafts for framing" she laughed.

"The guy who left the papers and prints said to tell you that his kids were delighted to receive your signatures" she added.

"Jesus Christ, this is all a bit embarrassing Leah" replied David.

"Well my famous brother, I think you better shrug off your shyness because I foresee a lot more of this just around the corner for you and Lionel. I love it and at lunch I had quite a few people who I've never spoken to in lectures come up and introduce themselves!" she boasted, very proud of her big brother.

"Seeing as we are speaking so openly there's something I need to let you in about Leah, but this does not go further than you and I. The only other people who know are Lionel and his American girlfriend, Tammy" said David.

"Pray tell, David. I'll say nothing about it to anyone until you give me the green light" she said.

"Alright, here it goes then. I've met someone too! You guessed it the other night. She's the one who has been putting such a smile on my face the last few months" said David.

"I knew it! But this is wonderful David, why be so secretive? I'm sure she's special this girl especially for you to have ignored Loren like you did for *Shabbos.* Poor girl must have spent a fortune on her hair alone and you gave her maybe 2 quick glances. She is probably telling her friends you are gay" laughed Leah.

"Well that's mom's fault for trying to match make me with a Jewish girl!" he said, making them both laugh.

"So then, who is this mysterious lady who makes my brother so happy?" she asked.

"Her name is Shakira and she's very beautiful. She's not Jewish either" said David.

"Well that's hardly a surprise, really. That's a gorgeous name. Is she Spanish by any chance?" she asked.

"Leah, she's not a gentile. She's Muslim" replied David softly.

After what felt like a really long silence Leah replied, "Oh Jesus, no David, please tell me I misheard that part about her being Muslim". He could sense the utter shock in her voice. He had expected her to be surprised but not this shocked.

"Yes Leah, she's from a secular Persian Shia Muslim background on her mom's side and Sunni on her father's. She's no different from you and me otherwise. She's not only very intelligent, she also happens to be very beautiful too. She looks like an old Hollywood movie starlet. We met at varsity last year and she's completing an Honours in Accountancy working towards a CA qualification" he said.

"David, how the hell did this happen to the both of us *at the same time*? Mom and dad are going to freak out! How serious are you with her, David?" she asked, still in shock.

"Well my sister, let me say that you aren't the only person in love. We've been seeing each other for just over 6 months now and we are getting even closer. We decided the afternoon of the Shabbos mom hosted, that we would introduce each other to our families. That's how serious this is. Shakira has already broken the news to her mother this week?" he replied.

"Oh yes, and how exactly did that go for her then?" Leah asked.

"Difficult at first but the mom is open-minded and quite worldly. She studied art and history in Paris after high school. She wants to meet me in private next Tuesday and I guess that will determine how things progress for Shakira and me. If I pass the test she will inform the father who sounds like a strict, pious man" said David.

"David, I'm sorry if I seem so shocked but this really was the last thing I was expecting to hear from you! I have no reason or right to judge you considering I'm doing the same thing, but with a gentile. You've got *both* the religious and racial thing to deal with, it's no wonder sometimes I've seen this conflict boiling inside you. Then in the middle of all of it I drop my baggage on top of you too. I'm so sorry" she said with tears in her eyes.

"Leah, stop. I have never been happier in my life, honestly. This girl is incredible, she's the best thing that's ever happened to me. She knows all about you and can't wait to meet you!" he told her.

"Really? Wow! Do you have a photo of her?" she asked.

"Look inside the glove compartment. There's one of the two of us sitting on the Green Mamba that she got some stranger to take" said David. She did as he instructed.

"Wow, wow, wowzers!" she exclaimed. "My goodness, she's more beautiful than you described David and I'm sure I've noticed her on campus. Look at those green eyes and olive skin. Body looks pretty fine too!" his sister exclaimed.

"She looks very Spanish or Mediterranean. Persian, you said, right?" she asked.

"Yip, mother's side Persian like I said" replied David.

"I have to say you guys look very well suited and incredibly cute too" she giggled.

The picture was one of them with David half sitting on the trunk of the Green Mamba hugging Shakira who was leaning back into his embrace. It was a wonderful night out, just the two of them and the big smiles bore witness to their mutual happiness.

"You guys look totally in love in this photo. Now I truly understand what you meant when you told me that a love like this between any two people can't be wrong. This is exactly what this photo tells me" she said.

"I was just telling her how well you two would get on. She's so curious about Jewish culture. I'm also not her first Jewish boyfriend. She dated someone from Jewish aristocracy when she lived and studied in Paris after she matriculated. His family were really nasty to him when they found out she was Muslim. She broke it off in spite of him standing up to them but she didn't want to cause a rift between him and his family. Now, along comes this schmuck, who she falls for after promising herself never to date another Jew again. Can you believe that?" said David.

"My brother, she's just as lucky to have you. I know what my friends have said about you to me over the years. She's not the only one with looks and talent in your relationship!"

"Well look, I wanted you to know before I break the news to our beloved parents after the French Open. You deserve that much from me and I trust you. Tonight is about you and Michael though and I'm looking forward to meeting the man who has won my little sister's heart" said David.

“Thanks David, I’m excited too. You should really keep this photo in a more protected place than your glove compartment though. It’s a very special photo of you guys. If there was ever a photo to explain being in love, this is it, even if you were still wearing your tennis outfit” she laughed, placing it back in the glove department.

David pulled into the parking outside Schmaltz’s Diner, a small kosher restaurant in Umhlanga Ridge. The restaurant was quiet and Michael had arrived and was already seated. When he saw them entering he immediately stood up to greet them.

“Hello David! I’m Michael, it’s so nice to meet you although the way Leah speaks about you I think I almost know you already” he said, whilst extending his hand out for David to shake,

“Good to meet you too, Michael. I believe you’re a fellow horsefly?” said David, shaking Michael’s hand firmly.

Before answering Michael hugged Leah warmly and gave her a peck on the cheek.

“Yes, yes, I was a few years after you, I think. My whole family, going back a few generations, attended DHS including my father who was actually head boy back in his day” responded Michael.

“Is this your first time in a kosher restaurant then?” asked David, as they seated themselves.

“First time in this particular one yes, but no I’ve eaten in ones in Brooklyn and Jerusalem” he said, which quite surprised David.

“Did you have Jewish friends you were with that you ate there?” asked David.

“Oh no, not at all. I was just curious. I just wanted to understand the difference between kosher and non-kosher and if it differed between Brooklyn, which is mostly Ashkenazi, and Jerusalem which has many Sephardim” said Michael.

David couldn’t help but laugh at his answer. “Sorry, I don’t mean to sound condescending but you must be the only non-Jew on the planet voluntarily wanting to put themselves through eating kosher food at a restaurant. I would never bother if it wasn’t for my darling sister having become *frum*.”

“Oh no offense taken. I think I’m probably a bit strange at wanting to experience all sorts of weird things in life! I think I’m just one of those strange people who likes to try understand why people do or think the things they do. It sometimes keeps your sister in hysterics when I do things I think are completely normal but which she considers *meshuggeh,* I think you call it in Yiddish, right?" he laughed.

"Yes, you got it right, it is *meshuggeh*" replied David chuckling.

"Anyway, I just wanted to tell you that I really don't care whether you are Jewish or not. It really makes no difference to me. I only want someone who treats my sister well as she's very precious to me. She says you are kind and thoughtful towards her so that's good enough for me although I honestly never saw her having a gentile for a boyfriend and ... especially not one thinking of the priesthood!" laughed David.

"A bit too early to say for sure whether I enter the priesthood yet but it is a possibility. I'm studying theology and a number of other areas too so anything can happen. I don't think my father will ever speak to me again if I do wind up going down that path but that may not be such a bad thing either" he laughed, ironically.

"Don't worry, you in good company there, Michael. Our father is not too wild at David's choice of being a tennis professional" said Leah.

"Well, that is really a damn pity because I watched you practicing on Sunday morning at Mitchell Park with that Perreira guy. Man, I really admire you guys. You are like artists, man. I was fascinated how you were able to outsmart a bigger guy who hits a lot harder than you by using your guile" said Michael.

"Oh yeah, and specifically how did I do that?" asked David, curious as to what he had observed.

"Well, as much as I love watching tennis, I'm certainly no coach or anything but after thinking a bit about it, I realised why you were hitting those looping top spins to the middle of the court" remarked Michael.

"Oh yes, and why was that?" asked David, curiously.

"No angle. You were giving him no angles to create from that position and kept him rooted to the baseline and away from the net. Well that's the way I saw it, anyway" he laughed.

“I think if the religious thing doesn’t work out you may have a career as a tennis analyst. You one-hundred percent correct, that’s exactly why I was hitting those shots. Are you sure you haven’t played the game?” asked David.

“I told you my guy was smart, brother!” said Leah, giving Michael a hug.

They were seated in the meat section of the restaurant and ordered steaks and salads. The conversation moved smoothly, varying from David’s career on the tour, to the political situation on UND’s campus, to religion and inevitably to the situation in Israel. David was more than a little impressed with the younger man’s knowledge on so many topics. It was more than obvious why his sister was so drawn to him. Not only was he bright but he was also full of passion for the truth and understanding it. He was very funny too. After they had finished eating he questioned David about his atheism.

“So, David please tell me if this is a bit personal because religion usually is, but Leah explained to me you are an atheist. Can you tell me how and why you became one?” asked David.

“Well it’s pretty simple, actually. After my *bar mitzvah* I realised that I was just observing religious rituals and holidays out of habit and not because I had faith in a deity. My grandfather and my Uncle Sol both became atheists as a result of the *Shoah* and their reasoning for doing so resonated with me. If there was a God, the Holocaust was the perfect time to show himself or herself and save The People of the Book from those Nazi scum. As a result of six million people expecting to be saved by this almighty power, they were instead murdered, going like meek lambs to the slaughter” explained David.

David watched Michael contemplating this before he said, “If those six million were my people I think I would feel the same as you. I’m going to sleep on that and say a few prayers for guidance before I give you my final answer” replied Michael.

“That’s certainly one of the better responses I’ve had from anyone to date” laughed David.

“I look forward to what you finally come back with beyond the usual blind faith answer which doesn’t hold water with me” said David.

He couldn’t help but notice how intently Michael looked at him, almost like he was searching for his soul. This kid was smart and deep. He liked him regardless of Leah.

"Hey, if you have some time tomorrow afternoon you are most welcome to come umpire for Lionel Perreira and me. It means most of the afternoon because we are playing a full 5 sets no matter what. You see I have to get ready for 5 set matches at the French Open. We only play best of 3 sets on the Challenger tour" said David.

"Are you being serious?" asked Michael in amazement at the offer.

"About tennis, I'm only serious. You know how to score in tennis, right?" asked David.

"Score, perfectly, play, not so much" laughed Michael.

"Then you're in but remember any close calls go my way!" laughed David.

"I'm in, count on me. What time should I be there?" he asked excitedly.

"12:30 p.m. sharp but doesn't it cut in with your lecture times?" asked David.

"Screw lectures, I'm not giving up the opportunity of umpiring Oppenheim versus Perreira, no way! Should I wear tennis gear?" he asked, making them all laugh.

"Not unless you planning on playing too! Now listen, I'm going to pay Shlomo for the meal and then I think we all need to get moving because it's nearly midnight and we all have a big day tomorrow" said David.

David cleaned up the bill and they moved outside.

"Thanks so much for dinner, David. Kosher or not I really enjoyed it and I can't wait for tomorrow's match. I'll be there early I promise" he said shaking David's hand.

"Thanks my Leah. It's been a lovely evening" he said giving her a hug and kiss goodnight.

Leah and David were back in The Green Mamba flying back to Glenwood.

"David, did I ever tell you that you are amazing?" asked Leah

"Not often enough, sis. You don't need to say anything. You've got a good man there. I like him. Let's just leave it at that for now" he smiled, as the Green Mamba munched up the kilometres.

Chapter 19

It had been more than 7 years since David had last visited Israel and lying back in his airline seat he was both excited and apprehensive for what awaited him. Dov had arranged one last meeting at the Economics Society where he had given David extensive background on Shakira's mother and brother Mo. He was impressed to learn that besides English, Farsi and French, the mother also spoke Spanish and Italian too. She had come from what was considered a wealthy home at that time in Iran. Her father was a senior government minister in the Shah's cabinet and her mother, a professor of international studies at Tehran University. The mother had been educated at the American school in Tehran and as an only child had led a privileged life. She was both academically gifted and sporty like her daughter and had made the Iranian junior national badminton team. After graduating high school her parents had sent her for tertiary education to Paris for 4 years where she studied art and music. During her university years in France she had serious relationships with 2 white men, one a local Parisian and the second, an American student. Both had ended amicably and had resulted in her becoming even more secularized. The family had been forced to flee before the Revolution, shortly after the mother had completed her university studies. They had fled to Durban where her father had relatives who accommodated the family for their first year until the father had found employment as a mid-level manager with one of the Muslim clothing firms, and her mother as a lecturer at the University of Durban-Westville, a then predominantly Indian university.

The move had been a major adjustment for her mother's family on many levels, both economic and religious. The mansion the family had enjoyed in Tehran was downscaled to a 2 bedroom flat in Overport and gone were the evenings of hosting twenty or more guests for dinner parties. The fine wines and whiskeys her father treasured were considered *haram* and no longer permitted as were the regular European holidays they used to take annually. The local community was insular and lived an archaic lifestyle as far as her mother was concerned and mixing with the more sophisticated and educated whites was off limits. It had taken them many years to feel comfortable and it was only when Shakira's mother had married Ismail, had they really been accepted within the community.

Shakira's brother, Mo, had been a rebel like his mother from early on and had been the source of frequent arguments between his parents for playing truant and giving the *mufti's* a difficult time at the Islamic school he attended. Ismail wanted to discipline him but his mother was always in the way making sure Mo escaped the worse punishments. She did not want to see her son's playful and rebellious spirit quelled by a bunch of archaic Muslim rules like most of her friends' kids had been. He was a livewire by nature and he fascinated her with his confidence and bravado.

In his second year of high school, Mo had been asked to leave due to his constant shenanigans and rather than join his father in his many growing businesses he had convinced his mother to allow him to finish his schooling at a boutique high school, which was more like a full-time party. He somehow managed to matriculate with a university pass and then spent two years studying very little at UND before quitting. Studying just wasn't for him he had explained. Then much to his father's dismay he had decided to invest in the nightclub scene with 2 of his other university drop-out friends. He had told Ismail that they spent so much time at the clubs that they figured they may as well buy them. The one partner was Jewish and the other one Greek and along with Mo made quite a formidable team with majority shares in about 15 clubs throughout the country. They were smart enough to invest in complimentary businesses like club music and audio equipment as well as handling security for the clubs. As much as it worried his mother that he was involved in a relatively risky industry, she was also proud that he had shown his father he was a capable businessman even if Ismail didn't approve of it exactly. He had been wise enough to have invested some of his profits in properties which would one day become regular rental income so he wouldn't be reliant on the nightclubs. He didn't have their daughter's academic smarts but he had plenty business acumen and she was proud of him.

Dov had also given him a more in-depth run down of his Israel trip. It was going to involve mornings of lectures, starting with basic Arabic followed by some psychology and history lessons. In the afternoons he would train with the top two Israeli juniors at the Tel Aviv Country Club which also had clay courts which David was still to experience. He would stay with Moshe's family. He would also have full access to all the facilities at the Tel Aviv Country Club including the modern gym and lovely pool.

Moshe had also made arrangements for him to visit Jerusalem and the Dead Sea, as well as Masada. Dov had also explained that he would be given basic instructions on weapon handling as well as a detailed fourty hour crash-course on Krav Maga by an IDF expert. Finally, a dietitian would analyse his bloods, sugars and fat levels to devise a very specific diet to increase his energy and stamina levels. It seemed like a helluva lot for only 2 weeks David thought.

As the Air Turkey plane jetted deep into the clouds above east Africa, David thought about his first meeting with the beautiful Shakira Mahomedy. She was far more beautiful in the flesh than her photos had done her justice. He had felt the first pangs of guilt for his deception soon afterwards, which Dov had warned him to expect. Their relationship shrink would help him navigate these emotions in Tel Aviv, Dov had assured him. With a beautiful girl like Shakira he was going to need to muster every ounce of restraint possible not to develop deep feelings for her. Their second meeting, their first date, having dinner in the VIP room at Legends had been perfect in every sense. She was interested in more than just his records, which he wasn't entirely convinced of after their first meeting in the SU's cafeteria. After their dinner date he was able to provide Dov with some info he didn't have about her having dated a Jewish man in Paris. Even these little snippets of information were vital Dov had emphasised to him in their last meeting before he flew out. David had made one visit to the Economics Society to refresh his memory about the various topics he and Dov had discussed in case Mossad tried testing him. He was as ready for the agency as he could be.

The rest of his flight to Istanbul and his connecting flight to Tel Aviv were uneventful and David slept like a baby after a few double whiskeys and soda. Before he could make his way through passport control at Ben Gurion International Airport, 2 huge IDF officers emerged from seemingly nowhere and instructed him to follow them. He wasn't going to argue with them. They took him past immigration and customs checkpoints and ushered him into an awaiting vehicle.

"What about my luggage, though?" asked David.

"That will be delivered shortly to you at Moshe's home" replied the one soldier gruffly.

As his ride drove through the various areas of Tel Aviv, David marvelled at the growth that the city had experienced in a relatively few years. Where there had not so long ago been desert, now tall buildings, hotels and office parks had sprung up. It really felt like a mini New York City both with the buildings and the obvious signs of the hustle-and-bustle of a big metropolis.

“A lot has changed since you were last here, soldier?” his driver said with a thick Israeli accent.

“After Silicon Valley, we have become the second largest tech start-up country in the world and the American tech giants are ploughing billions of dollars into investment here”.

“You right, it’s really incredible the development that’s happened here in the last 7 years” David replied.

“My name is Reuben, but you can call me Rubie like everyone else. I have been assigned to be your driver and security whilst you are here. You are not to travel anywhere without me. You can buzz me anytime twenty-four hours around the clock if you need to go somewhere and I’ll take you” instructed Reuben.

“There is a pager waiting for you at Moshe’s, so you use that” he added.

“How far is Moshe’s house?” asked David.

“He lives in Ra’anana another 10 minutes from here” said Rubie.

They had passed many signs of towns David recalled from his previous trip. Signs for places like Ramat HaSharon, Hod HaSharon, Petah Tikva and Herzliya flashed by. Ra’anana was like a little Sandton where the majority of South Africans chose to make *Aliyah* to.

“Is Moshe an ex South African?” asked David.

“No, not him but his wife’s family are from Johannesburg. He was born here but his wife is close with her family so they live in Ra’anana. They are lovely people and you are lucky to be staying with someone who is considered a hero here” said Rubie.

Soon they were pulling into the driveway of a lovely Tuscan-style home in a secure, gated community.

“You are going to feel like you are still back in South Africa because all the tenants living here are South Africans” laughed Rubie.

"Both my doctor and dentist live in this road" he said with the first signs of a smile.

It was only when Rubie got out the car did he realise just how big he was. He made his two colleagues from the airport look like shrimps David thought. *Kosher* ones!

"*Shalom* David and welcome to your other home!" announced Moshe, shaking his hand and giving him a massive hug. He seemed a lot bigger in the flesh than in the various photos Dov had shown him.

"Please, allow me to introduce my wife, Beverly, and our two sons, Avi and Dan" he said.

"*Shalom* David, we've been so looking forward to meeting you. Please, whilst you are with us treat our home like it's yours. We want you to feel comfortable here. The boys will help you with your things and take you to your room. They are both so excited to have a professional tennis player staying at us because they are both crazy about tennis. We have also prepared a delicious Israeli meal for you so when you've freshened up please come through. I hope you don't mind but my parents are joining us because they really want to meet you and catch up on what's happening in South Africa" she said, after giving him a warm hug and kiss on each cheek.

After shaking his hand firmly the 2 boys insisted on taking his bags from the vehicle to his room.

"Good night, David. As you can see, you are in very good hands here. I doubt you'll need me tonight but Moshe will give you a pager which you can contact me with should you need anything. If not, I'll see you tomorrow for your first day, but Moshe will explain everything tonight" said Rubie.

"Thanks for the ride, Rubie. I'll see you tomorrow then" said David.

The family home was spacious and beautifully decorated with a lovely selection of South African art. David also noticed framed photos of Moshe with many famous Israeli leaders including one with Golda Meir. Moshe had certainly given his life to the IDF with various pictures of him with tank battalions, sitting in fighter jets as well as on navy ships. He was a handsome man but his face wore the wounds of battle. It was easy now to understand why Israel revered him. Hopefully he would be able to learn a lot from this man.

“David, David, please can we look at your rackets? We want to see your tennis outfits too. What brand of shoes do you wear?” the 2 young boys asked in unison. Their mother had certainly been right about them being tennis mad. They were obsessed with John McEnroe and seemed to ask a million questions all about Mac at once. Had he met Mac? What was it like to face his serve? Was he taller than David? Fortunately he had hit a bit with Mac in Rome when his regular practice partner had caught a stomach bug at the last minute, so he was able to answer most of their questions. They were in awe listening to that story and pressed him for more until their father shouted for them to quit and give David a chance to shower and freshen up.

“Avi! Dani! David has only just arrived and you are already interrogating him. Let him shower my boys, please!” shouted Moshe from down the hall.

David was delighted he had been assigned to stay with Moshe. The home was very comfortable and the family were warm and welcoming. It was much nicer than staying at a hotel and Beverly had assured the home had a strong South African feel about it.

After David had showered and put on a change of clothing he wandered through to the living area where he was introduced to Beverly’s elderly parents. They were delighted to have a South African visitor and asked David many questions about the state of the country. They asked David about the effects of the state of emergency and how it affected his family’s every-day living, the rising level of crime with the political unrest as well as the general feelings of the local Jewish communities. They had noticed a slight increase in the number of South African *olim* who had made *Aliyah* because they were concerned with the inevitable change in government that everybody was anticipating. They were also very interested to hear about David’s family and their history in the Czech Republic and how they had made their way to South Africa. They asked him many questions about his tennis career and whether he had an alternative career path should that not work out for him.

“OK, mom, dad, everybody I’ve put dinner on the table so please come eat while it’s warm. Avi and Dani, please, enough playing with David’s tennis things” Beverly said, whilst the two boys removed David’s twelve rackets from his Head bags.

"David, please sit here next to Moshe. I've made a bit of a combined Israeli-South African meal so I hope you like it" said Beverly, as she helped her parents in to their seats.

Beverly had prepared a magnificent spread with a fresh Mediterranean salad and hummus and lamb falafels with some roast chicken. David was starving, having eaten very little of the airline food, and if he hadn't been so hungry he may have felt embarrassed for returning for seconds. He was fascinated how whether it was with a group of strangers in South Africa or Israel, how easily Jews embraced each other and felt so comfortable in their company. It was a good feeling and David enjoyed being part of their family.

"David, besides our work here we are looking forward to showing you some of the sites your forefathers would have ventured through. Dov said you hadn't seen much of Jerusalem and nothing of the Dead Sea and Masada, so Rubie will take you around. I think it's imperative that every Jew should understand their only real home and its history, and there's nothing like visiting it in the flesh. Books and photos don't do our beautiful land justice" said Moshe.

"*Baruch HaShem*, Moshe" said his father-in-law.

"At this point I would also like to make a toast to David. David, we are so delighted to have you here and we cannot express our gratitude for taking on what is a very important role for Israel. We understand how unexpected and even disruptive this task is for you, but as you will understand, we *are* you and you *are* us. You are our family David, and we look after each other. So here's to you and your family, David. *L'chaim*!" said Moshe, giving David a wink.

"Thank you so much for your hospitality, Moshe and Beverly. It's so lovely to be here and be welcomed like this. You do feel like family already. *L'chaim*" replied David as they clinked glasses.

The two boys then made sure to grill David with all sorts of questions over the South African bread-and-butter pudding Beverly served. Besides his recent tournament successes they wanted to know about the big majors. Had he been to Wimbledon? What about the French Open? How much money was he going to make his first year? Could they come watch him practice at the Tel Aviv club? Lots of questions.

"OK, OK, enough questions for a first night for poor David. He's not leaving tomorrow! It's time for you to go to bed now. You have school tomorrow. If

David says it's fine then you can watch him practice next week, but now off you go" he said, giving his sons hugs and kiss on the lips.

Soon after they had finished their dessert Beverly's parents excused themselves to go off to sleep and Moshe picked up a bottle of scotch whiskey and 2 tumblers and signalled for David to follow him. They made their way to the home's lovely garden and pool setting where they sat in lounges while Moshe filled their tumblers.

"David, I don't normally have time to have guests at our home besides my in-laws. Our enemies are keeping me and my colleagues very busy unfortunately but you are too important to all of us so I have taken a personal interest in you like I did with Dov all those years ago. I will be following your movements and progress very closely. You have already made a good start with the secondary target and I have no doubt that it will not be long before you make inroads with the primary target" said Moshe earnestly.

"Well, it's going to take a minimum of six months before I get to meet her family. She made this very clear to me on our first date" answered David.

"That's no problem but in the meantime you can get whatever you can from the daughter. Please David, every tiny bit of information, no matter how small you may think it is, can be the difference between people dying or living. Our enemies are receiving large funds that are being funnelled to them through various places and Durban is one of the most important. We don't know exactly how or who, but the prime target's name keeps on coming up in the chatter we are intercepting" said Moshe.

"Just last week a large payment was made from Durban to an arms smuggler in Russia for an order for 4 containers of AK-47 assault rifles and ammunition. They intend smuggling these rifles into Gaza and the West Bank through their tunnel network in the Sinai and Jordan. One of our operatives discovered this information, David. Those rifles will never make it there because that ship will be destroyed before it can make port in Egypt. Can you imagine how many Jews those rifles could and would kill, David? This is the value of intelligence, and using our training and your guile, you will uncover the mystery source and modus operandi of these collaborators in Durban. I have no doubt about that, David" explained Moshe.

"I will do my best for my Jewish nation Moshe, but please understand that I will not hurt anybody physically. I explained that very carefully to Dov but I want you to hear it from me now" said David firmly.

"David, we have people to neutralise targets when necessary. We're not asking or expecting you to do that" laughed Dov, "but we will nevertheless train you in case you find it necessary to defend yourself. In fact Ilan, the one giant who met you at the airport today, is an expert trainer in Krav Maga along with Rubie and will give you a crash course in it during your stay. It will improve your tennis reactions too as a side benefit" joked Moshe.

"What else will I do?" asked David.

"You will be taught weapons training but just with a hand weapon, no automatic rifles or the like. You will undergo psychological analysis and have psychological training in how to be a spy and coax the information we need from our targets. You will be shown how you can improve your tennis game through positive visualization which was developed primarily for our IDF soldiers but can be used in sports too. The two kids you will train with at the Tel Aviv Country Club underwent that training and the one is rated second and the other eighth in the world junior rankings. They may only be juniors but they will give you a good workout. I've told them to be tough on you!" and they both laughed at that.

"Your mornings will involve both physical and theoretical learnings and after lunch you'll be on the courts. It'll be intense but we have allocated weekends to rest and for sightseeing. David your instructors and teachers here are amongst the best in their fields in the world. We are investing everything we can in you" said Moshe, refilling their tumblers.

"You will eat breakfast with us at 6:30 a.m. and Rubie will collect you at 7:30 a.m. and you will start the day. Rubie will be with you all the time and drop you back here around 6:30 p.m. After dinners we will spend time together discussing things. David, except for Rubie, you are not to discuss anything operationally with anyone. The fewer people who know about this the better for their sakes as well as ours. We don't want to compromise your mission in any way" said Moshe.

"Understood, Moshe" he replied, draining his large second glass of whiskey.

"Good. You've had a long day *boychik*, it's time for you to go rest. We'll catch up again tomorrow night" said Moshe, gathering the empty bottle of whiskey and their tumblers.

"See you for breakfast at 6:30 am then, Moshe" said David.

"I wish. I'll be at base by that time already! Our enemies don't sleep, David" he laughed.

Chapter 20

When David's alarm went off at 5:30 a.m., doing beach sprints was the last thing he felt like, but the vision of Figueras doing them quickly motivated him to jump out of bed. He had arranged a 2 hour massage with his regular masseuse, Jeannie, to give him a good rub down afterwards before his afternoon session with Lionel at Mitchell Park Tennis Club.

It wasn't long before he had thrown all his kit in the back of the Green Mamba and was making his way on his regular route to North Beach. It was funny how quite a few of the early morning joggers would now wave at him as they recognised the Green Mamba.

Once again Durban had served up a perfect morning and the sea was a dark blue. This morning the ocean was a dark blue and the swell was just a perfect 4 foot. It seemed like every surfer in Durban had got wind of the news because the backline was lined up with surfers of all ages and there were even a few girls too.

After ten minutes of stretching, David began his routine and after thirty minutes he had built up quite a sweat. His ankles were holding up nicely and he could feel all the good chemicals in his body flowing through him. The last thirty minutes he worked himself hard, imagining that each sprint was to retrieve a drop shot Figueras had hit. He had no doubt in his mind that he would be chasing down a lot of those from Figueras and with the speed he was building up on the soft beach sand he felt confident he would reach them now.

The crisp, early morning sea was a welcome respite and David enjoyed body surfing in the shore break. This morning he wasn't alone as there was a Johannesburg school girl's hockey team who were staying at one of the beachfront hotels, also enjoying the water. He could feel them staring at him but just ignored them until two of them waded over to him half-giggling and asked, "Hi there, we sorry to disturb you but are you the tennis player who was in the newspapers yesterday? Jenny and I have been arguing whether it's you or not!"

"Yip, that would be me, David Oppenheim" replied David, half-dying with embarrassment."

"You see, I told you it was him!" the cuter of the two replied to her friend.

"You sound like a Jo'burger? Are you lot a sports team by any chance?" asked David.

"Wow! Do we really sound so different from Durbanites that you can tell we are from Jo'burg?" asked Jenny.

"Well it's more like Durbanites have such a distinct, almost British accent, that we can tell when someone isn't from here" laughed David.

"Ja, we're from St Mary's in Waverley in Jo'burg. We're here for the SA Schools tournament in Queensmead" said the cute one.

"We were watching you doing your sprints earlier and Bridget recognised you from the newspaper. Her brother is a big fan of yours. He told us you are going to be the next South African champion to break through. He will be very jealous we have met you" giggled Jenny.

"She's right about that!" laughed Bridget, whilst admiring David's physique.

"Well ladies, have a great day and I hope things go really well for you at the tournament. I'll be looking out for the results in the newspaper. Cheers then!" said David.

"Bye-bye David!" they replied, still giggling.

He was relieved when he turned around to make his way to the showers that Bridget and Jenny weren't able to see how red his face was. He couldn't understand how even young school girls could make him feel so shy. He was really going to need to speak to his father about this inflicted trait. He realised as he progressed through the ranks that he was going to have to become accustomed to this sort of attention without turning beetroot red.

Jeannie's home was not very far from the beachfront and David was delighted to see her. She was his regular masseuse back home and was the only one who could really get deep into his muscles. She also didn't annoy him like some of the others who spent the entire session giving him a rundown of their lives. This was a rest time for him where he could clear his head and focus on things he needed to. He smiled to himself when he felt Jeannie going deep into his hamstrings. This is *exactly* what he needed.

With Jeannie hard at work, David's mind wandered to his girlfriend and the meeting with Zara Mahomedy planned for the following Tuesday. What exactly did she intend telling and asking him, he thought. Was she going to tell him outright that she didn't approve of him and would only tell her husband if David persisted in seeing her. Was he just imagining things and she was going to be an open-minded, welcoming mother who was going to invite him into their mansion? Did her experience of dating two white guys during her time as a student in Paris work in his favour or not. He was going to be charming but not overboard. Like Shakira had told him, he needed to just be himself and not some *schmuck* trying to *schmoose* his way into their lives. One way or another he would soon learn whether his relationship with Shakira would progress to the next stage of meeting the brother and finally the old man. He still had some tall obstacles to hurdle.

"OK mister, time for you to turn over now!" instructed Jeannie.

He could feel her pressing deep into the balls of his feet which triggered a weird feeling inside his stomach. It felt really good, thought David. Then Jeannie got stuck into his angles and calves and that felt anything but good. He could feel the fatigue of the last week's beach sprints exertions working out of his body.

"David, what the hell have you been doing to your legs and ankles? They're stiffer than a corpse" she said, starting to sweat like crazy.

"Today, you've *really* got me working!" she laughed.

The second half of the massage was tough, even for David, and when she finished off with a few neck adjustments he was relieved it was over. He just lay there for 5 minutes letting his body balance. He paid Jeannie twice her normal fee and made 2 bookings for the following week.

"Jeannie, I wish I could afford to pay for you to join Dov and me at the French Open, man. I could really use you there especially if I get through any 5 setters!" said David.

"The way your game is going and your stamina is building I think that day is not far off. I really had to work twice as hard today with the extra muscle you are building. I don't know exactly what you are doing, but it's working" chuckled Jeannie.

David headed off to Mitchell Park and was surprised to find Dov there. He had gone straight to Tel Aviv after Morocco for some training and was only due back the following day. David laughed inside when he noticed that Dov was reading a copy of Gordon Forbes' "A Handful of Summers".

"This is a lovely surprise, bro! I thought you were only flying in tomorrow?" said David, giving Dov a hug.

"And neglect my investment? Not a chance! I changed my flight and flew in this morning and came straight here. The breakfast in the park is excellent by the way" he laughed.

"I'm going to have a quick shower and get this oil off me before Lionel arrives" said David.

"Good, I'm at a very interesting part of the book with this big Jewish oke, Big Abie, getting up to all sorts of his nonsense. Those were some Jews, hey Davie!" chuckled Dov.

Shortly after his cold shower Lionel arrived and David introduced them.

"So Li, this is the *schlemiel* of a coach I was telling you about, Dov Mendelson. He knows all about you and has been phoning me every night insisting on a detailed run down on of our daily training. He's also very intrigued with the 3 skill drills you showed me" said David.

"Howzit china! Thanks so much for looking after my boy here in my absence. I can't tell you how much we appreciate you helping out before the French. We going to get this *oke* in tip-top shape before he steps out on the court against that Figueras fucker!" said Dov, whilst shaking Lionel's hand.

"Great to meet you, coach! You've been doing an amazing job of late with this *schmuck*. His results have been really good" complimented Lionel.

Before Dov could proceed to tell Lionel about his school playing days for the B team at King David, David interrupted.

"Li, Dov here has brought back his own concoction of energy drink from Israel after I told him about your pink drink. He says it's something the clever boys from the IDF invented for the troops whilst in combat in the desert" said David.

Dov eagerly took out a few bottles of a purple-looking liquid from his bag and palmed one off to Lionel. He cautiously opened it and took a mouthful before spitting it out.

"Jaezus, that tastes like camel pee and methylated spirits, dude!" shouted Lionel.

"Are you trying to poison me so it's easy for David to beat me!" he barked.

“I’ll stick to my pink drink, thanks very much” he said, whilst David and Dov laughed themselves silly.

It was halfway during their warm up that Michael arrived. David had completely forgotten he had invited him the night before to umpire for them. He had said 12:30 p.m. and the kid was prompt and exactly on time. He quickly introduced Michael to Lionel and Dov and beckoned him to climb up and sit on the umpire’s chair.

“Now listen Michael, any close calls go my way, OK china” teased Lionel.

“Bro, too late I’ve already paid him off earlier” laughed Dov, who had now positioned himself on the court and looked like he was taking notes.

“Right Davie, you to serve then. Let’s do it. 5 sets here we go” said Lionel.

After the massage and cold shower David felt fantastic and everything he swung at went fizzing past Lionel with huge rotations. David could see from his obvious delight that Dov was very impressed.

“Beautiful, *boychik,* just like I taught you!” laughed Dov.

Before they knew it David had wrapped up the first set 6-1 and the usual small crowd had started to gather around the main show court. David was also impressed with Michael’s umpiring.

“Michael, did you do a crash course in umpiring this morning or something?” asked David whilst gently sipping on Dov’s purple medication so as not to hurt his feelings.

“I may have read something” replied Michael, with a huge grin on his face.

“I’m just enjoying watching you guys so much” he said, whilst sipping on a Coke.

“I’m not!” said Lionel, with obvious annoyance.

By the second set Lionel had found his game and David just edged it 7-6 in a hard fought tiebreaker. The standard of both their play had lifted and at the drinks break David smiled because the crowd had now mushroomed to about two-hundred people. He wondered if the photographers had got wind of them playing and would pitch up.

“You got lucky there, Davie, I’m coming for you now!” barked Lionel, knocking back a second bottle of the pink drink.

Lionel was wrong because whatever was in Dov's purple brew kicked in and David felt a burst of energy. He smashed Lionel from corner to corner and then tricked him with at least half a dozen drop shots. He finished off the set 6-2 with an ace down the T box, and with that he wasn't sure who was clapping louder, the crowd or Dov. David was particularly impressed with Michael's strong, clear announcement of the score which meant the crowd didn't need to. He could also see just how much the kid was enjoying the tennis and the atmosphere whilst playing umpire. He was pleased for him.

"I think I need to go to Jeannie also and maybe Dov can give me a bit of coaching too" said Lionel, exasperated.

"Seriously amazing tennis, Davie! You are definitely in the zone today. Do you mind if we rather do some drills than our planned 5 setter today because I don't think I can stand another 2 more sets of this" he joked.

"Of course yes. Dov wants to see them too" replied David.

"Lionel, you see what happens to my pupil when I'm around. He plays for us!" joked Dov.

Michael insisted on still staying seated in the umpire's chair whilst the two friends went through their drills, all the while Dov barking encouragement to his charge. The crowd had not moved an inch, mesmerised as the two players practiced moon balls and scrambling to reach balls. They also seemed fascinated at Dov's rather different coaching style of sometimes running up and down the court, shouting instructions to his charge. To most of them he resembled more of a football coach than a tennis one but judging by his pupil's fine play it seemed to be working somehow.

At the end of their drill sessions the crowd gave both of them a standing ovation although the way Dov was bowing and thanking them, one could have been forgiven for thinking it was for him and even Michael chuckled at the sight of him.

"Right lads, no more of this 3 set only shit tomorrow. It may be *Shabbos* but *HaShem* told me it's not the day off for you two. Lionel, you're asking for my advice for tomorrow? Drink my fucking purple drink. Only girls drink pink drinks!" he barked

They all had a good laugh at that.

“Talking of *Shabbos,* my mom will be lighting candles about now and it’s the only religious thing I give my family. I had better shoot but 9 a.m. tomorrow here, Lionel?” asked David.

“Of course bro. And Dov give me a bottle of that fucking purple drink as you call it” laughed Lionel.

David dropped Michael off at his home on the Berea en-route to his parent’s home for *Shabbos*.

“Thanks so much for this afternoon, David. It was thrilling to watch you pros and you are an incredible tennis player. *Shabbat shalom* to you and your family then” said Michael, opening the passenger door.

“Thanks man and great umpiring today *boychik*. Shabbat shalom to you too!”

Chapter 21

David cursed when his alarm went off early Saturday morning. He had thoroughly enjoyed the *Shabbat* dinner his mother had prepared the previous evening. He had really appreciated that his mother had only invited his Uncle Sol, whom he had hardly spoken to in weeks.

Uncle Sol was so excited to be jetting off to Paris and regaled them with some stories about the French lasses who had entertained him on his last visit there, twenty plus years before. The whole family were crying with laughter when he told the story about going home from a bar with a French miss, who only spoke 2 words of English, only to be chased out of her apartment at 6 a.m. by her husband. He swore he had no idea she was married but clearly recalled her burly husband chasing him down one of the small lanes holding a butcher's knife and cursing at him in high French. Just typical Uncle Sol, David thought. He and Dov were going to create one hell of a ruckus in Paris.

David washed, dressed and packed his kit for his morning session at Mitchell Park. He threw in 2 sets of Tacchini tracksuits and some more of their T-shirts that the local agent had sent him the previous afternoon by express from Johannesburg. The newspaper photos had been seen by the bigwigs and motivated them to ship extra items for him and Lionel, who they had noticed was wearing some of the Wilander range they had especially sent David. The stickers were even marked Lionel Perreira on the items which really amused him. Lionel owed him big time, at least ten percent chuckled David.

David left before his parents and Leah had risen for *shul*. Durban had served up another spectacular day and he was looking forward to a solid practice session with Lionel. He drove along the ridge until he was outside a neat little block of flats near his old high school. Dov was waiting patiently for him, all spiffed up in his Sergio Tacchini outfit and with a massive smile on his face.

"So, so, what you think of this?" he asked David, looking very pleased with himself.

"Dov, you've got fat! Too much good Israeli food and not nearly enough exercise. You lucky I don't fire you!" laughed David.

"I don't see you for a couple of weeks and that's all you've got to say? Who needs enemies when I've got friends like you, Davie!" he said, jumping in the passenger seat.

"What is it with this fucking city that everybody gets up at the crack of dawn, even on weekends?" asked Dov, as they drove past a group of joggers along Essenwood Road.

"Well that's why they aren't fat, Dov!" teased David.

"I didn't eat *that* much OK! I'm only carrying an extra 2-3 kilograms since Morocco" he said defensively.

"Bollocks! Make that 5-7 kilos at least" laughed David.

"OK, OK, I'll do some training before the French. Got to look good for that I suppose" he sighed.

"I'm just taking the piss, Dov. Relax!" laughed David.

Arriving at the courts they were both amused that a small crowd, who had somehow got wind of their practice routine, had gathered. They had come prepared this time with fold-up chairs and breakfast snacks.

"Davie, you think it would be rude to ask this lot for a contribution? I mean they would normally be paying to watch pro tennis, right?" asked Dov.

"Jesus, you are the reason for turning people into anti-Semites, Dov. Definitely not, please! Do I need to remind you that Mitchell is my home club and I do want to continue playing here" laughed David, not quite sure if his "coach" was being serious or not.

Lionel interrupted them as he came bounding down the stairs to the main courts. This time he was ten minutes late, not that he really cared. He waved at the small crowd like he knew them although they did half-wave back. He was going to have no issues settling in to the pro tour very quickly, thought David.

"*Schlemiel*! Even though you are only ten minutes late we have a little something for you. Some more clobber my sponsor sent me. They saw the photos from the papers and figured the bigger sizes I had requested were actually for you, so they sent these tracksuits and shirts marked for you on the packets" said David, throwing a bag to his friend.

"No ways, Davie! So they know about me, now?" replied Lionel in shock.

"Yip, I'll pass on your folk's telephone number to the rep next week. I've put in my best word for you so hopefully they'll kickstart you with some kit for the tour. I didn't mention I've been kicking your ass in practice so let's just keep that between us, OK" laughed David.

"Davie, these tracksuits are beauties man" he said putting one of the tops on.

"Look, if the tour doesn't work out I think you've got a chance as a Tacchini model, bro! That's a perfect fit on you" laughed Dov.

"Well, with us all decked out in their gear we look like Team Tacchini today!" joked Lionel.

After stretching out and warming up for thirty minutes they got down to some tough tennis and this time, after Lionel had clinched the fourth set, they played out an incredible 5th set. The better the match and tennis got, the more excitable and animated Dov became with his court walking and gestures. On quite a few occasions he had taken to quietening the now large crowd down, and after 3 sets he had appointed 6 kids to play ball boy. They were delighted.

After nearly 4 hours of fantastic tennis David was able to edge out the 5th set tiebreaker before both of them collapsed on the court, soaked in sweat. The crowd was enthralled and especially with an almost impossible to reach crosscourt forehand that David had finished the match with. David could only watch as Lionel gave a few bows of appreciation to the crowd. He was just too tired to acknowledge them beyond a sheepish wave as they clapped for both of them. He smiled, watching his "coach" clapping back at them. Dov was certainly a big character and he was glad to have him on his team.

"Brilliant tennis *okes*, really top stuff. I'm very proud of you both. Lionel, I can't believe how well you played today. You nearly got my boy. I told you my purple stuff would help you!" he shouted at them whilst giving Lionel a high five.

"Davie, c'mon get up china! Go lie on the bench, drink some purple and I'll give your legs a rub down with another concoction I got from Israel" ordered Dov.

David wasn't going to say no to a massage. If it wasn't possible to have Jeannie, Dov with his big mitts was a good second choice. His muscles had stiffened and he could feel the burn of the lactic acid.

"Please save some energy for me afterwards, coach. My whole body is fucked after those 5 sets even if I look better than Davie" asked Lionel.

"Guys, after I've given you a rub down and you've showered, lunch is on me. There's a cool new Thai place in Florida Road I hear is good" suggested Dov.

"Sounds awesome "coach" but please revive my legs. I felt better than this after that long 3 setter in the sun in Morocco, and you remember how buggered I was that day" said David, collapsing on the bench.

He watched Dov pull out a rather dodgy-looking glass bottle holding some sort of cream in it. He was too tired to ask any questions as much as he probably should have. The cream went on nice and cool on his hamstrings and calves whilst Dov used his big mitts to massage deep into his muscles. He explained to David that it was an IDF invention of virgin coconut oil, aloe vera and something called DMSO. Whatever it was, it was certainly soothing, until David started feeling a strong taste of garlic in his mouth.

"Oh ja, by the way the DMSO stuff will give you a funny taste in your mouth" laughed Dov.

"Dov! You tell me this after the fact!" shouted David, spitting garlic out of his mouth.

Lionel and Dov had a good laugh at him.

After a cold shower David felt much better. He was pleased with his level of play and soon his body and mind would acclimatise to playing regular 5 setters. He was starting to feel like he would be ready for the French Open.

"So Dov, are you joining us for the party tonight?" Lionel asked, after they had placed their food orders at Mo Noodles.

"I'm too bloody old for that stuff any longer. I leave the boogie stuff to young guys like you two!" chuckled Dov.

"Oh, I don't know the way you were moving up and down the court this morning was pretty impressive" said David, and they all had a good laugh.

"David is finally introducing me to this mysterious Shakira of his" said Lionel.

"Wait until you see her bud, she's bloody hot! This *oke* just got lucky because she's way above his pay grade" said Dov, teasing his charge.

"I've got to say though Dov, the last person I expected our friend here to be seeing is a nice little Muslim chick from Durbs" laughed Lionel.

“Likewise, but just wait until you meet her. She’s the full package man. Looks, brains and a lovely disposition too” said Dov, winking at David.

“You right I got lucky. If it wasn’t for those records that day in the SU I would have had zero chance and I’ll admit it” said David.

“Well the proof is in the pudding, or in her case maybe the chicken tikka, so I’ll let you know tomorrow Dov” laughed Lionel.

Chapter 22

David slept solidly his first night at Moshe and was woken up by the boys before his alarm clock could ring.

"David, David, can we come watch you play at the club this afternoon? Dad said if you OK with it then we can come" asked Avi excitedly.

"Sure, but only if you two ball boy for us" replied David.

"Oh wow! That's even better!" exclaimed Dani.

"Mom says breakfast is ready, if you can come through" said Avi.

"Tell her I'll be through in 5 minutes" said David, stretching.

The two boys ran off excitedly to tell their mother that they had been asked to ball boy for David and his 2 practice partners. He could distantly hear their excited exclamations which probably meant their mother was OK with it.

David had diligently packed his kit bags the night before and carried them to the front door in anticipation of Rubie's arrival after breakfast. He was surprised when he arrived at the breakfast table to see Rubie seated with the family, also eating.

"Shalom David! Did you sleep fine? You have a big day today, your first" Rudie greeted him.

"Good morning Rubie, good morning Beverly and good morning again boys! Thanks Rubie, I'm very comfortable thanks. It's just like a South African home that Beverly has made here that I feel like I'm still home" replied David.

"Ah, I'm so pleased!" said Beverly with a huge smile on her face.

"David, please help yourself. We have some fresh grapefruits and melons, cereals and I made some omelettes too. We've tried to make our own little piece of South Africa here in the Middle East. I even told the boys I'm thinking of teaching them some Afrikaans too!" she laughed, as the 2 boys looked up at David with turned-up noses.

"Well, I'm hoping to improve my Hebrew because I don't think I've spoken anything more than *Yiddish* phrases since my *bar mitzvah*" laughed David.

"Before that we want you speaking Arabic" laughed Rubie, giving him a wink.

"David, are you quite sure it's OK for the boys to ball boy for you this afternoon? I don't want them being a distraction whilst you are in training" asked Beverly.

"Oh no, not at all. In fact it'll be really nice to have someone else picking up the balls but boys please note, I only pay in milkshakes afterwards" teased David.

"We love milkshakes!" replied Avi, full of smiles.

After a wonderful breakfast David and Rubie set off for the day but not before Rubie had blindfolded David.

"Sorry, but on these trips to base camp there won't be any sightseeing my friend. That's for all of our safety" said Rubie.

On the drive to wherever Rubie was taking them David learnt that Rubie was far from just a chauffeur but had fought in most of the wars and intifadas with Moshe. He could see they were the closest thing to being brothers although they were unrelated. He explained to David that he was still involved operationally but in the intelligence side of things. Moshe would not allow anybody else to take care of him besides Moshe which made David understand just how important his mission was.

After about a thirty minute drive the car came to a stop and Rubie told him to remove his blindfold. They had parked in an underground parking but it was not long before they went a further few floors lower in a lift. As the door opened David's eyes were blinded by the bright light and his senses were assaulted by the vast number of people dressed in everything from military fatigues to white doctor's coats. Once his eyes had adjusted and he had stepped out of the lift he recognised the figure of Moshe in front of him with his big smile.

"*Shalom* David! Welcome to Mossad, *boychik*" he said, giving David a hug.

"Leave your bags here. Rubie will take care of them and then join us" he said, beckoning David to follow him.

"On this floor we start by giving your body the once over. This facility has the most advanced medical equipment on the planet. This morning we will be checking your bloods, your sugar levels, insulin and testosterone, the full works. We will do a full CT scan, body analysis, ECG and EGG. By the end of it you and we will know everything going on in your body, including your brain. We will know what your percentage chances are of developing any cancers or heart, brain or lung conditions the rest of your life and fix them now" explained Moshe.

Whilst David was listening intently to him he was amazed at how many people were either saluting or head bowing to Moshe. He definitely was revered.

"You will also undergo a psychological analysis by possibly the smartest shrink on the planet. She will help you over the next couple days how to improve your mind set in tennis. Dov will monitor that aspect as he travels the tour with you. Of course we've already done a rudimentary analysis on you and you passed that with flying colours but this will be a whole different level" continued Moshe.

"Jesus, does *everyone* undergo all this?" said David, shocked.

"Ha! Ha! You must be kidding! This is only reserved for a handful of operatives and prime ministers, *boychik*. Only for the most important amongst us. The cost of this exercise we are going to perform on you is worth hundreds of thousands of US dollars. This little country of ours would be broke if we did more than that otherwise" laughed Moshe.

"This level of testing is reserved only for the best!" chuckled Moshe opening a door for David.

Once inside, the new area was eerily quiet after the noise of the floor. Moshe motioned for a young lady dressed in white coat to approach them.

"David, this is Channah. She is one of the best young doctors to graduate from Hebrew University. She and Rubie will be your guides through the process this morning. Any issues and I will be notified immediately and come through. Wishing you luck" and with that Moshe departed.

"Shalom Channah! Very nice to meet you" said David politely, extending his hand.

"Shalom David, likewise. Thank you so much for doing this. It really isn't as bad as it sounds and besides both Rubie and I will be your chaperones" she answered, in a thick Israeli accent.

"Please follow me so we can get you all prepared. In this change room you will find a gown and slippers to change into. You will also notice a brown military bag. It has all your military apparel inside and once you are done with your medicals, you will be required to wear them for all future exercises. You will be a full member of the IDF for the duration of your stay" she explained.

"Oh yeah, so what's the pay like?" asked David.

"Financially unrewarding, emotionally the big bucks" she laughed.

David had forgotten just how sharp Israelis were.

"Then Dov really lied to me big time!" said David, as they both laughed.

Before changing into the gown and slippers David had a quick look through the military bag. There inside were brand new military browns with his name, Oppenheim, embroidered on the shirts together with sturdy brown soldier's boots. He couldn't help laughing at the irony that he was so determined to avoid conscription in the SA Defence Forces yet here he was with his own set of military apparel.

After donning his gown and slippers he joined Channah and Rubie to another room where David completed some paperwork and Channah drew blood for a barrage of tests. She told David that the results would be back within the hour.

Next up David was sent to the radiation department where he was made to strip for a full body CT scan. This was then followed by an ECG where Rubie had already purchased a pair of Nike runners and cyclist shorts for him.

"We know you like Nike's for tennis so we thought you'd like them for running too" laughed Rubie.

After all the traveling David welcomed the exercise on the running machine. Rubie was excited to watch too as he explained to David that the IDF set fitness challenges this way and he was curious to see how his charge stacked up against the best.

David was pleased when the machine started up and he got to stretch his legs. The machine had been programmed to increase its speed every 5 minutes but after 30 minutes he felt fine yet was quite surprised to see that the room was now filled with people. He looked over to Rubie who gave him an unusually big smile and thumbs up. He also noticed Channah furiously taking down notes and smiling. By 48 minutes he started feeling the first pangs of fatigue and muscle burn and he noticed the group starting to clap him on. Rubie had written a note which he was waving in front of him now that read **TWO MORE MINUTES BOYCHIK**. The last 2 minutes really were a strain but all the early morning beach sprints, all the endless hours jogging and sprinting around the tennis courts of South Africa helped him through.

Suddenly without warning the treadmill started slowing down as did David until it stopped completely. Only then did he hear the shouting and clapping clearly. Rubie picked him up from the treadmill shouting "New record, new record!"

As he sat down exhausted, Channah immediately got to work attaching various probes on his body as she took measurements of his pulse and recovery rate.

"David, we have only seen your sorts of numbers with Kenyan long distance runners and Olympic sprinters! This is amazing. Did you know that you are this fit?" she asked.

"Well look, I think I could have gone a bit longer actually" laughed David.

"My friend, we're only here to measure you, not kill you!" laughed Rubie, thrusting a purple concoction into his hands and instructing him to drink.

"David, it's only a minute and you are now nearly fully recovered" laughed Channah, shaking her head in awe.

After 20 minutes rest David was whisked away for an EGG with nurses inserting probes on all sides of his head. He was happy just to lie back though after the treadmill.

When he walked out of the room he was met in the corridor by Moshe who he really didn't expect to see so soon again.

"Jesus Christ, Dov said you were fit but he didn't tell us you were Sebastian Coe!" laughed Moshe, hugging him.

"You realise that you now hold the IDF treadmill record? I don't think you quite understand that? Some of our top generals sent a bunch of their people to witness it themselves because they couldn't believe it. *Mazel tov* David! Beverly will have to make your favourite bagels and salmon tonight and some champagne of course! I must go now but I'll be collecting the boys to come ball boy for you at the club this afternoon. I'm very proud of you!" said Moshe with delight. Before David could answer he was off again. Our enemies don't sleep thought David.

Rubie and Channah then escorted David for a light lunch of salads and some cold meats. After his exploits on the treadmill Rubie could not stop grinning and frequently spoke in Hebrew to other military dressed personnel, barking out things to them whilst gesturing to David.

Channah explained, with laughter, that Rubie's old brigade had never set this record before and their competing brigades had made sure to rub that in their faces but now it was Rubie's revenge, and he was loving it. Now David could understand all the long faces looking at him both in wonderment and jealousy. Over lunch Channah said his blood tests, except for slightly lower than normal iron levels, had been fine. She also asked him if he was aware that he was allergic to gluten, which he wasn't. The next port of call was with the world famous dietitian, Dr Sylvie Aaronson, who had flown in for her nephew's *bar mitzvah* from Los Angeles. He was very lucky that their trips had coincided.

"Hello David, I'm Dr Aaronson but please call me Sylvie" Dr Aaronson greeted him with.

David was quite startled by how much she looked like Shakira but 25 years older. She also had a soft, Californian accent to go with her looks.

"I've looked through all your tests and what you put down as your regular diet. I picked up importantly that you are gluten intolerant and if you had gone a little longer on the treadmill you would have had a dramatic decline in your stamina and recovery levels. Your diet is really bad. You are eating far too much bread and dairy not to mention sugars. What you do have are incredible levels for short, aerobic type exercises like the quick sprints involved for tennis but when you find yourself in 4th or 5th sets on a slower surface like clay, then you're dead. I need you to lay off the breads and dairies, especially. I'm going to recommend more plant-based meals. The one thing you are eating that I don't mind is your biltong. I have family in South Africa who smuggle that, and Appletiser drink, into LA when they visit us. My whole family love it!" she laughed.

"So you telling me no *pizza*?!" David asked.

"*Especially* no pizza, please!" she exclaimed.

"And I know this is almost an impossibility for South Africans but try eat a bit less red meat. Try more white meats like chicken and fish if possible" she chuckled.

David liked Dr Aaronson. She was not only attractive but had a good sense of humour. Just for her he would try stay off the steaks and chops he loved so much.

"David, I can assure you that within a month of adhering to my diet that I've prepared for you, you will see your stamina levels improve for those long 5 setters you will no doubt have one day. I have left my contact details with Rubie for you if you should have any questions for me. I really hope one day to switch on the TV to see you playing at Wimbledon or the French Open" she said, embracing him.

"*Baruch HaShem* Sylvie!"

Finally, David got to meet his shrink, the diminutive Dr Ilana Berkowitz, who was an ex-South African from Cape Town. She was a tiny little lady but spoke with an unexpected confidence and air of authority.

"David, I'm only going to ask you to complete this questionnaire today and then tomorrow we will begin our work in earnest. Some of these questions are of a very personal nature but are necessary. Answer them honestly because if I have even the slightest inkling you are being in any way untruthful, I will not hesitate to connect you up to one of our fancy lie detector machines, OK" she said sternly to him.

"I'm really not inclined to lie" said David, taking the questionnaire from her.

"That's what everyone says, my son, *until* they get caught" she said chuckling.

She was absolutely right about some of the questions being of a personal nature. Amongst others there were questions asking about his sexuality, how old he was when he lost his virginity, how many sexual partners he had had and many other revealing ones. David answered them as truthfully as he could before handing the questionnaire back to her.

"Thank you. I'll see you tomorrow then. Rubie will come collect you now" she said as she left the room.

She's going to be a tough one David thought to himself.

It wasn't long before David was blindfolded and back in the car with Rubie on their way to the tennis courts.

"How you feeling after everything they did to you today then?" asked Rubie with a big grin.

"Well the easiest part for me was actually the treadmill" laughed David, ironically.

"Thanks for that achievement by the way. I've been *giving it* to some of the senior officers from the other brigades which you may have seen at lunch. I haven't enjoyed something like that as much, ever. We announced your new record internally immediately and I can tell you my brigade were celebrating straight afterwards. By now the entire IDF is aware of it!" laughed Rubie.

"Did you or Moshe ever go through the same thing I did today?" asked David curiously.

"Not me but Moshe yes many, many years ago. Only the best go through it my friend and now you are part of that elite group"

The Tel Aviv Country Club was like an oasis in the desert with its beautiful gardens and exquisite clubhouse. Inside the entrance area were pictures of Israeli heroes like Moshe Dayan, David Ben-Gurion, Chaim Weizman, Theodore Herzl and many others. They walked through the club as many people greeted Rubie and made their way to the tennis courts. David was amazed that in addition to the 6 hardcourts to see 4 clay courts and 2 grass courts which were beautifully maintained. He also saw two young men knocking up on one of the hardcourts.

"C'mon, I'll introduce you to Eli and Ohad. They'll be your practice partners. Moshe and the 2 boys are on their way. It was really nice of you to invite the boys by the way" said Rubie.

"Shalom Eli, shalom Ohad, come meet Mr David Oppenheim. He says you look useless and he's going to kick your asses" shouted Rubie.

"I didn't say that all. He's talking nonsense!" laughed David, embarrassed by Rubie's remark.

The two kids were both excellent juniors and had well developed strokes and made sure David had a good warm up. By then Moshe and the two boys had arrived and they sprinted onto the court shaking the other 2 boys' hands and hugging David.

"Shalom David! Are you sure you up to this after the treadmill this morning?" asked Moshe.

"I'm always up for tennis Moshe, but thanks for the concern!" replied David.

David played a best of 3 setter against both boys, one after the other. They may have been amongst the top juniors in the world but David had too much guile for them beating Eli 6-3 6-2 and then knocking off Ohad 6-4 6-1 in less than 3 hours. What was perfectly obvious to all watching, is that the 2 boys had a lot more fun ballboying, than either junior had playing David.

"David, if anything they look like they've undergone the treadmill torture test today not you!" Moshe laughed.

"Dov seems to have perfected the art of undervaluing you. I had no idea that you were *that* good a player. You play like this I don't think it's going to be long before we finally have our first Jewish Wimbledon champion!"

"Well if that works out it won't be because of Dov's coaching, I can assure you!" laughed David.

"Right boys, seeing as you did such an excellent job I'm going to ask Rubie to take us for milkshakes!" said David.

"Daddy, please can we go with David and Rubie?" asked Dani.

"The way David performed all round today I can't say no, can I now?" laughed Moshe.

It didn't take Rubie more than ten minutes to get them to one of the new modern malls in Tel Aviv. The milkshakes were the best David had ever tasted and if they weren't half as delicious he may have felt guilty about Dr Sylvie's suggestion of no dairy products.

It had been a good first day and David was looking forward to arriving the next day in his military browns representing Rubie's Galani brigade.

He was ready for this. Bring it on he thought.

Chapter 23

David and Lionel arrived at Ronnyz just before 10 p.m. after having a couple drinks first at the Los Angeles Hotel on the Berea. David was particularly amused how easily Lionel had taken to his new fame at being recognised from their newspaper clips. David found the whole celebrity thing rather ridiculous but Lionel had no problems getting accustomed to it.

Within minutes of them arriving David saw EB's distinctive Golf GTi pulling up and both Miriam and Shakira getting out. He waved at them and marvelled how beautiful and sexy his girlfriend was in her tight-fitting, leather outfit. Miriam, without her traditional Muslim garb, wasn't half bad looking either. When David pointed her out all Lionel could remark was "Wow! He wasn't kidding, she's well above your paygrade! She's gorgeous!"

"Hello, my darling! Have you missed me?" asked Shakira as she proceeded to hug David and kiss him on the lips.

"Li, this is my Shakira and her friend, Miriam" said David as he introduced them.

Lionel didn't miss the opportunity to give both of them one of his big hugs.

"OK, OK, that's enough now" joked David.

"It's lovely to meet the famous Shakira. Are you sure you got the right guy though? He doesn't deserve a beautiful girl like you. Do you have a sister perhaps?" joked Lionel.

"Oh no, it's me who is lucky!" laughed Shakira.

"OK guys let's go in before this long line enters" said David gesturing to an ever growing line of people waiting to be let in.

The 4 of them walked to the front of the line where David greeted the long-time bouncers Brian and Eugene who let them pass. David had been given VIP tickets by Fat Frank, the regular Ronnyz DJ. David handed in the invites to the cashier and they each had their wrists stamped so they could go in and out easily.

They excitedly climbed the stairs to the next level as they felt the bass on the walls and the lighting suddenly changed to strobe lights only. David could clearly hear New Order's extended remix of "Blue Monday" playing and Lionel shouted, "Welcome to Ronnyz ladies! Now let's party" as they entered the club proper.

Ronnyz had started out as a gay club but over time had relaxed its admission requirements, allowing all the cool people of all persuasions entrance. One thing that had not changed though was that Frankie still played the best dance music on the planet.

The club was unexpectedly busy for early as it normally only really got going by midnight. David led them to the DJ box to say hi to Frankie and introduce the girls. He was delighted to meet them and gave them both big hugs, remarking how beautiful they both looked. He was happy to see Lionel too whom he hadn't seen for years. David was quite amused how Shakira was already sifting through Frankie's pile of vinyl.

"My darling, any special requests for you ladies tonight?" asked Frankie.

"Sure, are you able to play these?" she asked, handing a couple records to him.

"I see like your boyfriend you know your stuff! I'm impressed" said Frankie.

"She's the only person I know who has a collection more than double mine" laughed David.

"Well my brother is Mo Mahomedy. You probably know him from the club scene. I think he and his 2 partners may actually have a percentage share in Ronnyz" she said.

"Oh wow! Yes, you are right, Mo is a shareholder both here as well as Zodiac and Faces. He was here just this week actually, dropping off a bunch of remixes I had ordered. What a small world it is" said Frankie.

"Well I'm so glad you found yourself a nice Jewish boy like David. There aren't many of us left in Durban" he joked.

"Yip and it's amazing he was right under my nose at university all those years and he only plucked up the courage to introduce himself a few weeks before he finished" she said, teasing David.

"That's because you would have told me to get lost in first year!" laughed David.

David led the 2 girls upstairs to the VIP level whilst Lionel stayed behind in the DJ booth, obsessed with all the equipment and music Frankie was laying down. David greeted many of the old familiar faces from the early years of the club who had come especially for the Reunion Party. He arranged seating for them so they could overlook the revellers on the dance floor. By this time the dance floor was full and David thought he could smell the distinct smell of poppers which someone must have put in the air conditioning system. It definitely was a reunion David thought. David could also sense that Frankie had increased the decibels as more people moved onto the dance floor acting as sound absorbers.

David ordered a bottle of champagne for them and a lime and soda for Miriam.

"David, this is the best view to watch all the different types on the dance floor. It's such fun. Look at those 2 guys with the pink mohawks. They look like gay parrots!" laughed Miriam.

"What about that crowd over there in the dungarees and cowboy boots?" laughed Shakira.

"Aren't they just fab!" she continued.

"Well, it was originally strictly a gay club. They always have the best music and there's no aggression in their clubs either. A lot of them on the dance floor are the original members" said David.

"Hey, there's Lionel on the dancefloor!" shouted Miriam.

"He can certainly move alright. I think I'm going to leave you lovebirds for a bit and join him" she said, finishing off her drink.

"You go show them girl!" encouraged Shakira.

David chuckled as he watched Lionel having a good boogie on the dance floor. He was delighted when Miriam joined him and immediately grabbed her hand and gave her a whirl. Shakira loved it and gave a whistle. She looked at David, smiled and then got up and sat on his lap.

"So then, how are you feeling for Tuesday with my mom? Have you got your battle strategy all prepared like you do for your tennis?" she teased.

"I won't lie my darling I am feeling kind of nervous about it. I don't want to prepare anything because then it looks scripted" he replied.

"Well she has her poker face on with me this week so she's giving away nothing so I'm afraid I can't give you any intel there. As I said before, you just be you Mr O, you are wonderful in every way" she said, kissing him on the lips.

"Jesus, look at those two go!" laughed David, nodding at their friends on the dance floor.

"I would never have thought Miriam was such a party animal! They actually make a nice couple, don't you think?" laughed David.

"Oh just because she wears a scarf at varsity and comes across as conservative, doesn't mean much. You right, they actually do look like a couple the way they are dancing together. I'm definitely not getting involved in that though" she laughed.

"Tonight I have a little surprise for you, my angel. I'm not going back with EB and Miriam later. I'm all yours tonight" she said dangling some keys in front of him and then kissing him deeply.

"We have an apartment on the beach front and I want to watch the sun rise over the ocean with you" she smiled.

"You sure?" asked David.

"Yes David. I'm quite sure and I know my mom is going to love you" she said, cradling her face into his neck.

"OK, OK, either you get a room you two or you join us on the dance floor!" said Miriam, pulling them both up to join them on the dance floor.

"And Lionel says please bring him a glass of champagne" she said, before leading Shakira by the hand to the dance floor.

After pouring 3 more glasses of champagne David joined his friends. The music was thumping now and the dance floor was heaving, full of hot, sweaty, tanned Durban bodies. David could see Frankie in his element throwing back one cracking tune after another. Maybe the line "God is a DJ" was true after all and the revellers were his flock that he commanded, thought David.

He danced close to Shakira and could smell her sweet perfume. She pulled him even closer until her hips were against his and she could feel him harden. Her lips were on his again and she went in search for his tongue which he gladly offered. He could feel that tonight was different. They had passed that point of any doubts and were now fully committed to each other in every sense. *They* were ready.

After nearly an hour of partying and their bodies sweating they went to finish their drinks at a side table.

“For someone who doesn’t play sport you are incredibly fit girl. Also, who taught you to dance like *that*?” asked Lionel as he downed his glass of champagne.

“She was a very good ballerina when we were kids” laughed Shakira beating her friend to the punch.

“Well, very impressive. I’m super fit and look how I’m sweating” said Lionel.

“Miriam, I’m getting a lift with David. Are you OK dropping Lionel off please?” asked Shakira.

“Of course, I’m sure EB won’t have an issue with that. We arranged for 2:30 a.m. pick-up so we still have half an hour on the dance floor”

“You mean *you two* party animals have another half hour on the dance floor. I’m exhausted just watching the 2 of you. Besides we’re going to head out now and leave you guys to it. Be good and do everything I wouldn’t do!” laughed David.

“Davie, thanks so much for tonight. It’s taken me back to our misspent youth. So many of the old faces were here tonight and it was such fun” said Lionel pulling his dance partner back to the dance floor.

“Be good you two! See you tomorrow Miriam! Lovely meeting you Lionel!” shouted Shakira, winking at her friend.

The apartment Shakira lead him to was the penthouse suite of a tall frontline block of flats overlooking Durban’s central beaches.

“This is one of my brother’s apartments which I also happen to have keys for” she said to David whilst pouring them both water.

“What an amazing view! What an amazing apartment!” said David, walking around the lounge and large outdoor patio.

“Your brother has certainly done very well for himself in a short space of time” remarked David.

"Yip, he's quite the entrepreneur is Mo. I think he's even shocked my father although he would have preferred him to join the family business rather" replied Shakira.

"Come lie with me here and tell me a story, Mr O" she beckoned to him whilst lounging on a luxury sofa.

"Oh yeah! And what kind of story would you like me to tell you?" he asked, moving in next to her.

"Tell me the one about these 2 crazy lovers who everyone thinks are mad to risk it all, but they go for it anyway, my love" she said, pulling his face closer to hers. She was so incredibly sexy this girlfriend of his.

He kissed her long and passionately until he felt her taking his shirt off and then unexpectedly his jeans too. It was signal enough for him to do the same to her until their warm bodies were both naked.

"I know I've asked before, but just in case, are you sure?"

"Yes my angel, now make love to me please. We've waited long enough" she whispered in his ear.

David felt himself slide easily inside her as he heard her gasp. He could feel the hardened nipples of her perky breasts against his chest. With each thrust he could feel her breath becoming more ragged and then he would slow down to anticipate the next build up until she could take the teasing no more. He thrust deeper and faster inside her until his whole body tensed and then exploded inside her whilst she climaxed. He could feel her long fingernails digging deep into his back as she became lost in her pleasure.

"Oh my God, I don't even know what that was! I've never experienced anything like that before Mr O ... but I do know I want more please!" she giggled, out of breath.

"I think it's called being in love" laughed David.

"You right, my darling. I really am deeply in love with you" she said, gulping down some water.

The cool sea breeze drifted in through the open patio doors and cooled their bodies off. They lay holding each other for some time saying nothing yet saying everything that needed to be said.

Before they knew it the first strains of sunlight peeped over the horizon but by then they had already fallen into a deep sleep in each other's arms.

Chapter 24

The following morning David beat the boys to it and woke them up for school. They told him they couldn't wait to tell their friends how their guest had annihilated the 2 best junior players in Israel and that they had been the ball boys. They weren't able to make it again that afternoon because they had football practice but were free the following day. He enjoyed them and they felt more like his kid brothers.

Whilst dressing in his new army browns David couldn't help thinking about the history lesson Moshe had given him the previous night. He had covered everything from the War of Independence that both his father and grandfather had fought in. Israel was extremely grateful for the support given to her by South African Jews who arrived to defend her when she was attacked by 6 Arab nations. He explained how the South African air force-trained pilots essentially built the Israeli air force in the middle of the battle.

Then the hardships the *Yishuv* faced afterwards, being cast as political pariahs with no real foreign support even from the United States. America only assisted much later and only when it suited its own agenda. He described the ingenuity of the top brass in taking out the entire Egyptian air force in the 1967 6 day war and the enormous courage of the young troops in the 1973 war on Yom Kippur, when the Arabs had surprised them. He said it was during that war, that both he and Rubie had come close to dying, but *HaShem* had other things still planned for them. He described how many young men, some not even eighteen years of age yet, had died in their arms defending their young country.

"*Boychik*, after all we've struggled and come through as a nation it's hard to believe we can still smile or have kindness in our hearts. We, as a people, are here to shine a light unto others but *they* want to stay in the dark. They hate the light we have been shining for four-thousand years David because we are a tiny number but we have overachieved which creates jealousy in others. David, I am in the military to prevent wars not start them. If our enemies see how strong we are, they will fear us and not attack us" explained Moshe.

Beverly and Rubie were happy to see him arrive at breakfast and greeted him warmly.

"Here's my champion, Bev. He absolutely smashed their treadmill record yesterday and could have gone even longer he says" laughed Rubie.

"David, of all the things you could do for Rubie getting the treadmill monkey off his back is the best present you could ever have given him. By the way that uniform really suits you and if you ever visit the ladies' brigades you are going to be a very popular young man. I'm going to grab my camera to take a picture of you and Rubie" said Beverly.

"Unfortunately, no cameras" said Rubie gruffly.

"Of course not. What was I thinking?" replied Beverly.

"In any case David I've made you an Israeli equivalent of good old Jungle Oats porridge for you. Dov suggested it" she laughed.

"He's right, I do love it with honey and small cut up banana rings. Rubie you should try it!" said David to the big man.

"Sure, why not" replied Rubie much to David's surprise.

After breakfast it was the same routine of being blindfolded but the journey seemed much faster. David figured that for security reasons Rubie was not going to follow the same routes. Clever, thought David.

As the lift door opened on their level David and Rubie were greeted by the diminutive figure of Dr Berkowitz.

"Come on then David, we have work to do!" she seemed to growl, at which Rubie grinned and winked at David.

"Good luck with that. See you later" he chuckled.

Once they were seated in her office she pulled out a file.

"Well as per your questionnaire it's good to learn you have no homosexual tendencies so seducing the target should be a much easier thing for you" she laughed.

"Well, I think I got off to a good start after our first date" said David defensively.

She stared at him for quite some time before answering.

"You young guys of today really know nothing about women do you? You have one date where she mouths off about some idiot Jew breaking her heart and her wanting to see you again, and now you think she wants to marry you? Son, I've been doing this job for nearly fourty years and I've heard the same thing, time and time again. We are going to have to toughen you up a bit because this one is obviously very attractive and got you thinking with your penis instead of your brain" said Dr Berkowitz, point blank.

"First rule, she is not your future wife. Capiche? Second, she is your secondary target. A means to an end nothing more. Third, if you need to get laid to get closer to her go for it but just don't fall in love. This isn't a summer romance Mossad is arranging for you. You are on a mission which is why you are in army browns whilst you are here" she said, again with the long stare which made David feel very awkward.

"It's not all bad though. You have some good traits. For starters you are truthful so the lie detector won't be necessary. In spite of thinking too much with your penis around the target, you are sensitive and kind which will appeal to her. You are ambitious and determined and will see things through to the end even if you don't particularly enjoy them. You are loyal which is important to us although can easily be used to manipulate you. You're quite handsome too, which can be advantageous when it comes to romance" she continued.

"Phew! And there I really thought I was doomed" David replied, sarcastically.

Again the long, awkward stare.

"Do you want me to prepare you for one of the hardest jobs in the world - being a spy, or do you just want me to help you get laid? If you can't handle criticism from a little, old Jewish lady then you aren't right for the job. You will be putting many lives in danger starting with Dov's" she replied in a stern voice.

"I'm sorry Dr Berkowitz. I want to learn from the best not just for the mission but also to improve my mind for tennis" David apologised.

"Yes, about your tennis. You may think you are mentally tough but you aren't, certainly not from what I've seen. You have improved a little bit in the last few months but you still need more killer instinct. David, it's not about your mechanics, it's all about your mind. If you want to break into the top twenty in the world, which you certainly have the game for, you need to develop a real killer instinct on the court. Giving those 2 kids a few games because you felt sorry for them yesterday. Is that your idea of killer instinct? The other kids on the tour will eat you up for breakfast and shit you out before lunch" she said.

David was shocked to learn she had been watching him.

"You are right, Dr Berkowitz, I shouldn't have done that" said David embarrassed.

"I'm here to learn from the best so please help me all you can" he said earnestly.

"David, everyone here under this roof is the best in the world at what they do. We have to be otherwise we are dead, as in *literally* dead. I will help you achieve your best mentally if you work with me. In fact to make it crystal clear for you, everybody here is trying to give you their best" she said.

"I'm ready" said David.

For the next two hours the little Jewish lady explained the pleasure principals of human psychology and their differences between the sexes. She even went so far as to describe all the processes the brain goes through during orgasm.

She then moved onto the question of whether winners were born or developed, or at least could be developed. It was closely related to killer instinct and the art of training one's mind to achieve one's goals.

One of the most interesting topics for David was the difference in psyche between Jews and Muslims. Dr Berkowitz highlighted that many of their fundamental differences were as a result of the differences in the Torah and the Koran. For instance she explained how Judaism emphasized the importance of how one conducted oneself in this life and had nothing really to say about an afterlife or Heaven, whereas Muslims only led this life to reach Heaven. She also emphasized how all 3 books of the monotheistic religions believed that the Jews had been chosen by God to be an example of how to lead one's life. This had never sat particularly well with the other religions who then judged Jews and criticized them, by holding them to a higher standard.

Jews having been persecuted in large numbers over the years were also more introverted within their own communities whereas Muslims were open for proselytization, which had led to a huge growth in their numbers worldwide.

"David, under normal circumstances we would never have sent a Jew to do this work because we are such different people in so many ways but as you've seen for yourself, she has been heavily influenced by her secularized Persian mother. I mean how many Muslim girls do you know who drink French champagne, for instance? The fact that you are an atheist is a big advantage because if you were *frum* this wouldn't work. So please remain an atheist is what I'm saying. You can find God later" she laughed.

"And with that our time is up for today. You get to learn some Arabic now, *habibi*" she laughed, pointing to the door.

David was shocked to discover that his Arabic teacher was a conservative little Arab Israeli professor called Fatima Noor who was wearing a veil. An Arab Muslim was the last person he was expecting to meet inside Mossad. Surely Mossad could find an Israeli Jew who knew Arabic, David thought. It became even more peculiar when he discovered from Rubie later, that she was married to a secular Yemenite Jew who didn't care a damn about religion and allowed his wife to bring the children up as Muslims. All of a sudden his situation seemed perfectly normal in comparison.

"As-salamu alaykum, David" she greeted him with.

"Wa'alaykum salaam, prof" David replied instinctively.

"Wow! Very good. Has your lady been teaching you already?" she asked.

"Oh no, not at all. It's just there are so many Muslims living in Durban" laughed David.

"What's your Hebrew like?" she asked.

"Poor, I would say but I wasn't too bad at it in primary school but then I went to a non-Jewish high school which didn't offer it" he replied.

"Well I've been tasked with doing a crash course in Arabic to at least give you some tools in following a conversation. It's a difficult language as you'll soon see but we give it our best shot, what you say?" she asked.

"For sure, I'll do my best for us prof."

If Hebrew had been difficult Arabic was far worse. No wonder the Muslim kids always won the Hebrew prizes thought David. It must have been child's play for them after Arabic. Well maybe he would at least pick up a word or two that may come in useful one day but following complete conversations in such a short period of time wasn't going to happen. Thank goodness he didn't have to learn to write it.

After 2 hours of Arabic with Professor Noor, he was mentally exhausted and relieved to see Rubie and Channah.

"*Salaam habibi,* you look like you ready for lunch my friend" joked Rubie.

"Jesus Christ, I don't know if I can do Arabic" said David.

"Nor did the Ashkenazi's think they could speak Hebrew when they first stepped off the ships in Haifa but now look at us" said Channah.

"I wish it was only Hebrew I was learning, Channah. Arabic is a thousand times more difficult" replied David.

"David, we are starting you on a new gluten-free diet as of today. We are going gently on you at first with the sugars and salts, so today we're serving up fresh salmon on gluten-free bagels with some chicken salad. We need to build 5th set stamina for you for the majors one day" said Channah.

"More like for the 5th set with the Persian girlfriend. Have you seen how hot she is, Channah?" asked Rubie.

"Oh yes I have! She's beautiful David, especially those dark green eyes. You better not fall in love!" Channah answered, looking at David.

"You right, she is hot. The guys at varsity all check her out but she can come across as being quite aloof although she's anything but that. I had a first date with her already and she's lovely. I'm calling her tonight and I hope she still feels good about me" said David.

"*Habibi*, what girl wouldn't possibly fall for a nice Jewish boy like you? Isn't that so, Channah?" said Rubie, with a wry smile on his face.

"Yes, that's true Rubie" replied Channah, with a look of slight embarrassment on her sweet face.

After lunch Rubie took David to a much lower level in the building for his light weapons training. It felt like a basement level and housed an indoor shooting range. Rubie would be handling the course himself and was surprised to hear that David had never so much as even picked up a weapon, never mind having fired one before.

"I'm going to start you off with what I consider a toy gun then David, but first we run through the safety protocols which apply to any weapon. This Beretta 9mm is a nifty little weapon for close combat type situations and hopefully, at worse, this is all you will ever need if you are facing any danger. You only use a weapon if you are facing a life and death situation though" explained Rubie.

"Or else?" asked David.

"Or else run!" laughed Rubie, "or use the Krav Maga techniques you will be taught later in the week if you really have to but first rule of thumb is avoid contact wherever possible. Don't think with your ego, it can easily get you hurt or killed. Punching that kid when you were in high school is very different from what you could potentially face now and let's hope that doesn't happen" said Rubie.

"I liked the part you said about running actually" laughed David.

"Good, but that's not always possible and things happening quickly in these situations" said Rubie.

Rubie spent an hour running through the theory and then handed David the weapon to David who ran through all the checks Rubie had shown him.

"Good. Now let's see how accurate you are with that thing" he said moving on to the paper targets.

Rubie didn't seem too shocked how accurate David proved to be and at least hitting some part of the target from 50 metres out. David was enjoying himself but was curious as to Rubie's abilities.

"Rubie, show me how the pro's do it" said David, handing the weapon to Rubie after doing more safety checks.

Rubie placed the weapon in a holster he was wearing and when he was ready he retrieved it in a flash and fired 5 consecutive shots at 5 different moving targets at different distances. It all seemed to happen in a second and left David gobsmacked that holes had suddenly appeared in all 5 bullseyes.

"Jesus, incredible!" said David.

"No different from your tennis. The more practice you put in the better you get, right? That's why I'm still alive David" he said looking at David in earnest.

"We're done for the day here. Let's get you to your tennis. I really enjoyed watching you yesterday" said Rubie.

"Will Dr Berkowitz be traveling with us this afternoon or separately like yesterday?" David asked with a cheeky grin.

"Ah, he's got some *chutzpah*! I have no idea, I'm not in charge of *her* safety" smiled Rubie.

The trip to the Tel Aviv Country Club was much shorter than the previous day. Rubie was sticking to his protocols laughed David. It was Israel after all and it made him feel relaxed to be taken care of by the best.

As with the previous day the two youngsters warmed him up nicely before playing a couple sets. Before starting David had a good look around but if Dr Berkowitz was there he couldn't see her. So she didn't think he had killer instinct. He would show her.

To say that David annihilated the two youngsters would be a complete understatement. He took whatever pent-up anger from the bullying session Dr Berkowitz had reserved for him, and unleashed it on the kids. Poor Eli and Ohad looked like they had undergone their own private Holocausts and between them only managed 3 games off David in 4 sets. Rubie, sitting on an elevated bench sipping on a glass of Coke, was in his element, almost as bad as Dov with his constant clapping and cheering.

"Lovely, lovely David smash them up *boychik*! Give me more of that please!" he hollered, and David didn't disappoint.

"Sorry boys! I was just in a bit of a mood today and needed to release some steam" he said to them.

The whole ordeal had taken less than an hour so David took the extra time to run through a bunch of drills Clive had shown him over the years. He didn't want to break their spirits so he put them to training, encouraging them each in turn.

"Now Eli, Ohad where were *these* shots when you were playing me earlier? This is what I want to face tomorrow from both of you, OK. You can see the level you need to attain now if you are going to progress to senior level tennis. You both have the talent for it" encouraged David.

The long faces suddenly turned to smiles and David felt good that he could build them up and not leave them with crushed dreams.

"Jesus Christ, David. That was some tennis today" smiled Rubie, en-route to Moshe.

"Well, you said it earlier bro. Lots and lots of practice is what it takes to be the best, right? I've been playing this game since I was 5 years old and competitively since I was 8 years old. If I'm not improving by *at least* 10% every year, I'm dead in the water" said David.

"Well, whatever Dr Berkowitz said to you worked big time because you were ruthless today, like a killer on the rampage. I haven't seen anyone play better than that including Amos" laughed Rubie.

"By the way I'm staying for dinner with you tonight. Beverly is doing a barbecued chicken with special vegetables and then Moshe and I want to talk some tactical stuff with you afterwards".

"Rubie, if you going to take care of me you are going to have to use the word "braai" rather than barbecue. No South African worth anything would ever "barbecue." It just wouldn't be right. We are the world champions at that type of cooking, believe me. Every South African boy gets taught by his father from a young age how to braai" laughed David.

"Ah yes, that's the word Bev used but I just can't pronounce it" laughed Rubie.

"It's also probably why Bev is going to do the cooking rather than Moshe trying to barbecue" laughed Rubie again.

"By the time I'm finished my training I'll have taught you quite a few South Africanisms, don't worry" joked David.

Chapter 25

David woke after 12 p.m. on Sunday and through his sleepy eyes he could make out Shakira's outline on the patio, drinking what smelt like coffee. At some point she had covered him with a sheet and put a pillow under his head and he had slept solidly not even feeling her untangle herself from him.

"Hello my darling! I slept so well last night I didn't even feel you move. How did you sleep?" he asked, giving her a kiss on the cheek.

"Good morning, my love. I slept beautifully but what do you expect after the ending to our night. That was incredible" she replied, looking ravaging in a white bikini. She smelt fresh and David could see that she had showered.

"Would you like some chocolate croissants and orange juice or some coffee rather?" she said, getting up from her lounger where she had been tanning her beautiful figure.

"Croissants and coffee sounds amazing" replied David, following her inside.

"Do you mind if I call Lionel first, please. Neither of us will be in a state to play anything half decent today so I had better cancel our practice. Besides I would much rather spend it with you" he said, pulling her closer whilst she wiped some of the chocolate off his lips.

After calling Lionel, who sounded a lot worse than he did and sounded relieved that David had called to cancel, David went for a quick shower.

She surprised him by putting her arms around him and within seconds he was hard again. She really was full of surprises.

"I thought you had showered already?" he asked.

"I did but who said I had come for a shower?" she asked, cheekily.

"You little vixen you" he laughed, turning her around and lifting her up.

Her olive skin was almost bronze from the sun and her still-warm body was smooth and completely hairless. He entered her wetness whilst she was kissing his neck, and then his lips, and then his tongue. David moved more slowly and methodically than before and felt the excited tension build up in both of their bodies until they could contain themselves no more.

“Oh my God! Did you do this for all your lovers, my darling?” she teased.

“Nope, because I wasn’t in love with them like you, Shakira. It was just sex before” he said.

“Even the Jewish ones?” she asked.

“Yes because when it’s just physical it’s the same with anyone” he replied.

“Who would have thought a Jewish boy and a Muslim girl?” she laughed.

“Yes, and particularly in South Africa with the stupid Apartheid rules. If this is a crime then I’m ready for a lifetime of being a career criminal” laughed David.

“I think when it’s the real thing, love sees no colour, not even genders. It’s the purest, most natural potion out there” she said.

“And yes, this is it” he said.

“Shit. I better go phone Dov before he waits outside for me to collect him. Do you mind, my darling?” asked David.

“Come join me on one of the loungers on the patio afterwards” she said, drying herself off.

David caught his coach just in the nick of time.

“I was actually expecting this call much earlier. Well, that’s fine if you not working on your tennis game, at least you working on your other game, you lucky boy” laughed Dov.

“How do you know …” David began before Dov interrupted him with, “Davie, we know everything. I told you that a few times now. Pick me up tomorrow and don’t use all your strength this afternoon. I’m going to work you two boys hard tomorrow” he laughed, putting the receiver down before David could answer.

“How is Dov?” she asked, as he entered the patio and plonked himself down next to her.

“Dov is Dov. He’ll never change. I’m glad to have him traveling the tour with me. He’s a lot of fun and after a bad match he’s been able to pick me up quickly again. He’s a good man” he told her.

“So you were telling me last night your dad is off to Dubai and then Jordan soon? What sort of business is he doing in those places?” asked David.

“Well Dubai has always been textiles and clothing, along with India and China where he has clothing factories. I’m not sure about Jordan but he also has a good friend who he stays with on his trips there” she replied.

“Have you ever been to Jordan yourself? I would love to visit there but as a Jew I don’t think I would be particularly well received” at which they both laughed.

“I’ve been to the West Bank and Gaza with my dad but at that time he wasn’t going to Jordan, so no” she replied.

“But I will tell you David that the Palestinian civilians in both settlements, contrary to what people say, are very nice. They were so hospitable I can’t tell you” she said.

“Wow! Do you have family there still by any chance?” he asked.

“We had on my father’s side of the family but they fled Israel for South Africa just before the 1948 war. My dad has helped many people living in squalor in both settlements in recent years. We met quite a few of them and they were so grateful it had my dad in tears. That’s why he’s anti-Zionism although not anti-Jewish people. On that trip we even travelled to Tel Aviv to meet some of his Israeli partners whose tech start-ups he has invested in” she explained.

“He’s got Jewish partners in Tel Aviv? That’s so crazy!” exclaimed David.

“My angel, the Jews got him started in business in Durban when his own people wouldn’t even cut him a break. We have had all those men in the clothing business over at our house for meals! I’ve even been to one of the daughter’s weddings. As I say it’s not about Jews for my dad. It’s about the Israeli government which he detests. He’s also totally against violent groups like Hamas and Hezbollah who he feels have derailed any potential peace processes between the two peoples. He was definitely no fan of Arafat either. I remember him cursing him as being a fool and naïve and not being honest in his negotiations at Camp David. Sometimes I feel my dad is almost caught in the middle of this whole conflict. Unfortunately, it has put a bit of a dampener on his relationship with some of his Jewish friends but as he’s told them, this is for poor people not to finance terrorists” she said.

“David, when you get to really know my father you will understand that he’s a great man, and I’m not just talking businessman. I mean a great person with very strong morals and convictions” she said.

David was so relieved to hear this from her and couldn't wait to report back to Dov. Ismail Mahomedy was not their man. It was someone else which is why there was no money trail leading back to him.

"I know sometimes you make him sound a bit intimidating but I'm actually quite looking forward to meeting your father. He sounds like an amazing human and I'm sure I could learn a lot from him" said David.

"Stick to talking tennis and stay far away from Israel and you'll be fine" she laughed.

"He's actually a real softy if you really want to know. He cannot say no to my mother or me, hard as he might try. I think from both a sports and business perspective you will have a lot of things to talk about but first let him get to grips that you are white, and secondly, Jewish. My mom's going to have a lot on her plate explaining all that" she laughed.

"Well, that's assuming your mother even likes me" he laughed back.

"She'll love you David, don't worry. She's the easy one" she replied.

The late afternoon sun was shimmering the last of its rays off the sea which had calmed down a lot from earlier. Most of the Sunday beachgoers had packed up their belongings and were heading off. The surfers had seemingly had the best of the earlier 4 foot swell and had also called it a day.

"Spend tonight with me again please, my love. Tomorrow is a public holiday so no varsity for me and my mom is only expecting me home from Miriam's tomorrow sometime. Maybe I'll even come watch you and Lionel practice if I won't be too much of a distraction for you?" she asked.

"You will be but I would still love you to watch. When I drop you tomorrow why don't you invite Miriam and EB also? I may even invite Leah because I would love you two to finally meet" said David.

"That's actually a great idea. I think it's time I met her" she said.

"OK, so whilst you phone her I'm going to shoot out and get us a nice curry from downstairs" said David.

"Oh don't worry, they know us up here only too well. Mo and I run a tab with them which he settles up at the end of the month. I'll order for us to deliver then. There's a great 8 p.m. movie on M-Net tonight with Tom Cruise we can watch in the main bedroom which Mo had a surround sound system installed in. This is so exciting" she said, snuggling up to David on his lounger.

"Before we get too comfy let me just call my folks and let them know I'm still alive and will only see them tomorrow" said David.

"Perfect, I'll call Miriam after."

Leah answered the call and asked when he would be back. He asked her to convey the message he would only be in the following morning and just for a quick bite of breakfast and to grab his kit. She was delighted to be invited to watch him and Lionel practice and would ask Michael to join them too. She was especially excited to finally be getting to meet Shakira. David told her she would also get to meet her crazy friend Miriam too.

After her call to Miriam who was very touched for the invite and would definitely join them, their food was delivered. She had ordered a variety of things including the juiciest mince samosas he had ever tasted. He also just loved the fresh smell of naan bread. She had ordered two separate curries, mild for her and hot for her boyfriend. After her earlier experiences with him eating hot curry she came prepared with a tall glass of milk and bottle of water.

"I've got you covered this time' my love" she said, throwing him a towel to mop any sweat off his face.

"Nobody makes a better curry in the world than Durban. Man, when I travel I really miss them" he said, making them both laugh.

"You sound just like my dad. He feels exactly the same" she said.

After they had finished the delicious supper they went through to the main bedroom and jumped in beneath the silk sheets to watch the 8 p.m. Sunday night movie. David was feeling so much better having heard about her father's philanthropy in the Middle East. He looked forward to conveying that news to Dov first chance he could get.

With her lying in his arms and with them both naked, the 8 p.m. movie had no chance of competing and it didn't take long before they were making love again. Their bodies were a perfect fit in every way and David couldn't help thinking how Dr Berkowitz and the others had warned him not to fall in love with this beautiful woman, but he wasn't a robot and besides it was way too late for going back now anyway.

After their physical exploits of the afternoon and the sun tanning on the patio deck, it didn't take long for them both to fall into a comfortable sleep, with David cuddling her in his arms.

They were young and in love and life was good.

Chapter 26

After dropping Shakira off early David had a quick breakfast with his parents and then showered. His mother quizzed him a little about his whereabouts over the weekend whilst his father headed off to do more research work in his study. David didn't want to get into too much detail so he told her he had been running about with Lionel and Dov. He noticed the little grin on his sister's face as she sipped on her tea.

"Mom, I'm going to watch David practice with Lionel at Mitchell Park today so don't expect me until much later" said Leah.

"Oh, that's lovely. Hopefully one of these days he will invite your father and me too" she said wryly.

"You can watch me at the French Open, mom" said David before bolting upstairs to shower.

It wasn't long before he and Leah were heading off in the Green Mamba to collect Dov in Musgrave. When they arrived Dov, in a full Tacchini outfit, was deep in discussion with what looked like 2 old Jewish ladies.

"Ah, here's my guy David. Davie, Leah this is Mrs Goldberg and Mrs Levy. I was just telling them we off to the French Open in little over a week's time" said Dov.

David noticed whilst he was introducing them that Dov had gone and had "Coach Dov" embroidered on the front of his Tacchini polo.

"Hi there Mrs Goldberg, Mrs Levy I'm David Oppenheim and this is my sister, Leah. Nice to meet both you ladies" David answered politely.

"Hello son, so nice to meet a famous Jewish tennis player. May *HaShem* bless you and bring you much success. Please send our regards to your clever father too. He taught both our kids at university" replied Mrs Goldberg.

"*Baruch HaShem,* I will make sure to pass on your regards" said Leah.

Mrs Goldberg reached out for Leah's hand which she offered and held it with both hers and kissed it. It was then that David noticed the numbered tattoo on the little old lady's one arm. Leah immediately reciprocated, kissing her hands many times with tears in her eyes.

"Thanks *bubba*, thanks for everything your generation did for ours. We treasure you" she said, looking at both ladies with tears running down her cheeks.

At that point David had never felt more Jewish or proud to be Jewish than before. His people were the greatest survivors and Mrs Goldberg was living proof of that.

Dov was in a playful mood and started out by teasing David about Shakira.

"So yesterday, did you get it *all*?" he asked David.

"What you mean?" asked David.

"Did you get *all* your rest china, you know all your sustenance for today?" he asked, with that huge Dov-grin of his.

"Yes, thanks for your concern Dov. I'm feeling well rested today for practice" replied David.

"So not *too much* strenuous exercise then yesterday?" asked Leah, getting in on the action now.

"Alright you two, I know what you getting at! Maybe a *little* exercise then" he laughed in good spirits.

"*Now* we believe you!" laughed Leah.

"*Exactly*!" shouted Dov.

They arrived precisely on time at 9:30 a.m. like David had planned and amazingly Lionel was already on the courts practicing with a junior.

"*Howzit,* bro! I thought we had said 9 a.m. but then when I got here just after 9 a.m. and you weren't here, I realised we had said 9:30 a.m." shouted Lionel.

"Hah! I think that's the only way to get you to practice on time in future" replied Dov, who was already putting the frozen purple containers out to unfreeze.

Whilst he was stretching David noticed Leah hugging Michael.

"Ah, our umpire has arrived" remarked Dov.

"Hi chaps, thanks for letting me umpire again this morning" said Michael, waving at everyone.

“Jump in the chair young man but before you do that put on this Tacchini T-shirt, courtesy of Team O” ordered Dov, flinging him a packet.

“Oh, super cool! Thank you very much, David” said Michael.

“No problem, Michael. Just remember all close calls go my way OK” laughed David.

David was about ten minutes into their knock up when he noticed Shakira and Miriam walking down the stairs. They waved at him and he blew them quick kisses. Leah, noticing this, walked over to them and introduced herself. He wasn’t surprised to see Shakira giving her a big hug and kiss on either cheek. They were going to become good friends for sure.

It wasn’t long before a small crowd appeared and Dov managed to carole 4 kids into ballboying for them before making himself comfortable next to the 3 girls. By the time they were ready to start their match the little crowd had grown to a much bigger crowd. Durban was such a small city and word travelled fast, laughed David.

After a full day of rest the previous day David was ready to put on a show and proceeded to do exactly that. The first set went by in a flash with David whizzing passing shots, placing delicate drop shots and simply chasing down and sending back everything Lionel sent his way.

“Shakira! You should really come to the French and watch David because I’ve never seen him this motivated before” Lionel shouted to her whilst they were knocking back the electrolytes between changes of set.

“Oh I’m sure it’s all Dov’s coaching, not me!” she laughed back.

“Exactly and thank you, my sweet” he replied, acknowledging her compliment.

The first set score was 6-2 and Lionel only slightly improved his position by an extra game in the second set. David had managed to completely discourage Lionel from his strong serve and volley game and had him pinned to the baseline. The variety and pace of groundstroke that David was hitting were too much for his rival and he was able to impose his will. Dr Berkowitz’s work was paying off and his killer instinct was at another level. The crowd was mesmerised with David’s wizardry and every so often he noticed out of the corner of his eye that Shakira was sitting on the edge of the bench and clapping.

"Right, that's it, I've had enough of this Davie. This set is mine" said Lionel, pouring purple liquid down his gullet like he was pouring gas at a bowser.

The third set was closely contested and true to his word Lionel sneaked it in a tiebreaker to force at least a fourth set. David was surprisingly still feeling fresh by the close of the third set and put it down to the new diet he had observed as closely as possible for the past couple months. He popped two glucose sweets in his mouth before serving for the 4th set.

Lionel, probably through fatigue, could simply not sustain his third set levels and in an effort to shorten the points fatally chose to chip and charge the net. David picked him off easily, whipping cross court passing shots off both sides. Even though the crowd and ball boys all wanted a fifth set they were in awe of David's fine shot-making skills and guile and David settled the set 6-1 with an ace down the T of the deuce court. Even though the match had been less competitive than their previous ones, the crowd was appreciative of being entertained by two fine players gratis and gave them both a standing ovation.

David was used to the clapping now, but Dov shouting out his name to everybody and instructing them to look out for him playing at the French Open, caused him to blush instinctively. He was happy to look up and see both Shakira and Leah standing and clapping with the others. He winked at both of them and they both blew kisses back at him.

"Fucking amazing, Davie! You were on fire today, bro. Those passing shots of yours were as good as anyone's I've ever seen. You are more than ready for Roland Garros" said his great rival.

"Thanks Li, I just had a very good day today is all" replied David.

"You are having lots of good days now and that's how you win the big ones" remarked Lionel.

"David, that was spectacular. I am so privileged to have had the best seat in the house to witness that. My old man is not going to believe that I got to see this today. Hard lines Lionel you did very well to clinch that 3rd set" said Michael.

"No problem Michael. Glad you enjoyed it. We are just going to shower and then I'll take us all out for lunch somewhere" replied David.

"Wow Mr O you certainly gave me a show today!" said Shakira, who had wandered onto the court and was now hugging him.

"Thanks, my angel. I had a good day. I think you brought me luck today!" he said giving her a big kiss on the lips.

"Now, now lovebirds let David go shower before you get a room" laughed Miriam, who was now also on the court giving both him and Lionel high-fives.

"Hey Miriam, I'm so glad you could come this morning but where's EB?" asked David.

"He had a golf game booked with some mates at Papwa so couldn't stay unfortunately. He's very disappointed but I'm sure you'll invite us again?" said Miriam.

"Absolutely, of course. Let us go shower and I'll take us all out for lunch. Let's go to that seafood place on the harbour. I know it's kosher for Leah" said David.

The happy crew were seated at The Fish Haven overlooking Durban's harbour entrance. It was a great spot to watch the giant container vessels and others entering and exiting Africa's busiest port. It may not have been pretty like Cape Town's foreshore with its dramatic views of Table Mountain, but it certainly was a very interesting one. Sitting in the restaurant it felt like one could almost reach out and touch some of the ships.

"How are you two boys feeling after all that exertion?" asked Miriam.

"I was really feeling it after that 3rd set and wasn't sure if I was going to make the 4th. To be honest I was half relieved Davie rolled me over so quickly in the 4th!" joked Lionel.

"Surprisingly, I actually feel pretty good still" replied David.

"It's my purple drink I'm telling you" barked Dov, which had the whole group laughing.

"Michael, how was it up there in the chair today?" asked David.

"I loved every second of it, man. I love the way you guys have the tools to pivot to a different set of tactics when something isn't working for you. Like you in the 3rd set Lionel. I noticed you were being a lot more selective as to when you were going to approach the net. Your first touch volleys were also far more penetrating" noted Michael.

"Wow, china! Tomorrow you start as my new coach. Dov, sorry but you are fired!" chuckled Lionel, having them all laughing.

"You are very observant Michael. I think I'm going to pass on some tapes Dov managed to rustle up of this Figueras dude I play in the opening round at Roland Garros. Do you mind watching some of his matches for me?" asked David.

"Are you being serious?" asked Michael, quite astounded.

"When it comes to music and tennis I never joke" said David in a serious tone.

"Cool. I would love to do that for you. Who knows, maybe as a novice without any preconceptions I may even pick up something for you" said Michael in an excited tone as Leah hugged him.

"There you go. Your first professional job. I'm sure my brother can pay you in apparel" laughed Leah.

"Anyway, enough shop talk for now. I want to know what you two ladies were so busy talking about at Mitchell Park? Be honest because I'll have to ask Dov otherwise" said David, looking at his girlfriend then his sister.

"Oh, we were mostly talking about varsity life and our courses really. I was just telling Leah that your dad had taken me for English 1 first year. Don't worry, my darling, we weren't gossiping about you" she smiled, hugging David closer.

"Yes, Shakira was also telling me she thinks you were so good today because you two had such a good rest yesterday" teased Leah, with her wry little grin.

"Oh, I bet!" laughed Miriam, causing Shakira to blush.

"Yip, the view from Shakira's brother's apartment is incredible. It's a pity you and Lionel hadn't come with us but then again you were *far too busy* on the dance floor, right?" replying with a grin.

"Let's order people. I'm hungry and thirsty after all the work this bugger had me doing this morning!" Lionel interrupted.

"Great idea. Me too" said Miriam, whose cheeks were also blushing.

David suggested ordering 2 giant seafood platters and salads for everyone to pick on as well as a bottle of champagne and light drinks.

Shakira started discussing Judaism with Leah and her reasons behind her stricter observance. Leah explained that if anything it had been Michael's influence and how the clarity of his explanations of God and spirituality had set her on this path. She explained how Michael was studying Theology which could very well lead to the priesthood.

"After today I'm thinking more along the lines of tennis umpire or analyst" joked Michael.

"I certainly know my father would approve more of that than studying Theology" he continued.

"You mean one day we could all be calling you Father Michael?" asked Dov.

"Yes Dov, but if that does happen it will be in many years to come" chuckled Michael.

Shakira continued by explaining that her mother's side were Shia Muslims from Iran who had followed Sufism too. Leah was amazed to learn that Islam also had saints and a mystical side to it along the lines of Jewish kabbalah.

"I thought only the Catholics had saints? I had no idea that Islam did too" she said.

"I think like Judaism, Islam is also a rich, spiritual tapestry with many, many facets to it" added Miriam.

"As we discuss our religions more I realise just how many commonalities we have. We really just approach praying to the same God but from different cultural perspectives is all" she said.

"Yet religion has resulted in *how many wars*?" asked David.

"But that's man David, not God. You have to separate the two" interrupted Michael.

"Yes, please everyone tell my heathen brother here that God exists!" laughed Leah.

"Not me! I'm still a SWIP" said Lionel, adding to the conversation.

"A what? Sounds freaky that!" asked Dov

"A SWIP. You know, a Spiritual Work in Progress" explained Lionel to everyone's amusement.

"Well, there's at least some hope for *you,* Lionel" said Leah.

"I'll tell you this much though, God or none, the tennis gods weren't smiling down on me this morning like they were on my heathen opponent!" said Lionel, having the group laughing again.

The conversation turned from religion to politics and the impending unbanning of the African National Congress and the inevitable release of its leader, Nelson Mandela. The general atmosphere of the country was one of expectation, excitement as well as a certain amount of fear among the minority races. Would Mandela be able to control the militants within his party, now possibly looking to extract their revenge on their Apartheid oppressors? How would the far right white groups react to this loss of white rule? Would many of the highly skilled minorities emigrate with their money and skills to Europe and other white-majority countries? Was crime going to spiral out of control? There were so many unanswered questions but David's group were positive young adults looking to contribute to building a new, united and strong nation and even Michael who had won a scholarship to Cambridge University, had decided to stay on and study in Durban.

"And you two can finally stop being a *crime*!" Lionel teased.

"The only crime these two have ever committed is being too damn beautiful!" said Miriam proposing a toast to them.

"Here, here!" the others responded, clinking glasses.

"It's a crazy country isn't it, guys? But hey, it's our crazy country so let's go show the world. Davie, we'll be doing that in just over a week's time my bro. To Team O taking on the tennis world in Paris" Dov proposed.

"You go boys! Go smash them in Roland Garros!" Lionel shouted as they clinked their glasses together once more.

"Thanks Li, you'll be there right with us" said David to his old friend.

The lunch arrived shortly thereafter and was devoured hungrily by the group.

"Wow! I haven't had a feast like this for lunch for a long time, guys. The best part is to be included with all you amazing people. My family never do anything like this" said Michael.

"Well Father Michael, welcome to the looney tunes. David and Shakira are crazy doing what they doing, you and Leah hot on their heels and then Miriam and Lionel aren't what I would exactly describe as all there, either. I'm the only sane one here really if you think about it!" laughed Dov.

The entire group packed up laughing at the thought of Dov considering himself sane.

"Here's to my coach and general menace, Dov!" shouted David, standing up and toasting him.

"Dov, l'chaim" said David, clinking his glass with Dov's.

After lunch Leah suggested to Michael that they drop Dov, Michael and Lionel off and go have a late tea at the Jungle Garden Nursery in Sherwood. David and Shakira then dropped Miriam at her home and headed off to the beachfront apartment.

"This has been such an amazing day, from watching you play tennis to our lovely lunch. I would love a bit of an afternoon dip in the sea. What do you say Mr O?" asked Shakira.

"Let's do it!" said David

The ocean was picture-perfect and still warm after a long day of sun. The majority of beach goers who had flocked to the beach on the public holiday had left and the two of them had the beach mostly to themselves. The two of them frolicked together in the waves for about half an hour before walking back to the apartment.

"C'mon then, let's have a bubble bath, my darling" said Shakira who was already naked. David admired her slim, sexy body. Her skin was sun drenched from the day and was a bronzed olive colour.

David didn't need a second invitation and climbed into the bath full of scented bubbles next to her. They gently washed each other's bodies, building the anticipation for that which they both knew was coming. David picked her up in his arms and pulled a towel gently around them. He kissed her passionately and before they could even reach the bed he was inside her. She surprised him and flipped him off her and mounted him. Whilst delicately kissing his neck she rode him until they both came. She flopped next to him, out of breath but laughing.

"Was this the *rest* they were teasing us about earlier today?" she giggled in between breaths.

“I believe it was” he answered, pulling her into his arms.

They stayed holding each other for nearly two hours before it was time to take her home.

“Good luck with my mom tomorrow, my love. This is too perfect for us not to be together. We’ll talk tomorrow night when I get home from lectures” said Shakira, giving him one last kiss.

What a perfect end to a perfect day David thought as he watched her enter the giant electronic gates and wave at him.

Chapter 27

David was relieved he had eaten the full powerhouse breakfast Beverly had prepared for him that morning once he discovered Dr Berkowitz was his first lesson for the day.

"So, you do have it in you after all then, young man. I bet you didn't even know it was in you, right?" she laughed, lounging back in her chair.

"You are talking about yesterday's tennis I take it, Dr Berkowitz? I didn't notice you there" David replied.

"That's because I wasn't *there*" she chuckled.

"I don't understand then?" he asked, confused.

"David, those floodlights at the courts have high resolution cameras in and tape your practices. I watch the tapes later in the evening to analyse your attitude on the court and your body language" she explained.

"Ah, thanks for the explanation. *Now* I understand fully" laughed David.

"I really liked your positive body language and your ruthless mind set. I've analysed the mind set and body language of thousands of champion athletes, David. Although some may interpret it as arrogance I prefer to call it *chutzpah.* For instance your heroes Bjorn Borg and John McEnroe radiate a sense of supremacy and positivity from the moment they step on the court to the time they step off it. They are able to do it not because they are necessarily better athletes than their opponents, but because they have trained themselves to believe it. If you don't believe you can beat the opposition, you won't David, it's that simple. Your *mind* is your biggest weapon. Never forget that" she went on.

"Yes, Dr Berkowitz" he replied.

"Yesterday, you had a skip in your stride and everything about you screamed you were the big dog and positivity to me. You didn't feel sorry for them one bit and made it very clear that just because you are older than them that you were *not* going to give them an inch. That's what you are going to need on the pro tour because that's what your opponents will be giving you. What you did yesterday was also what we call compartmentalising your emotions. You separated your feelings of big brotherliness towards those kids from them being your opponents, your enemy. Today we are going to work on that further because you are going to need to separate your feelings for this girl from the inevitable guilt that will follow from spying on her family. If you don't, your work will be that much more difficult and you won't be as effective" she said.

"So are you ready David?" she asked.

"I'm ready doc" David replied.

Their session lasted 2 hours and by the time he left her office his head was swimming with all sorts of theories she had taught him. He was almost relieved to spend 2 hours learning elementary Arabic with Professor Noor.

Rubie then collected him and they travelled further underground to an incredible gymnasium with basketball court and a full complement of the most advanced gym equipment he had ever seen. The gymnasium was full of soldiers but the moment they entered everyone stopped what they were doing and saluted Rubie, which he returned, and they then returned to their exercises. David realised to the full extent just who Rubie was in the hierarchy of things in the IDF.

"OK *boychik,* I'm going to instruct you in Krav Maga. Let's move over to that mat in the corner out of everybody's way" ordered Rubie.

David looked around the giant hall and was impressed to see huge, ripped men doing some team drills.

"That's the Galani Brigade, the best of the best. They are training for a specific operation related to the work you will be doing back home" said Rubie.

"If there's a hijacking of any of our planes those are going to be the guys who go in to fix the problem. If we need a facility blown up in Iran it's them who we look to" he said.

"Well, I would hate to be *their* problem" laughed David.

"Rubie, shouldn't we be changing out of these though?" he asked, pointing to his military browns.

"Do you think your assailants are going to wait for you to change into your ninja outfit before attacking you?" laughed Rubie.

"We go as is!" instructed Rubie.

Rubie explained to David that the martial art of Krav Maga had been developed originally by a Hungarian-born Jew living in Bratislava, to defend his villagers from anti-Semitic attacks. He explained it as being a combination of aikido, karate, judo, boxing and wrestling and was passed on by him to the IDF specifically, but then later to civilians too.

"Look, we know you know how to throw a left hook so maybe we spend less time on the boxing!" joked Rubie.

David was relieved that after an hour of being thrown judo-style over Rubie's shoulder, on to what he considered a totally inadequate gym mat, and then nearly having his head knocked off his shoulders by his roundhouse kicks, Rubie called it quits.

"Enough for one day *boychik.* You did well" said Rubie.

"What do you mean? I did nothing but act as a ragged doll being thrown and kicked everywhere" said David.

"Yes, but you did *that* well is what I mean!" laughed Rubie.

"David, there's no tennis this afternoon. After lunch I'm taking you to Masada and we'll be meeting Moshe and the family there. It's important you see it" said Rubie.

They were joined for lunch in the cafeteria by Channah and Dr Berkowitz. He got to see the human side of Dr Berkowitz outside of her office and could see she was a lovely person. She told them about a special skiing holiday she was taking her 2 teenage grandchildren on later in the year to Switzerland.

"Do you ski yourself, Dr Berkowitz?" asked David, whilst munching on a delicious chicken salad and gluten-free roll.

"Oh yes, we all grew up skiing in winter in Europe. I definitely won't be skiing black slopes any longer like I did as a kid but I'll be OK on the gentle slopes" she laughed.

"These little old legs of mine aren't quite ready to be put out to pasture yet" she said.

She told David that her late parents had both been Holocaust escapees from Hungary/Poland and they had arrived in what was still the *Yishuv* in the early

1940's, when she was still a teenager knowing at best a few Yiddish words only.

She had completed her high schooling in Israel and then attended NYU, followed by postgraduate studies at Columbia. They had arrived penniless but her academic talents had been identified early on and her higher education studies at NYU had been sponsored by the Jewish Fund, until she was awarded scholarships to further her studies at Columbia. She had enjoyed her time studying in New York but always yearned for her true homeland where she wanted to contribute to and build the new fledgling nation. Rather than remain in academia or private practice, Mossad required her to immediately form a study program in the psychology of warfare and terror. This had then been her life for the better part of nearly fourty years and she was the leading expert in the field.

"Fortunately or unfortunately, I was in the perfect location with the subjects surrounding me so I had a big sample size to choose from" she laughed.

"I believe Rubie is taking you to meet Moshe and his family at Masada after lunch. A very special experience David. I remember taking my two grandsons there. We had an amazing picnic and watched the sun set" she said.

The drive from Tel Aviv to Masada took them a little over 2 hours but Channah joined them too and their conversations seemed to make the trip feel shorter. Channah, her siblings and her parents had all been born in Israel but her grandparents had escaped persecution in Poland. She had studied Medicine at Hebrew University and then specialised in anaesthetics in New York before returning home. David could tell how intelligent she was and was not surprised Mossad had recruited her after her first year of basic training in the IDF. She also proved to be an excellent tour guide and knew the history of the country exceptionally well as they passed towns and villages, the names of which David recognised, but knew very little about. He could see a small grin appear on Dov's face as Channah became ever more animated in describing their histories. He had heard her give this commentary before but not nearly as animated or with such passion.

Just after a sign for the Arab Bedouin city of Rahat, Rubie took a turn-off to a petrol stop which was full of tourist buses.

"Sorry guys, but this old man's bladder is nearly bursting. Let's have a fifteen minute toilet break before Masada" announced Rubie.

David went inside the convenience store to load up on some beverages for them. He overheard a bunch of grumpy old Americans complaining that they weren't going to be able to have a sunset on Masada because of apparent maintenance work announced late that afternoon.

After a quick break they were back on the road again, sipping on cool drinks.

"Rubie, I overheard some Yanks back there going on about Masada being closed for maintenance this afternoon?" asked David.

"Yes that's true, we closed it so we can *maintain* your love of your people!" Rubie barked out, making them laugh.

"Rubie, you are the reason people hate us" joked David.

"David, this is how important you are to us. You *are* us" Channah said, looking intently at him now.

Within half an hour they had arrived at the Masada National Park and David could see Moshe and his family waving to them. Except for a handful of armed IDF soldiers the place was abandoned and eerily quiet, considering it was Israel's second most visited site.

"Shalom David, Channah and Rubie! A special welcome to Masada for you David" said Moshe, giving him a big bear hug.

"We are not hiking but going up with the cable car. We want to have some sundowners up there so let's move" instructed Moshe.

Once they had summited Moshe led the party to the western side passed the last of the Roman ruins which had been excavated. On the way Moshe explained how 960 Sicarii Jews, an offshoot of the Zealots, had taken refuge from the Romans after the fall of the Temple in 70 AD. Rather than submit to Roman rule they had eventually 3 years later taken their own lives. The only survivors were 2 women and 5 children.

"David, in spite of all these civilizations trying to take our freedom away, *we* have outlived them, outwitted them and survived them all. They are still trying to obliterate us David! Hitler murdered nearly half our people but we beat him and today the children of Abraham and Moses have multiplied and thrived. We can only do that by every single one of us, wherever in the world we are, understanding Israel will be our last stand, our modern day Masada. For your people David, our people, to survive we have to protect Israel at all costs" explained Moshe.

As they got closer to the western edge of the fortress and with the sun quickly falling closer to the horizon, David could see that a small group of IDF soldiers had prepared a small bonfire and were grilling food for them. They had laid a beautiful table for them to eat on as well as a table of drinks. The skyline was a beautiful shade of pinks and purples as the sun was setting and Moshe used the opportunity to pull the group together, including the soldiers. He looked at David intently and began a special prayer asking *HaShem* to bless the Jewish people and their land of Israel. He also said a blessing for David and his family and for *HaShem* to shower them with good health. Finally he asked for David to be blessed with great success in his tennis career.

"*Amein*!" the group shouted.

"*Baruch HaShem*!" David shouted.

David couldn't help notice Channah smiling at him but with tears streaming down both cheeks.

"Thank you, David!" she said unexpectedly, throwing her arms around him and giving him a hug.

Whilst watching the last of the sun set and answering a million questions fired at him by Moshe's boys, David could not help but feel an incredible closeness and love for these people. They were right about one thing. He was one of them. They were *his* people. He also at that moment felt how deeply he was missing Shakira and wished she was with him, laughing and joking around the crackling bonfire.

The dinner the IDF guys had cooked up was outstanding and David ended up wolfing down 2 steaks he was so hungry. For non-South Africans he was rather impressed with their *braaing* abilities and told Beverly as much.

"Well, that's because they are all from ex South African families!" she laughed.

"That certainly explains it then" said David.

"David, we have one last surprise tonight for you and you can thank the boys for this one, and the fact that it's a full moon. You are going to have a swim in the Dead Sea under the light of the moon" said Moshe.

"Oh wow, that's just awesome!" said David, with genuine excitement.

"Hopefully it helps my body heal after the number of judo throws Rubie performed on me" said David to a grinning Rubie.

After dessert and after thanking the IDF boys for the delicious meal, they descended in the rickety cable car and headed over to one of the Dead Sea beaches. The boys were first in, running and screaming as they ran into the salty water. The water was surprisingly warm and well-lit under the full moon.

Floating on his back in the water, looking up at a star-filled sky, David wondered how many ancestors of his had done the same thing over the centuries. He decided there and then that when he returned to Durban he would do a family tree to see how many generations back he could get to. It would be interesting to manage to trace back to his last living Israeli relative to see where in this magical land they had lived. Were they forced into exile or had they left voluntarily, looking for greener pastures? Had they been carpenters, traders, fishermen or maybe scholars or rabbis? How he would love to hear their stories he thought.

"Moshe, how far have you been able to trace your family roots back to?" asked David.

"Funny you should ask that as I have had the genetics and genealogy guys looking into that the last year or so. They have uncovered through my father's side that I have a direct lineage to King David" he answered.

"That's incredible, Moshe!" exclaimed David.

"Being such a small gene pool and a scholarly nation our family trees are not as challenging to put together compared to others, because a lot of our history was written down" said Moshe.

"Would you like me to ask them to look into yours for you? It's often quite fascinating to see who we are related to" he asked.

"I would love that but it seems a bit unfair to ask someone to do that for me" said David.

"No it isn't. You are Mossad now and information is our game so it's no problem for them. I'll tell them to get started tomorrow" said Moshe.

"Thank you so much, Moshe. I'm very curious to learn that history because so much of it was destroyed during the *Shoah"* said David.

"The exile of our people from our homeland is a fascinating journey my friend. They don't refer to us as "Wandering Jews" for nothing. What warms my heart though is the number of *olim* returning to their homeland from all parts of the world, both young and old. They are often highly skilled like so many of the Russian *olim* who brought with them technical scientific and mathematical skills. Then we had young Israeli-born ones like Channah who went abroad to study and returned having learnt skills from the West. I think we now have some of the smartest tech and medical scientists in the world. These stars are not only uplifting our nation but sharing their inventions to help the whole planet. You would no doubt have noticed all the development that is happening all around you in our beautiful little land. If we can just convince the Arabs to recognise us as a legitimate state they will benefit so much for our expertise. Don't forget *boychik* we have achieved all this without a drop of oil or water" said Moshe.

"Yes, Israel is a miracle land, a beautiful country of our people. It has to succeed for the world's sake" remarked David.

"And yet the rest of the world, except a handful of countries, don't understand that" said Moshe, with a note of sadness in his voice.

"Well, my home country is also going through major strife and changes now. Soon Apartheid will come to an end. The business sanctions are in the process of crippling our economy and we are just too isolated to continue with all these obstacles. White South African parents are also sick of sending their young sons off to the army to fight a silly war for nothing. It is inevitable that change has to come and the country will be ruled one day by Mandela and his ANC party. My Uncle Sol started moving his capital out to both here and the US years ago because he knew this day was coming. He told me that a man must never sleep where his money is. I'm not sure exactly where but he has bought property on the Tel Aviv beachfront just in case we need to flee" laughed David.

"History proves to us that the world and life is not static, David. If nothing else the *Shoah* proved never to get too comfortable. That can be a very dangerous thing for Jews" warned Moshe.

"David, what is important is that you uncover the source and manner these funds are managing to leave South Africa for these terrorist scum to buy weapons to kill our people. We had a report from a kibbutz in the south, close to Gaza, of terrorists shooting a bunch of kids who were playing soccer outside. Can you imagine killing innocent kids like that, David? Imagine how you would feel if they were your family?" asked Moshe angrily.

"I abhor violence but I would track them down and kill them!" replied David.

"Well, we did that, yes! But we have to stop this continual violence at some point. We have to make peace. We cannot keep on killing each other generation after generation. This isn't a solution. Violence only begets more violence" said Moshe.

"Yip, a political solution is the right answer but do the Arabs really want that?" asked David.

"Only time will tell, *boychik*" replied Moshe.

David lay back in the salty water staring at the starry sky above. He longed for the day when he could bring Shakira to this amazing land and float in the Dead Sea in peace. One day he thought.

Chapter 28

After a restless night of very little sleep David waited patiently for Zara Mahomedy's arrival in the Musgrave Centre library. He had arrived 15 minutes early armed with a box of the Turkish delights he had bought in Dubai, as well as a bunch of pretty flowers. He was hoping they would at least create a good first impression for him. Except for a few old ladies sitting in the front reading, the library was deserted.

At 9:55 a.m. exactly David looked up and noticed a very attractive lady with a black headscarf approaching him. As she got closer she smiled at him and gave a small wave of acknowledgement. David stood and extended a hand to greet Zara Mahomedy.

"Hi Mrs Mahomedy! I'm David and it's really nice to meet you" he said as she shook his hand.

"Hello David! Thanks for meeting with me like this and please call me Zara" she said in her perfect English.

"Well, firstly I brought a little something for you. I was playing in Dubai recently and Shakira said these were your favourite" said David, passing the Turkish delights and flowers to her. He also noticed she was wearing the same Calvin Klein perfume her daughter liked.

"Yes, these are absolutely my favourites. Thanks so much!" she said, appreciatively.

"There's a little balcony outside over there which is a really private place to chat, David. Should we go sit there" she said pointing to a door on the side that David hadn't noticed.

Once seated outside Zara decided to take the lead.

"David, I'm sure Shakira has told you that we are a close family. A Muslim family, although my side is quite secular as opposed to Ismail's, who are religious. My daughter has explained that you are from a secular Jewish home and consider yourself only culturally Jewish. To me this is all far less important than you being good to our Shakira. She's a very special child because after Mohamed was born I was advised by my gynaecologist that I wouldn't be able to conceive again. Then out of the blue a few years later I fell pregnant with her. She is a very special little girl to the both of us and especially to my husband. I'm sure you are aware that she is a very, very talented girl too and Ismail has earmarked her to run his extensive business one day. Now my husband has Jewish business associates right from his early business years and we have also become friends with many of them, but for Shakira to be dating a Jewish boy is another thing altogether. In our culture you only date with the intention of marrying that person, not just for fun. These last few months I could see how happy someone was making Shakira but the last person I expected it to be was a Jewish boy. No offense David because neither Ismail nor I have anything against Jews, please.

Shakira is totally in love with you and she has told me how good you are to her. I can see just having met you that you are a kind and thoughtful, young man. When I explained some of the challenges involved in mixed race and mixed religion relationships she told me outright she doesn't care and will not under any circumstances break it off. She wants you to come home and meet the family which is a really big thing. Before I can agree to that I will have to get my husband's approval but before I even do that I need to know that your family will do the same for my daughter. I'm not going to disrupt my husband's life if your family is not willing to accept my daughter's place in your life" she ended.

Whilst she was explaining all this to David he couldn't believe how closely she resembled an exact older version of Shakira with the same high cheekbones, beautiful green eyes and soft olive skin. She was also beautifully dressed in what looked an expensive, suit-type outfit. She was also well spoken.

"Zara before answering, I just have to say how you are the same beautiful carbon copy of Shakira. I feel I could be talking to her in thirty years just listening to you talking!" David said.

"Yes, that's what everybody says when they meet the two of us" she laughed.

"I'm head-over-heals in love with your daughter. I've never had that before whether it was with Jewish girls or others. We especially waited 6 months before committing to each other and within that time we have either seen or spoken with each other every day including on my overseas trips on the tour. I don't think I could live without your daughter and my parents will understand that when they meet Shakira. I want her and your family to come to my family's home to experience *Shabbat* with us on my return from playing the French Open. I believe our love can overcome these obstacles. I can understand how religion can be too big an obstacle to overcome for some, but I don't think that would be the case here. Your daughter has met my religious sister Leah recently and they are now non-stop chatting with each other. I'm not so sure that's necessarily a smart move by me, by the way" he joked.

"Yes, Shakira has spoken to me about your brilliant sister as well as your very smart father who many of my book club ladies also know. Many of them follow tennis too and have wonderful things to say about you and how you could be the next great South African tennis player after Kevin Curren" she said.

"I'll tell you after the French Open" David laughed.

"Please Zara, speak to your husband, I beg you. I can assure you it will not be an issue for my family, they are very open-minded Jews. Shakira and I are tired of sneaking about having to hide our relationship. Next year my father has told me from his friends in the ANC leadership that Mandela will be released and the Apartheid laws will be repealed so the race thing will no longer apply. In any case Shakira looks foreign like you and nobody has ever questioned us about it" said David.

Zara looked at him directly for quite some time before replying.

"David, if I do this you need to promise me you will never hurt my Shakira and protect her from anything and everything. She and Mo are my world. They are everything to Ismail and me" she asked, now with tears in her eyes.

"You have my word, my promise. There is nothing I will not do to make sure she is safe and loved. I promise that to you" said David, quietly and sincerely to her.

"Alright then. I'll talk to Ismail for you two. I also want you to know David, and I'm going to trust you not to share with anyone beyond us, including Shakira, that I know about her heartache with that Rothschild boy in Paris. I don't want to see her go through that heartache again which she tried to hide from everyone. Now you may understand some of what I'm telling you and why" she explained.

"This won't be shared with anyone else and I am so touched at your love and care to protect your daughter. I could never hurt somebody I love so much" he replied.

“I see that and it’s the only reason why I am agreeing to this. You two aren’t the only ones who have faced religious issues in your lives by the way” she said with a small smile on her face.

“Ironically, Ismail has already mentioned your name a few times to us, including last week with those photos of you in the newspapers. Shakira and I had a good laugh to ourselves over it, truth be told” she chuckled.

“Well I really hope he feels the same way about David Oppenheim when you break the news to him. Shakira told me on our first date that if he found out he would hunt me down and shoot me!” David laughed, causing her to laugh too.

“Ismail’s bark is far worse than his bite I promise you. He simply adores us and always gives in to his girls, eventually. He is the kindest, most honourable man I know. I am proud to be his wife and Shakira is proud to be his daughter, David” she said.

“Anyway, enough serious stuff. I want to hear about some tennis gossip so I can impress the ladies at my book club next week” she laughed.

David spent the better part of an hour telling Zara about his progress over the previous 6 months on the tough Challenger tour. He told her quite a bit about his ongoing rivalry with Lionel Perreira from their first meeting all those years ago in the Coca Cola final at Westridge. He even spent some time telling her about his family’s European history and how many of them had not been so fortunate to escape the Holocaust.

She in turn spoke about her wonderful upbringing in Iran before the Revolution and having to flee, and her special years in Paris. She spoke about how much she missed her home when they were forced to move to Durban and how difficult it was to break into and be accepted by the local Muslim community. She was surprised when she was readily accepted by her white colleagues at the University of Durban-Westville, where she had lectured for a while. It was only when she had married Ismail had her own community in fact accepted her and her family.

She also spoke how her son have driven her up the wall with all his naughty pranks but her parents had reminded her that she had also been a prankster when she was little. She expressed her pride that Mo had not relied on his rich daddy for an income but had gone out on his own and was doing very well for himself. She was looking forward to him settling down though and marrying a nice girl from a good family and giving her grandchildren.

“I have to tell you, Zara, that my conversation with you is as easy-going as my chats with Shakira. On our first date we spoke non-stop for nearly 3 hours like we had known each other forever. I feel the same with you. I think it’s because you are so worldly and obviously well-travelled” said David.

“Ha Ha! You could very well be right about that David and I feel the same way about you. Most importantly I can feel you love our daughter as much as Ismail and I do. Mo is also very close to her and is the model of a protective big brother. He holds no jealousy in his heart towards her that she is being groomed to be Ismail’s successor in the business. You will need to meet him after I’ve broken the news to Ismail. He believes in and trusts his sister implicitly so if she’s chosen you, it will be for the right reasons and he will respect that. You are lucky because I wouldn’t like to get on his wrong side!” she joked.

“There is one last thing I would like to touch on but I don’t want to make a big deal out of it” said David.

“What is it?” she asked.

“Shakira and I discussed the obvious Muslim-Jewish thing right from our first date. I did explain that my family, except for Leah, are secular but we are pro-Israel but not in an aggressive manner at all. Shakira said your husband is very pro-Palestinian which I fully respect, and that he tries to help them financially which I have no issue with either. I just would hate it to become an issue when it doesn’t need to be” said David.

“Yes, Ismail has been to both Gaza, the West Bank and Israel a few times and has developed relationships with some Muslim aid agencies whom he tries to support. He feels terrible, especially for the Palestinians kids who have been orphaned and don’t have access to decent health facilities or educational institutions. It’s not an anti-Jewish thing at all, David. It’s not like he is helping any of the terror groups like Hamas or Hezbollah, I can assure you. Like me Ismail abhors violence and wants to see a peaceful solution between Arabs and Jews so they can peacefully co-exist again. Having said that I don’t know how much longer he will continue this philanthropy because just like whenever money is involved, there’s potential for abuse” she sighed.

David was hoping she would elaborate on these abuses which seemed to tie up with Shakira's story but she didn't.

"Well I'm glad we've had an opportunity to get this sticky one out the way because I don't want it to become an issue where there is none. I admire your husband for caring for the poor Palestinian kids and if I had his wealth I would like to think I would do the same for them. Hopefully one day" he chuckled.

"Thank you David. Ismail is a very good man. His trips to the Middle East have brought him closer to God in his later life and he wants to be a better person. I wish my kids and I were on the same level as him but they are secular like my family and are happy to be at that level for now. He told me that one of his most special times was praying at the Al Aqsa mosque and then watching Jews praying at the Wailing Wall in Jerusalem. He said something quite profound and what I truly hope is prophetic. He said for the first time, first cousins were praying for the same thing for the land, just a couple of metres apart. Both were praying for peace in the land!" she exclaimed.

"Wow! That's quite surreal. I really hope that comes to be. Imagine that? It would be like the ancient days when Arabs and Jews lived peacefully together in the Holy Land" replied David.

"As we Muslims say, Alhamdulillah" she said.

"*Baruch HaShem* as my tribe say!" said David, which had them both laughing.

"So I believe you fly to Paris over the weekend to start your French Open preparations, Shakira tells me. I hear your family and your friend Lionel are traveling there with you. I think that's lovely for you" she said.

"Yes and I hope in the not-so-distant future you and your family will be able to join us to watch me play at one of the majors" he replied.

"Well, try your best to make it Wimbledon please! I love strawberries and cream ... and Pimm's but don't tell Ismail that" she joked.

"David, it's been so lovely meeting you. You are a fine young man. My daughter has impeccable taste! Thank you so much for these lovely gifts too but I'm already late for another engagement so I need to make tracks" she said, getting up and extending her hand.

David obliged and took her hand in both of his and kissed it gently.

"Thank you so much for being nice to me, Zara. You are lovely just like your daughter" responded David.

After she had left, David sat back and relaxed. It had gone splendidly with Zara, much better than he had expected. He could hardly wait to tell Shakira later that afternoon but even more so to tell Dov that Ismail Mahomedy's money was in all likelihood not going to the charities for purposes he intended it to be used for. His girlfriend's father wasn't Mossad's man, whatever the chatter they were picking up was. Whatever his donations were being used for his only intention was for it to be used to help the destitute children of Gaza. David decided whatever it was going to take he was going to uncover who was involved in intercepting the funds for terrorism.

Chapter 29

The drive back to Moshe and Beverly's home took the better part of 2 hours in the dark. Both boys were so exhausted from the afternoon's activities that it didn't take them long to fall asleep in the back of the car, lying all over poor David. He wondered to himself if he and Shakira would have children together one day and whether they would be sons or daughters or both. As much as he was enjoying his experiences in Israel he was starting to miss her and his family. He was missing his Durban with all its bumps and bruises.

David's human alarm clock woke him at 6 a.m. that morning but it took a lot of tickling from him before the boys finally dragged themselves out of bed.

"David, dad says this afternoon he has a special surprise for you and we will get to ball boy again" said Avi.

"Oh yes, and who or what is this surprise, then?" asked David.

"I asked dad the same question but he said if he told me it would no longer be a surprise" replied Avi to much laughter.

David had really enjoyed a day's break from the tennis and the salt water had massaged his stiff muscles, including the ones in his back from Rubie's judo throws. His mind was also refreshed from the fresh air on top of Masada and he managed an early telephone call with Shakira that morning. Her voice was like a breath of fresh air and gave him sustenance for the last days he had ahead of him in Israel. She said that the accounting work she was doing for one of her father's businesses was keeping her busy but not busy enough to be missing him. She also told him that she had managed to source a Japanese pressing of a Lloyd Cole & The Commotions, which she knew he would love, as well as an out-of-print Led Zeppelin album. David chuckled, thinking that no Jewish girl he knew would ever get excited about Led Zeppelin. She was definitely his match, he smiled.

David told her about his trip to Masada with his "host family" and just how much he wished she had been with them.

"One day my angel, I will bring you with me to this amazing land and introduce you to these beautiful people. They are so kind and generous with their hearts I cannot explain" he had told her.

"I'm counting the days and hours now until you are back home with me, my Mr O. I can't be without you for so long. I'm going to have to travel with you during my varsity vacations next year" she said.

"Well, I only have a few days of practice left and then I'll be home, but I just wanted to tell you I thought of you so much last night on Masada and wished you were with us. You would have loved it so much and the dip in the Dead Sea afterwards. I was absolutely caked in salt and took about 20 minutes under the shower getting it off me" he laughed.

"When you take me there we'll have to go skinny dipping" she teased.

"That's it, I'm booking a trip for us today first thing!" he laughed.

The morning's lessons then seemed to fly by, even the second lesson of Krav Maga with Rubie who instructed David how to defend himself best if attacked, beyond just administering a good left hook. Before he knew it David was back in the car blindfolded and en-route to his afternoon of tennis at the Tel Aviv Country Club. He was curious as to the surprise the boys had mentioned earlier that morning.

He *was* surprised when he arrived at the courts to see nobody there and expressed his surprise to Rubie.

"Well *this,* is definitely an unexpected surprise!" he exclaimed.

Rubie ordered him to sit at a covered table which David duly followed. He suddenly felt something tugging at his shoe and put his hand down to feel what was doing it. He could feel nothing. When he felt it a second time he bent down to look under the tablecloth and to his shock came face-to-face with Dov's laughing face.

"Surprise!" shouted Dov, killing himself with laughter and full of smiles.

"You cheeky bugger you!" shouted David, whilst pulling his friend from under the table.

"You miss me, Davie?!" he guffawed whilst giving his protégé a massive bear hug.

"I hate to admit it but yes, maybe just a little" laughed David.

"*Shalom* Rubie!" laughed Dov, giving him a hug.

"Ah, here are Moshe and the boys with your other surprise" said Rubie, pointing at them.

"Is that who I think it is walking with them?" asked David, looking at a short, stocky, Israeli in tennis kit.

"Yip, I got you Amos after I heard you were smashing the juniors up. I can't have you not having proper competition to practice with" boasted Dov.

"You mean, *we,* got Amos" laughed Rubie, winking at David but by then Dov had already moved on to greet them.

"David, I've been watching your progress from a distance. It's really nice to meet you" said Amos, in a thick Israeli accent.

"The pleasure is all mine. I watched you win the SA Open a few years back in Jo'burg when I was still playing juniors and followed you and Shlomo throughout your careers too" replied David, shaking Amos's hand firmly.

"I have a dream to follow your path if I'm fortunate enough and make the top twenty in the world rankings like you" replied David.

"Ah *mazel tov,* I see Dr Berkowitz is succeeding with your positivity too" laughed Amos.

"Well, both Moshe and Rubie explained to me that you have been annihilating our two top juniors, so I've offered my services for the next few days. I'm getting a bit old so go easy on me please!" he joked.

"I'm so touched you would come out of semi-retirement to help me, Amos. I believe I will follow a similar journey to yours on the tour if I get really lucky so honestly there's nobody better to learn from than you. If I didn't have such an experienced coach already in Dov, I would have offered you the position" David said, with a twinkle in his eyes.

"Best you don't forget that either *boychik*!" barked Dov, which had everybody in laughter.

David noticed for the first time that Moshe's two youngsters were glued to every word that came from Amos now, rather than him. He had been supplanted by the older Jewish statesman of tennis already, he chuckled. One day you king, next day you peasant again. That was the tennis world, he thought.

"Amos please, whatever shortcomings with my game or advice you can give me will be greatly appreciated. I need every bit of help for the tour. I've played a couple of events on the Challenger already and those kids are tough. Jesus, even the teenagers want to kill you!" laughed David.

"David, unlike you who has had a relatively privileged upbringing in white South Africa with a good education, some of these kids literally have nothing besides tennis. Some of them have been born in the favelas of Brazil or Argentina, the slums of Delhi and some of the Africans, even worse. You are the obstacle between them escaping that life or remaining stuck in misery and poverty. If it means killing themselves to beat you, they will do it" explained Amos.

"I have watched your game and it's a good one for sure, but I've seen many talented David Oppenheim's not make it on the tour. They either didn't travel well and missed home too much, came from wealthy homes so lacked the necessary hunger or just burnt themselves out because they weren't well managed. My question is, who are you David? Do you have the hunger? Do you have the killer instinct which enables you to clinch the big points in a match? Do you have the tenacity to come back from 2 sets down to win in 5 sets? Does this mean enough to you to make the necessary sacrifices required to break into the top one-hundred, or even the top twenty, where you become a threat to all players at a major. And then ultimately, do you believe you belong amongst the best? That's what I need to understand about you, my friend" explained Amos.

Before he could even think of answering, Dov said in a steely voice, "Listen old man, my kid has got all of that in spades and if you don't mind to stop *hakking* so much, he'll show you how to break into the top ten. Let's get playing now!"

There was an awkward moment's silence before they all burst out laughing. All of them except for Dov who was now looking seriously at David without the slightest hint of a smile on his face. It filled David with pride because at that very moment he saw something in himself that until then, only Dov had already seen. He *did* belong in the top handful of players in the world. He understood that now. Little did he know that this would not be the last time Dov's words would motivate and calm him in times when doubting himself.

Dov's confidence in him put a real spring in his step and he played with a freedom few professionals display. Dov was quite correct. He **was** a top tenner for sure. Amos may have been a former top twenty player and had the experience to show, but he was no contest for a young man who was fast reaching his prime. David showed no signs of letting up as he smashed balls to all parts of the court, destroying his opponent's second serve just like some of the young kids had done to his before Clive had improved it.

Amos was still in tip-top physical shape and pressed David as hard as he could. It was in vain though as David romped through a first set, losing only two games in the process. The second set was an ever bigger disaster for Amos with David unleashing such a variety of strokes that Amos could literally not find any sort of rhythm. Amos was fortunate the set didn't end in bagel but he managed to hold his service, once. David almost felt sorry for his opponent, especially with Dov shouting things like, "kill him now David" and, "step up your level David", on the sidelines. In fact, there was nothing that was going to wipe the smile off Dov's face. He had never seen David looking so supremely confident. A real sense of *chutzpah* that only champions seem to possess. He knew he had managed to get David to another level mentally. Dr Berkowitz, Shmerkowitz, thought Dov, smiling incessantly.

"Very, very good my friend. I can't remember losing that badly in a long time!" laughed Amos, whose face was as red as a beetroot from all the scrambling David had forced him to do.

"Of course. We've been working really hard in Durban the last few weeks. You know, us spoilt white South African boys, I mean!" Dov barked at Amos.

Amos saw the humour in it and laughed back.

"David, I won't be able to compete with you but I will be able to teach you a few things about tactics and other things, like for instance travelling, etcetera on the tour. Dov, I take it you will be handling the back office things like traveling arrangements, booking courts and practice times, David's diet, etcetera?" asked Amos.

"I am the front office, back office and every other fucking office for Team Oppenheim!" shouted Dov to Amos's amusement.

"But I would appreciate any input you can share, Amos" he said.

"Well, Amos is coming for a South African dinner of lamb chops and boerewors at us tonight Dov, so you guys can chat there" said Moshe, who had been watching from the sides of the court with Dov.

"David, whatever change is happening within you is incredible to watch. We all thought you may lack the killer instinct to progress far in the professional tennis world, but you have proved me, us, wrong. To be honest and to his credit only, Dov saw this in you" he said. motioning to Dov.

"I never doubted *my* Davie for one fucking second!" said Dov, grinning like a Cheshire cat.

Dov was just so full of surprises thought David. Maybe he had underrated the level required of playing B team tennis at King David.

Chapter 30

It was lunch time and David flew in The Green Mamba to meet Shakira at the SU. She was waiting for him on tenterhooks and had taken in absolutely nothing during her morning lectures.

As he walked into the SU and she saw the big smile on his face, she suddenly relaxed.

"You were right about your mom, my darling. I think she really likes me!" he said, as she jumped on to him.

"I told you it would work out well for us with her! I knew you would charm her by just being yourself. What exactly did she say? Tell me everything please" she begged.

They left the SU and went to Shepstone Gardens where it was more private.

David gave her a rundown of his conversation with Zara Mahomedy.

"It was kind of freaky speaking to her though. You are her spitting image and I felt like I was talking to you in your early 50's. She even talks just like you. Your mom is a very beautiful, classy lady, for sure" said David.

"She loves you very deeply and just wanted to make sure that this Jewish hoodlum will take good care of her daughter otherwise her husband and son will sort me out" laughed David.

"She said whaaaaat?!" asked Shakira, shocked.

"Got you! I was just kidding about the last part but she does love you very much" he replied.

"You kidder, you! Come on now though, what else did she say David?" she pressed.

"Before speaking to your father she wanted to make sure with me that my parents would be accepting of you, which I told her they would be. I even said that I would like to invite your whole family for *Shabbat* at some point, which I think made a big impression with her. We then spoke openly for at least an hour about my tennis, her earlier upbringing in Iran, a bit about your prankster brother, as well as a bit about Israel and Palestine. Your mom was saying how much your dad was donating to children's charity causes in Gaza but that he may stop because the money doesn't seem to be reaching the right people?"

"Wow! She even told you about that?" she said.

"Yes, doesn't sound like a good thing money not reaching the kids it's meant to help. Who would do such an awful thing?" David asked, shaking his head.

"You right and my dad is furious about it. You know sometimes it's the ones closest to us that turn out to be the biggest disappointment."

"Well, I hope you don't mean me?" said David.

"No of course not, don't be silly. I mean my dad's cousin who is in charge of the main charity. My dad suspects he may be siphoning those funds off for his own personal use. My father is doing his own investigations now but being a family thing it's super delicate because it could affect family relationships" she explained.

"Oh boy, I can only imagine because over the years we've had lots of family *faribels* and it never ends well. What annoys me is that here's your father doing such a charitable thing and others are taking advantage of his kindness" sympathised David.

"Well, they picked on the wrong donor to mess with because when my dad uncovers the truth there's going to be hell to pay, I promise you. My father is nobody's fool" she chuckled.

"Anyway, what else did she say?" asked Shakira.

"She said that because I clearly loved you with all my heart and because I swore to her that I would protect you and never hurt you, would she would talk to your father" he said.

"Oh thank god, David! She will get through to him, don't worry" smiled Shakira.

"I'm sure while you are at the French Open she will tell him. Then it's up to you to break it to your folks. Just imagine, no more sneaking around having to tell white lies. I can't wait to tell everyone you're mine!" she shouted.

"OK, now it's time for lectures young lady. You've had enough excitement for one day. Go study now, OK! I'll call you tomorrow. I have a practice session with Lionel this afternoon but I'll call you tomorrow and we'll go do something with Leah and Michael. Michael says he's got one or two suggestions for me after watching Figueras's tapes. That kid is a smart one. Must have some Jewish blood somewhere" laughed David.

"OK, my darling. Well done with my mom. I can't wait to chat to her about you later. Say hi to Lionel and Dov and call me tomorrow, please. I love you" she said, jumping into his arms again and planting a juicy kiss on his lips.

They parted company and David headed off to collect Dov for their afternoon session. His coach was ready waiting outside for him.

"Ready for a good workout this afternoon, Davie?"

"Sure thing, but before then I have *very* important intel for you. I met with Zara Mahomedy this morning in the Musgrave Library about seeing her daughter. During our conversation she mentioned about donations her husband has been making to a children's agency being diverted to other causes. He's even thinking about cutting his funding, she told me. Then I met up with Shakira afterwards at varsity to fill her in on our conversation. I mentioned that her mother had told me about this unfortunate situation and she told me her father suspects it's some cousin of her father who is misappropriating the cash for his own purposes. Ismail is now carrying out his own investigations to uncover who is behind this. They gave no reason to make me feel they are not telling the truth and I think the agency need to find out who is behind this and expose them to the father. It sounds like he's really pissed off and will handle them himself. That way none of us are involved and we can stop the flow of funds to these scumbags. Everything inside me tells me the father is a decent human being. I think he's been deceived into something he had no intentions of supporting. This has nothing to do with the way I feel about Shakira, Dov. They are *good* people. The mother is a very classy lady and you can see the type of person Shakira is. She's the product of good people" David explained.

"This is amazing news, Davie, but are you *one-hundred percent* sure? What about the photos of him with those Hamas thugs and the fact he's become a lot more religious, and looks more like Prophet Muhammed than Businessman Ismail?" asked Dov.

"I thought about that on the drive here. Firstly, Zara said that his trips to the Middle East have caused him to become more religious which explains his physical transformation and secondly, I went up to the Economics Society and took another look at *that* photo, and he doesn't look very happy to be in that picture. Take another look at it yourself. In fact, I think, after *that* photo he realised his money was being spent on arms rather than food and nappies for poor Palestinian kids. I don't know *how* he's schlepping the cash out of South Africa but I'm going to ask my Uncle Sol, without arousing his suspicions. If there's a better *smokkelaar* in this country, I doubt it. He managed to schlepp a lot of his business profits out of here to buy properties in Tel Aviv. My mom says he has property in California too" laughed David.

"What you are saying makes a lot of sense, bro. I'll let Moshe know tonight and let them check out your theory. It would be good to get the father's cousin's name but maybe Mossad intelligence can get that for us. In the meantime see if you can coax that info out of your uncle. That will give us a place to find the source of funds and maybe his method of schlepping it outside the country. I think it may look legit on the surface but if you scratch deeper you're bound to find something" replied Dov.

"I hope you've uncovered the truth Davie because I really like Shakira, and the father actually sounds like a *mensch* for his philanthropy, and besides, I like you two as a couple. I think, as your friend now and not your coach or handler, that she's good for you but that's *strictly* between us two" said Dov.

"Thanks Dov. I do appreciate your friendship and you've actually surprised me how quickly you are adjusting to the tennis world. You have been good for my tennis" said David.

"OK, OK, let's not get too soft now. We have lots to accomplish starting with your opening match against Figueras" barked Dov.

They arrived at Mitchell as Lionel was arriving. He had a surprise for David in the form of Clive Jaikins, his favourite coach from his teenage years.

"Hello son, Lionel phoned me to invite me to watch one of your practice sessions. I also saw you chaps in the paper the other morning so I thought I would drop by to check on you!" laughed Clive.

David gave Clive a hug. He was suffering with cancer and he had thought of inviting him but then changed his mind, not wanting to bother him with the fight he had on his hands.

"Clive, please meet Dov Mendelson. He's taking care of me these days on the tour" said David.

"It's such a pleasure to meet you, Clive. David has spoken about you so many times now and how you shaped his game into to what it is today. Any help you can give us before the French will be invaluable" said Dov, humbly shaking Clive's hand.

"Well, I'm only too happy to watch them play and add my 5 cents worth where possible. All I can say is how proud I am of both these young men. I've watched them develop from kids into the fine men they are today" said Clive.

"Thank you Clive for all you gave me as a kid. I would never be the player I am today without your coaching in my earlier years or for the help you gave me with my serve and returns last year. You can ask Lionel the difference it has made to my game"

"Ja, thanks for *nothing* Clive! He's used that to smash me 3 love our last couple practice matches" chuckled Lionel.

"I look forward to seeing more of that so you guys get playing, whilst I chat with Dov for a bit then. If I see anything I'll let you know after" replied Clive.

Whilst knocking up David thought how strange it was having both his previous coach and his current one watching. He also felt so good about the way things had gone that morning with Zara Mahomedy and the information about Ismail. It was time to flex his muscles on the court and put all the efforts he had put into his game the last few months into action.

Try as hard as he could Lionel felt himself always a foot behind David, especially on the big points. There was a certain mental toughness that his friend had developed that he hadn't seen before. It was like he had an inner strength and belief that radiated from his psyche. Without saying as much he radiated an air of almost arrogance although it wasn't quite that, just an inner confidence. It said, "I know I'm better than you – just watch me", and Lionel wanted that too. It didn't matter how hard one trained. It was mental.

Once again, the two young men put on a show for the crowd that had slowly gathered around the 2 coaches. After the first set, which David clinched 6-4, he glanced up to see Dov beaming and trying to explain something or other to Clive, who was also smiling and nodding in agreement. It didn't take Dov long to rope in a few adults to act as back court ball people. They seemed to be loving it, with prime seats.

The second set was a little closer but with even better tennis than the first. The crowd seemed to be enthralled and David hit out freely, in full control of his game and his emotions. As hard as Lionel chased him it was obvious that he still needed work to be done to catch David. The end came for Lionel with a signature Oppenheim topspin cross-court forehand pass off a very nifty first serve slider which David had read. The crowd stood in appreciation and gave both players a standing ovation for the spectacle they had put on for them. David particularly enjoyed seeing Dov and Clive standing amongst them and clapping too. Both players acknowledged the crowd before towelling themselves off.

"I'm getting a bit pissed off losing all these practice games to you, *china*! I really hope Clive has some tips for me" said Lionel, giving his opponent a gentle swat with his racket on the *tuches*.

"It's in your mind, Li. There's nothing wrong with your game. Did you read that material I gave you written by Dr Berkowitz. She's the best in the world at mind stuff."

"No, not yet, but I'm going to start now because I think I'm some way behind you in that department" he replied.

"OK gents, go shower. Let's go grab a lunch afterwards at the restaurant in the park. I have some things for both of you, especially you Lionel. Thanks for putting on a great show, by the way. You two are both looking like professional tour players now. I really enjoyed it together with Dov" said Clive.

"I can't wait Clive, honestly. If all it costs me is a lunch then it's the cheapest lesson I've ever had" laughed Lionel.

The Blue Zoo restaurant looked like it had a pensioner's special on that afternoon it was so full of little old ladies, quite a few of whom had been watching them play earlier. Some of them at some point or other came up and thanked them for the exhibition and wanted to know if they would be playing more during the week.

After the waitress had taken their orders Clive began his analysis by starting with Lionel.

"First things first. You are tossing the ball too high on your first serve. It may be helping with power but except for your slider where your toss is perfect, it's making it hard for you to get your placements closer to the lines. Rather sacrifice a little pace for better accuracy. You'll see it'll win you a lot more points. Both your forehand and backhand are terrific, in fact some of the best looking groundstrokes I've seen, but you are standing a bit too close to receive service. Trust your groundstrokes a bit more like you see David with his forehand return when he lets loose on it. Then the other thing I see is a slight lack of patience in the rallies. You don't have to rush the net so early and so you are too easy a target when you chip and charge. I counted 11 passes David fired passed you today. More patience needed, son. Finally, just a word about your body language. You're not projecting a positive one at all times which openly signals and gives encouragement to your opponent, but otherwise everything looks good, *especially* the backhand. You have all the makings of a super professional, strong on any surface" finished Clive.

David couldn't help himself but smile. In a short space of 2 sets Clive had summed up the holes in Lionel's game, perfectly.

"Unbelievable! In 4 years of college tennis my varsity coach didn't pick up any of these things. As you were saying them, I could envisage exactly what you were saying and you are right. Thank you so much!" said Lionel.

"David, wow! Your serves both have plenty of zip and pop on them now since we worked on them a couple months back. Returns have improved fantastically too. My only comment to you is to just trust your strokes and don't be shy to be more aggressive. You've always had great groundstrokes. Don't be shy to use them to do more damage, otherwise you are ready for the French Open. I can see Lionel and Dov have done an awesome job in getting you prepared so go out there next week and make us all proud. One last thing, ease up on the training a little this week. You've done your hard yards and now it's time to play. Finish off the week with some light drills and then on Sunday play a couple sets with Lionel on your practice court they will allocate you. Your game is just perfect for clay so it won't take you more than a couple of sets to be ready. You move so beautifully on the court it will only take a set before you get used to sliding on the surface.

I haven't watched his tapes yet but Figueras is a wily, old journey man who will use guile to move you around. Be patient and give him back a dose of his own medicine and break him down. Move him about until he can't move any longer. No letting up from the first to the last point, son. I want to see a "W" next to your name on Tuesday morning" said Clive, as they all nodded in agreement.

"Thanks so much Clive. I'm so touched you could make one of our sessions. It means the world to Dov and me, I cannot tell you" said David, with tears in his eyes.

"Right gents, here comes the lunch which today is on Team Oppenheim" said Dov.

"So, what you really saying Dov is that it's on *me*!" laughed David.

"Exactly!" said Dov, having them all laughing.

Chapter 31

The rest of David's week of elementary Arabic lessons, compartmentalisation and relationship exercises with Dr Berkowitz, and weapons handling and Krav Maga lessons with Rubie, just seemed to fly by.

Much to David's entertainment Rubie put on an exhibition match with Dov, who much to David's amazement put up pretty good resistance. Ultimately though he couldn't hold out against Rubie and took a couple of hefty throws on his back and one or two kicks to the kidneys for good measure. He did however manage to put Rubie on his back once with a bit of nifty footwork. Hr proceeded to let the entire gym know about it too!

Dov also put David to work on building up his core for the gruelling weeks of overseas tournaments lined up on their busy schedule. It didn't take a rocket scientist to notice how far advanced the gym equipment was compared to that in their old varsity gym.

For David's last day Moshe lined up a visit to Jerusalem to visit the sites and pray at the Wailing Wall. David was fine with forming a minyan but praying would be a bit hypocritical, but he would go for the ride. Moshe had hired a minivan for them all as both his family and Dr Berkowitz and her 2 grandsons wanted to join the group too, along with Channah of course. Rubie had been assigned driving duties once again. The little group had really started to feel like family to David but still he was looking forward to returning home to his Shakira. Throughout his time in Israel she had never been far from his thoughts.

It didn't take very long before the small entourage had parked in a spot reserved for the IDF and entered the city through the Jaffa gates. As they moved through the Jaffa Gate and walked through the market, David could smell the spices the stallholders were selling which reminded him immediately of the Victoria Street market of his hometown. The stores were full of bright clothing,silks and textiles as well as gold jewellery. A silk shawl hanging on one of the racks outside one of the stores caught his attention, so he stopped to feel it.

"Habibi, you are not only a scholar and a gentleman, but also a man of great taste too. The lady in your life will love you long time, my friend" joked the storekeeper.

"How much can I take this off your hands for, boss?" asked David, who had learnt the art of haggling on his trips to buy his clothes at Mahomedy's.

"Habibi, normal price is $80.00, but today a special price for you, only $60.00" replied the storekeeper.

"Boss, did I do something to insult you?" David responded with his best effort of a distraught look.

"Ah habibi, because you make me laugh I give you killer price of $40.00 only, but be quick before others buy it first!" laughed the old trader.

"$30.00 and you wrap it up quickly" David counter offered.

"Habibi, you killing this old man. We meet at $35.00 and its yours"

"Done. Wrap it up and here's $35.00" replied David, passing the cash over.

The rest of his party had been watching the negotiations with utter amazement and amusement too.

"There's no flies on my boy folks, and if there are any believe me, they are paying rent!" barked Dov, as they all had a good laugh.

"Nice one, David! You are a man of many talents" laughed Channah, admiring the lovely silk shawl David had just purchased.

"From now on, David does all the negotiating for us lot" laughed Dr Berkowitz.

"And there I thought you lacked killer instinct, David" she said, amid much laughter.

After ascending above the market to its rooftop, which had incredible views of the Al Aqsa mosque, the Dome of the Rock, the Wailing Wall as well as the Mount of Olives, Moshe took them to what he claimed was the best falafel joint in Jerusalem. He wasn't wrong either and David simply could not refuse the offer of a second one.

"I see your motherland has given you an appetite, David! That's wonderful" said Moshe.

"I think those were the best falafels I've ever tasted" said David, rubbing his full belly.

"Yonatan, did you hear that? Our brother from South Africa thinks your falafels are the best in the world" shouted Moshe to the man behind the counter.

"Of course they are, Moshe. They're from Jerusalem!" shouted Yonatan, giving David a thumbs up.

"Right ladies, we part company here to take David to the wall. We meet back here in an hour?" suggested Rubie.

"Sure thing. Enjoy David, we'll see you soon" said Channah.

It was quite obvious as they approached the Wailing Wall, with the increased IDF presence, that with Rubie and Moshe he was in the presence of IDF royalty. The soldiers, some who looked no older than 17 years of age, were almost star-struck seeing the two men, instantly saluting them with them returning the greeting. They simply couldn't believe two of their heroes were walking amidst them.

"Here, I brought a bunch of *kippas* for us" said Rubie, motioning for their small group to take one from his bag.

The one and only time David had been to the Wailing Wall was as part of a youth group on a tour of the Holy Land. The boys in the group had been far more interested in getting to know the young Israeli army girls than in the historical or religious significance of one of Judaism's holiest sites. The Wall was, after all, the only remnant left standing of the Second Temple that the Romans had destroyed, with the Dome of the Rock, Islam's third holiest site, built on top of its ruins. The atmosphere with his group felt very different from that occasion as a school boy. He felt a real sense of purpose and belonging, like this was exactly where he was meant to be at that moment.

The area around the Wall was buzzing with people and David noticed what looked like 2 *bar mitzvahs* being conducted closer to the Wall.

"David, next time you visit we should arrange ahead of time for you to celebrate a second *bar mitzvah* here" joked Rubie.

"Jesus Christ, no way the first one was nerve wracking enough thank you!" David exclaimed.

"Sorry but Jesus Christ is the other way!" laughed Dov, pointing at a sign for the Holy Church of the Sepulchre.

Typical Dov, laughed David. He just couldn't resist.

The wall was packed mostly of Chassidic *frummies,* all bedecked in their black outfits liked they had just stepped out of Eastern Europe in the 1800's. Rubie and Moshe along with Dr Berkowitz's two grandsons immediately moved to empty spots along the wall and began *davening*. He and Dov also found spaces and he could hear Dov asking HaShem for good health for his family and friends, and great success and safe travels for the two of them at the French Open. David looked around and could see the two *bar mitzvah* boys, dressed in very smart suits, reciting their part of the Torah. It cast his mind back to years earlier when he had passed the same rite of passage to manhood. David could now see Jews of all colours and creeds praying not just the religious ones amongst them. They were *all* his people even if he didn't believe in a deity. This was a special place and he could understand why it was held sacred by his people. He took the piece of paper from his jacket pocket and found a hole between the rock bricks to place it. He had decided earlier that if he wasn't going to pray he was going to write down his wish of peace between Israel and her Arab neighbours. This was all he really wished for. He could see the irony that the Al Aqsa mosque was only metres away from this holy of holies of Judaism, and hoped one day Muslims and Jews and Gentiles would be able to pray in peace with each other.

After the wall they met up with the ladies again and Beverly suggested a walk to the Mount of Olives. She had bought some delicious fruits and drinks from the market in the interim, and thought it would be a wonderful place to view the old city from. The midday heat had subsided and it was a perfect viewing spot.

Whilst eating some juicy peaches and admiring the view, Moshe had some interesting news about his family's background for him.

"Are you aware that on your Oppenheim side in Czech, you come from a line of very famous rabbis?" asked Moshe.

"I had no idea about that! They must be very proud of my sister, Leah, but rather disappointed with my religious status!" laughed David.

"Yes, your great relative, Dr. Berthold Oppenheim, whose father Rebbe Joachim was also a rabbi, was responsible for building the Olomouc synagogue which was destroyed by the Nazis. He replaced the very famous, Rebbe Azriel Gunzig, as rabbi of Lostice when he moved to Antwerp and built up a strong little Jewish community in that town. That's the little town where your grandparents and parents lived and escaped from during the Shoah. Their Gentile neighbours were very good to both your father and mother's families by hiding them in their homes and church before they could escape to Switzerland. Those Gentile families are, without doubt, the *only* reason you came into this world, David, and I think when you find the time you should really go visit the place. The local community were even good enough to maintain the Jewish graveyard and restore the synagogue, which the Nazi's had used as a storage facility. Today, many groups, especially school kids, visit the synagogue which is used as the Centre for Respect and Tolerance and to exhibit the history of the local Jews. The amazing thing is that all the Jews of the town were slaughtered during the Shoah, sadly, including your rabbi relative, Dr. Berthold Oppenheim, who was murdered by those animals in Treblinka, yet the local gentiles did all this with the little money they had, out of respect for their Jewish friends!" said Moshe.

"*What*? You mean there were *no Jews* living there and they still did that?" asked David, incredulously.

"It's true, David. I checked immediately with one of rabbis, also from Moravia, and he visited this little town a few years back and confirmed this for me. He also gave me a bit of excellent history about Lostice. The Oppenheim's go back at least 7 generations as rabbis and Rabbi Joachim's father was Rabbi Bernhard Oppenheim. Your namesake, Rabbi David Oppenheim. was Joachim's brother and was also a much loved member of the Moravian community. With all these rabbis on your father's side I have *no idea* where your atheism originates!" laughed Moshe.

"There weren't only famous men from your parent's little town. Rabbi Eschel tells me that the daughter of Rabbi Neuda, one Fanny Neuda, wrote the first hymn book for Jewish ladies and it is displayed in the Lostice Synagogue for viewing. The other brilliant mind that was born in this village was one Lara Langer" he continued.

"You talking about **my** mother?" asked David, in a state of shock.

"Yes, your mother, David. She attended the local school or gymnasium as they called it and was identified as having extraordinary academic talents. If you consider your father and your sister as being academically brilliant you will be shocked to learn that she was singled out to attend a special school in Prague for the gifted, but never got there because of the war. When her parents arrived here they were penniless and your mother, as a young girl, had to forget about the luxuries of an education and find a job to support the family. Any monies were spent on her brother's university education, which enabled him to become a wealthy man. Without your mother's sacrifice your uncle today would not have anywhere near his wealth. I found out his property holdings here in Tel Aviv and I can assure you he's a very, very, wealthy man.

Your mother's family were largely traders and academics unlike your father's. Before the Shoah they had shareholdings in clothing, textiles and glassmaking concerns, and even a local cheese making business. They were wealthy but when they fled they left with nothing but whatever they could fit into suitcases. Whatever cash they had was used to bribe people to get them out of Europe" explained Moshe.

"You found all of this out in the last 2 days?" asked David, absolutely astounded.

"David, we are in the information business, boychik. We are the best in the world at this so it was easy" he laughed.

"I have another valuable piece of information for you. You wanted to know who your last relative to leave Israel or Judea as it was then known. I can tell you" he said.

"Well come on, who then?! Don't keep me in suspense!" shouted David.

"David, they believe you are related to one of the 5 surviving children from Masada!"

There was a long protracted silence as the whole group who had been listening intently, digested this fact. Moshe eventually broke the silence.

"They think this little girl was then taken to modern day Iran where she was adopted by a childless couple. She had a family of her own who spread far and wide within the Diaspora and eventually settled in Moravia. So, your roots were last here in 78 A.D. or thereabouts. They have not been able to go further back then that but to think you are a descendant of one of our most famous survivors is just mindboggling" chuckled Moshe.

David was at first speechless and then out of nowhere, he began to sob. This was just all too much for him. He had only a few nights earlier been enjoying a lovely meal with drinks on top of Masada, and now this.

Without thinking, Channah immediately moved to him and embraced him in her arms where he sobbed for a few minutes, quite uncontrollably. He hugged Channah and kissed her in a brotherly way on her forehead. She was a wonderful girl and he longed for the day she would be loved by a man the way he loved his Shakira.

"Thank you so much for your kindness, Channah. I don't know what just overcame me but I just couldn't control myself" he stammered.

For the first time he noticed that she too had tears running down her cheeks.

"It's a lot, David. I told Moshe too but he said it was the right thing to do" she said, holding his hand and wiping the tears away.

Their entourage had taken a stroll and had left Channah to comfort him alone. The sun was setting and David's mind had cleared and he had regained control of his emotions.

"Shakira is such a lucky lady, David, and I hope she knows it" said Channah, now leaning against him.

"Promise me that should anything happen, you won't forget me!" she laughed.

"Channah, how could anyone forget you. I promise, I won't ever forget you" he said, hugging her tightly.

As the last of the sun disappeared over the horizon the group returned with each one of them giving David a big hug. They understood full well his emotions and wanted to express their support.

David was so emotionally drained that in spite of the ruckus the group caused with all their joking on the way back to Moshe, he fell into a deep sleep, lying all over Channah who put a sheet over him.

He dreamed of Shakira and that she was lying with him on the top of Masada, surrounded by his family.

Jerusalem had been a life-changing experience in ways that he could never have imagined it would be.

Chapter 32

The rest of the week of doing countless drills with Lionel and two early mornings of beach sprints, seemed to fly by.

David had chatted early on the Wednesday morning with Shakira and that night they had taken Leah and Michael for a dinner at the Durban harbour. Michael had indeed been very helpful and much to David's surprise had correctly picked out a few weaknesses in Figueras's single-handed backhand. He had also picked up in his more recent matches how much stamina he had lost and unless he was going to close out the match in straight sets he tended to lose far more of the longer matches than he had won. David realised he had to make sure he won either the first or second sets, at least, to prolong the match and drag his man into the deep waters.

Thursday had seen David and Leah rushing about to the French Consulate to sort out last minute issues with visas for themselves and Lionel. It took most of that afternoon to accomplish the task but they got it done. That evening his Uncle Sol, Dov and Lionel came for supper at their home in order to check on all their arrangements before flying out the following evening.

Uncle Sol had been generous enough to book and pay for extra rooms for Dov and Lionel at their lovely hotel, as well as business class tickets for them too. Considering the magnitude of the event they were traveling for he thought it only correct to do this for them. In any event, he didn't have any children to spend it on anyway.

"David, whatever you do, don't leave your bloody game behind. Anything we've forgotten we can always buy in Paris" joked Uncle Sol.

"Uncle Sol, are we going to take some whiskeys over in our luggage?" asked Dov.

"Is the Pope Catholic!? Of course we are. I've already loaded up on those small airline Jonnie Walkers in my suitcase, my boy, and I suggest you do the same!" chuckled Sol.

"Go see my mate, Benny, at Solly Kramers near Davenport and tell him I sent you. He'll sort you out with great prices" winked Sol.

"Sol, you not going to get us arrested at the airport *again,* are you?" his sister asked in a most unimpressed voice.

"You do know they make lots of wine there?" she asked.

"Lara, my dear sister, the Frogs can only make bloody wine but not whisky, and I don't drink wine" Uncle Sol explained.

"Alright my Sol, have it your way then but I'm not bailing you out of any French jails" she sighed.

"OK people, can we kindly check through all documents one final time before we eat dinner?" asked David's father, who had been quietly watching the chaos unfold.

"I think it's best I hold all the passports and other documents like the airline tickets and hotel reservations etcetera" he continued.

It took them about half an hour to sort out all the documents, mainly because Uncle Sol had just thrown all his things into his overflowing business bag which seemed to contain his entire life's story in it. They were all starving by the time they finally sat down to dinner.

"So Dov, you got all the tennis arrangements done?" asked Lara.

"Yip Mrs O, practice courts booked for Saturday afternoon for 2 hours and then Sunday morning for 3 hours so Davie will be nice and fresh for Figueras on Monday afternoon. Team O is ready and prepared to annihilate that Spaniard. I went over the tapes of Figueras with both Clive Jaikins and someone else and we spotted a few weaknesses in his game. I'll share them tomorrow night on our long flight with you Davie" said Dov.

"Uncle Sol, was there no way you couldn't have got flights on any other night *except Shabbas*?" asked Leah.

"My girl, I thought about you and made a special arrangement with Rabbi Goldstein. He said we should have Shabbat on the flight. I've already ordered kosher food for you, plus a nicely baked challah and kosher wine which a mate at SAA has organised *especially*" he said proudly.

It never ceased to amaze David how enterprising Uncle Sol was and how he seemed to have a "mate" who worked at every business there was out there. He was definitely a guy you wanted playing in your team with his endless *chutzpah*.

"Oh God, Sol! Is any of this *actually* legal?" Lara asked, much to everyone's amusement.

"Legal, shmegal, Lara! Stop giving me a hard time and enjoy your life, my darling sister!" he said, with a huge grin on his face.

"Well thanks, Uncle Sol. Having *Shabbos* on a plane should be a novel experience" said Leah.

"Yip, just like joining the mile high club, but different" remarked Sol, creating much hilarity.

"God Sol, not now, we are eating, you *meshuggenah*!" castigated Lara but also half laughing at her crazy brother.

Lara had cooked up a magnificent roast lamb with potatoes and French salad and they ate like it was going to be there last supper for a while. Uncle Sol spent a lot of time questioning Lionel about his time at college in the United States and Lionel was more than happy to describe his time there, and the various courses that were on offer to him.

"Do you think you could ever come back and live in South Africa again, now that you've lived there for 4 years?" asked Sol.

"It's a tough question. There are so many things that make South Africa so special, starting with the people. South Africans are generally far more open and giving than Americans but America is the land of opportunities which has so much to offer us younger people. I think South Africa may be a place to consider retiring to one day but my immediate future can only happen for me in America" replied Lionel.

"Where do you think things in South Africa will go when Apartheid ends and we have one-man-one-vote?" Lionel asked.

"That's the million dollar question, my boy. No doubt there will be major changes and I think the smart ones will keep their options open so if things don't go peacefully in the transition they can hop to safer pastures" replied Uncle Sol.

"Don't be like the Holocaust Jews who didn't give themselves options until it was too late and the only place for them was the ovens of Auschwitz. You're not Jewish, Lionel, so you don't see dangers as clearly as we do. I'm sure you know the saying, "when the Jews start to leave you better start packing your bags too." Just make sure you have options available to you, is all I'm saying" advised Uncle Sol.

"Guys, please excuse me but I still have plenty of packing to do before we depart tomorrow night and I don't feel like a wild rush tomorrow" said David.

"If you need me, I'm upstairs in my room otherwise I'll see you tomorrow I guess" he said, getting up from the table.

"Mom, you outdid yourself tonight. The roast lamb and potatoes was out of this world. Thank you."

David went to his room and closed the door. He had arranged a 10 p.m. call with Shakira and didn't want to miss it. She answered on the first ring.

"Hello love. How was your dinner with everybody?" she asked.

"It was fantastic actually. Sol kept us all entertained with his mad sense of humour. He knows how to get my mom's goat up and she takes the bait every time. I think Lionel and Dov enjoyed the whole thing too. Only thing missing was you, my angel. I can't wait until you can join us too" he said.

"I know. I spoke with your sister earlier and she really wanted me to join you all tonight" she responded.

"My mom and I chatted a bit more about you. You really made a good impression and she was eating some of your Turkish delights tonight. That was such a smart move, you clever thing" she laughed.

"Do you have a better idea when she's intending on breaking the news to your father?" asked David.

"Yes. She said only next week because he's been under a lot of pressure this week and she wants him just to relax a bit over the weekend. She knows him best. I trust her intuition" said Shakira.

"Do you have any time tomorrow to see me before I leave?" asked David.

"I have nothing in the morning and only 2 late afternoon lectures, if you want to get together in the morning?" she asked.

"Perfect. If I collect you early why don't we have a morning swim in the ocean and then a shower at your apartment? Then we order up some breakfast. I'll pack all my bags tonight then so we can at least spend a few hours together before I fly out to Paris" he said.

“Ooh, a swim and a shower. That sounds perfect, Mr O” she said.

“Fantastic. Let me get to packing then and I’ll collect you at 6 a.m. my darling.”

“I cannot wait. Sleep tight, my love” she said, before ending the call.

Chapter 33

David awoke on Friday morning at 5 a.m. after only 4 hours of sleep. He was still tired but didn't care because he was going to spend the morning with Shakira before flying off to Paris with his crew. He had been meticulous with packing his bags and was prepared as he was ever going to be for Roland Garros.

Shakira was ready for him precisely at 5:30 a.m. and greeted him with a massive smile and kiss.

"An early morning sunrise swim in the ocean with my lover. What more could a girl ask for? You still look a bit tired. my darling. Try get some sleep on the flight tonight please" she said.

"With Dov, Uncle Sol and Lionel with us I don't think there's much chance of *that*!" he laughed.

"I may have a few whizzos with them which may help me nod off for a few hours, if I'm lucky. I'll probably have more luck sleeping a bit at the hotel in Paris on Saturday morning. Uncle Sol got me my own suite fortunately, so I'm not sharing with anybody. Then I'll go have a 2 hour hit at the stadium courts in the afternoon" he said.

"This is so exciting, my darling. This is it now! You really are breaking into the big time" she said, excitedly.

"Yip, I am getting excited but quite nervous too. I can see my future just sitting in front of me ready to be grabbed, and now I need to do it" he told her.

When they arrived at North Beach the first rays of light were just emerging from the horizon. They both quickly removed their clothes with Shakira revealing a 2 piece bikini which David couldn't take his eyes off. The water was still and surprisingly warm for so early. Shakira coiled her body around his and kissed him deeply. He could immediately feel himself respond.

"I'm going to need you to bring me my towel before I get out of the water" he joked with her.

"You damn right! I'm not letting any ladies see what is all mine" she giggled.

By the time they got out of the water the sun had completely risen and the water was full of surfers and the promenade busy with runners and cyclists. They didn't bother showering in the open beach showers but walked briskly to the apartment. By the time they opened the apartment door they were both naked and he was already inside her.

"I'm going to miss you so much, Mr O. I don't know how I'm going to be without your body, your touch for so long" she whispered in his ear.

"I love making love to you Shakira. I can't wait for you to be able to travel with me one day" he responded.

He could feel her body starting to quiver and her hips pulling him deeper inside of her. The intensity of her climax excited him that he didn't take long to follow her.

"So much for making the shower my darling!" he laughed.

"Why don't you order up a breakfast and then come join me in the shower" she said.

They showered together for half an hour and by then their breakfast order had been delivered to the apartment. The sun had fully risen and from the open patio they could hear the daily goings-on of tourists, businesspeople and others.

"What more has your mom had to say about speaking to your father?" he asked.

"She still plans on letting him unwind over the weekend and then she will break the news to him next week. She has asked if I can sit in with her when she tells him. I think she needs me to express the feelings I have for you, myself, rather than through her. It is only fair" she said.

"Have you thought how you are going to approach it when you get back?" she asked.

"Not really. I'm trying to just focus everything on the French Open for now and then I'll figure it out when I'm back. I still say I've got it easier than you on this one" he half-laughed.

"Well I hope I gave you some good motivation this morning to do well next week ... and come back safely to me!" she laughed.

"Oh yes, you did!" he said, pulling her closer to him.

After breakfast they went to Clicks to buy a few toiletries and other items David still needed, and then he dropped her at university. She gave him one last lingering hug and kiss before heading off to the Law library.

"Goodbye, my angel. I know you are going to make us all proud. Don't forget to call me every night. I will be waiting for your calls."

On his arrival home things were starting to become chaotic as his family were panicking because they had left their final packing late. David excused himself and laid down for a nap and was awoken 3 hours later by Leah.

"David, come on, everyone has been calling for you! Lionel, Dov and Uncle Sol are all waiting downstairs and the taxi is on its way" said Leah.

"OK, OK, I just need to change into new clothes. I'll be down in a minute" replied David.

Uncle Sol had ordered a mini-van to get them to the airport and it was just as well, with all their suitcases. David was relieved he had managed a bit of a catnap and was feeling refreshed as the taxi made its way to Louis Botha Airport, in the south of Durban. He felt sorry for the driver as with everyone trying to speak at once it must have sounded like a market place inside his van.

His entourage arrived in good time and in fact even had time to shrink wrap their luggage, which Uncle Sol insisted on.

"I don't trust those Frogs one little bit with our luggage" he complained.

Soon they were airborne, sitting very comfortably in their business class seats. Within half an hour of take-off one of the stewardesses approached Leah with a freshly baked challah and some kosher wine. Uncle Sol hadn't been kidding the night before. His sister had also come armed with kippas for the men as well as some little candles as a symbolic gesture. Leah gestured for all of them to gather around as she said a blessing over the ceremonial candles, which she had Dov hold. She then surprised David by asking him to say Kiddush and bless the wine and challah, before he passed the wine for everyone to have a sip and then broke the bread and passed it to everyone.

"Lionel, we'll make a good Jew out of you yet, *boychik*!" Uncle Sol teased.

"*Shabbat shalom*, Uncle Sol!" said Lionel, and they all laughed.

"Good *Shabbas* to all of you lovely people and a special thanks to you, Leah. I'm sure Rabbi Goldstein will be ecstatic to hear about this *simcha*" laughed Uncle Sol.

"Good *Shabbos* everyone!" wished David.

"*Shabbos* Davie! You are the reason we are all together tonight and we are very proud of you" his father, who had been sitting very quietly, added.

"Absolutely! Go smash them this week, Davie! For all of us. *L'chaim*" said Dov, toasting his protégé.

The 10 hour flight to Paris was over quickly and in spite of the raucous laughter from Uncle Sol and Dov as they finished off a bottle of Jonnie Walker Black, David was able to sleep for a couple of hours. Before he knew it they had landed in Paris and were en-route in another minivan taxi to their hotel.

Hotel Chateau Frontenac was everything Uncle Sol had said it would be and more. It was perfectly situated within a few minutes' walk of Avenue Champs-Elysees and the Arc de Triomphe, and about a 30 minute brisk walk to Roland Garros. The hotel was located about a 7 minute walk from the River Seine said Uncle Sol, who was about to begin a sordid tale of a damsel he had picked up there all those years ago, until his sister shook her head for him to stop.

It was still early French time so Uncle Sol suggested they have a breakfast in one of the hotel's restaurants before their rooms became available. The hotel manager emerged from one of the back rooms in reception to welcome them all.

"Ah, Mr Sol Langer, welcome back sir. I see according to our electronic register it has been almost thirty years since we last had the pleasure of hosting you. Was our service not up to your expectations all those decades ago?" he joked.

"Ha Ha! No my friend, not at all, it was excellent but the authorities wouldn't let me back in your beautiful country after one or two shenanigans!" he laughed.

"But I'm back better than ever as you can see and I've brought my family with!" he shouted.

"Well, on behalf of Chateau Frontenac I would like to sincerely welcome you all and because you have come as a group I would like to offer you a complimentary upgrade to a higher floor with the best views of the Eiffel Tower, as well as a complimentary breakfast this morning" he said kindly.

"That's wonderful and I can assure you we will be back here every year as my nephew, David, is a very famous professional tennis player who will one day win your tournament" boasted Uncle Sol, pointing at poor David who was dying of embarrassment listening to all this.

"Magnifique! In which case, may I offer you a free daily ride to and from the stadium in our stretch limousine you would have seen parked outside? Now would you prefer a hot English breakfast in our art deco-style restaurant, or a continental one, on the patio. Both are excellent" said the manager.

"I don't trust any restaurant that doesn't serve egg and bacon, so it'll be the first one" replied Uncle Sol.

"Er, Mr Sol, I don't mean to be rude, but the bacon ... it isn't *kosher*" said the little manager, sounding embarrassed.

"*Perfect*! Just the way I like my bacon. Which way is it?" barked Uncle Sol, to everyone but Leah's amusement.

"Follow me, sir. I'll have housekeeping make sure your rooms are prepared by the time you are finished breakfast then. Your luggage will be upstairs too" he said, leading them to the restaurant.

"Uncle Sol, you are a *mensch* and a rock star!" said Dov giving him a high-five.

"Your uncle is quite something, bro. I could get used to hanging around with him" Lionel said to David.

"Oh no, Lionel, I'm not going to allow my brother to be a bad influence on you. Dov, I can see is a lost cause already but you are still innocent enough to save" laughed Lara Oppenheim.

After a sumptuous breakfast in the beautifully decorated hotel restaurant the entourage made their way to the 8th floor which indeed had beautiful views of the Eiffel Tower. David was grateful that Uncle Sol had reserved a suite for him with his mountain load of luggage. He unpacked his tennis gear and then told Dov and Lionel that he was going to have a shower and a nap before their afternoon practice session.

David slept deeply after his shower on the soft mattress and silk sheets. He dreamed like he had on so many occasions of his beautiful Shakira except this time they were together in Israel. He was walking with her and Rubie, Moshe, Dov, Dr Berkowitz, the boys, Beverly and of course his Channah. This time it was different though because Channah was walking hand-in-hand with twin little girls. David could smell the spices and perfumes and the famous Jerusalem falafels, of course. It made him think back to the sad farewell he had with all of them and the tears he had shed when he had said his final goodbyes to his little family. They had been so kind and caring towards him. That trip had opened his eyes to *who* he really was and *where* he came from.

"Right, that's enough sleep, *china*! Put on your kit and let's meet downstairs at the limousine. We have a job to do and Lionel is ready to give you a good workout. It's 1 p.m. and your uncle and father have gone to some art museum your father has on his bucket list, but your mom and Leah will join us" barked Dov, pulling the duvet off David.

David washed and dressed in minutes and joined Team O in the fancy stretch limousine as their chauffeur drove them along the famous tree-lined boulevards of Paris, including a slight detour past the magnificent Eiffel Tower. David had never been to Paris before and was astounded by its natural charm and beauty. He understood better why Shakira had loved it so much. Not only was the weather beautiful but there was a real sense of life about the city with people jogging in the streets and the parks, young families pushing their new editions in strollers, the cafes buzzing with young people and tourists and a feeling of joy in the air. It excited David.

It was just as well they had taken the limo because they discovered it was about 30 minutes ride by car, and closer to an hour walking. His Uncle Sol had certainly got that part very wrong but then redeemed himself with the free limousine service. As the limousine pulled up to the main entrance of the stadium, David sucked in some air and slowly moved out of the car.

Dov had received guest passes for their guests and players' passes for the 3 of them, including Lionel, and instructed them all to hang them around their necks. David laughed when he noticed amongst the hundreds of items Dov had in his coach's bag, were at least 8 bottles of "the purple stuff" as it had become known. He loved the fact that Dov had also arranged with the Tacchini rep to have Team O T-shirts made for them which they were all wearing now.

"Mr Oppenheim, coach, welcome to Roland Garros. Your court will be available in 5 minutes if you would care to follow me" said a very official-looking gentleman wearing a very smart black Dior suit.

"Who are all these people? I thought play only starts on Monday?" asked Dov.

"We allow a certain number of people come watch the players practice, coach" answered the gentleman as they walked past the beautiful main stadium.

"We have allocated you court 14 and they are nearly finished cleaning it for you. You will find balls, drinks and towels available for you, coach" he said.

"Well that's what we expected!" barked Dov, like this was all just old hat for them.

"Jaezus, Davie. Isn't that Wilander playing over there?" asked Lionel.

"It sure is, bro. He's wearing *your* Tacchini outfit Lionel" joked David.

Court 14 already a smallish crowd of 300 spectators, waiting eagerly in anticipation for the next practice session. Leah and Lara found seats amongst them and at exactly 2 p.m. Lionel, David and Dov stepped onto the hallowed, red, clay courts of Roland Garros for the first time. David could feel all the nerves down his back tingling and his legs wobble just a bit.

"Who the hell are you lot?" shouted some Yank in the crowd.

"As soon as I've put these bags down I'm going to come up there and tell you exactly who, meathead!" barked Dov, which immediately had the crowd in hysterics. Only Dov, thought David, but he had won the crowd over at the same time.

"Why don't you drag your fat Yank *tuches* over here and play ball boy for us because you could certainly lose some weight!" he laughed.

"His name is David Oppenheim from Durban in South Africa. Don't let me hear you ask that question ever again!" he shouted to him, to the amusement of the crowd.

"OK Li, this is it. Let's put on a show for these *schlemiels*" said David to a very nervous-looking Lionel Perreira.

From the first sweet contact David's racquet made with the ball, the red clay just felt like it was made for him. He had felt the same when he had first experienced the surface in Morocco earlier in the year. Paris felt even more like home though. As the two of them warmed up hitting a variety of strokes, David could feel a buzz of excitement and the odd bit of laughter as Dov stalked the side lines, occasionally barking out encouragement to the both of them.

“OK, that’s enough guys, let’s get some practice sets in. They’ve only given us 2 hours today!” barked Dov.

The two rivals began what turned into quite a riveting 3 set match. David was just too experienced on clay for his old rival and ripped through the first set 6-2 before Lionel managed to scrape through the second 7-6, after finding his feet on the surface. By now the crowd was closer to two-thousand hungry fans, enthralled with the match they were being treated to.

The third set was a thing of beauty with neither of them giving an inch. Lionel managed to push David to 8-6, with David sealing the match with a beautifully disguised forehand drop shot.

The crowd loved it and gave both boys a standing ovation. David even noticed out of the corner of his eyes that Wilander had been watching them from his practice court.

“How you like them apples, Mr Yankee Doodles?!” shouted Dov to the very overweight American who was stuffing his face with a chocolate croissant, half of which had melted on his chin.

“Just beautiful, the both of you!” shouted Dov pushing yet another purple drink in both their hands.

“Now let them ask who the fuck we are” he laughed.

“I’m going to get a quick drink with the 2 ladies whilst you two follow that young kid over there for the nice ice baths I booked you” he laughed, pointing at one of the young ball kids waiting for them.

“Coach, how about you do the ice bath to calm down a bit and Davie and I go for drinks with Leah and Mrs O” laughed Lionel, but by then Dov was already heading towards the exit.

“Jaezus, I *really* loved that, Davie. I thought when I saw Wilander I was going to pee my pants but then when we started knocking up all the nerves went and I felt great. I really think we belong here!” said Lionel.

“I can’t tell you how much I appreciate you bringing me along for this” said his long-time rival.

“We’re friends, Li, and that’s all there is to it” replied David.

Their first day had been eventful and even the thirty minute ice bath had not seemed that bad. He couldn’t wait to tell Shakira later after Uncle Sol had taken them all out for dinner at one of the cafes on the Champs Elysees.

Paris was proving to be a blast!

Chapter 34

That night Uncle Sol insisted on taking their group to Le Cinque on the Champs Elysees for dinner. It was only a fifteen minute walk from their hotel through the lovely boulevards of the 8th arrondissement. Paris at night was a truly beautiful sight, especially with all its lights, and the weather was perfect for an evening stroll.

After arriving back from their practice and ice baths there were 2 surprises in store for David. First was the funny sight of both his father and Uncle Sol, totally intoxicated and singing piano songs in the hotel's bar area. He had never seen his father drunk and it was quite a hysterical thing to witness. Apparently they had gone to two museums before Uncle Sol, bored out of his mind, insisted they do some bar hopping. The second more sobering surprise was a box containing at least a dozen pairs of Nike shoes of his size but of different styles, with a note that they wanted to meet and talk business with him the next day before his practice time in the morning.

"Davie, listen to me *boychik*, I know exactly how to handle these *skelms*. Let me do the talking. They think you are this nice, little Jewish boy from South Africa who just stepped off the boat. They in for a massive surprise tomorrow, believe me!" laughed Dov.

"OK Dov, I trust you but please don't fuck it up for us. We both look pretty cool in Nikes" replied David.

The dinner at La Cinque was simply outstanding and both his father and Uncle Sol got funnier as their alcohol consumption increased. He had no idea his father even possessed a sense of humour yet he kept them in stitches of laughter throughout their dining experience. Shortly after dessert David excused himself early under the pretence of needing to repack his bags and get an early night's sleep. It didn't take him more than ten minutes to get back to his room.

She answered on the second ring.

"Hello, my angel. How are you? Was it a good flight? Isn't Paris beautiful? How is the hotel? How was your first practice session? Tell me everything, *please*" Shakira blurted out.

"Well, the flight was fun and Sol kept his word to Leah and we had *Shabbos* at 30,000 feet in the air. I managed a couple of hours sleep and then a few more at the hotel in the morning. The hotel is magnificent and probably in one of the finest areas of the city. We are only about a ten to fifteen minute walk from the Arc de Triomphe and the Champs Elysees, and even closer than that to the River Seine. The hotel has very kindly upgraded us to better rooms with stunning views of the Eiffel Tower. They've also offered free rides daily to and from Roland Garros in their stretch limousine. Even my father is having a ball and Uncle Sol got him rip-roaring drunk this afternoon and they've both been telling all sorts of jokes and sing-alongs. I didn't even know my dad knew any jokes!" laughed David.

"Well, good for *him*!" laughed Shakira.

"Practice was amazing and Lionel and I put on a bit of a show for our little crowd. I have a feeling Nike want to offer me a deal tomorrow. I think they must have had a rep watching this afternoon" said David.

"You go, Mr O!" she exclaimed.

"I've agreed to allow Dov to represent Team O in the initial talks tomorrow. I hope I don't regret that later although Diadora may be in the mix too" he laughed.

"I think it's an excellent idea you don't represent yourself in these negotiations, my angel. Rather have someone in between and Dov is the *perfect* guy" she laughed.

"I really missed you not being with us today, my angel. I can't wait for us to experience Paris together. Tell me your news. How is everything with your family?" asked David.

"We all fine this side. I learnt from my mom that most of my father's stress at the moment isn't from the business, which is apparently going very well, but the trouble his annoying cousin, Goolam, is causing him. You remember we spoke about this character he suspected of misappropriating his donor funds for his own motives. I hope he doesn't mess things up for us next week by causing too much stress for my dad. He's such an idiot, this guy" said Shakira, sounding annoyed.

"Well for your dad's sake I hope he doesn't have your surname" said David.

"Unfortunately he does which is *why* the level of stress for my poor dad" she said.

"Your father is a smart man, my angel. He will know precisely how to uncover and handle this" replied David, reassuringly.

"I really hope so" she said with a sigh.

"Anyway, this call is costing a fortune so let me say good night. I love you to infinity and beyond and will call you again tomorrow at the same time" said David.

"Thank you so much for the call, my darling. Sleep tight and have an awesome day tomorrow. Please send my love to everybody, especially Leah. She told me she would call me if you get up to any mischief there!" she chuckled.

At breakfast the next morning both Sol's looked quite awful, testimony to the previous day's revelry. Dov was the only member of their entourage missing which David found quite hypocritical in light of the stern awakening he had given him the previous day. In spite of their poor condition both Sol's insisted they wanted to come along for the ride and get a taste of Roland Garros. Lionel, he thought, was looking the part in his Wilander Sergio Tacchini outfit. He no doubt was hoping to make an impression on Mats if their practice schedules had to coincide with the 2 time French Open Champion's.

Dov finally appeared, looking very ruffled and with only minutes to spare before the limousine set off for the stadium.

"I'm so, so, sorry but those bloody prawns last night didn't agree with me so I had to rush out this morning to grab something at the pharmacy" he explained.

"Serves you right for eating shellfish, Dov" castigated Leah.

"Well, you don't *look* bad. You OK to do this thing with Nike this morning, bro? We can always tell them tomorrow or during the week rather" asked David.

"Oh no, believe you me, I'm ready" laughed Dov.

They arrived with only minutes to spare before their practice court number 14 was prepared for them at 10 a.m. On the walk to their court David had noticed a lot more spectators and certainly when they stepped onto court 14 he noticed a lot more waiting for them than the previous day.

“Where’s that fat Yank?” asked Dov, surveying the crowd.

The third surprise in less than 24 hours came about when David opened his kit bag for his shoes and in that moment he understood the true reason Dov had faked his earlier stomach ailment.

“Dov, what are *these*? Where are my fucking Nike’s?” asked David to the two smiling faces before him.

“To answer your question, Davie, those are a pair of Adidas clay court tennis shoes” laughed Dov.

“Yes, a blind man could see that but where are *my* tennis shoes?” asked David again.

David noticed that Lionel had also put on a matching pair of Adidas’s.

“They’re actually really nice, Davie” he said, bouncing in them.

“Bro, yesterday you told me you trusted me to deal with Nike, right?” said Dov.

“Yes and I must have been out of my fucking mind to have agreed to that!” replied David, still in shock.

“I’m going to talk to the 2 suits there trying to get my attention and teach them about Jewish negotiating” laughed Dov.

“The other thing I need to tell you before I go and raid their riches is that in my chats with Clive, whilst watching the Figueras tapes with him, he emphasised wearing down his single-handed backhand with high bouncing topspin. He said that he will only be able to withstand those for a limited amount of time. I think you two have played enough sets and you should take it a bit easier today with some drills rather. That’s *my* advice to you as your coach” he said before walking off to introduce himself to the suits.

“This guy just keeps on surprising me” David said to Lionel, nodding in Dov’s direction.

“I know he doesn’t look it but he’s plenty smart, Davie. You damn lucky he’s on Team O” laughed Lionel.

“You right” said David, shaking his head in awe.

After a bit of a warm up the two of them put the drills they had shared with each other in Durban into practice. Once again the red clay surface felt like it was his tennis home. The balls seemed to just glide off the face of his racket exactly as he intended them too. Out of the corner of his eye he did manage to catch Dov laughing loudly as the 2 suits threw their arms around in an animated fashion. Had the Italians just bought out Nike, he wondered.

At about half an hour into practicing drills Dov wandered onto the court armed with the purple stuff.

"What's that purple concoction you have coach?" asked an elderly gentleman in the front row.

"Sir, I could tell you … but then immediately afterwards I would have to kill you" said Dov, with the straightest of faces as the crowd packed up laughing.

"So Davie. I have some news" he said rather nonchalantly.

"So, did we get our asking price then?" asked David, nervously.

"Nope we didn't" said Dov.

"Oh fuck. I guess we should maybe think about Adidas in that case" replied David, sounding somewhat disappointed.

"That won't be necessary because … I got quadruple that!" shouted Dov.

"Say that again?" asked David, in bewilderment.

"I told the *schnorrers* that was what Adidas were offering and you guys were wearing their shoes because we were planning on signing with them over lunch" he laughed.

"You cheeky bugger!" laughed Lionel.

"What else did you say?" asked David, still in a state of shock.

"I'm going to put it like this. I learnt how to haggle from some young Jew in the marketplace in Jerusalem who was buying a silk shawl for his girlfriend and haggling with the Arab storekeeper. So I told them that I wasn't the guy who had been with their wives and daughters and why were they offering us such a shitty deal when it was clearly a case of mistaken identity" laughed Dov.

"Jesus Christ, Dov! I only asked that Arab if I had done something to offend him *not* that I had molested his wife or daughters!" laughed David.

"Exactly what I said" said Dov, much to the 2 younger men's amusement.

"Oh, by the way, give the 2 suits a big wave please. You too Lionel. I told them we don't want that *drek* they sent you yesterday as bait. We want the good shit. I told them to send it across to our hotel tonight along with the contract. I told them to send you a dozen pairs too Li. It's the least Davie and I can do as thanks. Oh yes, one last thing. Your Nike shoes are in my bag there. Please put them on for the suits now, and the Adidas ones back in my bag. I need to return them to their rep tonight" he laughed, wandering off back to the suits.

"Where the *fuck* did you find him?" asked Lionel, lying on the floor with laughter.

"I didn't. He found me!" laughed David, shaking his head in awe whilst waving to the 2 suits.

After fuelling up on the purple stuff they spent the next fourty minutes with David hitting elevated forehand and backhand top spin strokes to Lionel's backhand. With an hour left of their allotted practice time David suggested finishing off with a set.

"Li, this crowd is baying for more than just practice drills. Let's give them a set at least" said David.

For the following fifty minutes the 2 two great rivals played one of the most entertaining sets they had played to date ,with David hanging on to win it 7-5. They had both played with freedom, hitting out at everything, which made for a thrilling spectacle. When they had finished David could sense the crowd's disappointment. They wanted more.

"Sorry folks but that's all for today. You want more come watch my guy here next week, please" Dov told them.

Dov had arranged a ninety minute deep tissue massage for both of them. It was just what the doctor, or in this case, Dov, had ordered and left David feeling revitalised. They went through to Head's on-site offices afterwards and collected a dozen new rackets they had very kindly strung for David. They were all nicely packed in two branded carry bags with Team O silkscreened on both which was a nice touch.

"I thought I recognised one of their reps watching you guys in the stands yesterday" laughed Dov.

"He must have been impressed with what he saw" he continued.

In spite of Uncle Sol's protestations, David declined his offer to join them at another outdoor café along the River Seine for an early dinner. He wanted to order some room service and get an early night's rest after speaking to Shakira. He did manage to get Dov alone for a few minutes to let him know to check out one Goolam Mahomedy, purportedly representing some Palestinian aid agency.

"Oh wow! This day just keeps on getting better, Davie" responded Dov.

"Tell Moshe that her father is quite sure it's him and intends on handling the situation diplomatically because of it being a family member. Ask him to be mindful of that when he decides on how to respond please" added David.

"Moshe will be as discrete as possible I'm sure, but the priority is to stem the flow of these funds to buy weapons. If it can be routed for humanitarian aid then Moshe will be only too delighted so my guess is that will be his aim" replied Dov.

"Davie, this information is invaluable. Now your only focus is your match tomorrow. A good omen is the tournament director says it's scheduled for court 14 so you will feel very at home. I'm going to make sure our gang behaves tonight and doesn't disturb your rest, so you enjoy your room service and get some good shut eye. I'll wake you tomorrow morning for another good massage. I've already had the hotel order me a masseuse table delivered to your suite" said Dov.

"Dov, are you sure you didn't play for the King David *A team*?" laughed David.

"Oh shut up with that already!" barked Dov setting off to round up the Team O group for an early dinner.

Whilst waiting for delivery of his chicken salad meal, David was surprised to hear the telephone in his room ringing.

"I couldn't wait another hour so I thought I would surprise you, my darling!" she said excitedly.

"This is a really nice surprise though! I was just sitting here checking on my bags for tomorrow and waiting for my dinner to be delivered" he replied.

"I was hoping you would be in. I'm quite surprised you didn't go out for a dinner, but lucky me" she laughed.

"Yip, the rest of the crew have gone to some café near the River Seine but I want an early night before my big match. I do have good news about Nike though" he said.

"Pray tell. Did Dov get the deal?" she asked, eagerly.

"You were right to tell me to leave the negotiations to him. He got more than just the deal. He got me *quadruple* we originally were thinking of asking, the pirate" laughed David.

"Yay! Dov, you the best" she shouted down the line.

"And he got them to throw in a whole lot of extras too!" laughed David.

"From the minute you meet a character like Dov you know he's the guy you want in your team" she said.

"We've also been allocated our practice court, court 14, for my match against Figueras which I feel really comfortable on" he said.

"I think the stars are aligning perfectly for you, Mr O. Tomorrow, go out there and give it your all" she encouraged.

"I am starting to feel some nerves for the first time though" he confessed.

"That's good. It means you are ready, you're in the zone for this David."

"Oh boy, I think that's my food at the door."

"Well, let me love and leave you my darling. I look forward to celebrating your win on the phone tomorrow night. Have a good sleep and have a decent breakfast tomorrow morning. Go eat your dinner then have a relaxing shower and sleep. Good luck and I love you" she said, before ending the call.

This was really it now. Everything he had wanted as a young kid grinding away endlessly on the hard courts back home, the gruelling and sometimes heart breaking last 6 months of the Challenger Tour spending nights questioning his decision to become a professional. Now that the opportunity he had spent years dreaming of was finally on the doorstep, he was almost too scared to reach out and grab it.

He was going to need to have a serious talk with himself in the morning he knew.

Chapter 35

Dov let his charge sleep in until 7:30 a.m. before David was awoken by the sound of Dov's cursing whilst trying to assemble the masseuse bed.

"Jesus, they should really include *instructions* with this thing" he grumbled.

"Right Davie, get up on the bed. I'm going to give you a deep tissue rub, *boychik*" he instructed.

He hadn't been kidding either as David felt Dov's giant mitts working deep into his hamstring and calf muscles, followed by his shoulders and neck.

"I need you feeling loose and comfortable out there. He's going to try work you all over the court today and attempt to wear you down. He's got one helluva surprise coming his way that old geezer because you are going to work him over like he's never been worked over before. We've grafted too hard to allow some guy who has already experienced his glory days to block our path Davie! You were made for tennis greatness ever since you were a *kid* and you know that. If you aren't going to beat this codger for yourself and your family then you do it for *me*, you *hear* me. You owe me this David. I want it and need it for *us*" he said, moving onto David's feet.

"I'm going to do it for *us*, Dovi. For all those fucking endless hours in the heat, waking up at ridiculous goddamn hours to run and do drills and for those heart breaking losses we both had to endure. This one today is for us Dovi, nobody else."

"That's my *boychik!*" said Dov.

It was not going to be necessary to have that talk to himself after all.

Breakfast that morning, the limo drive to the stadium and stepping onto court 14 for his match with Figueras, were all just a blur to him. Later he could not even recall the lady umpire calling heads or tails or him greeting his opponent, but as soon as he hit the first ball in the knock up all his focus seemed to come back. All he could see was the ball and tennis court. He didn't even notice the crowd until much later in the match.

It took David at least 5 or 6 games to overcome his initial nervousness but by then his wily opponent had managed to break his service and finished off the set 6-4.

David felt good though and the purple stuff was starting to work its magic too. There was nothing specific about his opponent's game he hadn't seen before and his backhand was most definitely the chink in his armour. David started the second set peppering Figueras's backhand with high-bouncing angled topspin and if the reply from his opponent was a short ball, he would either hit drop shots or short angled slices back. The ploy worked and at the all-important seventh game he broke his opponent's service and evened up the match by winning the second set by the same margin as he had lost the first.

At the changeover he could hear his opponent breathing heavily and sensed he may be tiring. He knew from the outset that he had to win one of the first two sets, and he had accomplished that. His movement around the court was smooth and quick and he had retrieved any drop shots Figueras had attempted. He must have looked like a hungry young lion to the journeyman. Now he needed to put the knife in.

The third set David hit out freely and moved his opponent all over the court. He even managed 3 freebies by surprising Figueras with a couple of moon balls, mid rally. No doubt Lionel would have enjoyed those, he chuckled. Figueras hung in there valiantly but David could sense his tired, old legs were giving in. It was at this point that for the first time he sensed the crowd, and then he heard Dov.

"*Now* Davie, *now*! Remember, killer instinct!"

That was all the motivation he needed to finish off the third set 7-5.

At the changeover he looked up to the players' boxes to see his entire entourage on their feet and egging him on. Lionel was pointing to his head reminding David to think clearly and that it was all in his mind. What really caught him by surprise was to hear his father shouting out.

"C'mon Davie, you're *too* good!"

He felt tears swelling up in his eyes and then reminded himself to get control of his emotions as he took a final sip of the purple stuff.

The fourth set was quite simply a whitewash. That was the only word to describe it. David was totally focused and punished Figueras by running him all over the court. His valiant effort was not enough and David made sure he knew there was simply no coming back. David could tell from Figueras's body language he was a beaten man and duly obliged by finishing off the set 6-1.

The brave journeyman was almost relieved to shake his hand at the match's conclusion, pick up his gear and make a quick beeline for the change rooms. The full impact of winning his first match in a major championship only truly hit him when Canal+ conducted his on-court interview, in front of a fully packed court 14. Signing a few autographs was one thing but being interviewed on global television was quite something else.

"This win was for me and a very special person today, just the two of us" said David, when he was asked how he felt.

"I would like my coach, Dov Mendelson, to stand up please" he requested, pointing to his box.

Sheepishly, and with some goading by Leah and Lionel, the big unit rose in the players' box.

"I would respectfully ask everyone to give him a big hand because this win today is as much his, as it is mine" said David.

The crowd duly gave Dov the applause he deserved as they appreciated David's humility and the appreciation the young man had for his coach.

As David signed autographs for the young kids on his way back to the locker room, for the first time all afternoon he felt fatigue in his legs. When he checked his watch he understood why. They had been playing for just under three and a half hours although it had only felt like an hour.

Dov was the first to greet him in the change rooms, with tears in his eyes. His bear hug almost broke David's ribs but he didn't care. Lionel's followed straight after.

"Beautiful Davie, just beautiful! You were magnificent and I couldn't believe those moon balls" he laughed.

"Right Davie. Your family is waiting outside to congratulate you. Go see them and then straight into the ice bath for you. We have another match in 2 days" ordered Dov, getting straight back to business.

All four members of his family were in tears as he exited the locker room, even his father. His mother was so emotional that Uncle Sol had to gently pry her away from her embrace. David wasn't sure if she was going to let him go.

"Tonight, Uncle Sol, we celebrate!" shouted David.

"*Boychik*, tonight I take us to Beaujolais to celebrate. You have made your family and your people very proud" said Uncle Sol, kissing his nephew on the forehead.

"Wonderful. You lot go back to the hotel and relax a bit because Dov and I need to get me through another ice bath" said David.

David had seen a telephone in the member's lounge and couldn't resist phoning Shakira to share news of his win. He was hoping she had finished her university lectures and was home already, but instead her mother answered.

"Hi Zara, its David. I hope this isn't a bad time?" asked David.

"Oh, hi David! This is a nice surprise but aren't you supposed to be playing a match?" she asked. "I'm afraid Shakira isn't back from her lectures yet but I can always pass on a message?" she asked.

"Please, if you could Zara. I'll phone her tonight anyway but I just wanted to let her know I won today."

"Oh wow, that's fantastic David! I'm delighted for you as will Shakira be too. I hope you are going to celebrate it tonight with your family? I think MNet will show it later tonight, right?" she asked.

"I'm not sure if South Africa will show it or not as they usually only cover the seeded players' matches, but I really hope so. Is there any chance you could record it for me if they do, please? My uncle is taking us all out to Beaujolais for dinner this evening to celebrate and yes they are over the moon with my win, thank you."

"That is a *beautiful* restaurant. I think it has 2 Michelin stars if I recall so you must really enjoy it. I will pass on your message to Shakira as soon as she steps in *and* I'm going to phone Mnet immediately to see if they are showing your match later. Once again, congratulations and all the best for your next match David" she ended with.

The dinner at Beaujolais was a gastronomic delight and too sophisticated for Uncle Sol to get out of hand which was precisely the type of celebration David wanted considering his on-court exertions. Dov was beside himself with pride and happiness and toasted David at least half a dozen times that evening. He was also pleased that the 2 suits he had "negotiated" with had been true to their word and had a pile of "the good shit" delivered to their hotel for both David and Lionel. Dov said he would get his uncle in Johannesburg to scrutinise the contract they had also dropped off because he didn't trust "those sharks."

"Davie, at long last you've also earned some decent cash with this victory too, not that loose change stuff they paid out on the Challenger tour" laughed Dov.

"Well, I guess I have that to look forward to now" sighed Lionel.

Throughout dinner, as delicious as it was, David was longing to talk to Shakira and the minute he got back to his room he dialled her immediately. This time she answered and he could hear the joy in her voice.

"Big congratulations, my darling! I told you last night that we would be celebrating your win tonight. I could just feel it last night so when my mom relayed your news I was delighted but not surprised. Tell me how you feel?" she asked.

David described in detail the match with Figueras and how from the warm up he had felt good about his game. Figueras's ranking had dropped just out of the top fifty but in years gone by he had regularly been ranked in the top twenty, so this victory was no mean feat. He told her about Dov's lecture before the match which calmed and motivated him and how emotional he had been in the locker room afterwards.

"Then to celebrate, Uncle Sol took us to Beaujolais and I have never experienced fine dining like that before" he said.

"I know, I think I went twice with Jared and it was mind blowing."

"Yes, but tonight it was missing *you,* no matter how fine the food may have been. Today was my difficult day without you, Shakira."

"Me too! I may as well not have been at lectures today. All I could think was about you on that red clay court and imagining the score" she said.

"You are right, my darling, we are going to have to find a way for you to travel a bit with me on the tour" he said.

"My mom says she wants us to sit down tomorrow evening before dinner with my father. If all goes well it won't be long before I can join you."

"I can only imagine Paris with you. It's just so beautiful here. I think it's fast becoming my second favourite city after Durban" he said.

"Well, my darling, I'm starting to feel tired after a big first day but I'll be dreaming that you are with me in Paris tonight. I'm holding thumbs your dad is in a good mood when you sit with him."

"I hope so too. My mom thinks he suspects it has something to do with Mo but it's another surprise instead" she laughed.

"Oh yes, your match will be screened at 1 a.m. so I will be staying up with my mom to watch that and record it for you" she said.

"Ah, that's awesome, it'll be interesting to watch it with you when I get back" he said.

"Sleep tight, my angel. We are so proud of you but you need to sleep. I love you."

Paris had served up a peach of a day and within minutes David fell fast asleep, clothes and all.

Chapter 36

Dov woke him at 8 a.m. for both an early morning massage and to let him know who his next opponent would be.

"Davie, I think *HaShem* is blessing us. Your opponent is the twenty-eighth seed, some Yank called Buster Johnson who got a walk over in the first round. He was lucky too because he's a serve-and-volley specialist with a horrible clay court record. I think you can take this guy apart with your superior baseline game" he reported.

"I think today Lionel should put you through serve-and-volley drills for ninety minutes and then take a break for the rest of the day. We should go up the Eiffel Tower and just take our minds off the tennis. On another note, Moshe has informed me that they've made contact already with the problem guy in Gaza. Your information was amazing, David, and the father won't even need to worry about dealing with it. The money will keep on flowing but to the *right sources* who need it desperately. Shakira's father is a decent man like you said. He's no supporter of terrorism. They still don't know how he's getting the cash out but that's not our business and good luck to him. Anyway you've done an amazing thing for your people, David, and your little family in Israel have sent a big bouquet of flowers and Israeli fruits and nuts for you for your victory yesterday. They are praying for you *every day,* David" said Dov.

"I miss them and I can't wait for them to meet Shakira in Israel one day" replied David.

"I honestly think *HaShem* brought us into your life so you could meet her, Davie. You have also taught all of us that true love transcends all barriers whether religious or racial. I've watched how you two look at and talk to each other and I'm envious. I only hope I can find someone as amazing as her to share my world with one day. In Shakira, you have found someone *very special* my friend, and ironically in the most unusual of circumstances"

"I couldn't help myself Dov even in spite of the training from Dr Berkowitz. She's just too beautiful a person, both inside and out. I'm not too proud to say that there were times I looked at her and wondered why someone like her would even bother looking at *me,* never mind giving me her heart" David replied.

For the first time in months the weight of the conflict within him melted away. The thought of having to betray Shakira's trust in him, and then on the other side, of not protecting his own people who were on the receiving end of the possible actions of her father, had worn heavily on him. So often he had laid on his bed unable to sleep and feeling racked with guilt. Betraying the only girl he had ever loved would inevitably have meant the end of the relationship and caused her deep hurt, but not doing anything to prevent the arming of Hamas and Hezbollah with South African money to kill more innocent Jews, would have been just as bad if not worse. Whichever side he had chosen would have brought heartache and pain. Having both Shakira and helping his people had *never* at any point seemed like a possibility to David, until now. At times the pressure of his situation had almost seemed so unbearable that he had once, in a moment of anger, thought about walking away from it all. It had only been a fleeting moment, but still it had crossed his mind.

"Wow! I know I'm going pretty deep into your neck muscles but it is incredible how it feels like your entire body has just gone like jelly" said Dov, who had been digging deeply into his neck and shoulder muscles with those big mitts of his.

"Now you may be able understand how much stress this whole situation with the father has caused me, Dovi. Today she and her mother are going to break the news of David Oppenheimer, who also happens to be Jewish, being his daughter's lover. Poor Shakira is all I can say! This is going to be especially hard because she rejected the poor dude her father approved of. Some hot shot kid of one of his business associates and a friend of her family's. Instead, she's chosen a white guy and Jewish on top of that! As we both know he's a strict, pious Muslim father and she's his everything and being groomed to take over his business empire" laughed David.

"Yip, it's a lot to take in!" laughed Dov.

"It could go a number of ways including him banning her from seeing me. The last thing I want to do is to damage her relationship with her parents. I don't know if I could live with that on my conscience, and then there's the thing she's already had her heart broken before by a Jew, whose family rejected her.

Imagine if she's got to go through the reverse situation with her family rejecting *me* because I'm Jewish?" said David.

"*HaShem* will deliver the right result, Davie. If the father saw you two together he would understand how you two are a perfect fit. Everybody who has seen you two together has commented how perfectly you match. Even her friend, Miriam, told me that at the seafood restaurant we all went to by the harbour. She told me she's never seen Shakira so in love with anyone before" said Dov, digging deeply into his calf muscles now.

"I think if the father saw us together right now he would probably *shoot me*!" laughed David.

"I don't know, if he loves her as much as you say he does and she tells him how she really feels about you, along with her mother's approval, I think you'll be okay" said Dov, reassuringly.

"Anyway Davie, it's out of your hands now so let things take their natural course and you focus on the tennis. It's going to work out fine. I also wanted to say that just because this thing with her father has been resolved I'm still here for you if you still need or want me" said Dov.

"Don't be bloody *meshuggeh*, Dovi. You are both wanted and needed as Team O's coach. I couldn't do this without you now. You are my family and there's no escaping this I'm afraid!" he replied.

"Unless you have something *better* to do?" asked David, cheekily.

"And you call me *meshuggeh*? No chance, we got lots of matches still ahead of us, you meathead" laughed Dov.

Upon arrival at Roland Garros there was a noticeable increase in the volume of spectators even those just watching the players practicing before play proper got underway. David and Lionel made their way through the crowds in their new Nike sneakers to court 14 which looked like it was going to be their fixed practice court for the week. The stands were jam-packed but they had become accustomed to the crowds and both Lionel and Dov were even waving at a couple of them they recognised.

"Ah, I'm very pleased to see you back to watch us, sir. Today we are putting on a baseline versus serve-and-volley clinic for you and because you are a loyal supporter I have something for you!" shouted Dov, throwing the elderly gentleman a bottle of the purple stuff.

"Thank you, young man. Very kind of you. Will it help me with my wife?" he joked and causing much laughter.

"If she's twenty years old, then yes, but if she's your age or thereabouts, it may be a bit late!" laughed Dov.

The slower, bouncier clay was no surface to be testing a serve-and-volley game against the baseline strokes of a David Oppenheimer. Lionel knew it and was unsurprised when David sent return after return off his hard first serves and kicking second serves whizzing past him, or fizzing at this feet, which then left easy shots for David to pick him off with. When Lionel tried to take some pace off his first serve and hit wide sliders the results were even worse for him because David was able to generate even more acute-angled returns which had Lionel sliding all over the slippery clay surface.

During one of their drink breaks Dov had spotted the Nike gents standing near the exit of the main stand and suggested that all three of them wave to them, which was duly returned by "the sharks".

"Don't worry, boys, I'm not finished with those fuckers yet. After you've beaten the Yank tomorrow they are going to be paying for our team's lovely dinner rather than Uncle Sol tomorrow night, you watch me" he said, giving them a friendly second wave.

"I should be hearing from my uncle tonight if their written contract is good without any "fuck you" clauses in smallprint, Davie. These *schmuckos* mustn't think we Saffers are thickos" he laughed.

"By the way, if you guys haven't noticed yet, we have an interesting spectator sitting at the top of the stand behind me. Don't both look at once but I think its Wilander, in dark glasses with his coach next to him. I can assure you he's not here to see what his Tacchini styles look like on you guys. So for the last thirty minutes let's not give him any pointers. He's in our half of the draw, Davie, and if you get through you could play each other in the quarters. But let's not get ahead of ourselves ... he may not even make the quarters!" barked Dov loudly.

For the last thirty minutes David practiced his volleys which gave absolutely nothing away. He noticed after about ten minutes Wilander leaving the court although his coach remained another ten minutes or so before doing the same. He could hardly think of making the quarters in his first major but playing against one of his boyhood idols, who had already won the French *twice*, was beyond a dream. The mere fact that Wilander was watching him, a mere wildcard, practice at all, added to his confidence. He must have recognised him as some kind of a threat possibly.

After their practice session SABC who were covering the championships via radio broadcast, requested an interview which David managed to coax Dov into joining.

"Listeners, I have with me our own David Oppenheim and his coach, Dov Mendelson. For those who don't know David he was our top-ranked junior in his under 18 year and graduated at the end of last year from the University of Natal in Durban with a commerce degree. He has been doing very well this year on the Challenger tour and was granted a wild card entry into these championships as a result. He won his first round match yesterday against a journeyman Spanish clay court specialist with a fine display, and is scheduled to play the twenty-eighth seed, American Butch Johnson, in the second round tomorrow" announced Trevor Quirk.

"David and Dov, a warm welcome from all of us. How are you feeling David?" he asked.

"Thanks, Trevor and a big "howzit" to everyone back home in SA. To answer your question, and I think I can also speak for Dov here, we are so excited and feel fantastic. We are in one of the most amazing, beautiful, cities in the world and living our dream" replied David.

"You feeling confident for tomorrow, young man?" asked Quirk.

"Without getting ahead of ourselves I would say that Dov and I have done everything possible to prepare for anybody. These last few months, besides the regular Challenger tournaments hosted all over the world, we have got up at the crack of dawn to train, we've spent endless hours on the courts doing drills and practicing and lots of other things to achieve good results. We are ready for tomorrow, sir" said David.

"And you, big man? How do you rate your chances tomorrow, coach?" asked Quirk, moving his attention to Dov.

"Before that Trevor, I need to thank our wonderful sponsors ,Head and Sergio Tacchini, who have been so supportive right from the beginning and Nike, who we are about to sign a deal with. Trevor, David was born to be a tennis champion and now *he* believes it. He's in the top two-hundred in the world and should he win tomorrow he could be as low as one-hundred and twenty so there's lots to be motivated for. I've got him in the best shape of his life so now he needs to go out there and show the world he's a top twenty player" said Dov.

"Wow! *Top twenty*, that's confidence right there. Coach, we've seen you dishing out in the practices and then David drinking it during his match yesterday. What is that purple concoction he's drinking? It looks like turpentine to us. Care to elaborate?" asked Quirk, humorously.

"Yes, it is turbo fluid for tennis players, possibly mixed with a touch of turpentine to add zing!" barked Dov, with his trademark grin.

"Well, whatever it is it's working and my co-commentator Edwill has requested if you could bring some for your next interview!" laughed Quirk.

"Finally, David, any messages for the people back home before we let you chaps go?" asked Quirk.

"Yes, but before we do that I would like to give a special thanks to my friend and practice partner, Lionel Perreira, who has given a lot of himself and his time in helping Dov and I prepare for these championships. He's been an essential part of Team O and keep an eye out for him because he's going to crack the top one-hundred even faster than me. I also want to send out a message to my little family in Israel who I miss so much and love very much. There's also a special little lady back home, no names mentioned, who I hope is listening to your broadcast. I love you lots, my darling" said David.

"Thanks gents, and go make our country proud tomorrow" said Quirk, ending the interview.

With his duties at the courts done for the day David went directly back to the hotel. He told Dov that after the call he was expecting from Shakira he would do the Eiffel tower tour with their entourage and then head back to the hotel for an early night. Fortunately, the organisers had given the players and their families free Express passes for the tower for the week and Shakira had stressed he should take advantage of the opportunity.

The telephone in his room rang just before 5 p.m.

"Hello, my darling, how was it?" asked David nervously.

“Hello, my David. Well it went much better than I had anticipated. First off, my mom told me in the morning that my father received an interesting call late last night from Gaza. Turns out my father was correct in his assumptions about his erstwhile cousin but the man grew a conscience and took it upon himself to confess his crimes to the agency director. The man felt for him and gave him an ultimatum to leave Gaza immediately, otherwise face prosecution for theft and fraud in an Israeli jail. He phoned my father late last night to explain the situation and also to ask him if my father wouldn’t take him in here and set him back on the right path. My father, being the kind, generous man he is, agreed to this, so Goolam will literally work for Mo under his thumb. Mo is not nearly as forgiving as my father so he’s in for a really tough time. Anyway, the point is my father was in a really good mood and my mom says he has even increased his donations to make up for the funds his cousin misappropriated.

My father was dreading our meeting though because he really thought poor Mo was up to no-good so he was almost relieved when we told him. He was really shocked though that you were both *white* and *Jewish* but considering how many Jewish business partners he has, I think he realised it would be a tad hypocritical using that angle. He actually didn’t say much until we told him your name and then after a moment of silence, he actually burst out laughing. Your picture of you being interviewed yesterday with a whole long article about you was the back cover story of this morning’s Natal Mercury and he had read it only minutes before we sat with him” she explained.

“What?” he laughed.

“I kid you not, my angel. After our call I will fax a copy of it to the hotel. It’s a fantastic article and you look amazing in that Tacchini outfit I selected for you” she laughed.

“After my mom had spoken so glowingly about you, and then I told him my feelings, he only had 2 questions for me. First, he asked me how long this had been going on for, and second, if you treated and loved me like he does. When I told him about how both you and Leah treat me like I am already part of your family I did see just a tiny grin on his face. Then he left telling us that it was a lot for him to take in and he would discuss it further tomorrow night. He just needed to let it sink in which is exactly what he does before making a big business decision. My mom thinks it’s a good sign, my darling” she said, sounding very hopeful.

"Well, it's a helluva lot better than an outright no, which I was hoping wouldn't be the case!" laughed David.

"I hope he doesn't need the extra time to arrange a French hit man for me!" he joked.

"Not after the way my mom spoke to him. She reminded him how difficult his family had been towards them wanting to get married and how it has soured many things between them as a result. We owe her big time. She knows just how to talk to my father" explained Shakira.

After chatting a further few minutes to Shakira he bid her farewell and headed out to join his entourage in the hotel bar and then on to the Eiffel tower.

Uncle Sol had managed to charm a very well-spoken American lady, staying at the hotel for business in Paris. She had relatives in Johannesburg and was also following the tennis. Much to Lara's disgust she was at least 25 years younger than Uncle Sol which made her even more attractive to him, and she had agreed to join them for the trip up the tower. Fortunately the championship organisers had been generous with the Express tickets and they had one for her too.

The view from the tower was magnificent, in spite of the throng of tourists, many of whom glared at them in envy as their crew zipped to the front with their Express cards. Their timing was just perfect as they caught the evening's sunset and a 360 degree view of the City of Lights. Right there and then David decided if he were ever to propose to Shakira, this was the place he would do it. It was obvious why to so many this was the most romantic city in the world.

After the tower David parted company with his entourage, who were off for another dinner, to order up room service again, the chicken salad once more, to not break his winning routine. He was delighted to hear how the situation with Shakira's father's cousin, Goolam, had been so easily resolved without anyone being eliminated and that the funds would keep on rolling, but to the rightful charities. He had no doubts that some of the beefy lads from the Galani Brigade he had seen in Israel, had paid a visit to cousin Goolam and read him the riot act. Just looking at them probably scared the living crap out of him, David chuckled. Considering the number of Israeli deaths he was responsible for, he was very fortunate to still be breathing but no doubt Mossad would now use him for their means.

David could only imagine the crazy thoughts swilling around Ismail Mahomedy's head when he had discovered the South African tennis kid he was following had been secretly involved with his daughter for months. The same kid gracing the back sports page of his morning newspaper! It was hardly any wonder he needed some time to sort the whole thing out in his mind. Hopefully his 2 ladies had convinced him that David was good for his princess.

Only time would tell.

Chapter 37

The weather was warm and even a touch humid, a little bit like Durban's summer except the sun wasn't as biting. The sweat was pouring off David's brow but he didn't mind, in fact he loved it. It felt like home and the score line reflected it.

David had smashed Buster Johnson 6-2, 6-1 in the first two sets and was leading 4-3 in the third. The Yank knew nothing about his game or about David except that he was a wild card from somewhere in Africa. He had totally underestimated his opponent and came in with the attitude he would wipe him off the court. The electronic score board told a very different story and the Yank was becoming more and more frustrated as David whipped passing shots by him with regularity. Buster, in desperation, tried to change his game plan by staying on the baseline but that proved an even worse move so he went back to his traditional serve-and-volley style of rushing the net.

Two games later it was all over and a disconsolate Buster shook David's hand at the net.

"Where *exactly* are you from, again?" he asked in his southern drawl.

"Just that little country at the arse end of Africa" laughed David, unsure if Buster even really knew where Africa was.

His on-court interview was short and sweet like the match had been and he joined Dov in the locker room before his ice bath routine.

"Davie! *Mazels*, my *boychik*! You drove that poor Buster *oke* nuts out there. I knew you were going to smash him. Beautiful!" shouted Dov.

"OK, so you know the drill. Off to the ice baths for you. Canal+, BBC and ESPN have all asked for off-court interviews. I liked the Bud *oke* from ESPN so I gave it to him. We have to be at their studio in an hour so hurry up and finish your ice bath and freshen up!" instructed Dov.

David was quite sure that Dov had no idea the "Bud *oke*" he was referring to was the legendary Bud Collins, who had interviewed all the biggest names in tennis.

"So, David Oppenheim, welcome to you and your coach, Dov Mendelson to our studios here at the French Open. Let me start by asking you first, who the Hell are you and where have you been hiding? We really know nothing about you?" laughed Bud Collins.

Before he could answer, Dov jumped in "Well, you sure as hell know who he is *now,* Mr Collins!" to much laughter.

"We certainly know he's in the 3rd round of the French Open after knocking out both Figueras and Johnson but not much else I'm afraid" laughed Bud Collins.

"Well, I'm a native of Durban, South Africa where I went to college. I joined the Challenger tour end of last year full-time and was lucky enough to be given a wild card by the very kind French organisers" replied David.

"Well, you sure know how to manage your way around a clay court, son. We saw how frustrated you had our poor Buster today. I counted 28 passing shots off his serve alone. Did you grow up on clay in Durban?" he asked.

"No sir! No clay or grass courts in South Africa. I learnt how to play on clay overseas on the Challenger tour. I feel very at home on clay though and I feel especially at home here in Paris" he said.

"And your two big wins are showing that. We've calculated you should be around one-hundred and sixteen in the world rankings after your victory against Johnson. Do you know who you face in the 3rd round?" asked Bud.

"Nope. Are you able to tell me?" asked David.

"Yes I can and will, young man. You're up against Juan-Carlos Sanchez who was a semi-finalist last year here and made the same stage a few weeks ago in Monte Carlo. Any thoughts about that one?" asked Bud.

Once again, Dov answered for him. "We love eating Spanish. We had espetada on Monday for 4 sets and we'll order the same on Friday for lunch" he laughed.

"We will treat that match no different than our last 2 matches, Mr Collins. Dov and I are nobodies with everything to gain and zilch to lose. Imagine how seeded players must feel losing to a wild card? That's a lot of pressure" laughed David, hoping this interview would be heard by his opponent.

"I have to say you two look so relaxed you could be on holiday!" chuckled Bud.

"Who says we *aren't* on holiday?" barked Dov, with his big grin.

"Well, you two, congratulations on making it this far. David you play a beautiful game and we look forward to covering that match which my colleagues tell me will be on one of the stadium courts" said Bud.

"Remember the name *David Oppenheim*! And Mr Bud we look forward to our next interview with you sir" shouted Dov, before an amused Bud Collins could sign off.

"And that ladies and gents is the coach of Mr David Oppenheim, Mr Dov Mendelson" said Bud to much hilarity in the studio.

If nothing else they were certainly getting plenty exposure thought David, eyeing his crazy coach.

That evening David allowed himself a couple of glasses of Dom Perignon at yet another of the amazing French restaurants. This time, true to his word, Dov insisted that the 2 suits from Nike join them so they could sign the contract his uncle had green-lighted. The suits also discovered that Nike would be covering the bill at Peregrine, another Michelin star eatery, where Dov ordered a couple bottles of DP to celebrate.

David was amused to see Uncle Sol had invited his new friend, Rachel, to join them again for the evening and they were really cosying up to each other. It made him sad sometimes that Uncle Sol had not found a partner to share his life with and that they were his only family. It was no wonder his mother fussed over her brother like she did, more like a neurotic Jewish mother than his sister.

As soon as they got back to their hotel he dialled Shakira and once again she immediately answered.

"You won! I heard and watched your interviews too, my angel. Congratulations and thanks for not mentioning me by name" she laughed.

"I couldn't resist but then afterwards I did think I maybe shouldn't have said anything, because with your dad ..." he replied.

"Well, just the two of us went out for walk down by the harbour earlier this evening. He was very sweet and kind with me. He told me that he trusted me because I have always made smart decisions in life but he also wanted me to be sure of the difficulties we could face because we would be choosing the path less travelled, with all its unknowns. He watched your ESPN interview this afternoon which they showed on Mnet tonight and was very impressed with the way you conducted yourself. He loved Dov too and the way he is so protective of you.

David, to quote him he said, "I want to meet this young man who has won my princess's heart" so when you are back we'll set up a family meeting. He's already given his unofficial blessing to us by asking to meet with you. I think we are good! Now it's just for you to do the same with your parents" she said.

"Oh, by the way I spoke to Leah and she was saying your Uncle Sol may have a young American girlfriend?" she asked, chuckling.

"Yip, her name is Rachel and she's from New York City. She came out with us tonight again. She seems very nice and wants to come watch me play on Friday. The great news is that we've been upgraded to one of the stadium courts and the match will be televised live here" said David.

"Wow! This is now getting serious" she said.

"It sure is and at each stage the expectations get bigger, along with the pressure too, my angel. My sponsors are now also expecting more from me and when I walk out there sporting there brands I'm representing them too" he said.

"Never forget why you chose this path rather than enrol for your Honours degree, David. You love this game and as Dov said, you were born for it. Go out there and enjoy it" she replied.

"I'm a lucky man to have such a smart girlfriend who knows exactly the right things to tell me" he laughed.

"How are EB and Miriam, by the way?" he asked.

"All well and very excited for you. Miriam asks me every 5 minutes at varsity for updates on your progress and what you are getting up to in Paris. Everyone is excited for your next match and want to watch it live" she said.

"I'm going to suggest to my dad that we all watch it together on Friday after prayers. I can assure you there will be many prayers being said for you here, my love, whether you like it or not" she teased.

"Well, call me tomorrow night after you've eaten and let me know how you feeling" she said.

"Will do and I'm so relieved things have gone so well with you and your dad. I'll call you tomorrow then. Love you with all my heart and then some more. Sleep tight" he said, ending their call.

David was surprised to see he had slept so long when he finally woke at 9 a.m. Thursday morning. He was so used to Dov waking him up that he hadn't bothered setting his human alarm clock. He quickly threw on some clothes and wandered to see what the rest of his crew were up to, only to discover they were all still fast asleep. He could only assume that they had gone on quite a bender after he had parted company with them so he decided to go have a breakfast downstairs. The restaurant was busy as the hotel was filling up with more tourists and tennis fans as the weekend and second week of the championships was drawing closer. Quite a few of the guests were starting to recognise him from the local television broadcasts and were beginning to greet him now and shake his hand.

Slowly but surely individual members of his crew started to arrive for breakfast, all-bar-none looking worse for wear, even his mother. According to Leah they had wound up at some night club and after copious amounts of alcohol and lots of dancing they had dragged their sorry selves back into the hotel at 5 a.m. David had never seen either Dov or Uncle Sol looking so subdued and quiet before.

"Look, I think you lot should go back to bed and sleep off your hangovers. I'm off to visit Jim Morrison's grave at Pere Lachaise. I can't visit Paris and not see The Lizard King's resting place, which apparently isn't too far from here."

"Davie, we have an interview with the BBC at 3 p.m. and after that Head want you for some promotional stuff too. We should leave here just after 2 p.m., OK" mumbled Dov.

"Perfect, I'll be ready, now go get some shut eye" laughed David.

The Cimetiere du Pere-Lachaise was a twenty minute ride in the stretch limousine and housed some of the most famous artists, writers and poets of their time, like Edith Piaf, Chopin, Sarah Bernhardt, Oscar Wilde and of course Jim Morrison amongst many others. David always found it amusing that, just as in life Morrison had been mysterious, so was he in death. He had died under very mysterious circumstances in Paris aged only twenty-seven years without an autopsy being performed and only 2 witnesses to the body, both of whom passed not long after. As David laid the flowers he had bought on Jim's grave, he wondered if the man was truly buried below it or like many others suspected, he was still very much alive, working as a postman in some obscure little neck of the woods. One thing was for sure though, his music was still very much alive and kicking.

The walk through the cemetery was calming and peaceful with the wonderful flora and bird life, in spite of being home to more than a million poor souls.

He was glad to have found the time to have made the visit and enjoyed the eighty minute walk back to the hotel. The weather was wonderful and there was a feeling of joy and lightness in all the treed neighbourhoods he walked through. It was easy to see how artists and creative types drew inspiration from the beauty of this city.

On arrival back at the hotel David only had time for a quick salmon salad before it was time to depart for the stadium once again. Dov looked a lot better when he stepped into the limousine but there was no sign of Lionel who had made it very clear to all to not disturb him.

Roland Garros was pumping with spectators when they arrived and David was overwhelmed by the number of fans who still recognised him in casual clothes and sunglasses, demanding his signature.

"The joys of fame, Davie" teased Dov.

David thoroughly enjoyed the twenty minute television interview with the BBC. The interviewer was a former professional player who really understood the game and asked challenging and thought-provoking questions.

"David, when one of your idols, Mats Wilander, won his first French Open championship in 1981, you would have still been a young lad just starting high school. Did you watch him winning the final that year?" asked Chris Evans.

"I did, but not live though. One of my tennis coaches had a tape sent to him and so we watched a recorded version about a week later" laughed David.

"So how do you feel now, playing on the same courts and the same tournament as your schoolhood idol?" asked Evans.

"It's really surreal actually and I'm even wearing his line of Tacchini for the tournament too" replied David.

"So, you are both in the same half of the draw and should you both win your remaining matches, in theory you could face him in the quarters. Has that crossed your mind?"

"You mean, *when* we reach the quarters and, *if* Wilander should win his next two matches" barked Dov, causing a stir.

"That's my coach, Dov Mendelson, sorry. He gets very excited at tournaments" laughed David.

"It would be a dream to play Mats Wilander at any stage of the tournament. I would love to pit myself against him to see where my game stacks up against the best. To win majors you have to beat the best, it's as simple as that" explained David.

"How is it that without any clay courts in the country you grew up in and with only a few months of playing on the surface overseas, you seem to be so at home here on clay?" asked Evans.

"My guy is a clay court savant, is how!" barked Dov again, simply unable to resist and causing much hilarity. His hangover had clearly lifted, thought David.

"Sorry about that! No I don't think I'm any sort of savant but I've always had a strong baseline game and so clay is a natural fit for me really. It's hardly like all of this came overnight. I grew up on the courts of Mitchell Park and Westridge Park in my hometown of Durban and spent endless hours practicing there" explained David.

"How do you intend to beat a seasoned pro like Sanchez tomorrow then, young man?" asked Evans.

"As my coach is wont to say sir, I could tell you but then I would have to kill you straight after!" laughed David, bringing on huge guffaws from Dov.

"Well on that note, David, we have really enjoyed watching your tennis and would like to wish you all the best for tomorrow" said Evans, ending off the interview.

After the BBC interview Head needed to do some promotional shots of David for some posters they were going to hang around the stadium. It was easy work and didn't take more than thirty minutes. Rather than return to the hotel they decided to have dinner whilst watching Wilander play a young Frenchman.

David marvelled at Wilander's patience and understanding of the game. Even when the partisan French crowd became antagonistic and insulting as their countryman was being exposed he never lost composure or allowed it to affect him. He worked his younger opponent around the court effortlessly and never once looked rushed. Unlike his opponent, he seemed to have so much more time to execute his strokes.

"The guy is good for sure, Davie, but he's not unbeatable. I'm sure if you kept testing him you would find that chink in his armour. Everyone has one" said Dov.

"Well, if he has one please tell me because I can't see it!" laughed David.

"You will only expose a man's weakness when he's under pressure and this guy isn't under any real pressure from this French kid" observed Dov.

"Sure, but how do you put him under pressure to start with?"

"Show him something new he's never had to deal with. Whatever that is I don't know. *I'm* not the tennis player, don't forget. That would have to come from you. Maybe throwing in 2 first serves when you 40-15 up for instance?" suggested Dov.

"Dovi you are a lot smarter than you look, you know that?" laughed David.

"Tell me something I don't already know" Dov laughed back.

After watching Wilander annihilate his opponent in straight sets they headed home for an early dinner at their hotel.

"Right Davie, I'll wake you up early for a good rub down. Tomorrow is a biggie. Sanchez is your typical, tough, Spanish clay courter and we've seen dozens of those over the last 6 months. You know how to deal with them. You take them to the deep waters and drown them, is all. See you in the morning."

As he stepped into his hotel suite he could hear the telephone ringing and reached it just in time.

"Sorry, I'm a bit early tonight but I just wanted to hear your voice. We all saw your interview with the BBC a little earlier, my dad included. We just loved all

Dov's remarks and your embarrassed apologies for him. You guys make such a cute team" she laughed.

"We didn't look too Laurel and Hardy-ish?" asked David.

"Not at all. You guys looked fun but also serious about winning. My dad even had a good laugh at Dov and wants to meet him too, so we'll have to have him over" she said.

"So, last night my entire crew, including my parents, went out drinking and dancing and only crawled back into the hotel at 5 a.m. They all looked like a bomb had hit them at breakfast this morning. I decided to head off to Pere Lachaise and lay some flowers on The Lizard King's grave. I also walked around the cemetery and visited other famous artists' graves. It's really peaceful with all the flora and birds" he told her.

"That's fantastic, my angel. You've always wanted to do that, you said."

"I'm going to have to say good night now and get some rest before my big match against Sanchez tomorrow. They have us playing on Suzanne Lenglen stadium court tomorrow so there are going to be a couple thousand spectators which will be something new" he said.

"Alright, my angel, my whole family will be watching you live on MNet tomorrow. Now that you are the last South African in the draw all the focus is on you. It's so exciting. Go for it, my angel!" she finished the call with.

The walk back from Pere Lachaise had been good for David and within minutes of ending his call with Shakira he was asleep.

Friday was going to be the biggest day of his career yet.

Chapter 38

Like clockwork Dov woke him up at 7:30 a.m. and administered a particularly punishing sports massage on him. This time there was no need for any pep talks from Dov. David was confident and as prepared as he was ever going to be.

Even during the short thirty minute warm up that Lionel put him through on court 14, David felt good. All the good feelings as he ran through all his various strokes returned to his body and he knew he was ready by the time they walked on to Suzanne Lenglen at 2 p.m. The stadium was only a quarter full but that was at least double the number he had experienced before. He was happy to look up at his players' box and see his full team sitting there including his uncle's new interest, Rachel.

As with his match against Figueras it took a few games for David to overcome his nerves of playing on such a big stage and he lost the first set 6-3. By the second set his full repertoire of stroke making had come together and he took the set, 6-4. By that point they had been on court for two hours and the stadium was almost two thirds full and the crowd were starting to pull for him, the underdog.

In the third set Sanchez proved why he was the 8th seed and showed the same level of patience and calm Wilander had displayed the previous evening, whilst David pushed a little too hard. His opponent continued this through to the fourth set and at a changeover David found himself two sets to one down, four games to three down, and a break in the fourth set. He was staring down the barrel of the gun and he knew he had to change something. He sat back in the chair and sipped on the purple stuff and stared up at his box for some inspiration. He could hardly believe his eyes to see none other than the imposing sight of little Dr Berkowitz sitting next to Dov. She was the only one standing and when she noticed him looking at her she kept on beating at her chest. Courage! She wanted to see courage from him. It was exactly the inspiration he needed and he returned the signal by beating his chest too. He saw her smile and nod her head.

He decided if he was going to go down it would be on his terms so right from the start of Sanchez's service game he started hitting out freely like he had nothing to lose. At thirty-all for the first time in the match he noticed the first signs of doubt from his opponent and David pounced and broke back by winning the next 2 points. The crowd sensed a change in momentum and were now shouting "Allez, David, allez!" He could also hear Dov and Lionel screaming words of encouragement, some of which Dov was purposely shouting in Afrikaans!

David could feel a resurgence of energy and pushed his tiring opponent to all sides of the court for the next hour. At 5-2 in the fifth set, he finished off his exhausted opponent who was very gracious in defeat and wished him success in the next round.

The crowd had carried him through with their support and David thanked them sincerely in his on-court interview. He also made a point of thanking his surprise visitor in his box and he could see Dr Berkowitz wiping her eyes when he said it.

As he surveyed the stadium he noticed that there wasn't an empty seat and he could feel its energy radiating love onto him. He glanced at the stadium clock and was shocked to see they had been playing for nearly four and a half hours. He was really going to need his ice bath tonight, for sure.

The celebrations in his locker room were crazy, especially contrasted with the rather morose state his team had been in at the previous morning's breakfast. Dov had managed to find a ghetto blaster from somewhere and insisted on blasting out Queen's "We are the Champions" until one of the tournament officials came and confiscated it. That still didn't stop him from singing it and in fact if anything, was far worse. David had never seen Dr Berkowitz so emotional and she gave him a long hug. She was too emotional to even speak and just smiled continuously at David and laughed at Dov.

"OK, Davie I promised the Bud *oke* an exclusive if you won straight after the match, so we better go. Everyone, dinner is on Nike again tonight. We'll see you at the hotel in 2 hours!" shouted Dov.

"Good evening, viewers. We have David Oppenheim and his coach, Dov Mendelson, with us again tonight. Welcome gents. Firstly David, a fantastic match and congratulations on your come-from-behind 5 set victory. That must feel really special?" asked Bud Collins.

"It feels blood exhausting is what it feels! But yes, Dov and I are delighted with this one. I was starting to think I was a goner at 4-3 and a break down in the fourth" said David.

"So what changed it?" asked Bud.

"I think he got tight and I got loose is what happened" explained David.

"I told you we would be back for more interviews, Mr Collins!" shouted Dov.

"You certainly did, son!" laughed Bud.

"You did look like you were going to have a heart attack in the box at various stages though, coach?" said Bud.

"Yes, please tell David *not* to put me through that again, Mr Collins. He has no idea what I have to go through" laughed Dov.

"Well, we love having you two South Africans in our studio and I'm rooting for you guys to keep advancing through the draw. I have no doubt we'll be seeing you two again shortly. Good luck" he ended the interview with.

That evening David had promised Leah he would attend a *Shabbat* service with her at the Synagogue de Tournelles, in the heart of the Jewish Quarter. Even though David had played a four and a half hour match that afternoon Leah insisted they do the hour-long walk from the hotel to the *shul*. It was good in that it gave them an hour alone to just talk.

"David you are so lucky to have Shakira. We've been chatting quite often this week with early morning calls before she heads out for lectures. I'm so pleased things have gone well with her mother and father for you" she said.

"Thanks, it's a huge relief for both of us. But Michael seems a lovely man too" he replied.

"Yes, but there is something we have both realised and that is we fell in love with each other's *minds* not so much our hearts. We aren't in love like you two are, we are not destined to have that sort of relationship. I think us spending time around you two brought Michael and I to that realisation. We have mutually agreed to that and decided a friendship is what we both want. We are still talking every day and are just as close as we were. He is still hoping to be your friend too by the way."

"On the one hand, I'm sad to hear this because he's a fine young man, certainly many levels above the Myron Hirschowitz's of this world, but on the other hand, you have both handled the situation very maturely and I'm proud of both of you for that. I would certainly like to keep the friendship with him going because, being a fellow Aquarian, I find him brilliant and fascinating so please tell him that. It would have been lovely to have had him here with us actually" he said.

"On the positive side at least you don't have the pressure of having to tell our lovely parents any longer" laughed David.

"Actually, on *that* subject, I did have an ulterior motive behind insisting we walk tonight and not just preparing for *shomer Shabbats* in the future" she said.

"Jesus, please don't tell me you've had a change of heart about Myron Hirschowitz! *Anybody* but him Leah!" laughed David.

"Don't be silly, my brother! No, after much thinking and after seeing how in love you and Shakira are I wanted to help take some pressure off you so you can just concentrate on your tennis. I've seen the level of stress this has caused you having to sneak around behind mom and dad's backs as well as that of her family. It's not good for you and after a lot of thought I took it upon myself to break the news of what I've had with Michael the last year and about the seriousness of your relationship with Shakira. Please don't be angry with me but it's just not healthy for anybody, all this cloak-and-dagger stuff" she said very calmly.

It took at least a minute for David to get over the initial shock of Leah's revelation.

"What did they say?" asked David, his initial response.

"Well I think after all the Gentile girls you have seen they were better prepared. They still have open-minded European DNA fortunately so were pretty accepting of it from the get-go. They had both noticed the sparkle in your eyes so had suspected there was someone special in your life. Mom only wants the best for you, David, even if it's not her first wish of it being a nice, little, Jewish girl. I told them what a beautiful person Shakira is and how she is by far the nicest girl I have ever seen you with. They want to meet her as soon as we get back" she replied.

“So, they OK with it then?” he asked.

“Yes, my brother. If you are happy, they are happy” she laughed.

David, out of relief, put his arm around his sister as they walked.

“It was a bit cheeky and presumptuous of you but you did it with the best of intentions and it does feel like a weight off my shoulders” he said.

“You welcome!” she replied, cheekily.

The synagogue and Jewish quarter were lovely and David felt very at home walking passed all the kosher delicatessens and restaurants. He felt quite tired by the time they arrived and used the service to get some shut-eye until the rabbi called out his name to the congregation and said a special blessing for him. He didn’t even realise he had been recognised until he saw the grin on Leah’s face. He was touched how many of the worshippers came to greet him and congratulate him at the end of the service.

Leah conceded to a ride from the Jewish quarter back to their hotel because of David’s tough match. The hotel staff had prepared a special meal for his tribe on the outside patio of the restaurant with the best views of the Eiffel Tower. Dov and Sol were in festive spirits and soon had the entire restaurant singing songs, including the French national anthem at one point. At some stage the staff had moved some tables and chairs and made a make-shift dance floor to enjoy the occasion, and his crew obliged until late. David, although feeling the weight of the day, was so touched but all the while felt Shakira’s absence. He had only spoken briefly with her after getting back to the hotel from *shul*. He had just enough time to chat briefly about the match, fill her in on the discussion Leah had taken upon herself to have with his parents about them and that his last sixteen opponent would be a Frenchman, one Jean-Baptiste Leconte, the fourth seed. She sounded thrilled and had told him she would soon have a nice little surprise for him.

When he eventually got to bed at 1 a.m. on Saturday morning David fell immediately into a deep sleep and for once did not even dream. He was awoken by Dov at 9:30 a.m. for his customary deep tissue massage. Dov was feeling especially energised as he had met a young lass from Ireland with even more sass than him, the previous night. He could feel the fatigue evaporate from his muscles as Dov’s giant mitts dug deeper and deeper into them.

“So Davie, I watched a tape of Leconte. He plays a bit of everything, lefty with a good swinging serve. Tall, with good reach and surprisingly fast for quite a big guy. Also likes to get his partisan crowd worked up and behind him so it’s imperative we shut him and them up, quickly. I think he won’t like those short, acute slices you are good at. There’s a lot of him to bend down to scrape them back” assessed Dov.

David was quite positive that Dov had received some help from Amos because it was excellent advice. As Dov had told him during the Wilander match “every man has a chink in his armour” and now he knew Leconte’s.

He met up with his entire crew for a light, early lunch at a lovely café along the River Seine. In spite of another late night of partying they were all in good spirits and seemed to have something up their sleeve. He wasn’t sure exactly what it was but he could sense something was up with them.

After lunch his mother called him over and she and his father took him for a walk along the river. They each took an arm of his on either side of him which he found most unusual, especially from his father. He was also very surprised when his father began the conversation.

“Davie, I know sometimes I have appeared distant and often disinterested in you, but I want you to know that I have always loved you, dearly. You represent so many things I am not. You are brave, popular, determined to chase your dreams and you have the makings of a champion. I, on the other hand am a book-worm, totally absorbed in my own little world. I don’t tell you nearly often enough but I am very, very proud of you, my son. That’s all I wanted to say” he ended, with a squeeze of David’s arm.

David was caught completely unawares and speechless. His father had never expressed his feelings for him before. He felt almost ashamed at how he always assumed his father considered him a *rachmones*. Before he could respond his mother chimed in.

“Davie, we want to meet Shakira. She sounds lovely and your father and I are both delighted with how happy she makes you. We’ve seen that sparkle in your eyes that no other lady has brought on. As your father says, sometimes we may seem distant but you and Leah are never far from our thoughts!” she said.

“Yes, and Leah says she is *hot* too! *Mazel tov*!” his father chirped in.

"Thank you both for your understanding. I can't tell you what a weight this is off my shoulders. We've both had to sneak around behind your backs and it's been awful to be frank. She's a remarkable woman, beautiful, intelligent, sensitive and loving. From our first conversation I fell for her and dad you are right, she's *totally hot*!" laughed David.

"The only thing that is important to us Davie is your happiness. You are your own man and you go for what you want which we love and respect about you" said his father.

After returning from their walk the crew was determined to keep him busy and away from the hotel so they played a couple of rounds of backgammon and chess at a café close to the Arc de Triomphe. After wiping all of them at chess, Rachel only then told them, to Uncle Sol's amusement, that she had been New York State junior champion. Consequently nobody challenged her again. It was almost 5 p.m. when Leah arrived to collect them in the stretch limousine for an early dinner at the hotel, this time inside at the art deco-style restaurant.

For the second time within twenty-four hours his sister surprised him. As they sat down to dinner a lovely waitress approached them and it was only when she shouted out, "*Surprise*!" did he fully realise it was his Shakira. The entire restaurant seemed to have been notified as they broke out into equal amounts of laughter and applause.

David jumped up and swept her clean off her feet into his arms. This was the best surprise he had ever experienced. They told him later that Leah had arranged the whole thing and had sneaked off in the stretch limo that afternoon to collect Shakira from the airport. The hotel manager had suggested the waitress uniform.

"I can't believe this is really happening, my darling. Did they give you a sexy maid's uniform for tomorrow morning, too?!" he laughed, kissing her on the lips.

"Come on, let me introduce you to my parents and my Uncle Sol and his friend Rachel" he said, pulling her even closer to him.

"Oh isn't it wonderful to be in the city of love!" shouted Sol.

Everybody was delighted to meet Shakira especially Leah who now had a friend to gossip with.

“I am going to have to watch you and my sister a lot more closely because you are full of surprises, although nothing beats this one. I’m the Aquarian here who is the one supposed to be surprising people, not the other way around” laughed David.

The restaurant manager had also spoken to two of the local newspapers to arrange for their photographers to come take pictures of David and his team who had become the hotel’s local celebrities.

“It feels like I was just speaking to you on the telephone. How is it you are here, my angel?” asked David, still finding it hard to believe she was sitting on his lap.

“Your sister and I bugged my mom, to the point where she convinced my father to allow me to come over! Thank goodness I still had a long term visa for France so I packed quickly and caught the next flight out of Durban via Jo’burg this morning. And so, here I am. I told you I couldn’t stay away from you for long and besides you need my support, don’t you?” she giggled.

Whilst David sat chatting with the 2 Nike suits about his win that afternoon Shakira was deep in discussion with Leah and her parents about Paris and the multiple sights they had visited. He could tell her natural warmth and beauty were winning her major points and he knew all was going to work out well for them. She already looked like part of their family.

After supper the two of them retired to David’s suite and made love in the shower.

“OMG, I have missed you so much, Mr O, that even just watching your matches on MNet wasn’t enough for me. I needed to feel your warm body against mine” she whispered into his ear.

“I still can’t believe you are mine, my angel, I can’t believe you are here with me in Paris or that you are in my room” he replied.

It didn’t take long before they had both fallen asleep in each other’s arms.

Chapter 39

Dov woke them up at 8 a.m. with coffee and croissants,

"Sorry to disturb Shakira but I need to give our boy a good 90 minute rub down today before he goes to battle with Monsieur Leconte this afternoon" said Dov.

"Let me put some clothes on after this coffee then I'll come chat with you chaps next door" she said.

Shakira was very impressed with Dov's fancy massage bed and his dedication to preparing David by getting his hands dirty, or in this case, just oily.

"Today, because he plays a Frenchman they've put Davie on centre court or Court Central and their match will be the main focus for Canal+" said Dov.

"I'm quite sure it will be packed today which means about fifteen-thousand or so spectators which is 3 times more than we have ever played in front of before. The French public can be quite hostile to their countrymen's opponents so Davie must be ready to be sworn and whistled at" said Dov.

"Wow that doesn't exactly sound like a gentleman's game like tennis" said Shakira.

"When it involves big money I'm afraid gentlemen become ruffians overnight" laughed Dov.

"We need to shut Leconte out quickly, Davie. You have lost too many first sets to date. You need to shake off any nerves from the first point so as not to let the crowd in. They are a funny bunch the Frogs and if you impress them enough they have been known to do an about-turn and support the opposition player.

I watched one of Leconte's earlier matches early this morning Davie and you know what I realised?" asked Dov.

"What's that then?" asked David, cringing as Dov moved even deeper into his calf muscle tissues.

"Leconte is the exact copy of Lionel but a left-handed version" he laughed.

"Dov, how is it you have become such a smart tennis coach so quickly?" remarked Shakira, impressed with his analysis.

"Flattery will get you everywhere, my girl" he chuckled.

"So you mean he likes to do a bit of serve-and-volleying plus a bit of baseline too then?" asked Davis

"Yip he really fancies that swinging serve to a right handers backhand in the ad court. You can expect a barrage of this today both on first and second serves. His baseline is fairly solid but not quite up to yours. As discussed, he doesn't like anything too low at his feet. I think he's 6'3" tall, this dude" explained Dov.

After a light breakfast at the hotel he took Shakira for a short walk to the River Seine where they walked hand-in-hand as she reminisced about all the sights she had visited around the city as an art student. They were both surprised at the number of passers-by who stopped them to wish David luck or to have a photo with them. It was only after David noticed a picture of them on the back page of one of the local newspapers that he realised why. They purchased a couple of the copies the newsstand vendor had for their crew back at the hotel. It was one of all of them at the hotel's restaurant, with the focus on Shakira sitting on his lap. It was good advertising for the hotel too as it was mentioned by name.

David felt strangely calm on the ride in the stretch limousine to the stadium and even as they stepped onto Court Central at 2 p.m. to a packed and noisy stadium, he felt totally at home. After taking a seat and unpacking his bag he gave a glance up to his box. Shakira's presence added a sense of glamour and beauty to his crew which no doubt was bound to attract a lot of attention from the French cameramen. David chuckled when he noticed Colleen, the Irish girl Dov had taken a liking to, sitting next to Dov. Typical Dov, he thought.

Once again Paris had served up superb weather and from the first point David came out of the blocks firing. Dov was right about the Frenchman having a wide wingspan but the angles his opponent's serve created inadvertently allowed David to create returns with even greater angles. At first Leconte thought David was just getting lucky but soon he was cursing as return after return dipped over the net passed his outstretched racket. Like Lionel had done, Leconte decided to try outplay him from the baseline which was a huge mistake.

After ninety minutes David had secured the first two sets 6-3, 6-3 when, as per Dov's predictions, the French crowd started booing and whistling at poor Jean-Baptiste Leconte who was beside himself with frustration. There was simply nothing he could do to disrupt David so he resorted to silly things like serving underhand which just played into David's hands.

The third set was a complete whitewash and David handed his opponent a bagel in under thirty minutes. Strangely, the match had been his easiest of the tournament possibly because there was just too much pressure on the Frenchman from his local crowd. Whatever it was, he was pleased to be done in 2 hours.

He did feel sorry for his opponent when he literally had to run off the court amid loud boos, whistles and a smorgasbord of edibles that were thrown at him. Only the French, thought David.

In his on-court interview David made a point of thanking each and every one of his crew in the box with a special mention of his girlfriend who had flown all the way from Durban to watch him. The French crowd really appreciated that and French TV immediately focused on Shakira as the crowd wolf-whistled their appreciation for her beauty when she appeared on the big screen of the stadium.

David had expected to feel like a bit of a novice or uninvited stranger at his first time on centre court but it felt no different than playing at Mitchell or Westridge Park, just bigger. As he walked towards the locker rooms he wondered if Wilander was through. A quarter-final against one of his heroes. Fancy that he thought.

His entire team were waiting to congratulate him. They were ecstatic, not least of all Shakira, who was dressed in a beautiful green summery dress and beret. No wonder the French were whistling at her he laughed. They lacked manners but not good taste.

"Davie, we're in the quarter finals of the French Open, *boychik*!" barked Dov, giving his pupil one of his signature bear hugs.

"You were wonderful today, my darling!" said Shakira, hugging his sweaty body but not caring.

"Well, **your** presence inspired me, my beautiful girlfriend" replied David.

"Davie, sorry to cut short the celebrations but we need to interview with that *Bud oke* again. I did promise him" laughed Dov.

Chapter 40

"David Oppenheim and Dov Mendelson, two nice Jewish boys out of Durban, South Africa. What is it with you two giant slayers knocking out all these seeds? David, you made that look easy today?" asked Bud Collins.

"No, no that wasn't easy at all. Jean-Baptiste Leconte has been in the top ten in the world consistently for the last couple of years. I think the pressure of the weight of expectation from the French crowd was tough on him" explained David.

"I think you are just being respectful, young man. The fact is you played a different level of tennis today is all and now you are in the quarter finals of the French Open and will play your idol from your school days, Mats Wilander, next Tuesday. What are your thoughts on that?" asked Bud.

"What do they eat in Sweden because that's what we going to be eating on Tuesday" barked Dov, although the question hadn't been directed at him.

"Coach, let's bring you in then. What are your thoughts?" asked Bud.

"Mr Collins, after the performance David just put on against Monsieur Jean I would be *shitting* myself if I was Mats Wilander!" shouted Dov.

"I *love* your confidence coach" laughed Bud Collins.

"David, you feel the same?" asked Bud.

"Confident yes, but at the same time very respectful of Mats who is a legend of our sport. Still, I'm the wild card with nothing to lose and everything to gain" smiled David.

"Gents, I thank you again for your time and we can't wait to commentate your match next Tuesday on Court Central again" he said.

Before he could end off though, Dov snatched his microphone out of his hand with his big mitt and said "I promised I would say hello to her if I was on TV again, so I would like to say hello Colleen!" as he handed the microphone back to Bud Collins, who was killing himself with laughter.

"Ah David, sorry my director is screaming down my ear to ask you one last question, actually. We all want to know if that lovely young lady that the French cameramen kept on focusing on is your significant other?" asked Bud.

"Yes, I'm delighted to say Shakira is my girlfriend, sir" replied David, shyly.

"Well my director says well done!" laughed Bud and the rest of the studio.

David decided to skip the ice bath but settled for a ninety minute rub down from one of the local ATP-appointed masseurs before re-joining his crew who had been invited out for dinner to a beautiful Italian restaurant the Sergio Tacchini crowd booked out every night.

Their focus for the week, and correctly so, had been on their star player and cash cow, Mats Wilander, but in David they now could clearly see a future champion who would continue the legacy. Lionel was in his element at the dinner and made sure to introduce himself to all the company executives. He was happy to see Dov also helping to promote his friend to them and he had no doubt they would at least sign up Lionel as one of their sponsored players for the Challenger tour, which was a lot more than he had when he first started. He had suggested to Lionel that he use his design experience to put together some of his own designs for Tacchini to consider and he was going to make a point of suggesting it to the executives himself.

The food and atmosphere at the Il Brigante restaurant was out of this world. Uncle Sol was in top form along with Dov and had their Italian hosts in raptures of laughter, especially the story of him escaping the very irate butcher husband via the back alleys of Paris. The strong sports massage he had received a few hours earlier had relaxed David but best of all he had the love of his life with him. She had won over both parents big time with her natural, alluring charm and intelligence. She had fascinated his mother with all her tales of her 2 years in Paris and she had even opened up to a degree about her relationship with Jared. His mother could see she was a serious but also fun person, who was totally devoted to David. At some point towards the end of the evening Dov even suggested that the two love birds should go get a room because they were so attached to each other. David agreed and suggested that he and Shakira wanted a bit of a stroll through Montmartre where she had lived all those years ago and that they would meet them for breakfast at the hotel in the morning.

The walk along the cobblestoned streets from the restaurant up to the Basilique du Sacre-Coeur de Montmartre was full of buzzing little bistros and cafes which was impressive for a Sunday evening. Shakira knew the area well and David was impressed as she pointed out beautiful place after beautiful place along with their histories. Montmartre was truly a little village within a big city. The only disappointment was seeing a Starbucks coffee shop on one of the corners.

The view from Sacre-Coeur was truly spectacular and they could see the gleaming lights of the city below them, including the iconic Eiffel Tower and also the way the River Seine snaked around The City of Light. They found an empty spot on a bench to enjoy the gelato David had the restaurant put into containers for them as a take-away. They sat for quite some time just admiring the beautiful lights of the city before them, just holding each other quietly. After some time they made their way to one of the taxi ranks and took a cab back to the hotel. It had been a perfect end to an exciting day and they both climbed into bed, exhausted.

The following morning everybody including the Energizer bunny in Dov slept in until mid-morning when Dov emerged and woke the two of them up to administer another massage to David.

"Good morning, love birds! So how did the rest of your evening go? Or should I rather not ask?" grinned Dov.

"Montmartre is beautiful, Dovi. You should really take Colleen there if we have time. It's where Shakira lived for nearly 2 years when she was studying in Paris" said David whilst readying himself for more torture.

"You really should Dov, it's the most romantic little village in Paris" grinned Shakira.

"She left early this morning to do some sightseeing with her mom" replied Dov.

"Oh, so where did *she* sleep last night then?" asked Shakira with that cheeky, teasing grin of hers.

"In the hotel and that's all I'm prepared to say about that!" barked Dov.

After brunch on the hotel patio the group decided to take a stroll through the Marais district and have a late, light lunch at one of the cafes. Dov had decided it was best to not even spend any time at Roland Garros but to keep David distracted with other things. He had booked an hour's warm up for him with

Lionel on their lucky court 14 for the following morning before his afternoon match against Wilander. He would watch Wilander's fourth round annihilation of his seeded Chilean opponent with David later that night on Canal+ but other than that he didn't want him thinking anything tennis.

The fashionably hip Marais district, with all its boutique stores and galleries, was the perfect distraction for David and Shakira. David bought Shakira a beautiful brown, leather mini-skirt which showed off her lovely athletic legs, and she in turn bought him a smart/casual deconstructed jacket. David then purchased a beautiful painting of Paris that he noticed his parents drooling over, to commemorate their first visit to Paris. He finally had the money to do so.

The area had once been the Jewish Quarter so they humoured Leah and much to her delight agreed to eat at one of the many kosher restaurants. Rather than take the limousine back to their hotel they decided to enjoy an hour long walk back. Their route took them through the beautiful Jardin du Palais Royal as well as the Pyramide du Louvre and the Place de la Concorde with its fountains, statues and imposing Egyptian obelisk. Everything about this city was a piece of art, a piece of beauty thought David.

As they stepped into the hotel both he and Shakira were swamped by photographers who had discovered their whereabouts and were looking for a picture to put on their newspapers of the young, glamorous couple. That's when David knew immediately his life would never be the same. What the paparazzi hadn't factored in though was Dov. The big man immediately lifted a couple of them off their feet and gently plopped them outside the front door whilst David and Shakira made a dash for the elevators. The security were immediately inspired seeing Dov handling the photographers and marched the rest promptly out of the reception area onto the street.

"Jesus that was a bit scary!" laughed David when they were all in the escalator heading up to the 8th floor.

"I think you're now what they call "famous" my love!" said Shakira, packing out in laughter along with the rest of the crew.

"Well I think it was more your pretty face they were trying to capture my darling!"

“Well, it certainly wasn’t mine” his father said dryly, which had them all really laughing again.

David and Dov watched a replay on Canal+ of Wilander’s highlights whilst munching on David’s traditional night-before-a-game, chicken salad dinner. It was more a Spanish lowlights replay because his Spanish opponent was so full of nerves that he had sprayed balls all over the stadium worse than a graffiti artist.

“This is good for us, Davie. Wilander, unlike you, hasn’t had much practice or been even slightly pushed like you have. He’s not ready for a long, tough 5 setter so if you can drag him into those deep waters you have a chance, *boychik*. You have to come out firing though and surprise him. He’ll be thinking you’re going to be a bag of nerves in your first ever quarter final. Let’s surprise him with the exact opposite. Give him fuck all in the warm up too. Don’t show him how good you are. In fact show him your worse in the warm up like you are shitting your pants with nerves” he laughed.

Dov was right.

David could overhear Shakira telling her mother about the excitement of watching her boyfriend on centre court and how beautiful it was to be back in Paris again.

“Please send lots of love of to your mom and please tell her we are all taking great care of you. Send greetings to your dad and brother too!” he shouted to her.

“Mom, did you hear that from David? He and Dov are in the room next door watching a replay of his next opponent tomorrow, Mats Wilander” he could hear her say.

“David, my mom sends her love and best wishes for tomorrow, my angel!” she shouted back at him.

“Tell her thank you!” he shouted back.

“OK Davie, I’ll wake you tomorrow morning for the usual at 7:30 am. Don’t expend too much energy tonight, please. We need all your strength for our Swede tomorrow” he laughed, heading towards the door.

Dov was right *again*.

Chapter 41

The next morning seemed to whizz by and before he knew it they were in the limousine heading towards Roland Garros. Just before he had exited the room Dov had come through saying that some nutcase had been transferred by reception to his suite and needed to speak to David *urgently*. According to Dov, when he had asked who it was, the nutcase had told him, "never mind who the fuck I am or who the fuck you are, just put the *schlemiel* on the phone is all!"

"You want me to tell him to go get fucked or what?" asked Dov, looking most unimpressed.

"No, no, put him through. I know who the so-called "nutcase" is and I've been trying to get in touch with him for months now. Not even his parents know where he is!" laughed David.

"Huh, I don't think *he* even knows where he is!" barked Dov.

David knew from the minute Dov quoted him that it was his best mate Derek Reed, who he had gone through high school and university with. He and his girlfriend had decided to go off to Iceland to pack fish after he had graduated but he had not been contactable since. Dov was right about him being a nutcase and the two of them had got up to all sorts of really crazy things during their university years, including the infamous Commerce Students Council freshers' party.

"Knut, where the *fuck* are you? I've been trying to reach you forever" asked David, addressing his friend by his second Norwegian name.

"Bro, firstly tell that *oke* who answered the phone earlier I'm sorry for taking off at him but I'm phoning from a ticky box outside our kibbutz and I'm running out of money!" he shouted.

"*Kibbutz*? What the Hell are you doing *there*? I thought you were supposed to be packing fish in Iceland?" asked David, surprised.

"Bro, after a month of packing stinking fish if I had to look another fish in the eye I would have become one, so we decided to go work on a kibbutz rather than return home. Anyway don't worry about that shit. I phoned because Kate and I have been following your success in Paris and we both just wanted to say how much we love and admire you, bro. Go do it today for all of us and make us proud, Davie. I will phone you back later but my money is about to run out, my brother." He was right about that and as he finished his sentence the phone clicked dead. It was touching to receive his call and added to David's motivation.

The whole situation of being about to play his hero Mats Wilander in the quarter finals of the French Open, being a Mossad spy and now having a Muslim Persian princess as his girlfriend, all seemed beyond surreal. How had it all happened and so quickly too? Maybe he was wrong and there was a God after all, he chuckled.

Warming up two hours before his match on court 14 with Lionel, none of the earlier good feelings had left his body. The balls were zinging off his racket strings at high revolutions just as they had during his Leconte match and his serves had real zip in them thanks to Clive's guidance. After his earlier Dov-torture, his legs were feeling lively and energised. He had already drunk a litre of the purple stuff and he was *ready* for Wilander.

By 2 p.m. when he and the Swede stepped onto Court Central the stadium was jam-packed and from the decibels of the applause he received compared to his opponent, he could immediately tell they were supporting the underdog. The wry grin he noticed on Mats's face was evidence that this was hardly a new experience for him. The crowd had come to see if this was indeed the possible changing of the guard, with a newcomer out to overthrow an old champion.

At exactly 2:14 p.m. umpire Jac Berholtz called, "Mr Wilander to serve first set. Play!"

David's ploy of showing very little beyond being able to hit the ball back over the net during their warm up, but then aggressively hitting out from the first point of the match, paid immediate dividends. Mats had indeed assumed his young opponent was battling nerves and he wasn't prepared for the onslaught. He had reversed the tables on the champion and suddenly Wilander looked a bundle of nerves realising this kid was smart and good too. The break happened for David in the ninth game when Wilander uncharacteristically gifted David two double faults and then pushed a backhand passing shot wide. That's the pressure he thought. David was not going to return the compliment but instead fired off 3 aces and finished the game and set off with a beautifully disguised drop shot, which left his opponent sitting on his backside on the red clay. David had the first set 6-4.

He stared up at his excited box whilst drinking more purple stuff and nodded at them. The crowd was getting louder, sensing a possible upset from the young wild card. He could see Bud Collins and Johnny Mac, who had lost in an earlier round and was now co-commentating with him, sitting in ESPN's commentary booth. He had no doubt they were dissecting every play and sharing that with their viewers.

For the next 2 sets David discovered why Mats was the champion he was. He quickly brushed off the first set loss and showed patience and calm in finding his regular game. He had got used to David's penetrating groundstrokes and in return was flighting the ball higher over the net and deeper in the court, thereby negating David's harder hit ground strokes. He was also moving faster to and reading his drop shots better. David realised he was being outsmarted from the baseline and knew he needed to change his game plan for the fourth. He needed to take Mats out of his comfort zone. He was just too predictable and was playing the style Mats wanted him to play.

David figured he had worked so hard on his service that it was time to really put it to the test. It was his only hope really. So he totally mixed his service games up by serving and volleying for the first time in the match. He sometimes hit two first serves which caught the Swede by surprise and mixed that all up with a bunch of moon balls and then hard forehands to the middle of the court rather than out wide. It worked! This was the last thing Mats had expected and he laughed when he noticed his confused look at one of their changeovers. He hadn't seen this coming!

"Beautiful, beautiful, *boychik*! More! We want more, Davie! C'mon!" he heard Dov scream when he secured the break of service in the ninth game once more. He could sense the momentum back with him and Mats wasn't looking as composed as he had been during the second and third sets.

David stuck to his game plan and hitting mostly 2 first serves every point, secured the game and fourth set 6-4. For the first time he could feel a bit of fatigue in his calves and a glance at the stadium clock explained why. They had been on court for nearly 4 hours already and still had a fifth set to play. He glugged back nearly a half litre of purple stuff. Hopefully that would kick in soon, he hoped.

The fifth set was an utter dog fight and at the same time producing some of the best tennis of the match. The long baseline rallies were gruelling with neither player managing to establish an advantage. They were deadlocked at 5-5 when Wilander's experience showed and he managed the breakthrough, not through any fault of David's, but just the little extra patience he displayed. He broke David's service to lead 6-5 and was not going to let David back in. The end came in the following game with a well-directed serve that did enough to catch the line and skid beyond David's reach.

It had been the match of the tournament and David had pushed the Swede to the brink. When he shook his hand at the net he could see the relief on Mats's face as well as the admiration he had for David's efforts. He congratulated David for his amazing results in the championship and told him he was going to follow his progress through the tour.

Whilst sitting down and catching his breath and having one last swig of some purple stuff he looked at his box who were all standing and applauding him, along with the 15, 000 other spectators. They had been treated to one of the finest displays of clay court tennis they had ever witnessed and from a wild card at that. David felt no disappointment at his loss. Why should he when he had given his all. As he left the court to leave Mats for his on-court interview he felt the thunderous applause from the fans so he reciprocated by blowing them kisses.

His crew were waiting outside his locker room to both console and congratulate him. Both Dov and Shakira had tears in their eyes as they hugged and kissed him. The biggest hug though came from his father and for the first time David felt tears of joy welling up inside him.

"Fuck that! We're going out to celebrate Davie tonight with the biggest party ever. Tonight we take Paris!" shouted Dov.

"Hell yes!" shouted Uncle Sol and they all laughed heartily.

"Davie, go shower and quick. Everybody, and I mean absolutely *everybody* wants to interview you but that Bud *oke* comes first" barked Dov.

Nobody could liven up a room like Dov, smiled David.

"So David Oppenheim you just keep on blowing us away. You've gone from being a wildcard nobody to number fifty-eight in the world rankings. Do you realise in a couple of weeks from now that means you go straight into the main draw at Wimbledon? What do you have to say about that now, David?" asked Bud Collins.

"That was *never* in doubt!" barked Dov.

Bud Collins was getting used to these Dov outbursts but still couldn't help himself from laughing at his confidence.

"We feel great, actually. This has all been a dream for Dov and me. I didn't really get a chance to thank and congratulate Mats today. He is an incredible champion and showed everyone here today why. I thought after the 4th set I may have had him but he proved otherwise. I've learnt so much from today's match and so if you watch this later, Mats, I would like to thank you."

"Are all South Africans as genuine and gracious as you, young man?" asked Bud.

"No!" shouted Dov, once more causing many laughs.

"OK, coach, we can't resist asking how *you* feel today?" laughed Bud.

"First, I would also like to congratulate Mats but I told you he should have been shitting himself for this, last night. I also want to thank Davie for his courage and for bringing me along for the ride. This has been the greatest week of my life" said Dov.

"So, will you be joining David for Wimbledon then?" asked Bud.

"Why the hell wouldn't he be? He's my coach and big brother!" It was David's turn to butt in.

"Exactly! I'm always by Davie's side. Why the hell wouldn't I be going to Wimbledon with him?" barked Dov.

"Well gents, on that note, we bid you farewell and congratulations and we can't wait to see you on the grass courts of SW19 in a few weeks" Bud Collins concluded.

After a further 2 hours of television interviews and signing his signature, David finally entered their hotel hand-in-hand with his beautiful Shakira. The entire hotel staff were gathered in the reception area to applaud him and welcome him back after his terrific performance. He was very touched and told them all that if he was fortunate enough to be back the following year, Hotel Chateau Frontenac would be the only place he would be staying.

After putting on fresh clothes Shakira brought a facsimile room service had delivered, with a massive smile on her face.

"Read it my darling" she said.

It was handwritten on a fancy company letterhead and the paper was still warm, having just come off the machine.

"Dear David, we haven't met yet but we have a common love in my beautiful Shakira. She talks very highly of you as does her lovely mother, my wife, Zara. I am always a bit sceptical from past experiences when anybody talks so glowingly about someone I haven't met. This afternoon I happened to watch you play an experienced champion and all the character you displayed against him, in spite of losing, validates all they see in you. At the risk of sounding patronising or presumptuous your characteristics of courage and honesty remind me a lot of my younger self and are qualities I have the greatest respect for. I can see from the television footage as well as the newspaper articles the last few days that you treat and love my daughter as I would expect from her partner. Of course, it is no comparison to the obvious sparkle I see in her eyes when she talks about you. I would like to congratulate you for your tennis success in Paris and I look forward to receiving you on your return at our family home. Kindest regards, Ismail Mahomedy."

"David, my father has never spoken so glowingly about *anybody* before, my darling. He's giving you his blessing" she smiled, kissing him gently.

"I may have lost a tennis match but I've gained the love of my life today" said David joyfully, hugging her even tighter.

Chapter 42

It felt strange waking up on the Wednesday morning without Dov getting him up for his customary early massage. With all the interviews he needed to get through after his match against Mats, he had forgone his post-match ice bath and his muscles were feeling it this morning. It hadn't stopped him from making beautiful love to his Shakira who lay peacefully next to him now. How had he got so lucky?

The previous evening's celebrations at the hotel, where the staff had put on a special dinner and dance for all the guests in honour of David, was a blast and David had lost count of the number of glasses of champagne he had drunk ... but it was a lot. All 3 of his sponsors had attended and split the bill for the evening equally between them. As Dov had told him out of earshot, they recognised he was going to be a fantastic cash cow for them and in all likelihood a future, French Open champion. It had very little to do about friendship.

Dov had also told David that he thought it in David's best interests to add a "proper" coach to their team. He had a King David A team player in mind from his year but he was too busy and didn't have the time so he had chatted a bit with Clive Jaikins. It seemed like the aggressive chemo and radiation treatment had worked and he was starting to feel much better. He would consider Dov's offer seriously and give him an answer in due course. Dov had explained that he was best suited in his current role as David's all-rounder being his agent negotiating with sponsors and tournament organisers, arranging their logistics and interviews, dealing with paparazzi and other vermin as well as a world class masseur and purple stuff supplier. In other words, all the roles a big brother would take care of and then some. David had told Dov in return that he was indispensable to him.

After showering together he and Shakira joined everyone downstairs for a late breakfast. He was surprised to see them sounding so chipper and looking so spritely after the party of the night before. Lionel in particular was sporting a massive smile as he had used the opportunity to network with the sponsors who were going to discuss the possibility of starting him off with a little something for the Challenger tour. Once more he had Dov's support in helping with that, and who in their right mind was going to turn down the big man. He was very persuasive, David laughed to himself.

David had asked Dov, Lionel and Shakira to join him that afternoon to watch Lendl play one of the hard-working Spanish clay court specialists whilst the others went to visit some museums. Rather than take the limousine again they decided to take a leisurely walk along the beautiful, leafy, boulevards to Roland Garros. Sadly it was their last night in Paris before flying home where David could unwind and watch the semi-finals and finals live on MNet with everybody. He couldn't depart Paris without watching Lendl live. There was a lot he could learn from him.

Shakira acted as tour guide for their team, pointing out beautiful gardens, buildings and squares like the tranquil Square du Palais-Galliera with its beautiful treed garden and historic buildings on Rue Pierre Charron and the Place du Trocadero, with its unspoilt views of the Eiffel Tower. She took them to Pierre Herme Paris on Avenue Paul Doumer where she bought delicious pastries for all of them as well as a little box to take home for her mother.

The crowds at the stadium were quite overwhelming and after his match against Wilander it felt like everyone recognised them. Dov had his work cut out for him but they seemed to listen to him and were respectful in awaiting their turn for David's signature. A sweet little French girl with her mother had cut out a photo of him and Shakira entering their hotel hand-in-hand from the previous day's Le Monde, for them both to sign. She had bought a lovely bouquet of flowers for Shakira too, so she picked the little girl up and allowed her mother to take a picture of her daughter with them both. Shakira knew exactly how to endear herself to the French public and this would help winning them over for David's future matches in years to follow. Even wearing just casual jeans and a T-shirt she was striking and the paparazzi pushed to have her in every picture. It was no wonder they were so easily recognisable now.

After signing what felt like a thousand signatures they managed to make their way to the player's lounge at Court Central to eat their pastries and watch Lendl.

He was the ultimate professional and whilst not nearly as talented as Johnny Mac, he was equally effective with his disciplined game. Like David's parents he was Czech-born but had managed to obtain American citizenship too. Lendl could grind down any player barring Wilander from the baseline. That included the plethora of Spaniards who grew up on the surface and was precisely what he was doing to his younger Spanish opponent. Lendl's single-handed backhand was a thing of beauty to watch and he could smash it both down the line and cross court. Slowly but methodically he could see the gap between the two players widen as the match progressed. It was really just a question of time until the young Spaniard would capitulate.

Dov used the opportunity when Lionel and Shakira went to grab them drinks to address a developing situation. He had received a very early morning telephone call from Moshe. He had sounded distraught over the line and after he had explained why, Dov understood his feelings fully well.

"Davie, sorry to be the bearer of bad tidings at such a happy time for all of us, but Moshe called me in a panic this morning" he said.

"What's wrong now, Dovi?" asked David, fearing the worst.

"Moshe says that Mossad has finally uncovered Hamas and Hezbollah terrorist cells undergoing advanced training in the Karoo and possibly other places in South Africa" he said.

"No way, not in our country, surely?" asked David, incredulously.

"I'm afraid so. They've verified this via satellite and phone calls they've intercepted" replied Dov.

"So what does *this* mean then?" asked David, quite shocked.

"Moshe has asked if you can help again, David. He was thinking that we may, or rather, *you* may as you are now getting closer to Shakira's family, be able to manipulate Goolam into giving us more information on these scumbags. Once they are trained they head back to either Gaza, the West Bank or Lebanon to launch deadly attacks against Israel. Yesterday they did exactly that and bombed another school bus in Jerusalem full of young Jewish kids. Fucking cowards!"

"Jesus, Dov I really thought I was done with this spying thing. You have no idea the internal conflict I went through. Thank god Shakira is not aware of my assignment because she would end our relationship immediately and I don't want to lose her. You *know* how I feel about her, Dovi!" he said, sounding dismayed.

“I know David and nobody knows how you really feel like I think I do. It was the first thing that went through my head when Moshe was telling me this morning. I do know what your answer is going to be though as much as we both try to fight it and find logical reasons not to be involved” said Dov.

“They are *our* people, Davie, and we both know we are going to help them” continued Dov.

“You are the perfect cover being a pro tennis player. Who would suspect that you have time to be a Mossad spy too?” said Dov.

“I, sorry *we*, don’t have the time, Dovi! We have the grass court season starting now and then Wimbledon in a few weeks. I’ve never played on the stuff before! In fact the closest I’ve ever come to it is the one and only time I tried a joint with Derek at the CSC’s freshers’ party. Do you have any idea of how much work that’s going to be to get me ready, otherwise we are going to look like utter *poephols* when I get smashed triple bagel in the first round!”

“Relax *boychik*, relax! I have a plan in my mind already, OK” said Dov.

“Fuck sakes, you better tell them it’s going to cost them a shitload of vinyl this time. All collector’s items too” grumbled David.

“We will chat further about this tomorrow on our return flight. I have another call with Moshe tonight and he should give me more information. With the bombing of the bus yesterday he was in quite a state last night. But Davie, we’re not out of the game yet. We have another mission ahead of us and it isn’t going to be as easy as this last one, I can assure you” sighed Dov.

It didn’t take very long for Lendl to dismantle his opponent in straight sets and after saying farewell to the tournament organisers the four of them set off for a lovely little bistro in a lane off the main street that Shakira’s mother had told her about. She had been right to suggest it because it was a seventh generation family one with recipes passed down over the years. The food was delicious and David ordered a bottle of champagne to celebrate their last night in Paris.

“My angel, these couple of days have gone too fast. We need to come back here soon, but just for a break so I can show you more of this city. Who knows, maybe one day we even come live here for a few years” she said.

“With all this beauty, including yours, my darling, I could quite easily live here” said David.

"Davie, you're as much a Durbanite as a banana and you could never live away from Durbs for too long!" laughed Dov.

"It's true" laughed David, "but for the next few years good old Durban is just going to be a refueling station between ATP tournaments. You are right though, Dovi, I'm a dinkum banana boy!" David chuckled.

Before heading to bed, they joined the rest of the crew who had been visiting a few of the art museums that afternoon, for a night cap. David was impressed Uncle Sol hadn't dragged them to a whole bunch of bars like he had with his father when they had first arrived. Leah had made sure they went back to the Jewish Quarter to visit a museum or two there which must have bored the daylights out of poor Uncle Sol.

On the flight home the pilot announced that David was one of their special passengers which resulted in lots of young kids seeking his autograph. Shakira found the whole thing amusing and teased her shy boyfriend about his new found fame. After dinner and a glass or two of champagne, and because of a particularly busy evening they had in their hotel room the previous night, she fell asleep. David took advantage of it and switched seats with Lionel so he could continue his discussion of the previous afternoon with Dov.

"So what did Moshe have to say?" asked David.

"Well, firstly he's very grateful you are in for this one, Davie. He knows how hard it must be for you after you thought you were done with Goolam" said Dov.

"And?"

"Davie, this thing with the training camps is far worse than he thought. There are *at least* 6 different places including one site in Mozambique. Iran is sponsoring these useful idiots and the ANC is ignoring them in exchange for party "donations" and cheap oil. They have instructed all intelligence agencies to ignore any and all alerts about these training camps so we are up against our own country too" said Dov.

"Jesus, so we've been captured by the bloody Iranians?" asked David, shocked.

"Exactly right. We've become their proxy in all of this. Mossad are putting something together for us along with some of my ideas. I don't want to discuss anything here though. Too dangerous. We'll meet up at the Economics Society on campus next week with Carol. Until then let's just keep *shtum*" instructed Dov.

David switched seats with his friend again. Shakira rolled over into his arms, smiling as she made herself comfortable. Even with Dov's new announcement David knew just how lucky he was. He had solved the Goolam issue, he had reached the quarter finals of his first ever major tournament, he had rekindled his relationship with his father and he was in love with a stunning woman who felt the same way, and whose father had given his approval. Not only that but he had also qualified to play at the Holy of tennis Holies, at Wimbledon, in a few weeks.

Still, as much as he was looking forward to him and Dov traveling to Wimbledon they had a dangerous mission to perform for their people ... and there was no time to relax.

Glossary of Yiddish and South African (Afrikaans-derived) terms

boychik a term of endearment for any special male with whom one is familiar

boykie the South African equivalent of boychik

ballie can refer to either parent

barmitzvah religious celebration of manhood for Jewish boy at age of 13 years

Baruch HaShem blessed be G-d

challah bread traditionally served at Shabbat also know as kitke

charou South African slang for an Indian person

chutzpah cheek or nerve

drek ugly or unattractive

dorpies small, rural South African towns

faribel to bear a grudge

frum religiously observant, religious

gatvol South African slang for had enough

gefilte fish herring

goy/goyim a non-Jew/ plural : non-Jews

goyische in the manner of a non-Jewish person or place

hakking chasing or talking endlessly to someone

howzit South African slang for hello or how are you

kak South African slang for crap

klapped South African slang for giving somebody a smack

macher a big shot or big deal

mazeltov congratulations

meshugge senseless or crazy

meshuggeneh a senseless or crazy person

nogal South African slang for

oke casual reference to a guy or "dude"

olim Jews who have made Aaliyah or return to Israel from the Diaspora

pisher a nobody, a nothing

poephol literally an asshole

putz a jerk or a self-made fool but literally means penis

rachmones one you should have compassion for, possibly a bit of a lost cause

schlemiel inept/incompetent person or "fool"

schmuck/o a stupid/foolish or unlikeable person

schnorrer a miser

schweet South African slang for "cool" used typically in Joburg

seichel business acumen

shabbat the Jewish Sabbath

shiksa a female non-Jewish girlfriend

shmatte a rag or old garment or depicting the rag trade or clothing business

Shoah the Holocaust

Shomer Shabbat observing the strict rules of the Jewish Sabbath

shtum to keep silent about

shul synagogue or Jewish temple

simcha a celebration

skelms crooks or criminals

smokkel to smuggle

smokkelaar a smuggler

tuches butt, behind, backside

wit ou typical South African Idian slang for a white guy

yarmulke a Jewish kippa or skullcap

Yishuv the early Jewish settler community before 1948

Made in the USA
Middletown, DE
15 November 2024

64355839R00176